THE GREENING

THE GREENING

MARGARET COLES

HAY HOUSE

Australia • Canada • Hong Kong • India
South Africa • United Kingdom • United States

First published and distributed in the United Kingdom by:
Hay House UK Ltd, Astley House,
33 Notting Hill Gate, London W11 3JQ.
Tel.: (44) 20 3675 2450;
Fax: (44) 20 8962 1239. www.hayhouse.co.uk

Published and distributed in the United States of America by:
Hay House, Inc., PO Box 5100, Carlsbad, CA 92018-5100. Tel.: (1) 760 431 7695 or
(800) 654 5126; Fax: (1) 760 431 6948 or (800) 650 5115. www.hayhouse.com

Published and distributed in Australia by:
Hay House Australia Ltd, 18/36 Ralph St, Alexandria NSW 2015.
Tel.: (61) 2 9669 4299; Fax: (61) 2 9669 4144. www.hayhouse.com.au

Published and distributed in the Republic of South Africa by:
Hay House SA (Pty), Ltd, PO Box 990, Witkoppen 2068.
Tel./Fax: (27) 11 467 8904.
www.hayhouse.co.za

Published and distributed in India by:
Hay House Publishers India, Muskaan Complex,
Plot No.3, B-2, Vasant Kunj, New Delhi – 110 070.
Tel.: (91) 11 4176 1620; Fax: (91) 11 4176 1630. www.hayhouse.co.in

Distributed in Canada by:
Raincoast, 9050 Shaughnessy St, Vancouver, BC V6P 6E5.
Tel.: (1) 604 323 7100; Fax: (1) 604 323 2600

A catalogue record for this book is available from the British Library.

ISBN 978-1-78180-113-0

Printed and bound in Great Britain by TJ International, Padstow, Cornwall.

To my sister, Christina Myfanwy

By chance, I encountered the lost lady.
At that time I still believed in chance.
A candle burned, and by the light of the flame I embarked
upon the soul's solitary adventure.

1

"What do you want me to do? Trip her up at the airport? Lace her tea with arsenic? Stab her with a poisoned umbrella?" The newsroom fell silent as the other reporters waited to hear who would win this round in my ongoing battle with the News Editor.

"You're bloody useless, Meredith," said Milo, bringing his face uncomfortably close to mine. I could smell the whisky on his breath. "Joanna Useless Meredith, not a bloody clue."

My interviewee had pulled out with barely any notice, sending a message to say she had to leave urgently for South-East Asia. The interview with Ismene Vale, a distinguished anthropologist and environmentalist, had been scheduled for a two-page spread to be published the following day. The Editor would be furious.

Ismene Vale's secretary had been very mysterious about her sudden departure. I sensed a story, something beyond her views on the state of the environment, but had no way of following it up.

"How the hell can I interview someone who's in a plane heading for South-East Asia and nobody will say where?" I demanded.

"You're as good as your last story, Meredith. Remember that. Get onto this," said Milo, throwing some sheets of news agency copy onto my desk. "Simon will brief you. And for Christ's sake don't bugger this one up."

Seething, I grabbed the copy. I cursed Ismene Vale for letting me down. My frustration was intensified by my disappointment.

She was my childhood heroine. Her books about her travels among the world's forgotten and dispossessed had opened my mind and inspired my choice of career.

I quickly read the copy, which bore the Reuters dateline. It was background material rather than a news story. The subject was research into medicine to counteract depression. There was a lot of detail, describing the development of various drugs and their side-effects. It was not clear what I was expected to do with the material. I walked across to the news desk. Simon, the Deputy News Editor, was on the phone. He finished his call and said, "Take a seat, Jo. I need to talk you through this." Simon was a tall, sturdy Scot with an introverted, bookish manner. He had an air of self-containment and rarely said more than was necessary.

"This is big," said Simon. "International Pharmaceuticals has suppressed an internal report showing a link between one of their antidepressants and incidents of suicide. Their research director is going to blow the whistle. You're meeting him at 9:30." Simon gave me a full briefing on the interview I was to do and said, "You'd better get going. We don't want to keep him waiting."

I hurried from the building into the autumn drizzle and hailed a taxi. The day was chilly and the sky overcast. Twenty minutes later I arrived at the address Simon had given me, a 1930s mansion block in South Kensington. I pressed the intercom buzzer for Flat 11 and waited. There was no response. I pressed the buzzer again. Again, there was no response. After a few more minutes I pressed it again. I glanced at my watch. It was 9:35. I began to feel uneasy. I walked to the rear of the block and found another entrance, but that, too, was operated by an entryphone system.

I returned to the front of the block. Despite the need for discretion, I decided to press the buzzer for the concierge. The front door of the block swung open. I walked in and approached the reception desk. The concierge, a smartly uniformed man of about fifty, said, "Good morning, madam. Can I help you?"

"I'm visiting number 11," I replied, "but I can't get a response."

"The gentleman who occupies number 11 is out of town," said the concierge.

"I don't think so. He's expecting me. Would you ring him, please?"

"He's away, madam."

"Please, would you try? He is expecting me."

"The gentleman is away, madam. The apartment has been empty for the past three weeks."

I was becoming irritated. "Look, just try the number, would you?" I said.

"There's no point, madam. The apartment is empty."

"Are you being deliberately obstructive?" I asked, my temper rising. "Just try the number."

"I'm sorry, madam – " he began.

"OK, I'll check for myself," I said, walking towards the staircase. The concierge came swiftly across the lobby and blocked my path. "You mustn't do that, madam," he said. "I can't help you and I really must ask you to leave."

What could I do? I turned and left. The door swung to behind me. I felt desperate. There was a telephone box on the corner. I ran to it and rang the news desk. Simon answered. I told him what had happened. It was obvious that the concierge had been told to put me off. We needed to find out who owned the apartment and track down the whistleblower. Simon said, "Hold on. Let me brief Milo."

A moment later I heard Milo's voice. "What the hell are you playing at?"

"It's not my fault," I replied.

"It never is your bloody fault, is it? No doubt he got away while you were arsing around."

"I was not arsing around – " I began.

"Oh just bugger off," said Milo, slamming down the phone. His manner told me that I was off the story and had better stay out of his way until he cooled down.

Everything I had worked for, everything I thought I had achieved, my hope of a future and a successful career in Fleet Street seemed to be fragmenting around me. This would be the end. All the tension and worry of the past several months, as work had become increasingly demanding and difficult, coalesced in one moment of despair. I started to cry, leaning on the stand that supported the telephone receiver.

I heard the door open and a woman's voice ask, "Are you all right, dear?" I could not speak but nodded in assent. "Are you sure?" she asked. I could not respond. I pushed past her and gulped in the fresh air. A taxi was approaching. I hailed it and climbed in. I directed the driver to the offices of the *Correspondent* in the Docklands area of east London.

The world outside the cab window flashed by, full of people going about their lives as if it mattered. I felt I belonged nowhere. What was I doing with my life? The only thing that made any sense was my ability to do my job well and I could no longer count on that. The ground was crumbling away beneath me.

The Editor would be angry and Milo would put the blame on me. He would lay into me publicly and I would have to fight back. My self-respect, and perhaps pride, would allow me no less. I was used to fighting my corner. It had been my way since childhood. People thought I didn't mind. But I did mind. I found it frightening and debilitating and I had to summon up my courage every time.

My work was good, I knew that, but lately I always seemed to fail. The idealism with which I had arrived in Fleet Street ten years earlier, at the start of the 1980s, had dwindled away. In a hostile environment, my independent streak had deepened. I had grown a protective shell. If I was not as confident as I appeared to be, well, in my world appearances counted for a lot. But who was I? I no longer knew. And soon I would be out of a job. How would I pay my mortgage and the rest of my bills?

Then I remembered. I had to buy Patrick's birthday gift. He had specified a particular political biography – a nineteenth-century life of Disraeli – and I was determined not to disappoint him. I had tracked down a copy in an antiquarian bookshop in the Charing Cross Road and the bookseller had put it aside for me. He had assured me that it was in good condition. I hoped it would be good enough. I wanted to see Patrick's smile of satisfaction and approval and not the little frown that sometimes creased the skin between his eyebrows, making him look suddenly stern, as when a cloud passes in front of the sun.

We were travelling alongside the River Thames, heading east. The leaves on the trees had turned a golden brown. The sky was still overcast. I asked the driver to change course and take me to the Charing Cross Road. The door of the shop swung to behind me, cutting off the blistering sound of car wheels on wet tarmac. I stepped into a sanctuary. Rows of tall, narrow bookshelves created a maze of pathways, inviting exploration. The shelves were crammed, as though the books they contained had jostled and fought for space. Silence hung heavy, the sounds of the street deadened and the outside world removed to a place far distant.

I suddenly felt exhausted and I sat down on a stool used for filling shelves. I was in a silent, right-angled world with nothing to distract me, nothing but my thoughts. I felt completely alone. Nobody in my world knew where I was and, in a sense, neither did I. Who was I? Where was I going? They were questions I could not answer. My life had no purpose and no meaning. I feared the future. I was too sad to cry, too sad to know how sad I felt.

This place was unfamiliar territory. Bookshops I knew and frequented, browsing contentedly when time allowed among the new titles – the acclaimed biography, the recommended first novel – shiny volumes that enticed the eye.

This place was different. The books here were elusive: they did not clamour for attention; they needed to be sought out. In a place such as this, you never knew what you might find. It was the difference between being offered a selection made by someone else and discovering treasures that, I thought fancifully, had found their own way there, this destination being part of each one's particular journey. How strange it is that randomness can suggest an organizing mind when order and regulation may not. And where no one has chosen for us, what extraordinary choices might we make for ourselves?

Here were books that did not compromise. Old, worn books had been the silent companions of my childhood, treasures encompassing the author's soul, the most compelling born of toil and sacrifice and generated from the edge of being, where life meets the need to express itself, putting the past into the moment in defiance of those sorrows that cannot be explained, impelled by the desire to be known and understood.

Here were battered glass-fronted and open cabinets, packed with books, all shapes and sizes, none seeming to belong next to its companion, like strangers on a railway station platform. More books were piled into crates, littering the aisles: a heap of naval prints, another of gazetteers; a musty smell of dust, leather and old paper.

And here on a shelf were the thin, tattered wafers of folios that had fallen free of their spines, each layered upon another, their ancient bindings peeled and curled away in strips, like the dried bark of a tree. Wintering in a forgotten corner, like wan, frail old men whom no one had told that their time in this world was over, they emanated a naked fragility and vulnerability in their exposure to the light. In such a place as this, where life's slow decay moved imperceptibly at its own measureless pace, time would not be hurried.

And then I saw it. A glint of silver caught my eye, a sparkle of light among the dusty, faded covers. Curious, I rose and walked across and took from the shelf a volume bound in burgundy leather, its spine embellished by elaborate silver clasps. I opened the book and read:

> *By chance, I encountered the lost lady. At that time I still believed in chance. A candle burned, and by the light of the flame I embarked upon the soul's solitary adventure.*

I turned to the flyleaf – and took a quick inward breath. In faded black ink, someone had written "Find Anna. Begin your journey here. Reveal the truth. Find Anna and restore her book to her." It

felt like a blast of cold air that cleared my head. "Reveal the truth…"
It seemed as though the message had been put there for me. The
memory of who I used to be came into sharp focus. To reveal the
truth had been my aim and ambition and the motivation for my
choice of career. It had all been so very long ago, when I was a small
child and living with my great-aunt. Holding the little red volume,
which sat so comfortably in my hand, I remembered how she would
open her Bible at random, expecting the appropriate text to present
itself. On an impulse, I did the same. I read:

*You are beloved through all eternity and held safe in an
embrace that will never let you go.*

I began to cry. All the pain I had been feeling for so very long
poured out and I could not stop. If only I could feel safe in Patrick's
embrace, sure that he would never let me go. He seemed so remote
these days. He didn't realize how hurtful he could be, how deeply I
took things to heart. I was too good at putting on a brave face. And
I didn't want to lose him. I held the little book and cried deeply
from my soul. It nestled comfortingly between my palms, where it
seemed to belong. Could I be so loved? Could I feel so safe? If only
it were true.

I dried my eyes and turned the pages. It was a diary of sorts, a
personal confessional, which began with an account of a visit to a
place that had affected the writer deeply. I glanced again at the spine.
Inscribed in a delicate silver script, as though by an elegant feminine
hand, was the title, *Anna Leigh's Journal.*

I felt that I had chanced upon something intensely personal.
And more, this work had been valued by someone, perhaps even
loved. Why else would it have been bound, with consummate
artistry, in silver and rich burgundy leather? I fingered the clasps,
admiring the intricate design, the perfection of its proportions and
graceful delicacy of its flowing lines. I ran my fingers across the
softness of the leather and hardness of the clasps, taking pleasure in
the sensation.

There is a place to which life brings each of us, when we are ready. It is only later, when we look back over our lives, that we pinpoint the moment when the journey began. For the moment passes fleetingly, and the part that is aware is a stranger to us, we who do not know ourselves and vainly try to know others. That moment came for me. I was taken out of my hurrying life. My attention was caught and my footsteps guided gently from the wayside track that I had mistaken for the main causeway, and onto the path of the initiate.

I glanced at my watch and saw, with horror, that I had spent nearly an hour in the shop. I liked the comforting sensation of the little book in my hand. I would have it. I quickly paid for my two purchases and stepped back into the bustle of the Charing Cross Road.

I hailed a taxi. As it trundled through the busy streets of central London I began to worry. The battle with Milo was to come. A familiar uneasy sensation of queasiness and discomfort constricted my stomach.

The taxi arrived and pulled up at the security gates. I hurried through, passing below the name emblazoned above the gates – "Transglobal Media Corporation" – thinking, as I always did, that there ought to be an accompanying sign warning all those who entered to abandon hope.

As I crossed the newsroom, I spotted Milo hovering over the shoulder of a subeditor, shouting and gesturing at his computer screen. Someone was being given a hard time and I would probably be next. Milo looked up and saw me.

"Where the hell have you been?" he shouted.

I ignored him and walked to my desk. He came over. Milo was only in his forties, but years of excessive drinking had bloated his features. His hair was sparse and fair, his blue eyes bleary. He was mid-height but seemed taller because of his habit of coming too close and, when approaching someone seated, looming over them.

"What happened?" he demanded.

"I told Simon. He wasn't there."

"Well where the hell was he?"

"I don't know! I'm not psychic."

"The Editor has gone ballistic. What am I supposed to tell him?"

"I don't know, Milo. I went to do the interview – "

"Oh, for God's sake…"

"So it's my fault again, is it?"

"That's what the Editor thinks."

"And I suppose I can count on you to confirm that opinion?"

Milo grinned. His smile was, curiously, even more unpleasant than his customary limited gallery of expressions, which ranged from scowl to leer. Turning on his heel, he said, "Certainly can."

As I muttered, "Bastard," at his retreating form, he turned and grinned, saying, "Nice of you to notice."

My friend Alex looked at me, worried. Alex, who was in his early twenties, had joined the paper six months earlier and I had been helping him to settle into his first job in Fleet Street. He said, "You don't want to keep challenging him, Jo. Milo's dangerous."

"Mainly to himself, the amount he drinks," I said.

"If only that were true…"

"Has he been getting at you again? Try to ignore him," I said.

"Hah! That's rich, coming from you. His being permanently pissed, obnoxious, talentless and devious I can handle. But stitching me up with his bungling incompetence – that's something else."

"What's he done?"

"Never mind," said Alex wearily. "There's no point."

"I'll have a word…"

"Don't! I can look after myself. You don't have to take on everyone else's battles. You're not to get involved, Jo. Have you got that?"

"OK, OK," I replied.

I wondered how long it would take Alex to become as disillusioned as the rest of us. I said, "He should sack Milo. But that'll never happen."

"Our Milo's a talentless hack who's politicked his way to the middle and now no one can shift him because he knows where the bodies are buried," said Alex. "Well, at least he knows what he is; there's some saving grace there, maybe. Unlike our esteemed Editor. A third-rater who thinks he's God's anointed. That's the biggest con of all – when you con yourself."

I had liked Alex from our first meeting. I liked his lively manner, with its suggestion of curiosity and amusement. He was tallish, around five foot eleven, and slim, with longish straight dark hair that fell across his forehead, and deep-set brown eyes. He had caught the eye of some female colleagues but seemed unaware of his attractiveness. He had no vanity whatsoever.

I took the books I had bought from my bag and showed Alex the political biography. "Would you say this was in good condition?"

"Very good. Disraeli." He flicked through the pages. "Are you planning a political career? Oh, I know, it's for old Smoothie-Chops, isn't it?" I had confided in Alex about my secret relationship with Patrick.

"Don't say that." I lowered my voice. "You don't know him."

"I know enough," said Alex. "And how is your wimpish, ageing paramour? Still back-stabbing in the palace of power?"

"He doesn't back-stab. He makes strategic moves."

"Oh, like Milo, you mean?"

"Nothing like Milo."

"Really? I sometimes find it hard to tell."

Alex was becoming irritating. I said, "You're being unfair. Anyway, who ever heard of a wimpish back-stabber?"

"He's wimpish as far as you're concerned. He shouldn't mess you about."

"He doesn't," I said.

"Yes he does. All this 'My wife and I have an understanding' stuff. It's a load of cobblers."

"You're wrong. Patrick tells me the truth."

"Then you're the only one. Jo, he's the Minister for Spin."

"That's nonsense," I whispered. "You know he has no involvement with the media – other than being interviewed, that's it."

"Is that what he tells you? Well, they say love is blind."
Alex picked up the red leather volume with the silver clasps.
"What's this?"

"I don't know. Some kind of journal."

"Who's Anna Leigh?"

"No idea."

Alex opened the book. He said, "This feels good, good and solid.
Very nice."

I looked over his shoulder as he riffled through the pages. The
book comprised a series of entries, each passage notated by an
embellished capital.

Alex said, "Oh, this is a surprise. It's about a medieval mystic.
She's writing about Julian of Norwich."

"Never heard of him."

"Her. She was an anchoress who lived in a cell attached to St
Julian's Church. She took her name from the church." Alex had a
First in medieval history from Oxford.

"What's that?"

"An anchoress? A woman who devoted her life to prayer for the
community. Julian's an intriguing character. There's something about
her that draws people in. She had these visions of the crucifixion, in
which she received a series of messages, and she wrote a book about
them. It was incredibly risky. She was a very brave woman."

"In what way?"

"Well, the Church was preaching the wrath of God and fires of
hell for wicked sinners. Your only hope of salvation was forgiveness
and absolution, which only the Church could grant. And there
was Julian, right under the noses of the authorities, writing about a
God who is never angry with us, doesn't blame us and has already
forgiven us for anything we'll ever do."

"What would have happened to her if she'd been found out?"

"She'd have been condemned as a heretic and burned at the
stake. The thing that fascinates me is that she writes like a reporter.
She tells it like it is, even if it's an uncomfortable and inexpedient
truth – she tells it anyway."

After an exhausting twelve-hour day, I arrived home at ten o'clock, too tired to cook. I transferred a ready-made dinner from the freezer to the microwave and poured myself a glass of wine, before sinking gratefully into my couch. I examined the book I had bought for Patrick. Yes, he would be delighted with his gift.

I took up the second book – *Anna Leigh's Journal* – and flicked through the pages. I was intrigued by Alex's description of Julian the mystic. I wondered what it must be like to risk death for a piece of writing. I read again the message on the flyleaf, the message that seemed so personal to me. I had always known what I wanted to do with my life. It was a secret certainty that nourished me and delineated a clear path ahead. I would discover and reveal the truth. I wanted to understand and explain why things happened, why people did what they did. I wanted to expose lies and show what was real. Of course, as a child I did not express my desire, even to myself, in such clear-cut terms. It was simply an expectation and a knowledge that I would use words to communicate meaning. When had I slipped away from that intention? What had happened to the part of me that had been idealistic and full of hope?

I had come upon a mystery. I wanted to know, *who was Anna Leigh?* What was so special about her journal that it had to be returned to her? Why had it been bound so beautifully? Who had valued it so highly? Had it been Anna herself or the writer of the message on the flyleaf? There were no clues: no publisher's mark; not even the name of a printer. How had such a book, a personal journal, found its way to the anonymous, secret world I had come upon in the antiquarian bookshop? How long had it lingered in that repository of forgotten souls?

Most curiously of all, why did I feel that the message written on the flyleaf – like a message in a bottle that had washed up on the shore at my feet – had been meant for me? I began to read.

18 *August*

*By chance, I encountered the lost lady. At that time I still
believed in chance. A candle burned, and by the light of the
flame I embarked upon the soul's solitary adventure.*

*A clear, bright day in Norwich was drawing to a close. The
rays of sunlight slanting through the cathedral's stained-glass
windows were fragmenting into fine and glimmering strands.
As the light withdrew, I remained a moment longer within the
quietude of fading day.*

*I turned to leave, and my eye was drawn by a leaflet on a
table near the entrance. The leaflet, partly obscured in a display
of books and postcards, was decorated with a drawing of a
woman in nun's habit, holding delicately, between thumb and
forefinger, a tiny object that looked like a hazelnut.*

*I picked up the leaflet and read "Julian of Norwich is
believed to be the first woman to write a book in English. In
1373, during a severe illness, she received a series of visions
of the crucifixion, in which Jesus spoke to her of God's love.
For the next forty years she lived as an anchoress in a small
room attached to St Julian's Church, where she interpreted the
meaning of the revelations and wrote her book."*

*Julian of Norwich... I remembered her name from long ago.
Sister Mary Theresa had read to me from her book, comforting,
reassuring words of love, during a long period of illness when
I was eight years old. Sister had sat by my bedside, soothing me
with her cool hand on my forehead, her gentle, loving presence
and words of kindness.*

*Sister Mary Theresa had told me that God loved me, no
matter what I said or did, and that he could never be angry
with me because he was all love. I remembered the words "all
shall be well..." In that little time in my life, I dared to believe
that all could be well – perhaps because I so desperately wanted
it to be – to believe that my life could change one day and I
could be happy.*

*I opened the leaflet and found inside a map of the route to
St Julian's Church, which was some ten minutes' walk away.
My curiosity was aroused. A woman writer, like me, but one
who was a solitary and lived six hundred years ago. What kind
of life would she have lived? There was an hour to spare before
my train back to London. I decided to visit St Julian's.*

*The map led me to the outskirts of town, down dingy streets
with lock-up garages to a small, dark alleyway, where a sign
directed me to St Julian's Church. I stepped into a suddenly
cool, close place. I walked across the nave towards the altar.
To my right I saw a little door with a notice that read "Julian's
cell". Close up, I read "Julian of Norwich, the fourteenth-century
mystic, lived here. The cell was destroyed in the Reformation,
but was rebuilt when the church was repaired after being
bombed during the Second World War."*

*There was something in the air. Something indefinable
touched me in some forgotten, neglected part of my being.
There was something about the simplicity and quiet of the place
that spoke to me, as if the silence contained a message.*

*I was caught by the presence of the place. I sensed an
invitation to be rested and healed.*

In the margin was reproduced a note that Anna presumably had
added after the original entry. It read:

*But there was more. I believe I knew, deep inside, that in
acknowledging the truth of the moment I stepped onto the
path that was my destiny. I believe I knew that the path I chose
would take me on a hazardous journey into the lost land of
shadows.*

It reminded me of my own feeling of sanctuary when I entered
the unfamiliar world of the antiquarian bookshop. The main
narrative continued:

Someone had made this place, created its sacred centre. Her atmosphere remained. I wondered about her. If I turned my head quickly, I thought, I'd catch sight of the edge of her skirt; if I closed my eyes, I'd feel her touch at my shoulder, hear gentle laughter. She was unseen but substantial.

I entered the cell. To the right of the small space was a window, looking onto a patch of grass and flowers enclosed by the church wall. To the front was a plain table covered by a white cloth, upon which stood two candlesticks. High up on the wall, above the table, was a large wooden crucifix. Some little stools were stacked near the door. I took one and sat on it and closed my eyes.

Breathing slowly and observing the intake and outflow of my breath, I meditated for several minutes. A sense of elation welled up within me. I felt ecstatic, flooded with joy. The feeling was intoxicating and made my head spin. I wept, and through my tears poured out my hurt, anger and bitter disappointment with my life.

I felt a strong, feminine presence, the warmth of a woman whose love enfolded all those who entered the place, whose arms were opened wide to soothe a frightened child, whose tender caress touched me with understanding, whose gentle entreaty breached my resistant heart, whose compassion pitied my sadness, whose joy diminished the darkness touching my soul. I suddenly yearned to know the woman whose passion was imprinted on the place, whose mothering, limitless spirit sought out my sorrow and hurt and brokenness, desiring to hold me and make me whole.

I recalled the words from Anna's book that had so moved me, the words that had offered the hope of being held safe in an embrace that would never let me go. And here was Anna, describing my own feelings in a way that made me feel a kinship with her.

*I looked up at the figure of Jesus and observed that the head
was thrown back, the eyes wide open. I was brought up to
believe that Jesus died on the cross to pay for our sins and in
doing so had redeemed us and bought us a place in heaven.
But here was an aspect of his dying that I had not seen before.
The head was thrown back awkwardly and the eyes were
revealed. It was not only his nakedness, his powerlessness in
the hands of the people who ruled the society in which he lived,
not only these familiar aspects of his death that I observed. This
was different. The eyes were wide open, the soul laid bare, his
feelings exposed.*

*Suddenly I was taken back in my memory to the age of
fifteen. I had been holidaying with a German family, on an
exchange visit. One day they had taken me, without warning
or preparation, to the Memorial Museum on the site of the
Bergen-Belsen concentration camp. We went into a hall of
photographs, joining a queue of people that moved slowly, like a
procession of penitents, across and around the room.*

*Suddenly, as my hosts moved aside to allow me to see, I was
confronted by a sight that filled me with utter horror. Before
me was a pyramid of rotting, skeletal flesh – blackened eye
sockets where bright eyes had once smiled, emaciated limbs
flung indecently across a stranger's body, so many, many people
thrown away, like rubbish, with neither kind word nor prayer.
I caught my breath, feeling dizzy and sick. How was it possible?
How could this terrible thing have happened in this world where
I was growing up? I did not know what to feel or what to do.*

*To the right of the photograph I saw a glass-framed notice.
It was a report written by a journalist who had accompanied
the liberators of the camp. He had observed, he said, that each
of the bodies in the many similar piles he saw that day had
a small cut at the top of the hip. A survivor had explained to
him that, when the body becomes emaciated, this is the last
place where any flesh remains. The starving prisoners had been
gnawing at the dead in order to stay alive.*

I felt I was falling, falling backwards into a dark pit. I felt terror and I felt shame. I thought: We did this.

In that instant I knew what humanity was capable of and that I must be capable of the same. What would I have done? Might I have been a prison guard who committed such horrors? Or a guard who did not join in but looked the other way? Or one of the starving prisoners gnawing at the dead? Which of those parts might I have played?

I felt grief – for the dead and for those who had to live with what they had done. I felt shame. It is a terrible thing to kill someone. How much worse to kill his soul, to take away the part that is sacred? And how do you live among the people you love when you have compromised your soul? That day something deep within me changed for ever. My certainties dissolved. My childhood ended.

As I stood in Julian's cell, looking up into the eyes of the broken figure on the cross, I thought: We did this, too. I have looked at the cross many, many times, but now I seemed to see it for the first time. In the eyes of the broken figure everything was revealed – the anguish, the doubts, the fear – all the natural feelings of a man suffering terribly and close to death.

In those last moments, when Jesus bore his trial alone, he became the victim of our inhumanity. Like the numberless victims of our inhumanity throughout the ages, he was stripped of his dignity. And in his utter vulnerability, I realized, he compelled me to become a participant when I would have preferred to remain an observer, striking an image upon my heart that cannot fade.

I entered his private space, the space each of us strives to protect, hiding behind a mask throughout our lives, covering the shame we cannot bear to see in a place that no one else enters. What if the mask were wrenched away suddenly, exposing everything, exposing me as I really am? Could I bear it? Could anyone bear it if he has shame, and which of us does not?

*I remembered hearing a song written by a survivor of the
camps – "My sister Hana had green eyes, she looked after
me, my sister Hana had green eyes, she was murdered in
Treblinka." My heart moved; I felt it move as a constellation
moves in space, I felt it lift and move, as a heavy weight is
moved; a movement almost mechanical, of great power,
lifting my heart up and forward into a different space and
engendering a deep, sweet, mighty swell of compassion, brought
from unimagined depths with a force I could not comprehend
and moving me to tears of such heart-full sweetness that they
soothed away all hurt and horror, even the horror of the
atrocity that had inspired them.*

*As I looked at the wide-open eyes, I realized that the beliefs
of my childhood must now give way to a better understanding.
It was a necessary death, but the manner of his dying was
necessary, too. He embraced the worst that we could do, for us,
because we needed to be shown how much we were loved and
nothing less would convince us. And at the sacred centre of
the crucifixion a mystery unfolded, like the opening petals of a
rose, revealing the vulnerability that is at the heart of love.*

*I rose and walked to the window. In my mind's eye, I
saw the exposed and gusty shore of eastern England edging
the encroaching waters that claimed the outstretched land
time after time. At the bleak horizon, those brooding, restless,
rushing seas had no defence against the tearing force of wind
and weather, flung from a dispassionate, measureless sky. I
imagined all of this, unchanged yet ever changing, perceived
from the narrow confines of a tiny cell, through one small
window, snug and quiet in the dark, by Julian.*

*I wondered: What did she see and understand in her vision
of the crucifixion, what secret knowledge did she gain? How did
she distil her alchemical promise of unconditional love from
the crucible of faith and prayer, when her Church preached
fear and punishment? What made her risk a charge of heresy
and death at the stake to defy its teachings with her revelation*

of a God who is never angry? What impelled and sustained her? I wanted to know the beguiling woman who had walked a straight and steady path through such difficult and dangerous territory. And did her story have the makings of a play?

I left the cell and retraced my steps across the nave. Near the entrance to the church was a little table, upon which some pamphlets and books had been left. Among them were several copies of a little book with a pale yellow cover. Its title was Enfolded in Love *and it contained extracts from* A Revelation of Love, *Julian's book. Below the title was a simple line drawing of a homely figure in a rough garment, who was leaning forward to gather up a kneeling child in an embrace. The child's head was bent forward, exposing the nape of his neck, which was bare and vulnerable.*

I took up the book eagerly, glad of the chance to be reacquainted with the words that had brought me such comfort as a child. I opened it at random and read "He did not say, 'You shall not be tempest-tossed, you shall not be work-weary, you shall not be discomforted.' But he said, 'You shall not be overcome.'" Tears came to my eyes as I remembered how dear Sister Mary Theresa had touched me somewhere deep inside when she had read those words to me. And I was not overcome. It was true.

I put the specified £5 into the collection box and took my copy of Enfolded in Love. *As I made my way back towards the railway station through the dingy, now darkened streets, the image of the crucifix and the memories of my childhood travelled with me. How strange that the past should have surfaced suddenly, in such a profound and unimagined way. What could be the reason?*

What could be the reason? I echoed Anna's thoughts. For I, too, was being reminded of the past, of the person I used to be. Reading her words, entering the private world of her intimate thoughts and feelings, had brought me into a different space. I felt very calm.

But I was also intrigued. I wanted to know the rest of her story. And she was challenging me. What would I have done, had I been a guard at Belsen? How do you live among the people you love when you have compromised your soul? I hoped I would never have to find out.

At the office the following morning Milo was on top form, buzzing around with an air of self-importance that suggested a big news story was brewing. Alex approached, carrying a bundle of papers.

"Hi, Jo." He looked despondent. "Have you heard?"

"What? I just got in."

"Something big broke overnight. A mole in the Foreign Office says the government has lied about arms deals."

"Great! Who's got the story?"

"Chris," said Alex. "Imran and I are helping him."

"Terrific! Well done."

"Yes, it's a brilliant chance – but there's something more, something funny going on. The mole has a secret illegitimate child, apparently, and that side of the story's wanted. Only the boy doesn't know this chap's his father and I've been sent to doorstep the mother."

"Oh, God."

"I don't know what to do. What would you do?" Alex asked. He looked desperate.

"Well – Milo wouldn't give me that story – " I said.

"I know. He knows you'd have a row with him about it. And you'd get away with it because they wouldn't want to lose you. But what would you do?"

"It has to be up to you, Alex."

"If I refuse I'll be fired," he said.

"That's right."

Alex looked utterly miserable. At that moment Milo called to him, "Alex – get your arse out of here. What are you hanging about for?"

Alex grabbed his jacket and hurried out.

I looked around the newsroom and wondered how many people felt as I did. People were not happy. It was 1991 and conditions had changed radically in my time on the paper. The avuncular spirit of the old-time proprietors, rich men who ran newspapers for the pleasure of it, was long gone. Our employers now were powerful press barons who ran their papers for money and influence, but mainly for money.

So we had changed, too. People were less inclined to go the extra mile for the sake of the story. We were cautious and we watched our backs. How long would a young idealist like Alex survive? How long would I survive? I was a favourite of the Editor, it was true. But even he was under pressure and he was a weak man.

I had not been asked to compromise my principles, but I rarely wrote anything these days that I felt was of real benefit to anyone. The character of the paper was changing. Under the new Editor, its reputation as a principled and fearless investigator was diminishing. Insidiously, its pages were becoming increasingly contaminated by stories that lacked depth and meaning. I still dreamed, though, of writing copy that would change lives.

Anna Leigh had found meaning. I envied her. And I recalled the excitement and expectation I had felt when I read the message on the flyleaf of her journal. Would Anna take me on a journey of my own, as the message seemed to imply, a journey that would reveal the truth?

Patrick rang during the morning and asked me to meet him for lunch at his apartment in Westminster, near the Houses of Parliament. An assignment nearby made it possible for me to accept. As I entered the building, Vic, the concierge, said a respectful, "Good afternoon, Miss Meredith." I wondered if he believed I was there in my capacity as a journalist or if he knew the real reason. When I had shared my worries with Patrick, he had replied breezily,

"Vic's paid not to think, and handsomely. That man would die on the rack before he'd say a word against me. I have his loyalty. It's bought and paid for. Basic maths, darling. Everyone has their price. Simple matter of knowing what it is."

Patrick ordered in lunch from a local restaurant, accompanied by a carefully selected bottle of wine. For the first time, I felt a tension in our relationship. My lover was a junior minister in the Foreign Office. My newspaper was talking secretly to a Foreign Office mole, one of his civil servants. I would give nothing away, of course; but I felt uncomfortable. Looking back, I must have been pretty naïve not to consider the vulnerability of my position.

We planned to spend his birthday together in Paris. When Patrick had suggested it, it had seemed a madly risky idea. But he knew a quiet hotel on the outskirts of Paris and, as he always said, he led a charmed life. Patrick expected things to go his way because they always had. Eton, the Guards, a lucrative career in the City, a safe Tory seat and a junior ministership had all come his way with the ease that he considered his entitlement. Money and influence had smoothed his path all his life. His goal was a place in the Cabinet and – why not? – the highest prize of all.

But I could not wait for Paris. I was too eager to see his pleasure when I gave him his gift. "Here's your present," I said, handing him the carefully wrapped package.

He ripped off the paper, and said, "Perfect. Clever girl." He glanced at his watch. "I'm free till three. Gives us an hour." He took my hand, and, as always, when he touched me I desired him.

Patrick knew he was attractive. He was tall, well-built and elegant, Savile Row-suited with always the perfect matching tie. His hair was almost black and tinged with grey, his features fine, his eyes an intense and mesmerising blue.

"I can't really, Patrick. I have to get back," I said.

"Busy day, eh?" Was he fishing? No, Patrick would not compromise me. I never discussed my work with him; he knew it was off-limits.

I said, "It's always busy. You know how it is."

I felt uneasy. But Patrick was caressing me and every cautious, sensible thought went out of my mind.

"Come on, darling. What do you say? I'm off to Brussels tomorrow and won't be back for a week. You know I adore you…"

My resistance was crumbling. "I'll have to ring in with an excuse. I'll have to be back by three."

Patrick took me in his arms and, without a word, undressed me and carried me to his bed. When I was in his arms I could not resist him. It was a heady aphrodisiac – sex and power, intermingled with love.

The phone rang. "Jesus! Thanks, old chap. Jo, you've got to go."

"What!"

"That was Vic. My wife's here. He's keeping her talking. Hurry, darling, please."

I scrambled into my clothes. I was shocked and trembling. Patrick said, "Take this for a cab," handing me a sheaf of notes. I pushed his hand away, refusing to take his money. As he opened the door, he kissed me hurriedly and said, "Take the stairs. Quickly, darling, before the lift arrives."

I hurried through the lobby to find Vic waiting at the door, ready to hail me a cab. "Good afternoon, Miss Meredith," he said politely. I did not reply. I half ran into the street and walked for some way before hailing a cab. As I travelled back to the office I felt shaken and humiliated. Suddenly the whole situation with Patrick felt dirty and underhand. How dare he treat me this way. Had he been lying to me? I felt hurt and furious.

An hour later, as I worked at my desk, the phone rang. It was Patrick.

"I'm sorry, darling. That was a ghastly thing to happen to you. No, I haven't deceived you, how could you think it? Yes, of course she knows, but she expects me to be discreet. At least until we divorce. She doesn't want to be seen as the cast-off wife. We have to arrange things so it looks like an amicable separation.

"She never uses the flat. Always said she didn't like it. She hasn't even bothered to get it decorated. Apparently she'd been shopping and was tired and decided to take a nap before heading home. Look, this is nothing for you to worry about. I'll bring you something special back from Brussels. I'll make it up to you, darling. I promise."

I arrived home that evening feeling tense, troubled and angry. Patrick's breezy assumption that the incident could be smoothed over, his failure to understand how devastating it had been for me, how humiliating to be ushered out by the concierge, made me feel very vulnerable. It left me wondering what I had got myself into.

Patrick had pursued me with a determination that I found irresistible. It was thrilling to know that such an exciting and dynamic man had chosen me. When I had first met him, at a City dinner, he had made it obvious that he was attracted to me. I was flattered. And when he made his move, it was direct and daring. An interview over dinner, an invitation back to his apartment and a declaration that he had fallen in love with me.

I was thirty-four, old enough to know what I was doing. I wanted all of it, the passion, the sex, the intellectual stimulus, the feeling of importance because I had been chosen by one of the most exciting and powerful men in the country. The girl from rural North Wales loved every minute of it. But it had been more than a year, and I was beginning to wonder where it was going. When I dropped hints about the future, Patrick would simply say, "You're happy, aren't you, darling?" I was not happy. But I did not want to lose my chance with this man. I poured myself a glass of wine. Pushing away the sad and angry thoughts, I took up the journal.

25 August

Since my visit to Julian's cell I have been troubled by the depth of feeling and new understanding that came to me as I stood before the cross. The memory of it haunts me. I feel uncomfortable in my skin and a sense of expectation seems to hover within and about me; it feels as though every nerve and fibre in my body knows that something has changed and that more change is to come. The easy contentment of my ordinary life has been taken from me.

I thought I had left my past behind, but something that never made sense when I was a child has now emerged as a troubling question in my mind. How did Sister Mary Theresa, the one person I truly trusted, reconcile Julian's message of unconditional love with the fearsome sermons of Father James? Which message was true? Both she and Julian must surely have struggled with the paradox.

Julian's God is never angry. He wants us to repent of our bad ways and change but does not want us to feel guilty. He does not blame us and has forgiven us for everything we will ever do. Father James seemed to know an entirely different God, an angry old man in the clouds. And though Father said God loved us, he didn't seem to like us very much.

I am puzzled and troubled by these thoughts. I still find within myself the frightened child who does not feel safe. How I long to step into that line drawing on the cover of Enfolded in Love, *open and vulnerable as the child being gathered into the embrace of the homely figure who bends lovingly towards him.*

I remember how Jesus said that he longed to gather us up, as a hen gathers her chicks under her wings. How deeply I desire such a gathering up. But I have no right to hope, for I do not deserve it. I want to be better than I am. I want to be of use and value. My life is a selfish life, but it is not the life I would choose.

Illness during my childhood years brought me the gift of solitude. It is a gift I have always cherished. But it has left me feeling apart from the world and with my isolation comes a sense of shame. I am not good enough. I have kind friends, but I do not like to trouble them. I feel I am a burden, and they are not here. I am afraid I am incapable of a real relationship with a man. And so I shelter within my carefully constructed world, as I always have done, a world in which closeness and tenderness can be managed without. I find solace, as I always have, in the keeping of my journal; my conversation with an absent friend, a kind, patient friend who will understand me and not find me wanting.

What was the dark secret that made my parents unfit to enter God's house? The guilt still haunts me. Did everyone know, as I sat in the Children of Mary Bible class on Sundays, that I was a tainted thing? Did I contaminate the sanctity of the holy circle? Father James' warnings of hell and damnation and the punishments awaiting sinners return to me in dark hours when I feel so alone.

Sometimes even now I am afraid to go to sleep in case those dreams return – those terrifying dreams of devils with horrible claws and tails, who come crawling up from a dark pit, reaching out for me to pull me down. In dark clouds above the pit hovers the discarnate head of an old man, like some Medea, tendrils of long hair and beard swirling about his face. He points his finger at me, fixing me with a look of anger and contempt. I hold my breath as he shouts in a voice like thunder that I am cast out into the darkness, out of the world and out of heaven, out of the galaxy and out of the universe. I am dispatched to the place of desolation and there I must live, alive for ever, with no hope of escape or of seeing again the people I love.

Sometimes the dreams would trouble me so much that I felt unwilling to return to church, for surely my continued attendance would only perpetuate my crime. But I did return, not only because my parents wished it but also because I loved my teacher, Sister Mary Theresa. If you, my absent friend, imagined reader of my journal and companion of my lonely hours, could only have met her, you would have loved her, too. I used to think: She is like Our Lady.

I wish I could sit once more before the statue of Our Lady, looking up into her beautiful face with its alabaster skin and gentle blue eyes. She seemed so loving and kind, I could almost feel that she was real. There was such an atmosphere of peace and tenderness around the statue; it seemed to inhabit a space all of its own, where all was calm and everything would come right. I felt Our Lady did accept me and understand my heartache, which I confided in her but could never have shared with anyone else.

One long, hot summer, when I was eight, I became ill, haunted by the fearful imaginings that gave me no rest. I lay in bed for hours on end, headachy and feverish, wanting to be well again but feeling unable to summon up the will to make myself better.

Despite my parents' care and solicitude, the barrier between us that precluded real intimacy seemed even more impenetrable in my weakened condition. Because I longed more than ever to be wrapped up in the certain knowledge that we as a family deserved love, the absence of that certainty bit keenly at a time when I was bereft of any sanctuary, even the synthetic sanctuary of my everyday routine.

And then there came a tap on the door. The handle turned and my mother stepped quietly into the room. "You have a visitor," she said. With a sweep of her skirts, Sister Mary Theresa followed her in and came towards me, her wide smile, as always, seeming about to split her face in two, like an overripe melon. The Sister, I always felt, was so brimful of joy that it must have been fizzing about inside her like lemon pop.

Sister Mary Theresa's uncompromising, unquestioning gladness was one of the many things I loved about her. She would not, could not be daunted. She knew she was loved: no doubt at all about that, she would have said if anyone had thought to challenge her certitude.

It was as though a great flood of love was pouring into her from above and bubbling and spinning about inside her, reaching every part, like an angel doing its spring-cleaning, and flowing endlessly from her eyes and mouth and hands, in loving looks, kind words and practical deeds to help and comfort others.

She came and sat by my bed. My mother left, closing the door quietly. "Well, now, you're looking grand. They told me you were ill," said Sister Mary Theresa. She placed her cool hand on my

*forehead and said, "You're a little warm, but sure you'll soon
be back to your old self. And you'd better not be too long about it
because we're all missing you at the Children of Mary."*

*As I looked up into her kind eyes, I wished, I wished I could
open up my heart to her. But wouldn't that be a betrayal of my
parents? I said, "Thank you, Sister. I am feeling better."*

*The Sister stayed for some twenty minutes, while we talked
and laughed together and shared a prayer. As she was about to
leave, she took from her bag something wrapped in tissue paper.
It was a candle.*

*She said, "This is for you," as she placed it in the candle
holder near my bed. She took some matches from her bag and
lit the candle, saying, "This light symbolizes the light of Christ
in the world. Your journey is to follow it and always remember
that the light is also in you."*

*As evening darkened, I watched the candle's steady light,
my whole soul seemingly protected by its kindly, steadfast glow.
The face of Sister Mary Theresa, all one great smile, hovered
over my consciousness as I drifted into gentle dreams.*

I rested the journal on my lap. Anna Leigh's gentle, confiding voice
touched me. How strange to feel that I had become her absent
companion, the patient, uncritical friend in whom she confided; for
I felt she was inviting me, me and no one else, to respond and to
complete the circle of conversation she had begun.

And I would have liked to share with her the memories she had
stirred in me. For her descriptions of Father James and his hellfire
sermons and the loving contrast of Sister Mary Theresa reminded me
of my own childhood and the time I spent living with my great-aunt.

Like Father James, Aunt Vaughan served a stern and humourless
God. And like Anna, I had found refuge, at a time when I felt no one
understood me, with a loving and generous guide.

Michael… I had not thought of him in years. Michael was my aunt's
gardener. He was my friend, mentor and, I suppose, surrogate parent
in those long-ago days when I felt so very alone and misunderstood.

When I was seven my father, an Army major, was posted to India. The climate in India was deemed, bizarrely, unsuitable for children. So my sister, Louisa, and I were dispatched from our village in North Wales, where I had run free among the fields and streams and circles of stone, to live with my aunt in Shropshire. In her charge, my father informed us, we would receive a good Christian upbringing.

Aunt Vaughan belonged to a strict Presbyterian church, which favoured the fire and brimstone school of theology. The pulpit was a place of high drama, with much theatrical slamming-to of the Big Bible on the lectern when the minister wished to make an important point or wake up the surreptitious snoozers. Like Anna, I found myself listening to dire warnings of judgement and punishment. I used to wonder why people went to church every week to be told off. I got told off quite enough at home.

Not that my aunt lacked a sense of humour. On one particular day she seemed to have mellowed towards me. She handed me a sweet wrapped in a silvery twist of foil. I unwrapped it eagerly, happy to think that I must have done something right for a change. Inside the foil was a smooth, round pebble. How my aunt laughed. It was my first encounter with her sense of humour, and my last. I resolved to make it my life's purpose to annoy her as much as possible, in the hope of being sent to live somewhere – anywhere – else.

To be fair to my aunt, a rough-and-tumble child who climbed and fell out of trees and came home muddy and sometimes bloody, must have come as a shock. The photographs of me in those days show a brown-eyed little girl with a mischievous grin, her untidy dark hair in her eyes, who looks as though she is being held firmly in place by an unseen pair of hands for just long enough for the shutter to close.

My interview for the local Church of England school probably confirmed my aunt's initial impression that I was going to be trouble. Passing through the school gate, I observed that the noticeboard at the entrance described it as a "voluntary school". Did this mean, I asked the headmaster, as I sat under his stern scrutiny, that I didn't have to go when I didn't feel like it? He replied that impudence was an unattractive quality in a child, but one that was readily remedied. I had not a clue what he meant. I soon found out.

When I had been at the school a few weeks it became apparent that I was brighter than the star pupil, the headmaster's daughter. I counted this very bad luck. There was no means of compensating for my shocking lapse and he made my life a misery.

Aunt Vaughan insisted that Louisa and I accompany her to church twice on Sunday. We always walked the four-mile round trip, rain or shine. My aunt would never accept a lift from a neighbour because she thought it sinful to travel in a vehicle on the sabbath. I used to pray every Sunday that God would send me a horse. Nor did my aunt allow us to play games or even take our dolls from the toy cupboard on a Sunday. Reading was the only activity she would permit.

On one particular Sunday I was unwell and allowed to stay at home, with instructions to read an assigned passage in my Bible. The moment I heard the click of the latch on the front gate, as my aunt and Louisa departed, I suddenly felt much better. The sun was shining, it was a lovely day and the opportunity to run free in the garden, orchard and wood was suddenly too enticing to resist.

I skipped out of the house, calling my aunt's dog, Moses, to join me. Together we careered down the path to the wood. I remember singing loudly as I ran along the path, stopping to help myself to the Victoria plums of which my aunt was so proud. I pretended that I was a magical fairy princess who could turn frogs into princes. That put me in mind of the pond – what could be more fun than to find a frog and try out my magical powers?

That part of the garden fascinated me, because just beyond the pond my aunt had established a burial ground for her succession of dogs. Around the series of mounds that marked the grave of each departed canine companion she had planted gooseberry bushes. They yielded big, fat fruits which I would never touch, fearful that they would taste of dog.

I ran to the pond and stood at the very edge, peering in, hoping to spot a squelchy, shiny green frog. But there was no movement in the murky depths. The stagnant state of the pond had been the subject of discussion between Michael and my aunt. Michael wanted to clear it. My aunt, for some reason, wanted it to be left. I leaned over further. Surely there must be frogs. Every pond had frogs. Suddenly I lost my balance and I was in the water, struggling to swim in the slimy mass of smelly vegetation. I became afraid and started to scream.

The next thing I knew, Michael was running towards the pond. In seconds he had hold of me and brought me safely out of the water, spluttering and frightened. As I got my breath back, my first thought was that I was in deep trouble. Aunt Vaughan would be very angry. She had warned me sternly not to go near the pond and I had disobeyed her. Even Moses was dejected, putting his head down between his paws with a look that seemed to say, "Now you're for it."

"Well I don't suppose you'll do that again, will you?" said Michael, as I started to cry. "It's a good job I was getting a bit of work done, in peace and quiet – well, until you decided to go swimming with the fishes," he said. "Now, now, you're safe now. Come on, let's get you back to the house before Mrs Ogwen Lewis gets back."

Michael led me, dripping, back to the house. I rushed upstairs and changed. But what would I do with my wet, smelly clothes? I came down to the kitchen, where Michael had prepared tea and biscuits. He said, "Perhaps you should rinse out your clothes and put them in with the laundry. Jess won't split on you." Jess did the cleaning and other household tasks for my aunt.

I was amazed that a grown-up should suggest such a deception. Michael smiled his twinkly smile, as though he knew what I was thinking, and said, "Discretion is the better part of valour. Sometimes it's best just to keep people happy. But you must promise me you'll never do anything daft like that again. On your honour? Promise?" I promised. Michael trusted me to keep my word, and that meant everything. I had found a friend. I got away with it and my spirit soared. Anything was possible now. Aunt Vaughan was not invincible after all.

She was, however, a law unto herself. When she took it into her head to do something, she proceeded like a great swarm of killer bees, unheeding of any obstacle in her path. I used to watch in awe as she set off in gum-booted malevolence, circular saw in hand, to chop down dead trees – at least, she said they were dead.

It brought great pain to Michael. I became aware of this not long after my arrival, when I chanced upon him standing looking at a felled tree, tears in his eyes. He stretched out his hand and stroked the trunk sorrowfully, as though he were comforting some poor mortally wounded creature. I hid, realizing instinctively that this was a private moment.

But Aunt Vaughan did not get it all her own way. I discovered, with delight, that Michael frequently deflected her mad plans for the destruction of her property. He did it without openly opposing her, which, given her contrary nature, would only have made her more determined upon her course.

"These must come down," she said one day to Michael, indicating a row of perfectly healthy birch trees. "And quick about it."

"Right you are, Mrs Ogwen Lewis," said Michael. "We'll have them down next week. Mr Henderson talked you into it, then, did he?"

Aunt Vaughan and Mr Henderson, who lived next door, relished a mutual loathing.

"What has he been saying to you?" she demanded.

"Oh, nothing much. Just as how he'd like you to take these trees down. They're blocking the light to his fruit beds, he says."

"I've changed my mind," said Aunt Vaughan. "The trees will stay."

More memories came back to me, for the first time in many years, as I remembered with gratitude Michael's loving care and guidance. Whatever the difficulties with my aunt, the garden and wood always felt like home – because they were Michael's territory.

Every afternoon when I arrived back from school, I would throw my satchel into a corner of my bedroom, quickly change and run out to find him. There was nearly always some adventure to share – fishing, bird-watching, learning the names of wild flowers… Michael had seen my need for love and fulfilled my deep-seated longing to truly come home. As an adult, I had long since lost that sense of homecoming. But as I retrieved my memories of Michael, I felt a pain in my heart, a hunger to once again feel safe, comforted, accepted and loved.

Like Sister Mary Theresa and the extraordinary Julian, with her unbreakable adherence to her mission, Michael had found a straight path through life's turbulence and pain. What had sustained him? What had made him the man he was? Michael had found meaning. Could I? I was immersed in these thoughts when the phone rang. It was Alex.

"Hi, Jo. I've just got back." He sounded very downcast. "Fancy a drink?"

It was 10 o'clock. I was tired and still upset about Patrick. But Alex was a friend and he needed me.

"Sure." I arranged to meet him at an Italian restaurant near my house.

Alex quickly downed two glasses of red wine.

"I did it," he said. "I did it."

"How was it?"

"Awful. Have you ever done anything like that?"

"Once – well, not really like that, but something I didn't like doing."

"How do you feel about it now?"

"I wish I hadn't done it."

"I shall always regret it," said Alex.

He seemed to be in a bad way. My concern for him deepened.

"You're going to have to make decisions about this sort of thing," I said.

"I know."

"Why did they want to cover that angle? It makes no sense. It undermines the source. The mole must be very scared. Presumably he now knows he's going to be outed."

"Something's going on," said Alex.

"What? Bribery and corruption?"

"It's never that clear-cut, is it? You know how it works – a word here, a favour there. I'm not sure whose service I'm in any more."

"Whose did you think you were in?" I asked.

"Truth and justice. Hah! Even I think I'm pathetic," said Alex.

"You're not pathetic. You're a first-rate journalist. Don't let them make you forget that." But even as I reassured Alex, I was aware that I needed the same reassurance myself.

Alex asked, "Has Masterton said anything to you – about the story?"

"You know I'd never discuss work with him."

"That wasn't my question."

"Why do you ask?

"Because I don't trust him. I think he's using you."

"You're being paranoid. What's brought this on?"

"Never mind. Just something someone said to me."

"Who?"

"Geraldine Stephens, the woman I interviewed, the mother of the mole's illegitimate child, she used to be a civil servant. She let slip that she's afraid of someone in the Foreign Office, someone she described as ruthless and dangerous. She's really frightened. I promised not to put anything about it in my piece."

"Why should that be Patrick?"

"Dunno. He just gives me the creeps, I guess. Watch your back, Jo. God, I wish you would wake up and take better care of yourself."

Alex was beginning to annoy me, so I changed the subject. I said, "Tell me more about Julian. Anna Leigh agrees she was a very brave woman."

"OK. She was born in the mid-fourteenth century. Edward III was King. England was at war with France. Life was very hard. There were three plague epidemics before she reached her early twenties. The first killed a third of the population of England. While she was a young girl there was also an epidemic of something like Mad Cow Disease, which caused widespread starvation."

"It's hard to imagine suffering on that scale. I mean, it's what we see on television, in the Third World – but to imagine it happening here…" I said.

"Life was brief and horribly insecure. If you were poor, you were always hungry; you could get sick and die at any time, from any number of diseases. The water was polluted. The meat and fish were rancid – not surprising, since animals were slaughtered for the table in the ditches where sewage was dumped. Violence was casual and routine. Life was cheap," said Alex.

"No wonder the peasants revolted."

"Quite right. 1381, the Peasants' Revolt. The King imposed a poll tax to raise money for the war against France, which was then in its fortieth-plus year. It was the last straw. People had had it with authority – and that included the clergy and religious orders, who looked after their own interests while the people suffered."

"I'm trying to imagine this nice lady reflecting in her cell while the world went mad around her," I said.

"She would have lived through a huge amount of turbulence and civil unrest. And she would have been aware of it. She wasn't entirely enclosed, you see. In fact, she was a kind of agony aunt; people would come to her window to tell their troubles and ask her advice."

"Amazing that she managed to keep her book a secret," I said.

"If she hadn't, she'd have been forced to recant and repudiate everything she had written or be burned at the stake. And Henry Despencer, the Bishop of Norwich, would have had a personal reason for discrediting her message. He was a Crusader, known as the Battling Bishop, and he financed his expeditions by selling indulgences. These were documents that bought you time off from the sentence you were due to serve in purgatory in payment for your sins."

"So Julian's account of a God who is never angry and doesn't need to be bought off would have put quite a dent in his trade," I said. "She was a kind of revolutionary."

"In a way. But she was also a sincere believer in the Church and its authority to deliver the Christian message. She had to struggle with that paradox, and it was a very hard struggle for her. But she did what she had to do and she didn't compromise her integrity. Wish I could say the same."

I said, "But she did compromise, didn't she? But in a way that didn't matter." Our conversation had reminded me of something Michael had taught me. He had shown me a way of living peacefully with my aunt, and her endless criticism, without compromising my integrity. I told Alex about it.

I remembered it so very clearly, how I had gone to the wood to search for solace and Michael, feeling very sorry for myself after yet another bruising encounter with my aunt. I had found him digging out an overgrown patch of brambles in front of an oak tree. When I told him my woes, he had straightened up, rested his arm against the tree-trunk and looked at me very seriously.

"He started talking about my aunt," I told Alex. "He said, 'Not the sweetest cherry on the tree, is she?' I was amazed, because he'd always spoken respectfully of her. He told me I mustn't believe the things she said about me because they weren't true; that she saw things the way she did because of the way she was. All the same, he said, I shouldn't argue with her, just let her say what she had to say and not lose my temper. He said, 'Learn to dodge the blows. Box a bit clever. Play the Joker's card.' Well, it worked! I let her rant on until she'd finished. And when I handled it that way everything just went much more smoothly. And I didn't get nearly so upset.

"Michael taught me to be kind. He said, 'Be generous with your kindness because the world can never have enough. And always remember that you're a little star and your light will grow brighter and stronger every day, till it's strong enough to sustain you through anything.'"

Alex said, "Great bloke. So why are you always battling with Milo?"

"I'd forgotten. I'd forgotten a lot of things. Michael made me feel there was something in me that was worthwhile. He understood me and accepted me."

Alex said, "And loved you…"

"Yes. What he gave me was love. Nothing else can make you feel that good."

After rather a lot more red wine, we called it a night. When I arrived home I no longer felt tired. I curled up in bed with the journal, curious to read on in the knowledge of what Alex had told me about Julian and her world.

26 August

During those months when I was ill, Sister Mary Theresa often came to see me. I always looked forward to it. She filled the room with a comforting feeling of calm and repose. Even after she had left I sensed her presence. She made me feel that things could be different, that life could change. She made me believe there was genuine cause for hope. Where did that feeling go?

I believe it dwindled away long ago as I became accustomed to living with meagre expectations. Since childhood I have used familiar routines as a refuge from pain, from engagement with people.

I had to leave Cambridge and the stifling, protective routine of my academic world. I felt as though something inside was withering away. My survival depended upon moving on. In London I have felt as though a burden has been lifted from my shoulders. I am so lucky to earn my keep from what was once a hobby. I love the world of theatre. Being a legitimate part of it has allowed me to create a new image of myself, a new identity almost: someone who can be a little more daring. But at heart

the sense of isolation has remained. Now, though, I feel I am
being invited out of the shadows and into the sunlight.

This new feeling of lightness has come into me since my visit
to the tiny, simple chapel on the site of Julian's cell. I have, in
quiet moments, recaptured the gentle peace I discovered there.
The spirit of the place – a presence of its own or the imprint of a
personality or events that marked it for all time – remains with
me. I feel that Julian is still close by, a woman out of time with
a message I need to hear and understand.

I sat at my window this evening and watched night stealthily
overtaking day in the park, making the trees shadowy masses that
reflected the shapes of the dark clouds. I closed the window but did
not draw the curtains. I took up my copy of Enfolded in Love.

The preface reminded me of what I had learned from the
leaflet I found at the entrance to Julian's cell: she had written
an account of her visions of the crucifixion, first a short text
and then, after many years of meditation, a longer version. At
the heart of Jesus' message was God's assurance of his abiding
love. "Wouldst thou know the Lord's meaning in this thing?
Know it well. Love is his meaning," she was told.

The darkening gloom of early evening was making me feel
a little sad. I lit some candles. I closed the book and pressed it
between my palms, moulding it gently, my fingers sliding and
pushing against the cover. The book filled me with a desire to
know every part of it, and I felt instinctively that I would not
penetrate its meaning with my intellect. I knew that I must find
some other way to take it into myself.

I handled it urgently, as though its meaning could be
squeezed out through its fabric, through my skin and into
my innermost self. As I did so, something informed my
spirit that to take the knowledge within I must find the place
where it already resided. I handled the book and let my
imagination wander.

Julian.

*I hold the book now flat on my upheld palms. I open it. I am
in her cell. This is the city of Norwich. The year is 1383. I see
sunshine in a pale sky with soft clouds, and a carefree cluster
of spring daffodils, thrust into a jug. The water surrounding the
stems is limpid and cool, and there is a quietness enfolding the
flowers and spreading further now into the room, which opens
up around me, tiny but infinite in space.*

*My eyes are drawn to a candle's flame, and as I look the
heavy white wax becomes translucent and the steady gold
of the flame burns brighter and stronger, creating a light
that is spreading, penetrating every corner of the room, and
outwards, farther and higher, reaching and filling every
heart, so that every man and woman and child, every animal
and tree and plant and flower, every part of the sea and sky
and every piece of the earth receives and trembles as the light
enters it.*

*This little light from this plain wax candle radiates its power
from this small place throughout the world, and the stars, and
infinity. The flame draws me into itself, and I come slowly from
the heavy grief and disappointment of my life towards that
inner peace and calm and understanding that lives within the
heart of the flame.*

*I hold the book open now, my hands pressed on its pages as
though in prayer, awaiting benediction. Through closed eyes
I seek the place. My heart beats faster. Have I found the place
where I can begin? I read "He who made man for love will
by that same love restore him to his former blessedness, and
yet more." I read the passage again. "He who made man for
love..." I find it hard to believe that I was made for love.*

*I hold the book gently. It feels like a fragile bird, resting lightly
upon my palms, my fingers barely touching the pages. I wait in the
silence. I am afraid. I open the book again, at random.*

*"I saw that pain alone blames and punishes, and that our
courteous Lord comforts and succours, ever being gladness
and joy to the soul, loving and longing to bring us to his own*

*blessedness." Pain alone punishes? Indeed, pain does punish.
But it is surely the price of sin?*

*"I saw in truth that God does all things, however small they
may be. And I saw that nothing happens by chance, but by the
far-sighted wisdom of God. If it seems like chance to us, it is
because we are blind and blinkered."*

*How can it be that nothing happens by chance? When I
think of all the mistakes I have made, my fearful hesitation and
timorous withdrawals, all the disappointment and loss... All
this was planned? It makes no sense. All the pain and suffering
of the world, planned? If my failure to understand this is
blindness, I am indeed blind.*

*I am beginning to feel light-headed. The room still feels so
gloomy. The sky has become overcast and I think there will be a
storm. Perhaps I am allowing my imagination too much rein. I
shall close the book.*

*But this place is so calm and quiet. This place. Julian's cell,
dark, peaceful, candlelit. Outside it's a lovely, sunny spring
day, I can see it over the heads of the daffodils on the sill, and
they glow in their thick deep and pale transparent yellows,
they glow and glory in the sunlight. Why would she want to
stay indoors, in this small room, when outside there's an earth
and sky filled with glorious sunshine? The book seems to call
to me.*

*I read, "I saw, too, that his unceasing work in every thing
is done so well, so wisely, and so mightily that it is beyond our
power to imagine, guess or think."*

*Does this mean that I am not intended to understand?
Perhaps if I concentrate on the candle I'll be able to get a
grip...*

*"As by his courtesy God forgives our sins when we repent,
even so he wills that we should forgive our sins, and so give up
our senseless worrying and faithless fear."*

*If I could forgive myself would I lose my fear? But I do not
feel forgiven. I do not find it in my heart.*

I begin to feel sad. I need some air. I go and stand at Julian's little window onto the world. That's better. You have a lovely view, Julian, plenty of trees. I thought you would have been lonely, enclosed in your cell all day and all night long, but I can see so many people about, I expect they often stop by for a chat. It's such a beautiful atmosphere in this place, calm and restful and loving, they must feel drawn...

I can well understand the appeal of a peaceful, quiet corner, a place to be safe and free of the world... but how safe could it really have been? A woman writing theology in an age when women were forbidden even to speak in church – a dangerous undertaking.

I strike a match to light a cigarette and look into the blade of molten flame. I wonder about this woman who risked death to do what she believed she had to do. She embraced and lived a paradox: pursuing spiritual truth that had to be kept secret from the Church, whilst remaining faithful to it and believing in its authority to deliver God's message to humanity. What kind of person would have the moral integrity to make and maintain such a choice?

My questions seem suspended in the air. I hope for answers, but there is silence. The flame flickers gently. I feel very tired suddenly. I feel as though the weariness of years has settled upon me. I will sleep for a little while...

I slept and dreamed, or perhaps it was all a dream. I awoke and looked out of my window, across the park and up into the starry night. I opened the window and listened to the rustle of the wind in the trees, felt its cool caress on my forehead. I felt calm and refreshed.

A thought formed in my mind: I desired to know, so I was taken to the place of knowing, and knowledge was made mine.

I awoke with a start, suddenly catching my breath. I had dropped off to sleep in an awkward position and now my neck ached. The journal had fallen to the floor. I glanced at the clock. It was midnight.

I felt exhausted – *wedi blino'n lân*, clean tired-out… the Welsh that expressed the feeling so well came into my mind. My first language as a child was my treasure house, providing the depth and subtlety of meaning I sometimes failed to find in English.

I bent down to pick up the book and noticed a folded sheet of paper that must have fallen from it. I picked up the paper and was astonished to see written on it a song in Welsh. I hummed the tune that was annotated on the paper. It was a strange, plaintive melody, in keeping with the words. The song was about the spirit of the woods crying out to the spirit of the mountains of its weary longing for the sun. I was puzzled and a little disturbed. Why had providence dropped this Welsh song into my lap? Was there a connection between the song and the book? Why on earth would there be a Welsh song – and one I had never heard – in the journal? These thoughts bothered me as I lay in bed. I sang the song softly to myself – *"Mae ysbryd y coed yn galw ar ysbryd y mynyddoedd, mae'r gwanwyn yn ymdroelli ynddof i a dw i'n ysu am yr haul…"*

I was walking down a long corridor in a palace or temple made of light. Its tall columns and graceful arches reached high into the light blue and then deepening indigo sky. The walls I passed were constructed of myriad shimmering minuscule bubbles of coloured light, all fusing into one soft white iridescence. A figure in white approached – whether male or female I could not tell – with arms outstretched in welcome. As it drew closer I saw its beautiful countenance. The being smiled at me with such compassion and tenderness that I felt touched in my heart.

"Come," it said. "Come and see."

I followed as it moved ahead of me with a fluidity and grace that made it seem almost to be floating. It led me into a vast room filled with shelves containing row upon row of books. "You can rest a while here and learn what you need to learn before you go on to the next place," it said. "This library is for souls who choose to serve by healing. Healing takes many forms. You must search here to discover your own path of service."

I can remember nothing more of the dream. When I awakened the following morning I felt calmer and more rested than I had done for a very long time. I felt more confident, too, of coping with whatever the day might bring.

3

The next morning, as I walked across the editorial floor, I sensed a febrile, nervy atmosphere. We were in the throes of a big story. I could feel it and so, I sensed, could everyone else. That morning's issue had the arms story as front-page splash. A leaked memo from our embassy in Jakarta had revealed that the UK government knew that British arms sold to Indonesia were being used to repress the people of East Timor, which Indonesia had been occupying illegally for twenty-five years. The sale was a direct contravention of the UK's proclaimed ethical foreign policy and the memo gave the lie to a statement made by the Foreign Secretary to the House of Commons.

It was a very big story indeed. Patrick must be deeply involved in it, but he had yielded not a hint. I assumed we would continue investigating the story and run a follow-up the next day. Presumably, Alex's interview with Miss Stephens, the mole's former lover, would be used then. I had barely reached my desk when Milo called me across. I headed for the news desk.

Milo said, "I'm putting you on the FO story. You'll be working with Chris and Steve, with Caz, Imran and Alex for backup. The Editor's decided to run the mole's personal story tonight. Alex has got some useful stuff from the bastard kid's mother. Very heart-rending, just the job. She touchingly thought if she talked to us she could protect the kid. She's also said the mole's got an alcohol problem. Better and better." Milo punched the air gleefully. "Thank you, God!"

He continued, "Imran's in Bristol, chasing the kid at uni. Steve's chasing the mole's wife. If my luck holds – and I think it might – she's in the dark about the kid. The big interview is yours. The mole's at a conference in Oxford. He knows the game's up and has agreed to give us the works on condition we go easy on his family. Dr Trevor Newell. He's a specialist on South-East Asian affairs. If the FO press office rings you, act dumb. You know nothing. You're not doing a story. Chris is going to ask the FO for a comment just before we go to press, so they're put on the spot. You're doing a complete exposé, all the dirt, everything you can get. See what you can dig up."

As Milo briefed me, a hot and pricking sensation rose up my spine to the back of my neck. "Milo – why are we discrediting our source?" I asked.

"Why not? Two bites of the cherry."

"But it makes no sense…"

"Which planet are you on? We get another scoop tomorrow. Don't give me this crap, Meredith. Just get on with it." Milo called across to Simon, the Deputy News Editor, "Brief Jo on the mole interview."

Simon, who was on the phone, made a gesture of assent to Milo and indicated that he would talk to me at my desk in a moment. I walked back across the newsroom, the blood pounding in my ears and a jangling sensation in my brain. I was sweating and feeling sick. I was an experienced reporter. I was used to tackling difficult stories. I usually relished the challenge. But this time it was different.

The instruction to do something that I knew to be terribly wrong, knew to be a betrayal of the beliefs that informed my work and my life, delivered in such a sudden, brutal and matter-of-fact way, had knocked the wind out of me. Suddenly, just like Alex, I had to make a decision that I knew would affect the rest of my life.

I sat in front of my computer, staring blindly at the screen. I was in shock. Then I thought: *How could I have failed to realize that this moment would come?* As Milo had said, which planet was I on? How arrogant had I been to think that, because everyone knew what I stood for and the Editor particularly liked my work, I would be safe? I had been treading a fine line between an awareness of the insecurity of journalists in the new Fleet Street and a belief that I would never be pushed this far. Suddenly that seemed naïve and vain.

Simon arrived with a briefing and details of my appointment with Dr Newell. I was due to catch the train to Oxford in half an hour's time. I had a critical decision to make and no time to even think about it. I gathered together my papers, bag and coat and headed out to the main road, where I hailed a taxi.

As I sat on the train, feeling frightened and worried, my thoughts of the previous evening came back to me. I realized why. The sudden, shocking assault that had been Milo's instruction reminded me of Great Aunt Vaughan, and how I had felt when she had delivered her icy warnings that I would come to no good. Those verbal assaults had been like sharp poison darts. They came unexpectedly, when I was unprotected, making me doubt my sense of self, doubt who I really was.

Except for Michael. He had made all the difference. When I had run to him for comfort, he had shown me how to slough off my aunt's words. The balm of his friendship and the validation and confidence he gave me had made me strong. When I told him how well the Joker's card had worked with Aunt Vaughan, he had said, "Now you're getting it. Other people don't upset us. We upset ourselves."

As the train rumbled northwards through the outskirts of London, I thought again about the Joker's card. In adulthood, it had slipped my memory and I had tended to meet any onslaught in defensive, fighting mode, taking it all on the chin. Could Michael's Joker be the solution to this problem? Was there a way in which I could do the interview without compromising my principles? Or must I pull out of the assignment and lose my job, if I had the courage? I closed my eyes and allowed myself to drift off into a reverie. I opened my eyes and, looking out across the unfolding green fields of Oxfordshire, I began to see a possibility.

I arrived at Oxford Station and took a taxi to the Randolph Hotel, where I was to meet Dr Newell. The receptionist directed me to his room and I took the lift to the third floor. I knocked on the door of room number 37 and it was opened by a slim, grey-haired man in his fifties. He greeted me courteously and his manner was calm, but beneath the surface I detected a nervous apprehensiveness.

We sat together in armchairs at a large window that overlooked the busy street. I began by thanking Dr Newell for agreeing to see me. I said I would try to make things as easy as possible.

He said, "Your editor has promised me that my family will not be troubled any further. My wife is unwell."

I took a deep breath and decided to tell the truth, whatever the cost.

"Dr Newell, I'm afraid that promise will not be kept. I expect you know that one of my colleagues has already interviewed Geraldine Stephens?" Dr Newell nodded. "I'm very sorry to have to tell you this, but another colleague is attempting to interview your son. Both those interviews are scheduled for publication in tomorrow's paper. Another of my colleagues is attempting to secure an interview with your wife."

The silence that fell between us was deafening. The rumble of traffic in the street below seemed far away, as though we were detached from the rest of the world, cocooned in a moment taken out of time. Dr Newell's expression during those few minutes, as he took in what I had said and considered it, was something I shall never forget. The desperation and hopelessness in his eyes wounded me deep inside. I felt myself being stripped open, to reveal an inner worthlessness. I felt dirty, guilty and ashamed. It was still not too late. I could gather up my things, make an excuse and leave. The silence ended as Dr Newell turned to look me in the eyes.

He said, "It must have taken some courage to tell me that."

For the first time in an interview, I felt I was losing control of the situation. Tears were beginning to form in my eyes. Dr Newell leaned forward and put his hand over mine. "It's a dirty business, isn't it? Even those of us who try to do the decent thing get caught in the net. Should we accept what we are, do you think? Acknowledge our fallibility and weakness and ask for understanding?" He smiled wryly. "I don't suppose that approach would cut much ice with your editor."

I remained silent. Dr Newell said, "I can see that a lot of unpleasant stuff is going to come out that will be deeply hurtful to the people I love."

He stood up and walked to the window, and looked down on the street below. He said, "There goes the world, busy about its business, rushing here and there. We all do it. Until the moment when life catches up with us, and then we have to stop. Doing the right thing. I thought I was. Well, I had no choice. Sometimes there is no choice. People are dying in East Timor because we're breaking our own rules. Someone has to speak up and this time it fell to me." He returned to his chair. He looked desperate.

He said, "Help me." I thought he was about to cry and reached out my hand to him. He grasped it in both of his and then began to sob softly. Whilst the journalist in me was keenly aware that I had not yet switched on my tape recorder, the better part of me rejoiced. That omission felt like a victory.

I said, "I have an idea. Would you like to hear it?"

Dr Newell looked up. His eyes were rimmed red. He took out his pocket handkerchief and wiped his eyes and blew his nose.

I said, "We could make the best of the situation. We could reveal now everything that you know is going to come out eventually, the things that I am sure you would prefer remained private, and I could write up my interview from your point of view. I could try to present your story so that you receive the understanding you spoke of. I can't guarantee anything, but I can promise – and I will keep my promise – that I will write the story in that way."

"Give me a moment." Dr Newell crossed to the telephone and dialled a number. He said, "Darling, it's not good news. There's a journalist trying to get hold of you. Try to say nothing. Yes, of course. Don't you worry now. I'll see you later." He replaced the receiver and dialled another number.

"Geraldine? It's Trevor. I'm so sorry about all this. I know. I assure you, it's none of my doing. I'm trying as best I can to retrieve the situation. Have you reached Freddie yet? God, this is a disaster… the press are after him. Sorry. I'm so sorry. Please keep trying. We don't want a journalist telling him…"

He paused. I sensed that the person to whom he was speaking was giving him a hard time. He said, "You know, we made a terrible mistake. We should have told him the truth. No, I respected that. No, of course I didn't want to hurt him. But I do think we made a mistake. I wish you'd told him all those years ago. It would have been better. Of course I'm not blaming you. I'm the one who's to blame. Look, we'll get nowhere arguing about it. Please believe that I'm now doing what I can to save the situation, to put things right. Very well. All right. We'll speak again. Goodbye." He replaced the receiver and returned to sit opposite me.

"Very well, Joanna," he said. "We'll do it your way."

I said, "Just before we start, I have to tell you that my way isn't the way I was briefed, but I'm pretty confident that what I write will be liked and will be published." Dr Newell nodded his assent.

It was a strange experience to listen, like a priest in the confessional, to someone revealing the secrets of his life. When Dr Newell had begun his career, everything had seemed set so fair. A double First from Oxford was followed by a PhD in political science and then a professorship. He joined the Civil Service and rose swiftly. He was highly respected in both government and industry.

Well, that was the outer story. Behind the outer form was the shadow of someone who had aimed high and worked hard but never entirely shaken off the traumas of his youth. Dr Newell came from humble beginnings. He was brought up on a rough council estate in Glasgow, where knife fights and drunken brawls were regular occurrences. His mother had been unwell for most of his childhood and she died of cancer when he was nine. This left him in the care of his violent, alcoholic father. Dr Newell worked hard to make a life for himself. His diligence and natural brilliance brought him a means of escape – a place at Oxford.

But, in order to cope with the pressures, he turned to drink – the one thing he had sworn he would never do. He drank secretly, using it as a prop to give him courage and get him through. "I never really admitted to myself how bad it was getting," he said. "It's amazing how you can fool yourself when you really want to." It had taken him years to control his alcoholism and he had been dry for the past ten years.

In his thirties, soon after joining the Civil Service and still unmarried, he fell in love. Geraldine Stephens was a new recruit to his department in Whitehall. They were together for several months and by the time they had realized that they were not really suited, she was pregnant. She decided to end the relationship and make a clean break. She came from a well-to-do family and did not need his financial support. At this point in the story, Dr Newell broke off.

He said, "Look, I don't want to say any more about this. I don't want to blacken Geraldine's name. I understand she's told your reporter her side of the story, which is true – that she wanted to bring up our child alone and not involve me in any way. I felt strongly it was the wrong decision, yet I could do nothing other than honour her wish. But over the years I have been in touch from time to time, just to make sure she and Freddie have everything they need. He thinks I'm just an old friend of Geraldine. She wants to tell Freddie to his face. She gave the interview – she was afraid that if she refused they'd track Freddie down – on the understanding that it wouldn't be used before tomorrow. But he's away on some course and she can't reach him. She's in a terrible panic. You'll keep all this to yourself…?"

I nodded assent. I asked, "Does your wife know about Freddie?"

"Yes, of course. She's always wanted to include him in our family, but – well…"

"Geraldine didn't want that?"

"No. She thought a clean break was best. She says she's told your colleague all this."

Fifteen years earlier, five years after Freddie's birth, Dr Newell had met his wife-to-be. Theirs had been a very happy marriage. They had a son and a daughter, both now away at school. I said I would do all I could to keep them out of the story, that there was every chance of achieving this if I made the copy sufficiently sympathetic. Above all, Dr Newell wanted to protect his wife, who was suffering from cancer, and his three children. His story told, he leaned back in his chair and I switched off my tape recorder.

He said, "It's strange, isn't it? I thought I was doing something for my country. I suppose I thought I was doing something noble. I hadn't realized that it would cost me so much. The world doesn't see things the way the heart sees them."

I asked, quietly, "May I use that as a quote?"

Dr Newell smiled and said, "I can see you're good at your job. Professionalism is a great refuge, isn't it? But it's not enough."

I kept my promise. I wrote a sympathetic piece, putting into it every bit of energy and creativity that I could muster, trying to make it so good that its quality would speak for itself and it would go into the paper untouched by the subeditors, news desk and Editor. And it did. I stayed late at the office, to see the page go through for printing.

I arrived home feeling very tired but more confident and content with myself than I had felt in a very long while. I suddenly remembered Alex and wondered how he was feeling. I dialled his number.

He replied, sleepily, "Hey, Jo? Oh, hi."

"Oh, dammit. I was thinking you wouldn't be able to sleep and now I've woken you," I said.

"No, don't worry. I was slumped in front of the telly. Wazzatime? Blimey, midnight."

"What time are you in tomorrow?"

"Eight. Don't worry. I'm young and the magic dust will get me there," said Alex.

"What do you mean?"

"You know. Oh, not over the phone line, maybe."

"Alex! What are you up to?"

"What everyone else is up to, Jo, my little friend, my mentor and my guide."

"You sound out of your head."

"Well, it's a good place to be. Inside my head, now that's where it's all a bit dodgy. Don't want to go there too often…"

"I hadn't realized things were this bad with you. Are you on something?"

"It's just the time of the hour, time of the year, hair of the dog, year of the dog, dog of the year, Cruft's champion – and I miss my dear old dog, my dear old Rufus, every single day." Alex sounded as though he was about to cry.

I said, "Shall I come over?"

"No. I'm OK."

"Really, shall I come over?"

"No. I'm OK. I'll be OK. Listen – get your beauty sleep. I'll see you tomorrow. Thanks, Jo." Alex hung up.

Was Alex taking drugs? I wondered if I should go straight over to his place, but thought he probably would sleep and that he needed his rest. So did I. It had been a long, emotionally draining day. In bed that night, I recalled Dr Newell's words: "Professionalism isn't enough." I thought: *No, professionalism isn't enough – but it is a great refuge, at least for now.* I had played Michael's Joker and it had worked – hadn't it? Feeling far too restless to sleep, I took up the journal.

2 September

My hand is trembling, my heart's beating fast. I feel alive, I feel part of the world at last, because tonight something wonderful happened. I had given up hope and now hope fills me and surrounds me with a buoyancy that lifts me out of the shadows. Tonight I was noticed and admired and, perhaps, loved.

I saw him as I entered the room. He turned – almost as though he had been expecting me, waiting for me – and smiled. In that moment I felt that something passed between us, a recognition. He walked across to me – again, as though he had been expecting me.

There was a vibrancy about him and a lively curiosity in his expressive, soft blue eyes. I couldn't speak. But I didn't need to. For he was smiling at me with a boldness and confidence that made up for my tongue-tied awkwardness.

He introduced himself – his name was Mark – and asked me my name. Then he asked, "Do you often attend these seagull sessions?" I had no idea what he meant, so he explained, "You know, eew, eew, eew. The sound of us philistines being impressed by you thespians. I'm assuming you're a thesp and not a seagull? You don't look like a seagull."

I confessed that I rarely attend fund-raising theatrical events, not even for my own plays. He said, "But you should. A beautiful woman should be looked at and admired at every possible opportunity." As he said the words, I felt beautiful; I felt that the ease and confidence that comes with the assurance of one's own beauty might perhaps be mine. We talked and talked. He made me laugh. And all the while he looked at me, in a gentle and thoughtful manner, which I liked. I liked the openness of his face, the straight nose, finely drawn cheekbones and soft mouth.

He was exciting and amusing, with plenty to say; yet he seemed as keen to listen as to talk. We talked about serious and trivial matters – our shared love of the performing arts, his Labrador, Jasper, who seemed to be the light of his life. He asked so many questions; he wanted to know every detail – my likes, my dislikes, my work, my past, my hopes for the future. When he laughed, a lock of thick auburn hair fell across his forehead and I would have liked to gently brush it from his eyes.

Perhaps I drank a little too much champagne because suddenly Mark was saying, with an odd, desperate urgency, "I have to leave. But I must see you again." Moments later we were in Piccadilly Circus and he was hailing a cab. We climbed in and the taxi set off, rumbling through the brightly lit streets.

We sat very close together; then, without warning, he reached out for me and took me in his arms. He held me gently for what seemed like several minutes. Then, as I withdrew from his embrace, he kissed me on the mouth. He held me tightly and his kisses were at first gentle and then passionate. Though I wanted him to continue, I drew back, feeling shy and awkward. By the flickering lights of a continuous stream of lamp posts and neon signs, I looked into his kindly blue eyes. He said, "You're lovely. You're wonderful." I asked, "Why am I wonderful?" He replied, "It's wondrous that we've met."

And so it is. And I wonder now – as I replay and savour, moment by moment, the moving real-life picture that carried me along so swiftly and naturally – what made me choose to take the action that set the event in motion? Why did I suddenly choose, as the tube train pulled into Piccadilly Circus station, to leave my seat and push my way through the packed, rush-hour carriage, to quickly step through the closing doors? Something I remembered had prompted me to overcome my fear and shyness. I had thought of another woman, a woman who risked everything for what she believed in. I had thought of Julian's strong heart and that had brought a little courage to mine. And I have my reward. Tomorrow I shall see Mark again.

3 September

As Mark walked into the restaurant I felt as though everything around me were dissolving. He was handsomer than I remembered. There was a lightness of energy about him. I could hardly believe that this bright butterfly had chosen such an inconspicuous little flower. The time passed quickly. We are easy and natural together. I feel I have known him a lifetime. He loves the theatre and wanted to be an actor, but to please his father he joined the family firm and eventually took it over. But he was unlucky. He said, "The market changed and we were hammered by cheap imports, so the firm went bust.

*Unfortunately it happened a few years after I took charge."
It seems his father blamed him and never forgave him. After
that Mark spent ten years in the army and now runs a
security consultancy. He said, "My father can eat his hat now,
and his entire wardrobe. I now have a company of my own
that's going great guns. Next year I'm planning to expand –
bigger premises, more staff – prepare to be drooled over by a
multi-millionaire."*

*Mark has been married. He said, "I married impetuously
and it didn't work out. Passion isn't enough. There has to be
genuine respect and love." As we waited for the bill he said, "I
can't believe I've found you. You've knocked me off-balance.
I'm in a spin." He seemed anxious and afraid. He said, "Now
that I've found you, you won't run away, will you?"*

*Then, as we walked to his car, an extraordinary thing
happened. He said, "I have to go to Norwich on Thursday.
Would you like to come? We could have most of the day
together." I was astonished. I have been thinking so much about
Julian and wondering if I should return to Norwich, to carry
out research and find out if her story has the makings of a
play. Now it seems that fate is taking a hand. In two days' time
I will see Mark again. I can hardly wait.*

I was puzzled and disappointed. What was I to make of this
girlish, romantic confession? Anna had expressed such sensitivity
and depth of feeling in the earlier entries. In comparison, this last
seemed frivolous and shallow. But Anna was going to Norwich.
What might she find out about Julian? I turned the page and
continued to read.

5 September

"A cold coming we had of it…"

*I like the sense of isolation and endurance in Eliot's poem,
of striving against the odds. I would like to be the kind of person
who would be brave enough to set herself such a task. I would*

*like to have the belief and faith that some prize was really
worth the sacrifice. I like the image of the seed in the hard
ground beneath the snow and frost, the unbreakable promise of
life to come.*

*As I opened the door, Mark greeted me with a hug and a
kiss. "Are you ready for this adventure to Norwich?" he asked.
Something is happening between us, and happening so quickly.
A door has opened onto a path leading to companionship,
sexual pleasure, friendship, understanding, joy, fidelity, honour
and love. Ahead lies the hope of fulfilment, the chance to be
held in the embrace depicted on the cover of the little yellow
book. Shall I be allowed to walk that path and take those
pleasures and comforts that I so desire?*

*As we drove through London and towards the coast I stole
quick glances at Mark. I could hardly believe that he had
chosen to take me with him. Suddenly I wanted him with a
passion that I knew I must contain. His face seemed to change
at different times, and I realized I had not yet got a clear image
of it in my mind's eye.*

*He sang to me. He has a good voice, but he sings with an
American accent, which felt odd and a little uncomfortable. I
felt embarrassed to have him expose to me this part of himself,
with such a lack of awareness. In the small space we shared
there seemed to be nowhere to put that feeling. But when I
discovered that he had added five hours to his journey in order
to take me with him, I was thrilled. I felt valued and nothing
else mattered.*

*Mark was curious about my interest in Julian, though he
doesn't believe in God. He said, "If there's a God, why does
he let us make such a muck of things? I wouldn't want him
managing anything for me." He really has no concept of God;
religion seems to have passed him by.*

*Today has been a perfectly beautiful sequence of happy,
pleasurable moments. I have been so hungry for times like these,
so starved of being looked at with admiration and affection,*

being listened to with fascination and approval, being held with warmth and intimacy, being wanted, being needed, being loved.

We lunched in a little country restaurant just outside Norwich. We told each other about our lives, but it seemed as though we already knew everything about one another, from some time long past that I had forgotten. I probed gently to find out why Mark's marriage had ended. He said, "We wanted different things. Once the initial passion was over we just didn't connect. We couldn't talk, as you and I do. After five years of vase-throwing – by my wife, not me – shouting and slamming of doors, we agreed to disagree and go our separate ways."

We drove on to Norwich and along the dingy streets that I walked along so recently, to Julian's little church and the Julian Centre next door. As we parted, Mark leaned forward to kiss me gently on the cheek. He said, "No running off with any monks or vicars." Promising to return in three hours' time, he got back into the car and drove away.

As I walked towards the Julian Centre I turned my head, to see if Mark was giving me a final wave, and saw another car go by. The driver glanced towards me, and there was something in his eyes that I did not like. As I stepped through the doorway of the Julian Centre, I shivered. My emotions, rekindled in the past days and brought close to the surface, were making me more sensitive than was good for me. A few hours of sober research would bring me back down to earth.

The Julian Centre was a small space crammed with packed bookshelves. In a corner, a table and chairs had been provided for visitors. I received a warm smile and an offer of help from the administrator, along with tea and biscuits. I was surprised to see how much had been written about Julian. There were several hundred books, as well as historical documents and doctoral theses.

I felt the familiar sensation of curiosity and excitement that precedes a period of research into an historical character, with the promise of being led through unexpected twists and turns on a journey of adventure and discovery. It's always thrilling to track the elusive fragments of a personality that has touched and changed people or a place.

What secrets lay hidden, awaiting discovery? Who was Julian? Would I meet her and know her today? I indulged in the pleasure of surrounding myself with books, documents and papers. I anticipated sifting through them all for glints of gold: a seemingly insignificant fact, a line from a poem, a reported conversation – a detail that catches the imagination, an insight that reveals a truth, a scrap of information that captures the essence of a person. I believe the essence of each of us is in everything we say and do, but it takes practised perceptiveness, perhaps a kind of clairvoyance even, to see and to interpret. The great playwrights reveal the character's DNA in every line. How closely they must observe and how well they must understand. I long to do the same.

These clues, these hints of the individual's essence, are scattered, it seems, throughout our lives, but sometimes they are shy of the sunlight, like primroses sheltering in cool, dark undergrowth, waiting, in secret, to be discovered – an image from my childhood. As a child, I loved to go alone to the little park near my home. I loved the pale transparent yellows of the spring's first primroses, the soft fragility that declined to show its perfection because it bruised so easily in a thoughtless, hurrying world. I would lift aside gently the heavy, fringed leaves and steal my secret moments with the delicate little flowers; then carefully allow the leaves to fall back into place, feeling glad that the primroses were safe, where no one could hurt them, because no one knew they were there.

And as I remember, it makes me feel so sad. To even say that you cannot bear the light and the noise is to draw attention to yourself and to lose your place in the comforting shadows. By being anything more than motionless you attract life to you, and then you must deal with the pain it inevitably brings.

The pain is a constricting band around the throat, a tightness in the jaw, a dull aching in the ears – and tears are the only release. But the tears bring pain of their own and the memory of another pain that overwhelms and lays me low in fields of sorrow... Where is he, the friend who can lead me to the still waters? Where was he then? If I only knew the way I would go there quickly now.

Pain, exposure, vulnerability, release... I seek a connection but do not know why.

Yellow flowers. Why do I associate yellow flowers with Julian? Yellow is the colour of spring, birth, new life, new beginnings, the colour of hope. I selected and gathered together a heap of books and papers, including a copy of Julian's own book, and settled down to read.

As I read, a picture of Julian's world began to emerge. Julian was born into an age of turbulence and fear. Edward III was King and England was at war with France. Norwich was a prosperous, bustling city, England's second largest, with a population of six thousand. Its strategic position on the east coast had brought it wealth and status, through trade with the Continent.

How did Julian come to have her visions? What in her life led up to that moment? What made her seek the solitary life of an anchoress? I want to know Julian's character and personality as closely as I can. But there seems to be virtually no personal information about her.

Apart from her book, the only primary sources of information are a third-party account of a conversation with her and wills in which she was made bequests. Even her real name is not known. She took her name, as was customary, from the church where she was anchoress. These are meagre scraps. Can I learn enough to make her the central character of a play?

Some experts suggest she may have been a member of the well-to-do Erpingham family, whose head, Sir Thomas, fought at Agincourt. Some think she may have been married and lost a child to the plague.

As a young girl she asked God for three things. The first was to have the experience of witnessing the crucifixion, so as to be touched by it in the way God intended. She also asked for a serious illness that would heighten her spirituality. The third request was for "three wounds" – of "true contrition", "natural compassion" and "wish-filled yearning".

What could she have meant by the three wounds? Might the wound of natural compassion be some deeply hurtful experience that would teach her to empathize and feel for others who endured similar suffering? Julian says she forgot about the first and second requests but that the third, for the three wounds, was always on her mind.

Her requests seemed strange and even suggestive of instability, but apparently they were not unusual for a devout young woman of her time. They were the starting point of her journey, so I needed to try to understand their meaning and relevance.

As I made my way through the papers and books about Julian and extracts from her own work, my suspicions about instability melted away. There emerged a down-to-earth personality who would have had no time for self-indulgent fantasies. What happened to Julian was real and profound.

In a world of privation and suffering, a young woman received a message so important that it has been preserved for six hundred years, a message that is believed to have great relevance for us today. What might have been working within her, during those difficult and dangerous times, to prepare her for what lay ahead?

When Julian was thirty, her forgotten second request was granted. She became severely ill. She endured three days and nights of excruciating pain. Her mother and the others at her bedside believed she was at the point of death, and on the fourth night she received the last rites. But she clung to life for two further days and nights, coming close to death several times during the third night.

Then, on the morning of the 8 May 1373, she says, "I had no feeling from the waist downwards. I was helped to sit upright, to be better prepared for death. My curate was sent for; by the time he arrived I had lost the power of speech. The curate placed the cross in front of my face, to comfort me. As I looked at it, my sight began to fail and the room grew dark – but the cross alone remained lit, as though by natural light. Then I felt as if the upper part of my body was beginning to die; I became short of breath and felt my life ebbing away, and thought that death was imminent.

"Suddenly, all the pain was taken from me and I was completely well, especially in the upper part of my body. Then I remembered my request to be filled with the memory and feeling of Christ's passion..." There followed a series of visions of Jesus suffering and dying on the cross. Julian says, "I saw everything as if I were there. I suddenly saw the red blood trickling down from under the crown of thorns, hot, freshly, plentifully and vividly." Julian says she saw Our Lady, as a simple, humble young girl, little more than a child, as she was when Jesus was conceived.

Two years later, Julian was walled up in her cell, where she remained for more than forty years. Nobody knows if she was already enclosed when she had the visions, but experts believe she must have been out in the world because her parish priest and her mother were at her bedside during her illness.

If so, it would have been natural for her to join an enclosed order – but why choose the solitary life of an anchoress? Was it merely to reflect upon the meaning of the visions, or was there a more urgent reason? Julian's message of a God who is never angry with us, who has never accused us and does not want us to feel guilty – indeed, our self-recrimination is painful to him – would have been seriously at odds with the teachings of the Church.

Did the revolutionary nature of the divine message impel Julian to seek a place of refuge, where she could pursue, unrestricted, a faithful interpretation of the mystery that had been revealed to her?

I need to know the detail of her life, how she lived from day to day. Julian's cell was a few hundred yards from the main road that linked the centre of Norwich with nearby Conisford, where trading vessels docked at a bend in the River Wensum. Carts loaded with goods and provisions rumbled by, drunks and prostitutes passed under her window. How did she manage to meditate, contemplate and write?

She would have lived according to the dictates of the Anchoresses' Rule, which sets out a strict routine, including saying specific prayers at set hours. I mined the shelves and found a modern translation of the Rule.

It told me that Julian would have had three windows in her cell. One, covered by a curtain, looked out onto the world. Another, also covered by a cloth, gave onto an adjoining room, where a servant cooked for her. A third window gave her a view of the altar and allowed her to join in prayers and take communion. A wood-burning stove would have kept the cell cosy, and she was permitted to keep a cat – "but no other beast".

Was Julian an educated woman? She has the common touch, using simple domestic similes; she said the drops of blood falling from Jesus' brow were like raindrops falling from the eaves of a house, and that they spread like the scales of a herring. She describes herself as "unlettered" at the time of receiving her visions, but this could merely have meant that she did not read and write Latin, which was still being used for theological works. Chaucer, two years her senior, referred to himself in the same way.

There is speculation that she was educated at Carrow Priory, a Benedictine convent close to St Julian's Church, and even that she was a member of their order. But as an anchoress she could just as easily have lived independently of a religious order. That, I imagine, would have been her desire.

Julian wrote a short version of her book, comprising twenty-five chapters. Then, for a further twenty years, she prayed and pondered the meaning of the visions before writing the longer text, of eighty-six chapters.

During those early years, while she worked on the short text, she would have looked out onto a world of appalling suffering and social unrest. Henry Despencer, the Bishop of Norwich, was a merciless ruler. When the people's frustration and anger exploded in the Peasants' Revolt, he set an example to other regional authorities by suppressing the insurgency with armed force. He restored order in Cambridge and Norwich, gave the ringleaders absolution, in his capacity as priest, and then had them hanged. When sheriffs were granted powers to arrest and imprison heretics, in Julian's fifty-ninth year, he was among the first in England to raise the charge.

Throughout the years of civil unrest after Henry IV deposed his cousin, Richard II, Julian remained in her cell. As the new King fought the Welsh, the Scots and, inevitably, the French, Julian was working on the second, longer version of her book.

Julian would have seen the smoke and smelt the burning flesh of heretics, who were put to death at the stake in a pit at Mousehold Heath, on the outskirts of the city. She knew that her book would be considered heretical; and yet, there she was, in the heart of Despencer country, writing her revolutionary theology.

It may be that some people did have access to Julian's work in her time, but if so they would have been a trusted few. Is there a power we do not comprehend in the unseen written word?

Julian outlived her powerful contemporaries – the two Henrys and Despencer. The last recorded mention of her is in a will dated 1416, when she would have been seventy-three. Details from another will suggest that she may still have been alive at the great age, for those days, of seventy-eight.

I have unearthed the bare bones of Julian's life. I have more questions than when I began. But a picture is forming of a fascinating woman – a highly intelligent, perceptive, loving, brave, practical woman – who belonged to and yet stood apart *from the age in which she lived; timelessly hovering over the centuries, fresh and vivid, she seems so alive.*

I am getting a sense of someone who was clever enough to hide her cleverness. Like Mary, spirited away to Egypt after the birth of Jesus, she was somehow protected from the insecurities of powerful men.

Julian quietly survived an age when all dissent, religious or political, was crushed. In a disintegrating world, she articulated her best-known words: "All shall be well, and all shall be well, and all manner of thing shall be well."

One fact is clear: Julian's deepest concern was for ordinary people, her "even-Christens". In Julian's England, most people would have claimed to be Christian, so I suppose her dedication to interpreting and communicating the divine message was for the benefit of ordinary people, people like me.

Why has her book suddenly emerged in the past few years, with a proliferation of new editions? Was her message preserved through the centuries to come to light in our day? Are those of us who are alive today the ones for whom the message is especially intended? Has Julian been waiting quietly all this time for humanity to reach a place where we are at last ready to receive and understand its meaning? Into my mind comes a familiar image of a battered copy of a book being read by a prisoner in some forgotten gulag. For some reason it moves me to tears. Bringing messages from places that are difficult to reach to places that are hard to find... this was Julian's mission. No medieval knight could have embarked upon a more urgent or holier quest.

The afternoon was almost over. The brilliant sun captured me briefly in its dazzling light as it hung above the horizon in its final fleeting moments.

I selected documents to photocopy and purchase, among them copies of the annual Julian Lecture, which is given in St Julian's Church on 8 May, the anniversary of the visions.

As I gathered my papers together Mark arrived to collect me. While I paid for my purchases he was examining a poster on

*the wall – an illustration of Julian caught in a beam of blazing
sunlight, looking out through her cell window. Under the picture
were the words "Love is his meaning" – the very last words spoken
to Julian after she had pondered for forty years on the meaning of
the divine message. Mark asked, "What does that mean?" I replied,
"I don't really know. Perhaps you'll tell me."*

*We travelled back to London through the darkness. Mark drove
at great speed. I had a sense of hurtling through blackness with
no clear idea of where boundaries lay – our own and those of
the roadside and other cars and buildings flashing by. It was
disorientating and gave me a sense of danger. Paradoxically,
though, I felt I had been separated from the cold, black world out
there. I felt I had been chosen, deemed valuable and worthy of
being given sanctuary and brought home in Mark's loving care.*

*In my flat, I poured wine and he sat beside me on the sofa.
He seemed to me in that moment altogether beautiful. He was
vulnerable. His skin appeared to shine with an interior light.
The desire to kiss him was too strong to resist. I tugged gently
at his lapel and brought him towards me. As our lips and
tongues met I felt I was melting and dissolving. The embrace felt
familiar, as though we had shared many moments like these.
It felt natural and right to give way to the engulfing feelings of
tenderness and desire.*

*But he soon had to leave. He had to be up very early for
another long day. His work takes him all over the country
and he spends a lot of time travelling. But I shall see him for
lunch on Monday. He is coming to the rehearsal room where
I am directing my new play. Dear Mark, he is always in my
thoughts. I am falling in love.*

4

The following morning, as I crossed the newsroom, I thought it all looked quite different. Outwardly, everything was the same – people hunched over their computers, the clamour of ringing telephones, shouts and conversation – but there was something suddenly alien about the place. I had thought I belonged there, as a member of a team engaged in a worthwhile enterprise, but now I felt like a visiting stranger.

I had barely reached my desk when the phone rang. It was Patrick.

"Hello, darling. Congrats on your story. You kept that very quiet."

"Of course. What would you expect?" I was still angry with him and the suggestion that I might have told him about the story made me angrier.

"Oh I dunno. A bit of loyalty, maybe."

"Do you mean that?"

Patrick's easy manner returned. "No, course not, darling. You have your game and I have mine. And we're pitching on different wickets. Anyway, you've certainly put a crimp in my evening. I've been recalled from Brussels, as you will no doubt have seen on the wires. I'm on *Newsnight* later."

"The best of luck," I said.

"Won't need it. The BBC rottweilers don't trouble me." He was one of the few politicians who could deal with the most inquisitorial questioners without turning a hair. I speculated that, embarrassing as our story was for the government, Patrick would somehow pull it off.

He asked, "Are you angry with me? I'm really sorry about the other day, Jo. It couldn't be helped. You wouldn't have wanted my wife to walk in on us, would you? It was to protect you, too."

I wanted to be fair – and it was certainly true that I would have been horrified to have been discovered in bed with Patrick by his wife. And, after all, I had agreed to go to the flat. Could I really put all the blame on Patrick?

"I'll make it up to you," he continued. We'd better lie low for a bit – while this business is going on. I'll phone you in a couple of days' time, at home."

From a professional viewpoint, the day went well. My piece on Dr Newell had been well received; there was even a congratulatory memo from the Editor. Nonetheless, I felt a lassitude and restlessness. In odd moments, I felt something else, an emotion of sadness and pain that seemed to centre around my mid-chest. It had been a long ten years on the paper. Where had the time gone? I kept remembering Dr Newell's words: "Professionalism is a great refuge, isn't it? But it's not enough."

Dr Newell telephoned me during the morning. He sounded relieved. He said, "I just wanted you to know, you've done a very nice job, Joanna. I could not have asked for more. I'm going to have to face the consequences now. Don't mention this call to your colleagues. I'm being put incommunicado." I reminded him that he was welcome to telephone me at any time, at work or at home, if I could be of help in any way.

I was keen to talk to Alex. I was worried that he might be taking drugs. But I had no opportunity, as he had been sent to Newcastle on a story. When I arrived home I left a message at Alex's flat, asking him to call me. As I waited for the call I took up the journal. It had become a refuge, and one that I hoped would sustain me better than the increasingly insubstantial refuge of doing my job well. Anna was beginning to feel like a friend. And I was curious to know more about Julian.

9 September

*Mark was moved deeply by the rehearsal. He took my hand
and looked at me so lovingly, with tears in his eyes, and said,
"Darling, that was wonderful. I'm overwhelmed. You have
heart and soul and an extraordinary mind. I've never known
anyone like you. Your play was a revelation. I had no idea.
You write with a depth of meaning – things that have made me
stop and think about what I'm doing with my life."*

*I felt elated. Mark understands why I write plays. That means
so much to me. I said, "I want to write work that's of value, of use.
There are so many things I care about, things I feel helpless about
and can't change. I want to make a difference. I want to use
words to change lives. Does that sound vain?" Mark doesn't think
so. We talked about the terrible news from Ethiopia, the television
pictures, night after night, of people dying of starvation. I said,
"Once we know about the suffering and need, giving money isn't
enough. We have to respond personally."*

*I tried to explain about Julian, my experience in her
cell and the powerful realization that I can no longer turn
away. Mark looked rather taken aback and asked, "Road
to Damascus job, d'you mean?" I'm not sure I explained it
clearly, but I can't explain it clearly to myself. All this change
is coming so quickly. Mark took my hand and said, "I don't
really understand, but I do know what I feel. And the strongest
feelings I've ever had are for you. I'm in love with you."*

*I felt overjoyed and filled with happiness. My heart seemed
to open up and I felt such tenderness for him. I said, "I love
you, too." Smiling broadly, Mark said, "I'm a lucky man. We
have something worth working for."*

*I remained seated at the table while Mark went to collect his
car, to drive me home. I suddenly felt as though I were being
observed. I glanced around the restaurant. Most of the other
occupants looked as though they were on lunch breaks from
their offices; nothing seemed out of the ordinary.*

*As we left the restaurant, a man who was just replacing
the receiver in a telephone booth near the front door glanced
our way. Surely – but no, it couldn't be... I fancied that it was
the same man who had driven past me as I walked towards
the Julian Centre. Mark and I were almost through the door,
so I couldn't turn to look at the man again. My overactive
imagination was playing tricks on me. I must be careful. If I
give Mark the impression that I am over-emotional or fanciful,
it may put him off.*

*I hardly dare to believe Mark loves me. At last I can plan for
the future, plan a life that's happy and fulfilled. Everything is
possible now. I think so much happiness might just be too much
to bear. Mark has asked me to go with him on a business trip
to Cornwall. Suddenly, time – which has spread before me like
an empty ocean – is too small a space to accommodate all my
meetings with Mark and a busy rehearsal schedule.*

*As for Julian – there seems to be no time for her at all. Julian
belongs to quiet, introspective hours spent alone, when I have shut
out the harsh light and noise of the everyday world, to step into a
peaceful, silent space where my too-timid soul can emerge and be
free. But Julian, my companion of the lucid hours, still calls me
softly to her. So I will make the time to return to her. Encountering
Julian has felt like having an injection of some substance that has
gone into my bloodstream and changed me, in my heart, in my
mind, in my cells even. But how has it changed me, and what has
it changed me to? I can't say.*

*Late evening is Julian's time. And it was in the late evening
that I took up Julian's book. I knew I had very little chance
of understanding the original Middle English, but I wanted
to see how much I could grasp of her own words. I soon had
to give up and turn to a modern translation, by Father John-
Julian, an American contemplative monk. As I read, I was
dazzled. Perhaps the love I feel for Mark has softened my heart,
or fortified it, to take in the wealth and depth of magical,*

*profound beauty of meaning in Julian's book. I have found
simplicity and complexity, a treasure house of wisdom and a
profundity that calls for deep, intense analysis. I recognize the
fruits of a powerful intellect that stayed its own brilliance to
perform a professional task of eye-witness reporting, with all the
faithful, rigorous attention to detail that requires. I have a sense
of a personality who was faithful, courageous, self-effacing,
generous and transparently honest. Julian's book fills my mind
with images and questions. The more I learn about Julian, the
more I desire to know.*

*I want to know Julian, the real person. So much that we
think we know is only someone else's version of events: what
else is history, after all? And how often does history betray
those whom it promises to reveal? Facts alone cannot be relied
upon to reveal the truth. Imagination, it seems to me, is a more
reliable interpreter.*

*Who was this woman who sidestepped the restrictions of her
time, to create the conditions she needed to fulfil her mission?
Julian needed space, to contemplate and consider the meaning
of her visions. She needed independence, to live without
answering to others. She needed privacy, to compose her book
without outside knowledge or interference. She needed to be
outside the system and yet an accepted part of it. She needed to
pose no threat to anyone powerful. Most of all, to the men who
ran the society in which she lived, she needed to appear to be
under control.*

*But even as I search for clues, one thing is expressed so
clearly in Julian's book that I cannot ignore it. She asks us
to forget her and to focus upon God. Was it too fanciful to
imagine that the destruction of the church by a German
bomber had been intended to limit speculation and discourage
attempts to discover Julian's origins – and perhaps even make
a shrine of her burial place? Intriguingly, a few hours earlier,
an unknown young woman had taken her paints and easel to
the church and made the only picture of it that exists. Julian*

was probably buried in the original church, but now we shall never know.

I was gratified to see that Anna was at last back on Julian's trail. Now I hoped she would guide me into Julian's treasure house. I, who had always cherished books, was being drawn towards a book I had never read, never held, but wanted to read more than any other. I understood what Anna felt about Julian, because I, too, was beginning to feel a gentle, irresistible attraction. Something was moving and changing in my life.

The telephone rang. To my relief, it was Alex. He was just back from Newcastle and sounded on good form.

"How did the story go?" I asked.

"Great. Great story."

"How are you?"

"Great. Fine. You?"

"Fine. I've been worried about you. You sounded weird the other night."

"Oh, I was just pissed. I hit another bottle when I got home."

"It didn't sound that way."

"I'm a bit weird when I'm really pissed!"

"Alex…"

"Jo, I've got to go. I'll see you tomorrow. Are you OK? I hear Smoothie-Chops is going to be on *Newsnight.*"

"Yes. I'm about to switch on. See you tomorrow."

I turned on the television and heard the opening credits for *Newsnight.* They were leading on the illegal arms story. Patrick's interview came about ten minutes into the programme, after a package giving the background to the story: Indonesia's illegal occupation of East Timor, now in its twenty-sixth year, and the continued collusion of the UK and the US, despite ten United Nations resolutions calling upon Indonesia to withdraw. There was an interview with José Ramos Horta, East Timor's roving ambassador. There was some library footage that was several years old, but no recent footage, since journalists were not allowed into East Timor.

For once, Patrick's confidence had been misplaced. He took quite a bruising. As he might have put it, he was on a losing wicket. The government's position was indefensible. It had been caught out in flagrant contravention of its own avowed ethical foreign policy. The Foreign Secretary had made a false statement to the House of Commons – in anyone's terms, a resigning matter.

Patrick fudged around the issue, claiming that ministers had been let down by their civil servants. There had been massive errors in communication, he said: the wrong message had been conveyed. There was no substance to claims that Indonesia was using British arms to suppress the East Timorese. The blame for the miscommunication lay with a senior civil servant. He did not name Dr Newell as being at fault, but implied that he had in some way failed to be as rigorous as he ought to have been. Certainly, Dr Newell ought not to have spoken publicly, which was a grave dereliction of duty, said Patrick. His outburst, as Patrick described it, had put the country's security at risk. He did not say from which source, and I could not imagine that the East Timorese were about to let loose a campaign of retribution on UK soil.

The tough questioning to which he was subjected could not budge Patrick to say anything further. He would not explain why Dr Newell was not available for interview. The government was investigating and it would be improper to make any further comment until that investigation was complete. That was the official line and there it stayed. The government was bound to be given a rough ride in Parliament the following day, but Patrick's performance suggested that it intended to tough it out.

It had not been Patrick's finest hour. I had to admit it. I knew Dr Newell to be a man of integrity who had spoken out because his conscience had prompted him to do so. He had done the right thing. And Patrick? I was disappointed in him. As for me, I had come very close to the line. This new twist – the government's denial and sullying of Dr Newell's name – made me uncomfortable about being part of it all. In less than one week my life had been turned around, my conscience put on the line. Had I been blind or half asleep to be so careless of the dangers of the world I inhabited? Anna, who shared my desire to write words that would change lives, and the mysterious Julian, were making me question myself. And so, tired as I was and weary of the day, I had to return to one of the few things in my life that still made sense – Anna's journal.

30 September

I have two lives: my outer life with Mark and all the excitement of a passionate love affair. Then there is my inner life, with Julian, the intimate companion of my quiet hours. Sometimes I wonder why the repose in my heart comes when I am alone with Julian and her book and not when I am with my beloved. It is my failing, of course, my inability to believe and accept that the great gift of his love is mine. It is I who create the invisible veil between us – or perhaps there is always such a veil between lovers. For who can dare to be as close as breathing? It is terrifying. The coming together of flesh and surrender of one-ness is peril and adventure enough. I long for and yet shrink from the intimacy that puts me soul to soul with my lover, such nakedness, such vulnerability. Is it always like this, for everybody?

Mark could not do more to allay my fears. He is a most attentive lover, telephoning at least once a day, even while busy and far away. I am baffled by his perception of me as dazzling and glamorous. I have always known myself to be a quiet little mouse. "It's always exciting seeing you," he told me yesterday. "I'm always discovering something new about you to love."

Imperceptibly, it is Mark who is taking over my life, leaving Julian at the outer limits. My busy rehearsal schedule has to be amended continually, so that we can meet. Mark's working life is so unpredictable, with unexpected business meetings causing him to change our plans with little warning. He is always travelling and hardly ever at his flat. Our trip to Cornwall sealed our commitment to one another. We stayed in a little hotel overlooking the sea. While Mark was occupied with his

*meetings I spent my time walking along the endless beach,
which unfolded before me in promise of the years we will spend
together. I imagined us walking, arm in arm, towards the ends
of our lives, content and at peace to be small and insignificant
upon the vast canvas of land, sea and sky.*

*Sometimes I again had the uneasy sensation that I was
being observed. But there was rarely anyone in sight; just
occasionally a car parked up on the headland, facing towards
the sea. Each evening we dined in a restaurant at the water's
edge, the smiles and caresses we exchanged when we had no
need of words telling us everything about our love for each
other. When we walked together, hand in hand, the length of
the beach, under the stars, I felt that we, too, had our place in
the universe, a place that belonged entirely to us, like every one
of the millions of worlds whose far-distant splendour lit our
way. When we made love, it was as passionate, exciting and
joyous as I had dreamed it could be. I am completely happy
and more fulfilled that I ever imagined possible.*

4 October

*London seems too big and too loud. Mark's work schedule is
more frenetic than ever, with a great deal of travelling. And
rehearsals are occupying even more of my time. But nothing
can keep us apart. We spend every moment we possibly can
together. I am finding the need for clothes of a kind I have
never worn before. Last week Mark instructed me to "get my
glad rags on" for a charity event at the Savoy Hotel, one of
London's grandest.*

12 October

*The grand life suits me. It's a great surprise. I treated myself to
a black strapless sheath dress of jersey silk. It is very beautiful.
A diamanté buckle at the top right of the bodice holds in place*

a sweeping trail of the soft jersey fabric, which folds over my shoulder and undulates gently as I walk. I had my hair put up by a hairdresser, and for once the unmanageable curls came into their own, a carefully selected few spilling out to frame and soften my face. The lipstick I chose was a vibrant red. In my cowardly way, I chose a softer pink for my nails, which were manicured professionally. The reflection I saw in the mirror was of an attractive, sophisticated woman. Where had she come from? Where had she been hiding for the whole of my life? I glowed with love, from being loved. In the intimacy of making love to my beloved, had some essence entered me – as he had entered me, leaving behind his essence, gleaming and glistening upon my skin – an essence that had suffused me to cast upon my skin a delicate, shimmering glow?

I never thought that I could play the part of consort, of the pampered woman, whose appearance, expensive to maintain, was well worth the money and effort. I never thought I could walk into a grand room, full of grand people, on the arm of a man who was clever, witty, sophisticated and accepted in such company, and be introduced as his equal. I never thought I could keep pace with such people – though intellectually I had nothing to fear – with their knowledge of the world and their easy familiarity with the trappings money and position bring. This was another world and a far distant one from my modest childhood in a northern town and my adult experience of dusty academia. From Mark's behaviour, you would have thought he was accompanying some celebrated sophisticate. He introduced me as a well-known writer and theatre director. One or two people even pretended to have heard of me; that amused me, because they could not possibly have done, since I am small fry. We danced together. Mark moved beautifully and took me with him, so that I seemed to move beautifully as well. I was Cinderella at the ball and I wanted the evening never to end. After the party we walked, hand in hand, along the Embankment. We sat on a bench and looked across the River Thames.

I thought Mark seemed a little sad. He told me he wanted to sell his company in five years' time. He said, "Then you and I can sail away, just the two of us, and leave everything behind." He began to sing, looking into my eyes, "'Are the stars out tonight'… " He finished the song and said quietly, "I do love you, you know."

We remained there, Mark's arm around my shoulders, for several minutes. A sudden breeze rippled the water and made me shiver. Was someone watching us, away in the shadows beneath the trees? Why do I keep having this feeling of being observed? I turned towards Mark. He was looking at me with an expression of concern and worry. I asked if he was all right. He put his jacket around my shoulders, saying of course he was and that everything was fine. But I sense that he's worried about something. He never talks about his work, but I know it causes him a great deal of stress. His old Army contacts turn up from time to time, sometimes asking for money, he says. Mark is a generous friend and helps them out when he can. Once this play is over, I shall take time off, so that we can see each other more easily.

19 October

Yet another rushed lunch, stolen from a day of meetings, gave us hardly time to eat and to make love. But my desire, like Mark's, was too strong to resist. As he turned to walk away from me, and down the three flights to the front door of the block, I felt as though a part of me were going with him. I heard the entrance door close behind him and went to my window to watch him drive away. As his car turned the corner, to leave the square, my eyes were drawn back to the tall trees in the park, with their abundant autumnal crowns of russets and golds. Someone was looking up at my window. As I caught his glance, he quickly turned and walked away. It was the same man! The man I had seen in Norwich and again in the restaurant. I was suddenly fearful. What does he want, this intruder into my life? I have left a message for Mark at his hotel in Birmingham. I hope he rings me soon. I have just come in to find a message saying he will come to rehearsal tomorrow.

20 October

When I told Mark about the man the colour drained from his face. He says there's nothing to worry about, nothing he can't handle. I asked if the man was dangerous. He replied, "No. If he meant business we'd have known about it by now." That really scared me. He won't tell me what's going on, just that his work involves mixing with what he calls "a few low-lifes". I always thought he was doing security for computer systems and premises, but he says his company is also involved in rescue operations, when people are kidnapped. Now I'm really worried. I had no idea about any of this. Is the man a foreign spy, or a kidnapper? Mark says of course not, and that he'll sort everything out. He asked why I hadn't mentioned the man before, and I explained that I thought I was imagining it. He's promised me I won't see the man again.

27 October

It's been a week and I haven't seen the man again, but the thought of him continues to worry me. Mark will tell me no more than that he has discovered the man's identity and given him what he wants. I think that probably means money. But if the watcher wanted money, why didn't he just ask for it, instead of following us and frightening me? Mark will say no more about the stranger, other than that I mustn't worry because I have nothing to fear from him.

I was becoming concerned for Anna. What had she got herself into? What was Mark up to? I didn't trust him. I started to flick through the journal, to find out what had happened. Then I stopped. I would take my time. Each time I picked up the journal the passage I read made an impact on my life. I was coming to believe that I was meant to read the journal entry by entry, as Anna had written it, measuring the changes in her life against those in mine. I had no idea how prophetic that thought would turn out to be.

5

The following morning the *Correspondent* led on the government's response to Dr Newell's revelations. The Editor had decided to come out on Newell's side. Patrick's defence of the government's position had not played well with the broadsheet national newspapers, which reported his assertions of carelessness on the part of a senior civil servant with scepticism and ridicule. The government's decision to muzzle Dr Newell had not helped its cause.

The tabloids' take on the story was more mixed: whilst most were critical of the government, others painted Dr Newell in a poor light. I realized I should have known they would. Had I known? Had I pushed the thought to the back of my mind? I knew that any and all the newspapers could change position very quickly, and worried for Dr Newell. I was surprised but relieved to be assigned to a different story.

My feelings about Patrick were confused. I was disappointed, angry and hurt. Yet I worried about the personal criticism he was receiving. I loved him. I did not want to see him harmed.

Dr Newell's wife telephoned me at home, calling from a public telephone box. She could say nothing about the pressure her husband was being put under by the government but said he was quite stoical about the tabloids. He had had a long talk with Freddie, who had taken the whole thing surprisingly well and expressed admiration for his stand. Freddie's reaction had been a great comfort and relief, and the coming together at last of father and son – though so far only by telephone – had been tender and joyous.

Mrs Newell asked if I had seen Patrick's interview on *Newsnight*. Feeling uncomfortable, as though I were deceiving the Newells, I said I had. Mrs Newell said, "Trevor doesn't know what they're going to throw at him. This is off the record, Joanna, you understand that?"

"Of course." Nothing would have induced me to share any of this conversation with Milo. I was in too deep as it was. I was relieved that Milo had taken me off the story, which was now being covered exclusively by the political team.

Mrs Newell said, "He's going to resign and start afresh as a consultant. Our main worry is that he may lose his pension. But we'll manage. Once this is all over."

Alex and I snatched a hurried lunch in a coffee shop. He looked tired and unwell. "What was up with you last night?" I asked. "You were very evasive."

"Not at all. I was tired."

"Are you taking drugs?"

"Jo, if I were I wouldn't tell you. Is that good enough?"

"No, of course it isn't. And what about the boozing?"

"Well, you're not exactly abstemious," said Alex.

"I don't like it as much as you do."

"Men can accommodate more."

"Don't be flippant with me!"

"Sorry. Look I'm OK, OK?"

"The Editor's hot on drugs. If you get caught you'll get fired," I said.

"That's a laugh. I'd hate to think what goes up his nose."

"What goes up his nose is one thing. What goes up yours is another. Alex, you think you can handle it but you can't."

"Jo, you're becoming boring."

"Insults won't stop me nagging you."

"OK." Alex drank a mouthful of his coffee, then asked, "Did you hear about Imran?"

"What?"

"He's resigned."

"Why? He did a brilliant job on the arms story," I said.

"I don't understand it. You know, he got all the East Timor quotes, all of them, including those from inside the country. His uncle got him the contacts, he's an academic in the States, specializes in Third World politics, very well connected, used to be an opposition politician in Pakistan. I can't get anything out of Imran. It makes no sense."

That afternoon I made an opportunity to talk to Milo. I asked him what was happening with Imran. Milo tapped his nose knowingly, saying, "Wheels-within-wheels."

"What do you mean?"

"Our little friend has upset someone," said Milo.

"That's his job!"

"Wake up, Meredith. This isn't a kindergarten. Sometimes I wonder about you. I think you have a bit of a problem with objectivity."

"What do you mean?"

I was stunned. Now I wondered if this was the reason why I had been taken off the arms story, notwithstanding the approving memo I had been sent by the Editor. Was my position on the paper in jeopardy?

The news from Parliament that day was that the government was being given a rough ride but not yielding an inch. That evening I treated myself to a good bottle of wine. I drank more than usual and was on my third glass when the phone rang. It was Patrick.

"How's it going?" he asked.

"Not bad," I replied. "You seem to be holding the line. Do you really believe those things you're implying about Dr Newell?"

"Whose side are you on?"

"That's not a fair question, Patrick."

"Well, let me make it a little more specific. The United Kingdom or the enemies of the state?"

"You're being ridiculous," I said.

He became suddenly angry. "It's so easy for you bleeding-heart liberals, isn't it? You're all so good at pointing the finger and criticizing those of us who are doing our bloody best to protect this country. You write what you want to write, you and your little fifth columnist friends – so-called Brits when it suits them, happy to come over here and take everything this country can give them, but marching to a very different tune when the chips are down."

I was shocked. "What are you talking about? You sound paranoid."

"Oh forget it!" He slammed down the receiver.

I threw the phone onto the floor. It was so unfair. I had to do my job. Patrick should understand that. I had no sooner picked up the phone and replaced the receiver than it rang again.

"Jo?" It was Alex. "Sorry to ring so late. Are you OK?"

"No."

"Look, I've got something to tell you."

"What?"

"Not over the phone. Try to find time for us to talk tomorrow."

"Tell me now. What's wrong with everyone?"

"Tomorrow. Night."

Sleep would be impossible now. I took up the journal again, counting on Anna and Julian to bring me through a night that I knew would yield little rest.

3 November

My world has fallen apart. Mark is married. He told me, suddenly, as I was serving lunch. For a moment I thought I had imagined the words. I felt as though I had been slapped very hard. The room swam around me as I put down the dish of pasta and collapsed onto a chair. I felt giddy and sick and could not speak. Had he really said what I thought he had said?

The sudden, unthought-of savagery of it, the bald stating of a fact – as though it were some mundane, natural and acceptable thing – was shocking. My body recoiled from the force of what felt like a door slammed hard in my face. He said, "I'm sorry. I should have told you. But I didn't want to lose you." He touched my hand but I shrank from him. He said he hadn't meant to deceive me. He had been divorced but married again ten years ago. He says he's truly sorry and that he loves me. He wants me to trust him and give him time to sort things out so that we can be together. But how can I believe anything he says? He has broken his word.

The man who has been watching us is a former business associate with a score to settle. He happened to see us together, then decided to follow us and threatened to tell Mark's wife. Mark says his wife is unwell. He says he needs to take time and choose his moment carefully. If the truth about us were to come out now, he says, his whole world would fall apart. It felt as though Mark had thumped me in the chest, leaving a chasm where my heart used to be – the thought that he would have gone on deceiving me, but for the man in the park. But he says he would have told me soon and that it makes no difference. He still wants us to be together. He has begged me to give him time to handle things properly. He has taken care of the man in the park.

Mark's confession has shattered me. I feel as though I'm in a thousand tiny pieces and can never be whole again. I don't know what to do. I thought I knew him so well. How did I fail to see that something was wrong? Have I just been too ready to see what I wanted to see? How could he deceive and betray me? I trusted him with everything.

I can hardly bear to breathe or think or be. Every waking moment is torment. The thoughts revolve ceaselessly, taunting and torturing me. My poor heart is broken. I picture it as a sore, tremulous thing, very timid and afraid, and I am once again the child who learned to cry silently, her head bowed, her hair shading her face, hiding all signs of pain and vulnerability, in a pretence of reading her book. My heart's tender innermost self lies unprotected as a naked, newborn child. I feel this great rent as a heavy wound upon my soul. Despair.

*It's three in the morning. After hours of guilt and turmoil I
went to bed at midnight and sobbed myself to sleep. I'm grateful
for the refuge of my journal, for I have no other. Why has Mark
led me into this maze, where I am lost in my love for him but
no longer feel sure we have a future together? I thought I was
safe and secure, but I no longer know what to believe. In a brief
moment, the framework of my life has disintegrated.*

*I long to be with Mark. The connection between us is so
strong, I feel it can never be broken. But I can no longer allow
myself to believe I can have him. At the very moment when I need
to feel his arms around me, to comfort and reassure me, he is
with his wife. And how many times has he lied to me, pretending
to be away at meetings when he was at home with her? How can
I ever trust him again? Yet I know he wants to be with me. At last
real happiness is within my reach. Surely I cannot be meant to
give it up? But how can this be right? The thoughts go round and
round. I think I shall never know peace again.*

*It's morning and at last I feel a gentle peace in my heart. Last
night as, exhausted, I drifted into sleep, I saw a candle's flame
burning bright, illuminating the pages of Julian's book, and felt
the light taking me through the book and into another place.
There were the spring daffodils, in their jug by the window,
the light seeming to shimmer and glimmer around their yellow
heads. The place I had come to felt safe, a sanctuary.*

*A figure approached me from out of the shadows, a woman
in a simple medieval gown of brown cloth and a white wimple.
She was small and sturdy, with a merry, round face that was
creased and furrowed by the loveliest and most loving of smiles.
Her welcoming warmth touched me in my heart and made me
feel that I was, perhaps for the first time, home.*

*She called me by my name and asked me to sit with her by
her window, which looked out across a garden to a seascape
beyond and on to infinity. We were enclosed in a circle of light.
The smallness of the space within the vastness gave me comfort.*

She said, "My dear, love is to be found within yourself,
where God's love lives eternally. The search for love is the search
for God. When you are truly part of God, then you will know
how to give and accept love. Then the giving and accepting will
feel natural and right. You will not doubt or fear. Your heart
will be at peace."

"I am afraid," I said. "I have done things that are wrong."

"To feel miserable and guilty about our mistakes is
blindness. God does not judge us or blame us and we should
not blame ourselves. It is our own pain that blames and
punishes us and it will do so until we are led so deeply into God
that we honestly and truly know our own soul.

"God is endless love and there is no judgement and no anger
in him. If we sin, we have, through our shame and sadness, a
wonderful opportunity to be utterly vulnerable and childlike,
and in this state run to our Mother God, to find there immediate
acceptance and a continuing confirmation of our identity as her
beloved, her darling whom she will never abandon.

"God tells you that you are beloved through all eternity and
held safe in an embrace that will never let you go. But the love
he offers requires us to turn our lives upside down."

She smiled so sweetly and lovingly that I thought I should like
to stay in that quiet place for ever. "My dearest one, I want you to
understand that hope, authentic hope, always lies through and
beyond despair. To discover hope, we must move into the darkness
and risk the loss of the few remaining reference points that seem to
make some sense of the bewildering landscape. In time, each one
must come to Calvary, where hope and sorrow meet, and endure
the crucifixion of the earthly self. Always remember, nothing
happens by chance. One day you will give thanks that everything
in your life happened as it did."

I awoke in the early hours to find the light still on and the
journal lying, half-open, on the counterpane. I felt restless and
angry – on Anna's behalf and my own. I was angry with Patrick and

angry with myself. Why did love have to be like this, so full of hurts and snares and wounds? Why could it not be gentle, sustaining and kind? Maybe Mark loved Anna, but he was so weak, too weak for such a lovely woman. And did Patrick love me? If he did, why did he make me feel uneasy, unsettled and unsure? I continued reading the journal, hoping to find solace.

8 *November*

Julian, from whom I had wandered away in the excitement of my love affair, is suddenly back in my life, with her assurance of a love I can depend upon. When I take up my copy of Enfolded in Love, *I long to step into that line drawing on the cover, open and vulnerable as the child being gathered up into a loving embrace. If only it were that easy...*

There is at least one cause for relief: the stranger in the park was an opportunist blackmailer and not some far more threatening character from Mark's murky, terrifying world of kidnappers and ransoms. I need no longer worry about his safety. But the worry about our future is intense, as is the guilt about sleeping with a married man. Though I no longer go to Mass, those old traditions that were welded in childhood to my growing sense of identity retain their hold, like great iron gates of intricate design that clang together when my spirit fears its freedom. And, more than that, there is a belief I have, a principle that I respect. If I was never persuaded in my heart by Father James, I was taught well by Sister Mary Theresa the difference between right and wrong. Where does the loving act lie? My dream about Julian offers me balm for my pain, reminding me of the comforting assurance in her book that God does not judge or blame me... Can Julian's wisdom guide me through this nightmare?

I have been seeking guidance in Julian's book. She says sin is inevitable, that it had to be. Jesus told her "You will sin", but "I will hold you securely". She saw sin as "no thing", something

known only through the pain it causes. And though sin is vile
and we must fight it, "We need to fall and we need to see we
have fallen. For if we never fell we should never know how poor
and weak we are on our own; nor should we ever fully know
the wonderful love of our maker." We have only to acknowledge
our mistakes and fallibility – nothing more – to become humble
and accept the forgiveness that is always waiting for us. Julian
tells me that I must not allow my guilt to stand in my way,
because God understands and does not blame me.

I sit quietly and allow the healing balm to enter my heart.
The frightened child is soothed. "Rest, be still, accept the love
that surrounds you. Take it into your heart and hold it there."
These words come into my mind. I am comforted. I feel I am
loved for myself, just as I am. How my father, the collapsed
Catholic, would have welcomed such acceptance.

Julian was told in her vision that God allows us to sin
and will not punish us for it, and that the worse our sin,
the greater our glory and honour in heaven. I find this so
puzzling and perplexing. And so did Julian. She asked Jesus,
during the vision, how it could be true. Eventually, though, she
set aside her doubts and accepted a promise that everything
would be explained by a Great Deed, to be performed by God
"in the last day".

How hard must it have been for Julian, after a lifetime's
dedication to interpreting her visions, to set down her failure
to reach a satisfying conclusion? How hard must it have been,
when her intellect remained unsatisfied, to report faithfully and
to resist the temptation to trim the facts to make them fit her
limited human understanding? She had not been so afraid that
she had to cling desperately to what she knew.

I am reminded why I admire Julian so much and know
I can trust her as my guide. Her moral courage is beyond
question. She followed what she intuitively knew to be right,
to carry out her demanding and dangerous mission. But I
cannot hope to match her courage. My intellect has always

*been my bedrock, refuge and guide. And if God was never
angry with me and never blamed me, why do I feel so tainted
and unworthy? What must I do? The doubt and worry come
rushing in, against my will. "Hope lies through and beyond
despair…" I have come into Julian's territory. But do I dare to
brave the darkness?*

*Mark is as loving as ever, but an oppressive cloud hangs
over us. I no long feel easy and comfortable with him. He
accepts that I will not sleep with him again until he is free. He
constantly assures me that he will make everything come right.
His wife is as unhappy as he is, but there are complications that
he cannot explain. He asks me to trust him. "Darling, I won't
let you down, I promise you," he tells me time and time again. I
ache to know more about his marriage, but he says he is bound
by other people's confidences. He needs me to be patient for a
little longer.*

*I feel as though a great weight has descended upon my
shoulders. My life is spinning out of control. After my play has
been staged in two weeks' time, Mark wants me to go with him
to Ireland. I will go, but he knows I won't sleep with him and
says he doesn't expect me to.*

*As we parted today, he stood at my door and kissed me.
Then he held me close and buried his head in my neck and
kissed me again, near the vulnerable spot at the nape. But
as his lips touched my skin I was moving away; quickly I
realized, and moved back into the embrace, trying to recapture
the moment – but it was gone. He had drawn back and was
walking down the stairs. He turned to smile and call out, as he
always does when we part, "We'll speak on the phone."*

*The sky is darkening. The afternoons seem to draw to a
close very quickly and suddenly each day. I shall light one of
my heavy white candles. As I look into the flame's golden heart
I wonder why I feel that Julian is drawing me to her, when she
has made it clear that she does not want to be found.*

I look from my window to the inky-blue sky in the far distance, with its pale, glazed clouds and soft foreshadowing of night. I feel lost and adrift, with no bearings or compass. But I must not give way to despair. I must be disciplined and concentrate on my work – my work, which has always held me steady above life's stormy seas. I have unearthed a wealth of material about Julian, but I am not yet sure that I have the makings of a play. I hope I have not taken on more than I can handle. For I am beginning to realize that this is more than the search for a lady lost in time and space. My quest is for the Holy Grail itself.

6

As I travelled to work the following morning I thought again about the odd way Patrick had behaved the previous evening. He had said things that made no sense. Perhaps he had been drinking. My world no longer seemed to fit together coherently. It felt like a glass globe containing a snowstorm, which someone had picked up and shaken hard. Everything, including myself, was unsettled and out of place.

At mid-morning, Alex and I found time to go out for a coffee.

"Look, Jo, something very weird is going on. I think Masterton is involved. I've talked to Imran. Someone put pressure on his uncle, someone in our government. He was threatened. It was very serious. He was in fear for his life. The price demanded was that Imran resign from his job."

"That's preposterous! Talk about conspiracy theories!"

"Jo, it happened. You are not to tell a soul. I'm telling you because I think you need to protect yourself."

"From Patrick? Is that what you're saying?"

"He's using you, Jo. He's a very dangerous man. Get free of him."

"Why should anyone in the government care about Imran? It's ridiculous."

"He was a journalist that they could easily pick off. It was spite."

"And the Editor went along with this?"

"He takes his orders from Sharkey, you know that." Rex Sharkey was the proprietor of Transglobal Media Corporation, which owned the *Correspondent*.

"Wheels-within-wheels – that's what Milo said." I recalled Patrick's strange remark about so-called Brits with their own agenda. I realized, suddenly, that what Alex was telling me might be true. Was that why I was taken off the story? Because I had made it sympathetic to Dr Newell? That made no sense; my piece had been published. I was in shock. What should I do?

That evening I rang Patrick at his flat. It was too risky to meet in town. I said it was important and he gave me the address of a friend's house in Guildford, an hour's drive south of London. His friend was away. We arranged to meet there late that evening. While I waited for the time to pass, I read the journal.

13 November

The past few days have been busy, too busy. I have begun to feel unwell. I'm finding the days too long and am tiring quickly and having difficulty concentrating. Mark is away again. He must be particularly busy because he hasn't called for a couple of days. I hope everything's all right.

14 November

I feel certain something is wrong. Perhaps he has had an accident. I've rung him at his flat but there's no reply. Now that I know it's just a pied-à-terre and not his home, I suppose that's not surprising. I can only wait.

15 November

I am turning to you, my absent friend, the kind and patient reader of my journal. I wish you were real. I wish I could ask you to come and comfort me, for I am so alone.

16 November

It's over. This morning I called Mark at his office. He sounded his usual self. I asked if we could make arrangements for our trip to Ireland. He replied in a formal manner, saying I was welcome to come if I would like to. Then it all came spilling out. I was engulfed by a vast, terrifying torrent of pain and fury that shocked me into silence. He was desperately unhappy. He was locked into a marriage from which he could not escape. They each left a previous partner to be together. He said, "I know what pain that causes. There's no way I can put her and myself through that emotional devastation. The trauma she's been through is unbelievable. There's no way I can let her down."

The marriage has never been happy. Mark can't have children and he feels guilty because his wife agreed to stay with him during her childbearing years. The underlying tensions of years came to a head just before we met. When I found my voice, I asked, "What about you and me?" He said, "I don't know if there can be a 'you and me'. It's going to be virtually impossible, certainly in the immediate future. We've been having marriage counselling for the past few months. How can I leave her now?"

I tried to keep my head and calm him, fearful that he was slipping away from me. He says he loves me and wants to be with me but has no choice. It's insane. Of course he has a choice. The thing I most feared has happened. I dared to believe I was being offered something wonderful and, as always, it has been snatched away.

He copes by talking to Jasper, his dog, and crying it all out. I felt a passionate pity and sadness for the wretchedness of his life, intermingled with hope and fear. He talked to me about his childhood, how he had felt abandoned by his mother when he was sent away to school. He said, "I can't deal with feelings. I put them into a box. It's the only way I can cope with them. I have to see things in black and white. If I don't, I get swamped and I can't function. I've always lived my life this way, when I was at school and at university, always, since I was nine, when I decided I would never let a woman hurt me again." We have to talk. He agrees we have to talk. We're meeting on Thursday.

An hour has passed since our conversation and I'm still trembling. I feel very afraid that I'm about to lose something I desire and need very much. When we meet I shall have to be terribly careful to say the right thing.

17 November

Mark has cancelled lunch. He said he had to take his Land Rover to the garage. I slammed down the receiver. In utter misery, I stared at the telephone. I walked out of the flat, down the stairs and into the street. I must have walked some three miles. I found myself in a little park, where I sat on a bench and stared into the distance. Every bad feeling of loss and abandonment visited me there. I feel I have been torn away from the warmth and comfort of a pair of arms that once longed to hold me, as I long to be held. It is over. Love came to my door and I failed to welcome it and make it want to stay. The pain goes deep. It cuts like a tourniquet. Mark is pushing me away and the chance of happiness will not come again. I feel bereft and worthless.

What a rat. That was my immediate thought. I felt desperately sorry for Anna. She had trusted and hoped for so much. She deserved far better. Reading Anna's confessional had made me feel nervous and out of sorts. Now I wondered what I could hope for from Patrick. Had he somehow arranged for Imran to be fired? It seemed preposterous. I had to know the truth. How would I broach the subject? Was Patrick dangerous? Did he love me? I prayed that he did, that we would get through this difficult time and that we had a future together.

7

It was late when I arrived in Guildford for my rendezvous with Patrick, past 10:30. The house was in a quiet residential area and approached through wrought-iron gates. I parked my car on the driveway, next to Patrick's BMW.

He opened the door and kissed me. "Hello, darling. It's lovely to see you. It's been a long time." It had been a few days, but it did feel like a long time.

Patrick poured me a drink. He seemed familiar with the house. He said, "We've got the place for as long as we like. John's away all week. And I've got the night off." He came towards me and took me in his arms.

I said, "No, Patrick. We've got to talk. I can't go on like this." It was going to be difficult. I had to keep my promise to Alex. Was Patrick dangerous? The situation had become too confusing, my work life and private life hopelessly entangled. I felt as though I was becoming two separate people. I said, "We see the world differently."

He looked at me coolly and said, "We do. But it's been fun, hasn't it?"

"Fun?"

"Admit it. It's been fun."

"I thought it was more than that."

"Oh come on, Jo. We've had fun. Life is boring so much of the time, for both of us. Lighten up. We've had a good time."

"Is that all there is?"

"Well, what more do you want? Do you want to be like my wife? A couple of years with me and you'd be like her – complaining bitterly that you didn't get what you expected. I'm good at what I do. I'm not good husband material. And your little overactive socialist conscience would be prodding away at me all the time. It wouldn't be fun any more."

I saw in that moment that I had meant nothing to Patrick. How had I been so deluded? Now that I had forced him to show his hand, it was empty. There was nothing there for me. I seemed to be seeing him for the first time. Was it true? Had he arranged for Imran's uncle to be threatened?

There must have been something in my expression that he did not like, because suddenly his face changed. Had he guessed that I suspected him?

He said, "Don't get any ideas, sweetie, there's a good girl. You've a great career ahead of you. Pity to ruin it."

Tears came to my eyes. I turned and walked unsteadily to the door. Patrick caught up with me. He took hold of me, and caressed my neck lightly. "Queen and country, darling. That's the code. Never forget it."

I moved away from his touch. He said, "Don't worry, darling. I never leave fingerprints."

In tears, I ran to the door and from the house. I revved up the engine of my car and drove as fast as I dared into the night. I was grateful to be back in the sanctuary of my home. I was broken-hearted. Everything I had dreamed of had crumbled in ruins. There would be no sleep that night. I took up the journal.

18 November

I am in turmoil. Mark doesn't want to see me. Suddenly he has gone and perhaps I will never see him again. The thought tears me apart. Why did he fob me off so cruelly yesterday? Why hasn't he called me back? Why is he doing this to me? Who can help me now, when the one I love the most has withdrawn from me?

19 November

I have turned again to Julian, and read "He did not say, 'You shall not be tempest-tossed, you shall not be work-weary, you shall not be discomforted.' But he said, 'You shall not be overcome.' God wants us to heed those words so that we shall always be strong in trust, both in sorrow and in joy."

As morning has passed I have gained energy. Mark has broken my heart, but I know he did not mean to. I see that blaming and judging him only adds to my pain. None of the hurtful things he has done were done with the intention of hurting me. Having relinquished the need to blame or judge, I begin to feel calmer. I find that I am in a different space and I realize that he may have had good reason to cancel our lunch; he uses the Land Rover to draw the horse box when he and his wife attend riding events. Getting angry has clouded the vital issue of our future happiness.

My dream about Julian has given me a depth of perspective and an understanding that anger is self-defeating. I am governed and limited by fear – fear of not being loved by the people whose love I desperately need – and by memories of the times when the love I needed was not there. When I am fearful, it is anger that comes out. I have always played safe, choosing the sheltered path and taking refuge in high-minded principles that have no root in true morality. Now I am challenged, and I understand that the right path can be as narrow and painful as a razor's edge. But there has always been an alternative road and there have always been good reasons to take it. For every opportunity I have been given to become something more, there have been several invitations to become something less. I feel this pain

*is washing through me and stripping me bare. I see that
through my choices I have created the person I have become.
I feel I have been living a false identity. Is it imagined or
real – this sense I have that there is someone who desires
that I should be no less than all I really am?*

12 December

*It has been a while since I have felt able to write in my journal.
A great deal has happened. Mark phoned and said he loved me
and wanted to see me but would be away on business for a few
weeks. He sounded distraught. He suddenly became angry with
me. I have never known such pain as this. It drains me of my
strength. I feel savagely alone.*

13 December

*We have spoken again. He says he's sorry he's hurt me and that
he lacked the courage to be open and honest with me. He's torn
and doesn't know what to do. He told me about the difficulties
he feels are insurmountable, his guilt because he's been with
his wife during her childbearing years but couldn't give her
a child. He said, "My wife and I have been to hell and back
together, but I have no choice or freedom of action. My wife's
had a lot of problems. There are things I can't tell you about,
terrible things. I have to sort out the problems in my life." A
further complication is that his father-in-law has put money
into his company. He intends to repay him but can't do so at
present. He asked me to meet him for lunch in the new year. I
feel a huge sense of relief, knowing that I will see Mark again.
At the moment, that's all I have.*

Christmas Eve

*This morning I looked out onto the park and watched as a
neighbour played with her dog. I remember her telling me that*

the dog was a "Battersea boy", from the animal rescue home. As I watched the dog I took pleasure in his freedom and vitality, the joy he took in careering the length of the park and leaping, in crazy, headstrong bounds, to catch the stick thrown by his owner. There were moments when he seemed almost suspended in the air, frozen in time and space in an instant of perfection, symmetry and grace. I wondered how that felt.

Suddenly, for no reason, perhaps just because it is Christmas, a time when one remembers childhood, there comes to my mind a gift I received from my grandmother when I was seven, a book called The Isle of Wirrawoo. My grandmother had what seemed to me a treasury of old books. There they all were, some on shelves too high for me to reach, beautiful books with covers of Victorian and Edwardian design. There was something mysterious about their inaccessibility, the secret, closed worlds contained within their covers. It seemed to me that every secret there ever had been was hidden, somewhere, in a book. If I could read every book I would learn everything there was to know.

I imagined that they told stories of exciting adventures, of journeys to far-distant places and of the pleasures of summer-hazed afternoons when time stood still. I loved fairy stories, magic, tales about strange creatures, mystery and adventure. The Isle of Wirrawoo looked promising. The cover illustration showed a little girl in a place that was filled with luxuriant, exotic plants and trees, and among them glimpses of the furry muzzles and tails of wild and extraordinary creatures. In the background, a long way in the distance, was a mountain, upon which the sun was setting.

The book had made a deep impression on me. It was the story of a little girl who was lost and had to find a magical elf who could direct her to the top of the mountain. She had to reach it before the sun set, in order to come safely home. On her journey she met strange creatures, including a dugong, which, I discovered many years later, was the sea-cow – an ugly, endearing creature. There was a rhyme in the book that went "If you hear a wiffle-whoffing or a sound like someone coughing, that's the beetle in the big gum tree." There were gum trees because the island was off the coast of Australia. The elf the little girl had to find was called Mys.

And here I am, all these many years on, still looking for that elf. I am glad to have Julian's book by me. I am beginning to understand what she has in mind for me and for us all. She offers hope. She promises that I will become my real self as I become part of the whole that is God. And that, I believe, is the true Holy Grail. It is the greatest prize of all, the alchemical magic that gives us true selfhood and our real identity. I will become all that I was meant to be. But will I reach the mountain top before the sun sets? I think I can get there only through faith and by grace.

How strange it is, the way in which Julian's life now affects mine. She has made me examine myself, what I think and what I do. I had intended that she would be my subject. Now, it seems, I am hers.

It is early evening I have just been out among the shoppers and the bright lights. People were hurrying home, laden down with food and gifts. As I walked back through the park, I saw a man sitting alone on a bench. His face was hard, his features coarse. As I drew near, he lowered his eyes to take a drag on his cigarette, and I was able to steal a glance, unnoticed. I am curious about a man who sits alone in the park, in the cold, on Christmas Eve – a time when each of us wants to feel we belong somewhere. I wonder if there is someone in his life, the thought of whom makes his heart soften?

What can I bring Him, poor as I am?
If I were a shepherd I would bring a lamb.
If I were a wise man I would do my part.
What can I bring Him? Bring my heart.

Christmas was always such a special time. It was one day of the year when we did go to church as a family. Even since my parents died, I have always created a sacred space in my life for this time. I hope I can recapture the feelings of peace and security that Christmas brings.

Christmas Day

I feel dreadfully ill and entirely alone, but am comforted by the knowledge that I will see Mark again. It is a delicate thread that could break in an instant and I cling to it for dear life. Just beneath the veneer of comfort is a terrible fear, and in that feeling I seem to lose myself. I keep going over every detail of everything that has happened between us. I am planning how I will handle the next meeting. There's so much I want to say. Next time we will talk and I will give him the courage to take charge of his life. I won't allow him to throw away the wonderful gift of love we have been given.

The weather has broken. The thundery skies boom and rumble: I feel I am wrapped in their powerful embrace. And now here comes the pittering rain, in comforting release. My windows are uncovered and I see and hear the sleeting downpour, lashing the earth without restraint from a relentless sky that is edged with darkening clouds. They hang, heavy, along the horizon, like a pall of blackened smoke. Hailstones crack against my windows and hammer, hard and round, upon the sill. I surrender to the sound that envelops me, with the darkening night. I feel secure. The rain becomes gentle. Then a sudden loud thunderclap sounds like a trumpet call from the heavens.

I gave a start as the telephone rang, breaking across my thoughts. I glanced at the clock. It was nearly midnight. I lifted the receiver.

"Jo? Am I disturbing you? Sorry to ring so late." It was Alex.

"Oh, God, Alex. Now what? No, it's OK. Sorry. What's the problem?"

"I'm on late shift on the news desk. Thing is, someone's just dropped by wanting your phone number and I wasn't sure whether to give it."

"Who wants it?"

"Paul Huntingford."

"Paul Huntingford! But I – what d'you mean – is he there?" Paul Huntingford and I had known each other a very long time ago and my memories of him were not good. We had been at university together and though we had both become journalists – he was an acclaimed war photographer – our paths had not crossed since our student days.

"He's gone down to the picture library. He'll be back pretty soon. Didn't you know? He's joining the paper."

"No! He's leaving the *Observer*?"

"Already left. Some big kerfuffle over something. He told them to keep the job. The Editor got wind of it and nipped in quickly with the proverbial unrefusable, that's the word on the street."

"Well – what did he say exactly?"

"Not much. Just wanted your number."

"He didn't say why?"

"Nope."

I felt my jaw tightening and my mouth setting into a firm line. Alex asked, "What shall I do?"

"Don't give it to him."

"Er – well, what do I say?"

"Just tell him he can't have it."

"I can't be rude."

"You don't want to be nice to the Paul Huntingfords of this world."

"Oh, bit of a shark, is he?"

"What big teeth you have, Grandma..."

Alex laughed. "Oh, a wolf, then?"

"You're very smart this evening."

"He must have upset you big-time. Very bad career move!"

"Tell him you can't find my number," I said.

"Yeah, well, he'll know I'm lying. It's a bit awkward."

"Then he can go and ponder it. And maybe he'll learn to treat people with more consideration."

"OK. Sleep tight. See you tomorrow – or rather, today."

Paul Huntingford, of all people, asking for my phone number. It was the last straw. Another magnum-sized egotist thinking he could get anything he wanted at any time. No doubt he considered himself such a big-name, big-deal super-scooper that I would be thrilled and flattered that he wanted to talk to me. Presumably he wanted the phone number of a contact. Well, let him get in touch with me at the office in the morning.

I closed the journal and went into the kitchen to make coffee. Realizing that it would keep me awake half the night, I crossly tipped the coffee back into the packet and reached for the biscuit tin. I warmed some milk and took the cup of milk and the biscuits back to the couch, to try to relax before going to bed. Now I was beginning to wonder. What did Huntingford want? Whatever it was it would be something that suited his purposes and not mine.

Paul had always got his way. Women adored him. He could have taken his pick of the girls at university. He was six foot one inch tall, with broad shoulders and narrow hips, shiny dark brown curly hair, deep, melting brown eyes – and more than his fair share of sex appeal. But it wasn't just these attributes that attracted women. It was the way he had – a natural, easy charm, a likeability. It was extraordinary; he could get anyone to do anything. People just liked to please him. All this unmerited approval was really irritating.

Within a couple of weeks I was besotted, but he showed no interest in me. Well, at least I knew it and kept my dignity. The antics of some of the other girls, who plotted and connived to get a date with him, struck me as pathetic. I was independent enough to believe that if a man was worth having he would chase me. Paul never did. In any case, I didn't set much store by getting myself attached. I had been made to appreciate the value of a good education and did not intend to squander my opportunities.

I realized that my distrust of men echoed back to my childhood and my father's decision to leave Louisa and me with Aunt Vaughan; my mother had not wanted to leave us behind. And much of what I had observed since then had served to confirm my view that most men were a waste of time and energy.

The odd thing about Paul was that he didn't take his pick of the girls. He didn't seem to see anyone in particular during the first year. Rumours quickly spread that he was gay and were just as quickly dismissed by students of both genders and predilections.

Most of his free time seemed to be dedicated to good causes. I was studying political science and became passionately involved with several campaigns. This was the 1970s, and there were plenty from which to choose. We often bumped into each other at meetings and gatherings. I was impressed by his willingness to help anyone in need. I realized that people liked him because they instinctively trusted him.

Then, for several months, he did have a girlfriend. He had the appearance of being fond of her. It fizzled out. And then the most extraordinary thing happened. Paul asked me out. It took me so completely by surprise that I hardly knew what to say. He invited me to a concert in town. He had tickets for a touring production of *The Marriage of Figaro*. I spluttered an acceptance. Because of our different itineraries, we arranged to meet in the theatre foyer at a quarter to eight, fifteen minutes before the start of the performance.

I dressed up in my finery, including some ridiculous high-heeled shoes that pinched my feet, spent an hour applying make-up and arrived at the rendezvous a few minutes early. Five minutes passed and there was no sign of Paul. At five to eight there was still no sign of him. I looked around desperately. Had we somehow missed each other? Gradually, the foyer emptied and I heard the opening strains of the overture.

Perhaps he had missed me and gone on ahead to our seats. I ran up the stairs to the circle and quietly opened the door. The orchestra was in full flood and the auditorium a buzz of expectancy. And there, in the third row, was Paul. He looked happy and relaxed.

Seated next to him was Marcie, the pretty blonde Californian who was over on a scholarship. I saw her gaze up at him adoringly, squeeze his arm and kiss him on the cheek. He smiled and gently ruffled her hair.

I was speechless with rage. How dare he! Part of me wanted to storm down the aisle, yank him out of his seat and give him a good, hard thump. Fortunately, the rest of me realized that if I did so I would make a complete fool of myself and live to regret it.

I ran from the theatre, tears streaming through my make-up. I pulled off the uncomfortable shoes and padded, barefoot, to the bus stop. Half an hour later I was back in my room, pulling off my best frock, washing off my make-up and swearing that I would get my revenge.

I saw Paul the following day. To my amazement, he did not even attempt to offer an apology. I ignored him. A couple of days later I saw him again, in a corridor. He came towards me with a friendly smile. I gave him a frosty glare and marched past. It was near the end of the summer term and I was working hard. I made a point of avoiding him. On the last evening, he was in the bar with the rest of the crowd. He was being his usual charming self, surrounded by a group who were lapping it all up. Paul smiled at me and waved. I was outraged that he had humiliated me and was adding insult to injury by rubbing it in. I thought: *How easily people are fooled – but not me, mate.* I ignored him and turned away.

Paul did not return the following September. I heard he had won a scholarship to Harvard and would complete his degree there. A few hearts were broken. Perhaps mine was dented a little, but I knew very well that my heart was resilient and would mend.

Over the years, since those early days, I had come to admire his work. He had made a name for himself and carried off several industry awards. I always wondered, though, about his methods, how many people he had fooled and upset to achieve his success, and where that cruel streak I had witnessed fitted into his modus operandi.

8

I was in a foul mood when I arrived at work the following morning. Alex greeted me wearily, with a wide yawn.

"When did you finish?" I asked.

"Midnight. And I had to be back here for eight." He lowered his voice. "Have you spoken to Masterton?"

"It's over."

"I'm sorry. It's tough, I know. But believe me, Jo, you're doing the right thing."

I poured Alex a coffee and asked, "Did Huntingford come back for my number?"

"Nope."

"No? Well, isn't that just – "

"Course he came back. I said you'd told me to tell him to bugger off."

"Oh."

"Got you there, didn't I? No, he came back like a good little lad and, just to oblige you, I pretended to be a blithering idiot who couldn't find staff numbers on the system. So in all probability he'll try to reach you again."

"Oh dear. Why does life have to be so complicated?"

"Because you make it so, I suggest. You should try being straightforward about things. Find out what he wants. Maybe he wants to work with you on a story. Pity to lose out," said Alex.

"People don't change."

Alex eyed me quizzically. "Well, that's just not true."

"Here's one who doesn't," I said, spotting Milo heading our way. Milo poured himself a coffee and perched on the edge of my desk with an air of self-pity.

"Bloody, isn't it? Just my luck," he said gloomily.

"What?"

"This influx from the *Obs*. You know Paul Huntingford's joining? There's talk of a couple of bods from the news desk coming over as well."

I deduced that Milo was worried about his own position. "It's probably just another unfounded rumour," I said. "This is the place for them, after all."

"Huntingford has a lot of clout and he's bringing his mates in. But I'll have one powerful ally," said Milo, brightening a little. "Felicity hates his guts." Felicity Garner was the Features Editor. "They had an affair and he dumped her," said Milo, gleefully. "His wife found out what he was up to and gave him an ultimatum."

I felt the blood rising in my cheeks. Another adulterous, deceitful rat. Huntingford was even worse than I'd thought. Or he'd got worse over the years. I was tempted to make a disparaging remark about Paul, but knew that Milo would somehow use it against me.

"Yes, it was rather nasty," Milo continued, relishing the opportunity to spread bad news. "He'd shagged a native out in Kashmir and was stupid enough to marry her. Obviously forgot the elementary rule of foreign postings – stick to Reuters hackettes. They're glad of the action and don't expect you to write.

"When he was posted back here she stayed on in Srinagar, where Ma-in-law was dying of cancer. While the dusky-hued spouse is waiting for the old girl to croak, doting hubby's having a dalliance in the London fleshpots with La Garner. Wifey finds out and flies over in high dudgeon. Garner gets dropped like the hot proverbial. And back in Srinagar Ma-in-law kicks the bucket without the customary 'Cheerio, I'm off' to her daughter. Some people are complete bastards." Apparently cheered by this pronouncement, Milo placed his half-empty coffee cup on my desk and departed.

I was seething. Paul was clearly as big a rat as ever. Why were these men incapable of behaving decently? I determined to avoid contact with Paul at all costs. I thought he might show up in the office during the day, but there was no sign of him. So much for wanting my number, I thought. Then, late in the afternoon, as I was walking past the foreign desk, I overheard a snatch of conversation. Justin, the Foreign Editor, was talking to his deputy, and I heard him mention Paul's name. I slowed my pace and pretended to read a notice on the wall, in order to hear more.

"He's due there at nine. Get me a briefing then," Justin said.

At that moment the Editor appeared in the doorway of his office and beckoned Justin, who grabbed a handful of papers and hurried across.

So Paul had gone off on a story already. Could it be connected with whatever he had wanted to talk to me about? Now I wondered if I had missed out. But no, a foreign story was unlikely to involve me.

I finished work at eight o'clock and Alex, who was again working an evening shift on the news desk, suggested going for a drink during his meal break. He looked exhausted, his customary breeziness displaced by a weary despondency. I was surprised to see him down two whiskies in quick succession.

"Don't give me that mumsie look," he said. "It gives me an edge and it's better than drugs."

"It is a drug. And it's not the only drug you're on, is it? This is how addiction starts."

"Jo, you're imagining things. Anyway, I only drink spirits when I'm on late shift. And you're always whingeing on about the amount of chocolate you eat."

"Chocolate works. And it's not addictive. Just fattening."

"This works. And yes it is, chocolate, I mean. If you can't do without it, it's an addiction."

"Who says I can't do without it?"

"You do. Do we have to continue this circular conversation?"

"Not like you to be grumpy," I said.

"I know." He grinned. "That's usually your prerogative. Y'know, I don't know if I'll stay in this game long-term. I've a feeling that you eventually become disillusioned or someone you don't like."

"Or both."

"Or both. But then again, when you look at the kind of work someone like Huntingford produces… he's inspirational. He reminds me why I got into this game. Sorry, I forgot he's in your bad books."

"Oh, come on. I agree, he's produced some fantastic work. But I wouldn't like to think how many people he's walked over in the process," I said.

"You don't know that."

"What is it with you? Why are you defending him?"

"Things are rarely black and white," said Alex.

"Hah. That's rich, after everything you said about Patrick."

"I said rarely, not never. I'm not defending or condemning. How could I? I don't know the guy. Anyway, life's more complex than that."

"You're the one who was telling me to be more straightforward."

"Straightforward, yes. Simplistic, no."

"Any more criticism you'd like to chuck my way, while I'm already feeling like crap?"

Alex laughed. "Oh, poor you." He rose and leaned over to kiss me on the cheek. "I'm sorry you've had a rotten time, Jo. It'll get better. Gotta get back. I'll buy you dinner tomorrow evening."

"I'm OK."

"I'll buy you dinner. Don't be so obstinate," said Alex. "And don't stick pins in any dolls."

I arrived home feeling defeated by the day. I was cross with every man I knew: Patrick, Paul, Alex – and Milo, who, in his customary manner of sharing his bad mood around, had been particularly annoying.

I remembered that Anna had reached a crisis point. I wondered how she had coped with her brutal let-down. Why was she hanging on? She was being so hard on herself. I wanted to say to her, "You've got so much going for you – a good brain, work that you love, a kind and generous nature. You deserve so much better." But I had to ask myself the same questions. Had I been blind to reality? I had hoped Patrick's love for me would sweep me up and hold me in a tender embrace, like the homely figure, described by Anna, on the front of the book of extracts from Julian's writings. Was there any hope that I would ever know such a love? Why did it come to others, but not to me? I took up the journal.

13 January

We met today. As his eyes held mine I felt a great wave of love sweep over me, but I also felt terribly anxious. Mark was in good spirits. He looked at me with the sweetest expression of tenderness and love. We talked about nothing. I found it impossible to say the things I wanted to say. It had been so long since we'd met, I didn't want to upset him and frighten him off. Fear of someone else's fear; how complicated it has all become. Suddenly lunch was over and we were in the street. He is going skiing with his wife and will call me when he returns. He pulled me to him in a quick hug, holding me as one might hold an object, allowing himself no warmth in the contact.

I walked away, bravely while he was still in sight, then unsteadily, into Oxford Street, feeling as though my world had come to an end. Colours blurring, the noisy bustle of shoppers – I was not a part of it, I was walking through it, longing to be in the quiet of my home.

This evening I am beginning to recover. How could I have allowed the opportunity to pass without discussing everything and reaching some conclusion? Now my thoughts are occupied with our next meeting. Then I shall get some answers.

2 February

Mark has telephoned me several times. His company is in deep trouble and he's very worried. There have been signs of problems for several months, but he believed he could sort things out. Now he's no longer sure and terribly worried about the future. I can't help wondering if this has something to do with the stranger who followed us, but Mark won't discuss it. I feel so very sorry for him. He has worked so hard. It looks as though I shall have to wait for our talk.

14 February

We met for lunch today but all Mark could talk about was his work. He is waiting to hear from an American company that he hopes will go into partnership with him. Once again I walked away from the restaurant in deep despair. I need Mark so much. What does he want from me? I feel I can hardly push things now he's in such difficulties. It's agonizing to be kept in limbo, with so much left unsaid and unresolved. He promised that we'll meet in a few weeks' time.

3 March

We had lunch today. The Americans have agreed but seem reluctant to put in as much money as Mark wants. He's very busy, travelling around the country and to and from Chicago. He was stressed and worried, but happy to see me. I seem to cheer him up. It's six months since we first met. This routine with Mark is becoming unbearable. Perhaps he's planning to get out of his marriage and doesn't want to speak out until he knows he can be free. I need to know where I stand. But I'm afraid if I try to say what I want to say the conversation will go wrong. So I'm going to put it all down in a letter. I have to take a big risk to move my life forward. One way or another, the agony will end.

8 *April*

As we sat together in the restaurant, Mark was his usual chatty, lively self. At last, I plucked up my courage. I said, "I have something I want to say to you. I want to get it right, so I've written you a letter. I'd like you to read it now." Suddenly he looked serious. He took the letter and read it slowly and carefully. I noticed that his face turned slightly pink. Then he put the letter down and said, "I have nothing to say."

It felt like a body blow. From that point on the conversation disintegrated. I said I was simply asking for an answer, that he must tell me what he wanted and what he intended to do. He said, "You'll never get the truth out of people by being so direct. You should have warned me that you wanted to talk. I feel emotionally hijacked." He argued and blustered and changed the subject, drawing me into pointless arguments. I felt hurt, ridiculed and shamed. I asked if he was happy with his wife. He said he was; then said, "The fact that I say I'm happy doesn't mean I am." It was too much. I burst into tears, as I had determined not to do. Through my tears, feeling pathetic, I said, "I need you." I apologized for crying.

He took my hand and said tenderly, "It's all right to cry. I cry a lot. You know, I'm always here for you. Whenever you need me I'm always at the end of a phone line." I asked, "Why won't you trust me?" He said, "I do trust you. That's never been a problem, from the beginning. Can't we go on as we are?" I said I wouldn't continue in this way. I left the restaurant feeling even more bewildered and unhappy. In the street, he hugged me and kissed me on the cheek. He's going to Chicago for two weeks and will ring me when he returns.

I am utterly frustrated and desperate. I feel entangled in a web from which there is no escape. I long to be with him. I feel sure he longs to be with me. I'm caught between the desire to fulfil my needs and the knowledge that I may have to make a decision to abandon this love, abandon him to his fate, sentence myself to a lifetime's loneliness. The agony is acute.

29 April

*I met Mark again today. It's been three weeks since our last
lunch. I was determined to have a serious conversation. To my
joy and delight, he was willing to talk. He said, "I desperately
want to free myself. I want to be master of my own fate, but I'm
afraid of what will happen if I break the rules again." I asked
what rules he meant. Neither he nor his wife has any religious
convictions. He said, "The rules we have to keep, or society
would fall apart. I've been feckless one time too many. I've let
too many people down." He won't confide in me. He said, "I
can't. They're other people's secrets. I'm honour-bound. I'm
not a chap who can easily do the dirty. I'm afraid of being an
island. I'm afraid I'll end up hating myself."*

*Even though he was being so negative, I was overjoyed
that he was at last willing to discuss his feelings. My patience
was being rewarded. I trod gently, offering my thoughts. He
promised to think it all over and make a decision. I feel sure he
will make the right choice. We had such a happy time together
and were as close as ever. I was back with the old Mark, my
darling Mark, whom I love so much.*

*As we parted, Mark said, "You know, don't you, that I'll
always love you? I'm truly sorry for hurting you. I do want to do
the right thing, please believe that." He held me close and kissed
me tenderly. I could see in his eyes that he didn't want to leave
me. Mark is opening his heart to me once again. I need just a
little more patience, and all will be well.*

30 April

*The relief I feel is enormous. I feel sure now that everything will
come right. I felt almost light-hearted this morning as I went out
into the park to enjoy some fresh air and sunshine. My Mark is
coming back to me. Perhaps in a week or so he will come here
for lunch again, as he used to do, and we will be as close as we*

were. He must know by now how much I love him and that I will always stand by him.

4 June

Mark's business problems have suddenly worsened. The Americans are prevaricating. He says it will be impossible for us to meet for several weeks. I am bitterly disappointed. I had such high hopes after our last meeting. Now the old Mark seems to have disappeared again and I am again in limbo. I feel I'm losing control of my life. I've lost one commission because I failed to attend meetings. I'm living off my capital and that's a worry. Life no longer has meaning. I have been feeling below par for more than six months. I should see the doctor but can't face it. I have just enough energy to get through each day.

25 August

Late August already. The weather has been beautiful this summer, but I rarely go out. Everything is too much effort. Weeks have passed since we last met. My loneliness is unbearable. I feel as though all the energy is being sucked out of me. My creativity has dried up. My bank balance is dwindling and being further depleted by expensive treatment because my hair has begun to fall out. I miss him. Today I went to Brighton, to try to break away from this relentless treadmill of unhappiness. I walked along the beach and watched two boys riding their bikes at the edge of the water, careering, carefree, splashing in and out of the waves and laughing. I wondered if I would ever feel that way again.

It was much worse to be alone away from home. Wherever I go, there is no peace, no rest. It's never having been given a chance that hurts the most, seeing happiness come so close and then being snatched away. I walked the length of the beach, and it came to me that the only way forward is to stop trying to say the right thing, and to say exactly what I feel. That will release me and give me my freedom.

27 August

Yet another sleepless night. I tried to set my thoughts down in a letter I will never send. I've written "The pain I am enduring is almost more than I can bear. For nearly a year I have done everything that seemed right, with much thought, prayer and heart-searching. Last night I finally got to bed at a quarter to four and am up again at half past five, writing this. I don't know, finally, what to do with all this pain." I feel utterly alone.

29 August

Resolute in my decision to speak honestly to Mark, I rang him today. He sounded delighted to hear from me. I said I wished he would talk to me and deal with the problems between us. He suddenly became furious. "My feelings are off-limits. The issue is closed," he said. Then he asked me to meet him for lunch. I agreed to see him in three weeks' time. I replaced the receiver feeling confused, angry and hurt. Should I cancel the lunch, or simply not turn up? I can't go on this way.

18 September

In desperation, I have spoken to a psychotherapist recommended by a friend. He thinks Mark sounds like a codependent, which is someone who is perpetually occupied in blaming himself for another person's behaviour. He says Mark is in denial, and it's a coping mechanism, a means of survival. He said I shouldn't challenge Mark because he was

*not functioning at a rational level. He said, "If you love him,
your best course is to keep things superficial. Don't try to go
into those emotional areas where he doesn't want to go, or he
will become defensive and hostile and pull away from you." I
shall try to do as he advises – but for how long? I am in despair.
Mark needs rescuing but I cannot help him.*

5 October

*Autumn is here. It is just over a year since we first met. We met
today for lunch. Mark talked seriously for a while and then
became flippant. I realized I was not enjoying his company.
The person I knew seems to have become submerged. Mark
says he has aged ten years in the past year. He does look much
older. The soft auburn-brown hair has been cut shorter; it is
now coarse, with streaks of grey. His skin looks taut and pale.
There are etched lines of worry around his eyes and mouth. He
still tried to paste on his carefree manner, but mostly he looked
tired and sad. He seemed preoccupied and swore at the waiter
for spilling the wine, which is not like the old Mark. As he paid
the bill, I asked if he would like to come with me to an art
exhibition. Suddenly he became agitated and angry.*

"I can't come because I'm not free," he said.

"Why don't you do what you want to do?"

*He said, "I am. I'm happy with my dog, my horse and my
wife."*

*Our quiet conversation had suddenly erupted into a row,
as he began shouting at me. I became terribly upset. I said "I'm
afraid your denial will make you ill. That's what happens.
You could get cancer." I meant to say that he lived his life in
a cardboard box, but heard myself calling him a cardboard
man. I regretted it immediately, remembering how hurt he had
been by his father's opinion of him as a failure. He watched me
quietly and, to my surprise, tenderly.*

He said, "Thank you for saying you hoped I'd get cancer. Thank you for that tirade of virulent abuse." He rose and walked towards the exit. I followed him out of the restaurant. I said, "I've never abused you. I said I was worried that you would get cancer." It was freezing cold and I was shivering. He said, "It's not cancer that's the problem. It's IVF. We had treatment but it didn't work." With a complete change of mood, he said gently, "If things were different, it would be different, but they're not. I'll see you on the 28th." He put his arms around me, kissed me on both cheeks and walked away.

I was aware that I was nearing the end of the journal. I felt both eager to read the rest and fearful that there would be no satisfactory resolution of Anna's unhappy dilemma. I felt I had been drawn into a rather sad story about obsession. "But what about Julian?" I wanted to say. "You were getting so deeply into her story and I want to know more of what you discovered." I needed to know if Anna had been helped in any meaningful way by her attempts to assimilate Julian's teachings into her life. It had become very important that Anna – and Julian – should not disappoint me. I resisted the urge to quickly turn the remaining several pages. It was late and I was tired. I would finish the journal the following evening.

9

The next evening I took up the journal, sad to realize that so little of it was left but eager to read the last entries.

21 October

For several days after our last meeting I felt shell-shocked. As the date for our next lunch approaches I'm overwhelmed again by all the old feelings of fear and longing. These feelings, and the belief that the difficulties are a challenge I must overcome – like some chivalrous knight scaling a medieval tower to rescue a fair lady – have persuaded me to phone Mark. I hated being the one to make the call but as Mark is not accountable for his actions I felt I had no choice. As I dialled the number I had to control my breathing and try not to shake.

His business problems have increased and he's desperate to find another investor. He's on the road night and day. He can't make our date on the 28th. I said I had been very upset about the way things went last time. Suddenly his mood changed. He said, "I upset you! You were so bloody rude I had the distinct impression you didn't want to see me again." He accused me of hurling venom and abuse at him. He said, "You left me feeling a bit of a prat. I didn't see where you were coming from. I feel very odd about your reaction. I couldn't see the point in trying to pursue a conversation. There's so much pressure on me, I

can't take it. If I enter a discussion, then it becomes an issue
and progresses in some way. It's not going to happen."

My heart sank as he spoke. It seems incredible that he could
blame me when I've been so patient and supportive. I thought
perhaps the best thing was to end it there, end the pain; but he
asked me to meet him next month, on November the 9th.

9 November

I met Mark in a small town near London. He was his usual
cheerful, chatty self. It seemed extraordinary, after all that has
gone before, and somehow unreal – surreal even. My feelings
for him were still there, in the same old way, though muted
by the fear and discomfort that has become customary before,
during and after our meetings. He looked as handsome as
ever, but as he turned his head I was reminded of Will, my
first boyfriend, and in particular of a picture taken of us at a
party. In the picture he looked completely different. It was as
though the camera had caught him at an angle that revealed
something not usually seen. It bothered me at the time. Later,
after we had broken up, I realized that the camera had seen
more clearly than I had.

As Mark and I sat together at the lunch table, it felt as
though the situation had moved out of the sphere of reality.
It was agonizing to be playing what felt like a scene from
someone else's life. How could Mark sit and chat to me
about his life as though everything were normal and I was
just some casual friend or acquaintance? It was the lack of
acknowledgement, the apparent lack of recognition of who
and what I had been, was and could be that was somehow
shocking and very hard to take. But then, I thought, I suppose
this is what you do when you're in denial. He seemed to have
become desensitized to my feelings, and some of the things he
said hurt me deeply; but perhaps it was because I had become
so sensitized to the situation that everything took on greater
significance and was more painful.

He brought up the subject of marriage, informing me that it was always a disappointment after the first few years. I felt insulted. How did he know what marriage with me would be like? He had resolutely refused to give us a chance. He had thrown away something precious, perhaps irreplaceable. How dare he now rubbish it? How dare he categorize me with his wife? It was unfair. I had shown him something different.

I felt that in order to have any connection with Mark I was faced with being diminished, because he would or could accept only a watered-down version of me. Denying and diluting me allowed him to continue pretending that everything in his life was fine. I felt that he would give me only a cardboard cut-out of himself. How could I be myself in his company when he would no longer even touch my hand? All the things that had attracted him to me had to be kept under wraps. He made me feel like the invisible woman, like a butterfly that had been pinned to a board. I felt angry, frustrated and sad. I felt that colluding with him, shrinking to the pale figure in the corner of his picture of reality was the price I had to pay in order to be included. It felt as though I were killing some part of myself, consenting to be killed. I began to feel light-headed and detached from the scene we were playing out, but he didn't seem to notice.

Soon lunch was over and we were walking down the high street. We parted by his car. He kissed me on the cheek. He looked smaller suddenly, I thought, as though his body were shrinking around his shrinking spirit. I turned and walked away, wondering if this would be the last time.

I walked back down the high street. I felt I was floating almost, moving out of my body. My breath was coming in gasps and I started to panic. I was hyperventilating. The world seemed to be revolving around me. I leaned against a shop window, my head pounding, just managing to get my breath. I remained there for several minutes, then blindly headed back up the road towards the railway station. A London-bound

*train was about to leave. I ran and caught it as the doors
were closing.*

*For the next twenty-four hours I felt physically sick. I
had pushed myself too far and my body was rebelling. I
kept being overwhelmed by a feeling of panic, sweating and
hyperventilation. I would have to sit down, breathe evenly and
try to calm myself.*

14 December

*The panic attacks went on for five weeks but I haven't had one
since Friday, so I hope that's the end of them. Somehow, if I am
to regain my sanity, I must say my piece to Mark. Those feelings
need to be expressed, to end the torture and torment. But how?
Though I want to see Mark, the thought of it makes me feel sick.
I've gone beyond the limit of my strength. Nevertheless, what I
have to say has to be said to his face or I will again be cheated
of a conclusion. I must risk everything on one last card.*

16 December

*I feel strong enough to ring him. I've prayed that I will be able
to communicate with him.*

17 December

*I rang this morning. Mark sounded delighted to hear from
me, as he always does. We chatted as though everything were
normal. Work is still very stressful. I had the impression that
things are going badly. But he was cheerful and friendly –
until I said there was something I wanted to tell him. Suddenly
his mood changed. He said, "I don't want to hear you pour
out a lot of emotion. I had to shoot my horse last week, but you
don't hear me pouring out a lot of emotion about it." He said
he thought it selfish and unreasonable to ask him to rearrange*

all his plans if I wouldn't say what the emergency was. I tried to calm him, but it was impossible. He said, "The only alternative is to talk on the phone in the morning. I can be free of meetings and calls for about an hour." I feel utterly desperate. What shall I do?

18 December

I realized, during another sleepless night, that Mark was not going to listen. I rang and said I would leave things for the time being. Mark was friendly and cheerful. After we had talked for nearly an hour and a half about nothing in particular, I said I must go. I feel relieved and resigned. I can do no more, at least not for now. I do not feel any less unhappy. I long for peace of mind. Whenever I allow myself to recall my feelings of the past months I start to shake a little inside and reach for a cigarette.

5 January

Gradually, something has changed. It seems, curiously, to have been a physical change that has brought mental and emotional release. It is as though some intelligence within my body has made a decision for me. Some dam was breached and some mechanism activated to contain the flood. My body simply would not allow the situation to continue. If I pushed it any further, it seemed to be telling me, it would refuse to cooperate. But still, the hurt goes very deep. I feel there was something between us at so intimate a level that when he went a part of my soul went with him.

7 January

This morning I opened the study door and saw the slanting sunlight glancing across boxes, files and papers. There, on a corner of my desk, was the large red box that contained all my papers about Julian. Close by, in several untidy piles, were the books I had bought, including Julian's own book, A Revelation of Love. *I remember that I reached a startling conclusion when I last handled those papers: that I was on the trail of the Holy Grail itself. For the Grail is the cup that gives everlasting life, and the search for the cup of Christ is the search for the divine in each of us. But the wine in the cup has a bitter taste. In Gethsemane, Jesus asked if it might pass from him. He knew, as I am beginning to understand, that those who drink from the cup must undergo a crucifixion. And beyond that, I trust, the other side of vulnerability and exposure, lie redemption and release.*

And there the narrative ended. Had Anna reached a resolution? Had she found redemption and release? She seemed about to start on a second phase of her journey but, frustratingly, she had simply stopped. I had resisted all along the urge to turn to the end of the journal, anticipating a resolution of Anna's situation – and perhaps fearing that there would be none. Now that there was none, I felt cheated. But my quest for Anna Leigh was far from over. The yearning to believe in lasting love and meaning would not give me peace, for I had chosen Julian's path and in her footsteps I must proceed upon the journey of the spirit and the greening of my soul.

10

A week passed. I heard nothing more about Paul Huntingford's assignment. The row over Dr Newell rumbled on. But no charge had been made against him. Patrick appeared on television from time to time, holding the government's line that there had been a miscommunication and breach in security, which it was investigating. Every time I saw him I felt sad. Had he ever felt anything for me? How big a fool had I been? Where was the man I had loved? Had he ever been there at all? Why did I still love him, and fear him, and feel angry towards him, all at the same time? Despite everything, I still wanted him, and I did not like myself for wanting him.

One morning Milo appeared at my desk, saying, "Get over to Hampstead and talk to Ismene Vale. Your appointment's at 10:30. Simon will brief you. And this time, don't bugger it up." Milo headed towards the Editor's office for the morning news conference.

Simon was not at his desk. I was told his wife had been rushed into hospital and he had gone to be with her – leaving no details of my assignment. Milo would be in conference for an hour, so I would have to go without a briefing. I fumed. I was bound to make a poor impression.

The taxi took me to a quiet, tree-lined street in Hampstead, north London, and along a drive, edged with poplars, to Ismene Vale's front door. Her home was a large Georgian house with wide, tall windows, around which curled late-flowering pink and white clematis. As I waited at the door, I noticed in the front garden a long, pointed stone, placed upright, its rimpled grey surface catching the sunlight. Within and around it I seemed to sense a presence that commanded my attention.

The door was opened by a maid. She greeted me with the news that Miss Vale had been unavoidably delayed and had asked if I would wait. I followed the maid across the hallway and into a wood-panelled library. I felt tense and angry. I hoped Miss Vale would give me enough time to do the interview. But as I walked into the library, my mood lifted. I felt immediately at home. The room was elegantly and comfortably furnished, with inviting sofas and armchairs piled with cushions. It felt like a room that was used frequently, a sanctuary even. I could be at ease in such a place as this.

I walked across to a window that gave a view onto the garden. A magnolia tree sheltered a flagstone terrace. Beyond was a lawn interspersed with trees and bushes. The garden was private and proportionate, emanating an atmosphere of wholeness, contentment and ease – in keeping with my earliest impression of its owner. Ismene Vale… even her name had seemed exotic and mysterious in those far-off days when I was growing up, when her books had opened my mind and taken me beyond the unhappy and unchangeable present to a future filled with thrilling possibilities. Ismene Vale had seemed dauntless and unstoppable, and – in such contrast to my great-aunt – full of compassion. Naturally, her home would feel peaceful, restful and welcoming.

I rarely had times like this, moments with no urgent activity to fill them. I had admired Ismene Vale since I had first read one of her books more than twenty years earlier, when I was twelve. The book, titled *Voices*, reports a series of conversations with a diverse range of people – the rich, poor, content, wretched, influential and powerless. The book had inspired my choice of career. I had been impressed by her gift for getting people to open up to her. People instinctively connected with her and spoke from the heart, sharing their thoughts and feelings and revealing their inner lives. She knew how to listen, ask searching questions and report faithfully.

Her books had dazzled me. She had taken me to new worlds. Through the vivid pictures she painted with words, I could imagine I was there, feeling the atmosphere, hearing the sounds and almost tasting the air. She showed me the reality of other places and other lives. I was made to understand the suffering of people who saw their children starve because their land had been taken from them, who made a home along a railway track or under a plastic sheet at the side of a dusty road – for it was the stories of the dispossessed that affected me the most. I admired her ability to note tiny details. She reported small things that most people would overlook or think unimportant. And yet, those little nuggets of information – like a lover's glance – said everything. They encapsulated the reality of the individual's experience and brought the story to life.

One story in particular had touched me deeply. It was about a boy who lived among a colony of children in a Colombian sewer. The children were being hunted down and murdered by local gangs and had no one to defend them. This particular boy was a leader; he protected the others as best he could. He had one prized possession – a hat with a jaunty feather. The hat was a symbol, an assertion of the boy's individuality. He wore it with pride. Then, one day, he gave it to a friend.

I was astonished, not only by his generosity but also by his ability to let go something that was so much a part of his identity. What would make a child who had known little from the world but abuse, hatred and exploitation choose to serve others? And how could he, defenceless and vulnerable, bear to part with something that had become the symbol of his selfhood? It was a noble act, and more – an assertion of real independence. How are kindness and strength of spirit grown in such barren soil? What power is it that makes a soul shine clear and whole amid rottenness and decay? These were among my many unanswered questions. Ismene Vale did not hurry to supply answers, but she posed the kind of questions that made me want to search for answers within myself. I longed to inspire others in the same way.

As I gazed across the garden I realized how very much I wanted to do the interview. I had found most of the well-known people I met – business and political leaders and celebrities, people who were rich, famous and admired by the public – to be hollow shams, shallow and self-absorbed. They were little people who were perceived to be great. Ismene Vale – she was different... I must have stood there for several minutes, lost in my thoughts. Then the library door opened and the maid reappeared. "Would you like some tea or coffee, madam?" she asked. I glanced at my watch. My interviewee was twelve minutes late for our appointment. I began to worry: would she let me down again?

"Will Miss Vale be much longer?" I asked.

"I shouldn't think so, madam. It's not like her to be late. I expect it's the traffic. Would you like some tea, or some coffee?"

"I won't, thank you," I replied.

"If she telephones I'll tell you straight away," said the maid. She closed the library door quietly behind her.

A feeling of panic flooded me; the familiar sensation of fear and helplessness that engulfed me whenever I felt I was losing control of events in my busy life constricted my stomach and made me feel queasy. Ismene Vale was cutting it fine. Even if she gave me extra time, I was under pressure to get back to the office to do other interviews for the following day's paper.

I suddenly felt angry. I wondered: Was Ismene Vale all I had believed her to be? Stress and panic filled my mind with doubts. Ismene Vale was famous, successful, she could afford to override the day-to-day pressures of life. No worries for her about paying her mortgage or keeping her job – and no consideration for those who did not enjoy her privileges, I thought angrily. And her dedication to the world's impoverished and suffering had done her no harm financially, I observed, as I looked around the room. There were some very fine prints and original paintings. A glance at her shelves revealed rows of antiquarian books. Ismene Vale had a collector's eye and liked to indulge it.

I paced about the room, the composure and ease of a few minutes earlier displaced by anxiety. I felt trapped in this room that I might have enjoyed had I been in the right frame of mind. I ran my fingers impatiently along a row of books: there would be some gems here, I had no doubt.

And then I spotted it. A volume bound in burgundy leather with distinctive silver clasps. For a moment I thought I must have imagined it. But no; there it was, easily recognizable among the rest. I took a deep breath as I placed my hand on the spine and gently eased the book from the shelf. I was holding a second copy of *Anna Leigh's Journal*.

This copy bore no inscription on the flyleaf. But in every other detail – so far as a rapid examination could reveal – it seemed identical. My heart was beating fast. Was the mysterious Anna known to Ismene Vale? Perhaps I might be able to trace her after all.

At that moment the library door opened and the maid reappeared. "Miss Vale has just arrived. She asks if you will join her in the drawing room," she said.

I followed the maid across the hallway towards open double doors. I smelt a faint, indefinable fragrance – a hint of gardenia, and perhaps rose, and something else that I could not place. As I entered the room I felt as though I were stepping into a pool of light. The room was full of objects and surfaces that reflected the autumn sunshine. French windows opened onto a lush mass of green, gold, orange and red that seemed to stretch endlessly into the distance.

Ismene Vale came towards me. She was smaller and looked younger than I had expected from her television appearances. She was about five foot two and in her sixties, a rounded, comfortable figure with a sharp perceptiveness about her. She had a direct gaze and I had the sense that she missed very little. Her hair was grey, short and neat, her eyes grey-blue. There was a great warmth about her. She wore a matching skirt and top, with a brightly coloured floral scarf tied loosely around her neck. Her hand was small and soft but her grip was firm.

She greeted me, I fancied, rather like an old friend with whom she shared some special secret. The silliest of images flashed into my mind – a memory of secret campaigns I had organized at school, to outwit and confound the teachers. She seemed genuinely delighted to meet me – part of her gift, I thought. She asked the maid to bring us tea and led me across to the French windows, where we each took a comfortable armchair.

She asked, "Does that book interest you?"

I suddenly realized that I was still holding *Anna Leigh's Journal*.

I said, "It's the most extraordinary thing, because I have a copy of this."

It was Ismene Vale's turn to be surprised. "That is extraordinary."

I said, "I'm sorry. I didn't mean to help myself."

"But you didn't," she replied. "Books have a way of finding us. Clearly, that book intended finding you."

It was such an odd and unexpected remark – and at the same time so in tune with my own feelings about the journal – that I was caught off balance. It was as though she could read my thoughts. I told her how I had come upon my copy and that the two seemed identical, except for the message on the flyleaf of mine.

"But who is she?" I asked. "Who is Anna?"

"There I'm afraid I can't help you," she replied.

"Is it a confidence?" I asked.

"No – I actually don't know anything about her, except her name. The journal was given to me by a friend, my former publisher. She met the writer when she gave a talk at a literary festival in Winchester – it would be several years ago now."

"So your friend knows who she is? Who is your friend?"

"Frieda Bonhart." I recognized the name. "I'm afraid not," said Ismene Vale. "The woman gave Frieda the manuscript and asked her to read it and give her opinion. Frieda agreed to do so. But when she took up the manuscript, after returning to London, she discovered that there was no name and address or telephone number. This would have been odd in any circumstances, but in this case it was astonishing, because the manuscript was hand-

written. All Frieda knew about the woman was that she had introduced herself as Anna Leigh.

"Frieda became very much engaged with Anna's striving to
understand Julian's message of love and hope and to make sense
of it in the context of her own life. She felt very drawn to Julian.
She obtained a copy of Julian's book and was deeply moved by her
message of all-encompassing love. Frieda thought the manuscript
should be preserved – she always thought Anna would come back for
it – and had this copy printed. I had no idea there was a second and
I can't imagine how it would have found its way to the bookshop.
Frieda's health started to deteriorate and she gave this copy to me,
in the hope that I could do something with it some day. She felt a
responsibility towards the manuscript and gratitude towards the
author for introducing her to Julian, whose book gave Frieda great
comfort, particularly as her illness progressed. I put the journal on
my bookshelf and it has remained there until now. I knew that one
day someone, the right person, would be curious and take it."

"I don't think I understand... the right person?"

"Do you believe in serendipity? Apparent coincidences that
occur when the time is right?"

"I've never thought about it – at least, not until I read the journal."

"I don't believe in coincidences. Some things are meant to
happen. And some people are ready to take the opportunities that
come their way. You are one of those people, Joanna."

"I don't understand."

"You, Joanna, are what I call a truth dentist. By that, I mean
someone who is determined to extract the truth of the stories she
reports, who will not be fobbed off, who will not let go. It's all there,
in the quality of your work. You notice the details."

I was astonished. Ismene Vale, whom I had admired since I was
twelve, was saying nice things about my work. Was she teasing
or mocking me? Was she flattering me, in the hope of a generous
write-up? No, neither made sense.

"I've spent my life attempting to be in the right place at the right
time," she said. "That's important in your work, too, isn't it? Great

journalism happens when the reporter knows where to be, before the story happens. A great journalist would have known that a young teacher of unblemished reputation, who was very much loved by ordinary people, was likely to be executed for political reasons. A great journalist would have been on the spot, ready to cover the story – and perhaps one was. But it takes more than great journalism to interpret the meaning of the story. It takes the persistence to be a truth dentist and the courage to pull one's own teeth. It takes the determination to keep going when you're the only one who can see the point of the story. I think Julian was a great journalist."

I said, "I'd be intrigued to know what happened to Anna. But I don't understand why she would have given her personal journal to a publisher. As a manuscript it's pretty raw. I'm not sure one could even describe it as work-in-progress."

"It seems clear that she intended to use some of the material to write a play."

"But why hand over the whole journal? If, as you say, it was handwritten, then presumably it was the original copy, perhaps the sole copy. And why didn't she put her name on it? You know, I'd love to meet Frieda Bonhart and discuss this with her."

"That's impossible, I'm afraid. Frieda has Alzheimer's. She's really very ill and sees no one these days, except a nephew who manages her personal affairs and runs her publishing house. I discussed the matter with her when she gave me the journal. She said she recalled that the woman, who was in her mid-thirties, had seemed rather upset. But with the buzz and bustle of people who gathered around her after her talk, she had paid no attention."

"I'd love to know what happened to Anna and I intend to find out."

"I have a feeling that you'll find it worthwhile."

"Oh, and what about the song?" I explained how astonished I had been to find the song written in Welsh. Ismene Vale was intrigued. I said, "It's a strange song. I speak Welsh." I recited the words in English. "The spirit of the woods cries out to the spirit of the mountains, 'The spring stirs within me and I long for the sun.

The leaves open and fill the sky.' The spirit of the woods cries in pain, 'Where is the spring? I am old and weary with longing for warmth. I am old and weary with longing for the spring.'"

Ismene Vale said, "Those words remind me of songs I have heard in other cultures; very old songs. When one hears them, one feels as though they have come from the very heart of the earth." She was silent for a few moments, looking out across her garden.

Then she said, "It is a mystery, isn't it? For both of us now. Anna has crossed our paths. Her life has influenced my life. I feel she has more to teach me. Perhaps you will find that is true for you, too. Perhaps you will tell the rest of her story."

"The only clues are the plays she talks about."

"Frieda tried to trace Anna through her plays, after waiting a few months for her to get in touch, but she drew a blank. But with your professional resources, I expect you'd have a better chance."

Like looking for a needle in a haystack, I thought. I said, "There are other clues. She refers to an academic career in Cambridge."

"Not at the university. I'm afraid that has drawn a blank as well. Perhaps she disguised some of the details of her life, to protect her privacy in the event of publication."

"I'll make some enquiries, see if I can turn up any clues. In the meantime – this is rather embarrassing – I haven't been briefed and I'm afraid I don't know what it is that we're to discuss."

Ismene Vale turned her head to look out onto the garden and was silent for a minute or so. Then, her head still turned away, she said, "Have you ever seen a performance of Javanese shadow play?"

I vaguely remembered seeing on television some kind of Javanese performance in which strange, spidery-limbed puppets cast shadows to enact a story.

She turned to look at me. Her expression was serious and troubled. "It's part of Javanese mythic culture, the story of the puppet master who controls people's lives. To understand the culture and politics of Indonesia you have to understand the meaning of the puppet master."

I felt my heart miss a beat. Could the story I was to cover be connected with the East Timor arms story?

She continued, "An omnipotent god comes to earth. He rules the lives of others with an iron hand, and no one can stand against him. It is a story about total control. The shadow play came originally from Hindu tradition, but it has a particular resonance in Indonesia."

"I first went there as a young woman, during the 1950s. I began my career as an anthropologist. When I was twenty-one, I went to Jakarta for six months to study. I spent a lot of time in the islands, learning about the ethnic groups who live there.

"I fell in love." Her eyes had a faraway look, and I knew I must remain quiet now and allow her to tell her story. "Munir was a university lecturer in Jakarta. He was older than I, by nine years. I knew from the first moment that I had found the friend for whom I had always been searching. I hope you have or will have that kind of love. There is no greater blessing in this life."

I thought of Patrick and the way he had frightened me when the affair ended. I still felt deeply hurt and betrayed.

"We waited five years before we married. Munir was concerned about the difference in our ages and cultures. He did not want to deprive me of opportunities for a better life elsewhere. He wanted me to be sure of what I wanted. I continued to travel. My work took me to communities in Africa and South America. I began to write articles in professional publications.

"After we married, we set up home in Jakarta. It was towards the end of my time there that I wrote my first book, *Voices*, with material I had gathered during my travels. Munir and I had seven years of happiness together. Then things began to change. In the months running up to Suharto's coup and the overthrow of President Sukarno, Munir was arrested."

I cast my mind back to what I knew of Indonesian politics; the political ferment of the 1960s, when President Suharto seized power and killed a million of his own people suspected of being Communists. I thought of the old man's iron grip on the country since then, supported by the West, with aid and trade.

"He was held for six weeks and released. Ten days later he was arrested again. Munir and I were idealists. We wanted to help people, through education, towards better lives, but we were not politically active. Nevertheless, he was accused of being a supporter of the PKI, the Communist Party. It was a terrible time. Things happened very quickly. While I was trying to get Munir released, I was arrested and imprisoned, without charge. I was three months pregnant when I went into prison. Ten days later I lost my child. I was held for a further seven weeks. My family and human rights campaigners over here secured my freedom, but I had to leave the country without seeing Munir. I did not see him again. The Indonesians would not allow me to go back. Munir was held without charge or trial, and after fifteen years he became ill and died in prison." Her story was astonishing. I felt sure there was nothing on record about any of it.

"No, I haven't spoken of it before," she said, as though reading my thoughts. "I am telling you all of this for a reason."

A cloud had passed across the sun. I felt as though everything around us, all of nature, had become quiet and attentive to her story.

"The puppet master is driven by fear. He must control the lives of all those around him because he is afraid of what will happen if he allows them to be free. The puppet master is Herod, Stalin, Hitler and Suharto. He is the president of every multinational company that wants to rule our lives. He is the one who must always have more of everything, because nothing is ever enough.

"He is, you see, so very empty. Beneath the greed there is an unfilled space and an unsatisfied longing for love. But he cannot love himself, so how can he love others? You know, I believe that if we only knew the effect, the full, true effect of our hurtful actions we would change our behaviour." I did not agree, but continued to listen.

She said, "It seems to me that feelings are at the heart of our existence here. We learn through our relationships, and what matters most is the effect we have upon others. If we only knew how every action of ours, personal and societal, made others feel, there would be far more understanding and a great deal less neglect and casual violence. That's the point of my work, to bring to my readers an understanding of people who are very different from themselves. It's quite simple, really. But yes, the story I promised you. Come with me."

She led me into the hallway, across it and into the library. She opened a panelled cupboard and took out a small, rectangular parcel encased in plastic bubble wrap. As she undid it I held my breath, waiting for the sight of some ancient treasure, but what emerged was a video cassette. "Come with me," she repeated and led me back into the drawing room.

Ismene Vale put the cassette into a video player beneath her television and switched on the set. A procession of young people crossed the screen. They were dark-skinned, some wore head-bands, there were children among them, laughing and waving at the camera. They carried banners and were singing and chanting.

Suddenly, I heard the sound of gunfire and screams. As I watched, the young people began to run and some fell to the ground. I saw soldiers on tanks, armed with rifles, pursuing them and shooting them down. In less than a minute, the happy, peaceful scene had changed to one of carnage. I saw the young people running between gravestones, desperately looking for places to hide. I saw the soldiers pursuing them on foot, catching them and beating them savagely.

The picture was shaking. The person operating the camera was obviously crouching behind one of the gravestones. The camera lingered on a young man, his chest covered with blood, cradled in the arms of another man. The injured man was in the prime of his youth and vigour, but he lay silent, deathly pale, his eyes rolled back, as helpless in his friend's embrace as a newborn baby. To this day, that image is imprinted upon my mind as vividly as when I first saw it.

The picture disappeared from the screen. I turned to Ismene Vale. "What was that?"

"This massacre took place three days ago in the graveyard of Santa Cruz Church in Dili, the capital of East Timor. A peaceful demonstration was taking place through the main street of town, in protest at the murder by soldiers of a young man who had taken refuge in a church. The military arrived in tanks and trucks. The demonstrators, who were unarmed, were gunned down. Hundreds of people were slaughtered."

"This is incredible. What are you going to do with the film? Where's the person who shot it? Were you there yourself?" The film was a revelation. Journalists were not allowed into East Timor and this was the first proof of the brutality of the occupying power.

"The man who shot the film entrusted it to me. He was arrested, and just before the soldiers took him he buried the film in a grave. Several hours later he was released and he retrieved the cassette. I was asked to smuggle it out of the country. I was travelling on a false passport, as an Australian tourist – I am still not welcome in Indonesia – and was less likely to be searched. How did he find me? Let's just say I still have friends in the pro-democracy movement."

"Where is the cameraman?"

"He's still in Indonesia, but I can't tell you what he's doing there. Let us just say that he is completing his work. He asked me to get this film broadcast as quickly as possible."

I said, "You know, you could take this to the BBC or *Channel 4 News* – or anybody, in fact – and name your price. This is the first hard evidence of what's going on in East Timor."

"I have already spoken to *Channel 4 News*."

"Then, where do I fit into this?" My disappointment was immense. Suddenly, the front-page headline I had been imagining was being snatched away. "Wait, were you at the demonstration?"

"Yes, I was there."

"Then what about giving me the exclusive newspaper story, telling what you saw and how you obtained the film, for us to publish in the morning?"

"That's what I had in mind."

"What arrangements have you made with *Channel 4*?"

"They're sending a car to pick me up, with the cassette, at midday."

"We'll need to talk to *Channel 4* right away, to get pictures from the film."

"Oh, but you'll use your own pictures, surely?"

"Our pictures? What pictures?"

"The pictures taken by Paul Huntingford."

"Paul Huntingford – you mean he was there?"

"Of course. We met in Dili and went to the demonstration together. We didn't know the cameraman would be there, and of course we didn't know that this terrible massacre would take place. But Paul believed there would be trouble. A United Nations diplomatic mission was due and a protest march was being planned. He tipped me off. But I thought you knew all this. Didn't Paul discuss it with you? I know he meant to. He must have run out of time."

I felt myself beginning to blush.

Ismene said, "Paul's under cover, with the resistance in the mountains. He will have been trying to get in touch with your foreign desk, but tension is heightened at the moment and telephone calls abroad could put his companions at risk. He may be unable to make a call until he leaves East Timor. Paul wanted you to write the story. He said you were the best reporter for the job. He asked me to ring your news desk and to say that I would brief you and no one else."

As I sat, stunned, trying to take everything in, Ismene Vale reached further into her bubble-wrapped package and took out two rolls of film.

"Here are Paul's pictures," she said.

That evening *Channel 4 News* broadcast the footage of the massacre. Within twenty-four hours the film had been shown around the world. The morning after my meeting with Ismene Vale, my newspaper carried the front-page headline "Massacre in East Timor" over a story with Paul's pictures and my byline, with the word "Exclusive" next to it. For the first time in years, I had produced a piece of work that I considered to be of real value. It was a turning point in my life.

11

I travelled to the office the next morning with a light heart and a bubbling feeling of anticipation. Usually my heart sank lower and lower during the journey to our offices. Docklands was such a gloomy place. When I had joined the *Correspondent* our offices had been in Fleet Street, just along from the law courts, in the hub of the City. It was a buzzy, vibrant place, where work was fun. Our current offices were in a building constructed for Napoleonic prisoners of war, and it felt like it, despite its conversion to shiny, high-tech modernity. We mourned the loss of our old "village", with its familiar haunts and pubs and gossipy, clubby atmosphere.

This morning, as I walked through the entrance hall, past the life-sized portrait of Rex Sharkey the proprietor, those beady eyes that seemed to follow one felt a little less piercing than usual. As I crossed the newsroom, colleagues called out "Well done, Jo" and "Great story". Moments after I arrived at my desk, Milo came over.

"You kept very quiet about being a mate of Huntingford's," he said.

"I'm not a mate of his," I replied.

"That's not what I've heard," Milo said. "You'd better decide which camp you're in." He stomped back to the news desk.

Alex said, "Fantastic, Jo. Well done. Huntingford obviously thinks highly of you. Wonder if you'll get more opportunities to work with him."

"Not if he continues to be a perfidious worm," I replied.

Alex looked at me thoughtfully. "I wouldn't close any doors there."

I sent flowers to Ismene Vale, with a message of thanks. The next day she telephoned me. She asked if the foreign desk had heard from Paul. It had not, and neither had she. Nor had the organizer of the Indonesian human rights campaign in London, who was in contact with the East Timorese resistance. Ismene said Paul would undoubtedly lie low before making his way out of the country. To my surprise and delight, she invited me to supper the following Saturday.

This time, as I entered the poplar-lined drive to Ismene Vale's home, it was with pleasurable anticipation. This time I was a guest, invited for my own sake. The door was opened by the maid, who invited me in with a warm smile.

"Miss Vale is in the drawing room," she said.

I followed the maid into the room with the tall, wide windows. The flowers I had sent – creamy white lilies, irises, pale purple lisianthus and pink larkspur – were displayed in a cut-glass vase on the piano. As I entered the room, I again discerned the faint scent of gardenia and roses and something I could not place.

"Joanna, my dear, I'm so very glad you were able to come," said Ismene, crossing the room and taking my hand. "My housekeeper has cooked us something simple and wholesome. I hope you don't mind – it's a vegetarian meal."

She led me into her kitchen, saying, "I thought we might eat in here. It will be cosy. Do you prefer red or white wine?" I said I would be happy with either. She opened a bottle of Vouvray and poured me a glass, which she handed to me. The glass was exquisite, delicately etched with a pattern of purple grapes and intertwined dark green leaves. I thought it was probably antique and that I must be careful not to break it. I noticed that she filled her glass with iced mineral water.

Ismene helped me to a large portion of vegetable casserole, served with rice and a salad. Her manner was comfortable and easy, as though we were friends who often shared a meal. We talked about East Timor and she invited me to a reception she was holding the following week for supporters of the cause. As we ate, I told her how her book, *Voices*, had inspired me to become a journalist.

"That's a very great compliment, and I thank you for it," she replied. "And does your career match up to your expectations? Does your work fulfil you?"

"Well, writing the East Timor story certainly did. That quicksilver communication of events, by written word – it seems like magic when what you're conveying is important."

"Mercury – the winged messenger of the gods. Is your astrological sign Gemini?" I nodded. Ismene smiled knowingly.

She said, "I think we are all messengers. I believe we have a duty to pass on the knowledge that we have, to plant seeds by the wayside so that we may grow from one another. Every insight that one human being has can enrich another; indeed, every thought. Everyone has a story. Everyone is worthy of a hearing. Every voice should be heard. I have learned so much from the life experiences of others – often from people who faced terrible challenges that would have defeated me. I have received riches from people whom the world perceives as poor. You know, the effect that one life has upon another is so very important. If I had to put a measure on the value of a life lived, that is how I would do it." I thought of the child with the feathered hat in the Colombian sewer.

Ismene said "After reading Anna's journal I had to read Julian's book. Julian has influenced me profoundly. I think of books as secret weapons, opening hearts and minds and changing lives. A book that is the distillation of an individual journey, that puts down a marker to help others who walk the same path... a book such as Julian's, a great book... I feel a sense of wonder and privilege that such a book is mine for the taking. That is a true and precious freedom."

I said "It's such a shame that Anna lost sight of her objective when she became so obsessive about her wimpish boyfriend."

Ismene laughed. "Do you think so?"

I said "I liked her a lot and felt very sad for her. I did wish she would wake up and see that she was worth so much more. I really couldn't see why she persisted in trying to get him back."

"Ah, well, there's nothing rational about that kind of attachment, I think. I have read that obsession, or near-obsession – addiction, at any rate – creates a chemical imbalance that can be righted only by a regime of what the Americans call cold turkey. One can detach only by removing oneself from the substance or condition that perpetuates the addiction. And Anna did detach, eventually."

"Did things come right for her, I wonder?"

"I have a feeling that, with all she had learned, they did. Julian would have seen her through."

I said, "I think that love, that kind of passionate, desperate love – "

"You mean *eros,* as opposed to *agape*?"

"Yes, being in love, all of that. I'm beginning to think it's something we allow to happen – indulge in, if you like. Why do relationships break up? You fall in love. You get treated badly – or treat your lover badly. You fall out of love. And it hurts. Trouble is, there are too many strawberry thieves out there!"

"Strawberry thieves?"

"You know, the William Morris design. Emotional cheats, like Anna's chap. The bird that alights on the fruit, takes what it wants, then flies away without a care."

"Isn't this what we are so often encouraged to do? We are conditioned to be consumers – what an ugly word that is. Take this, we are told. It will make you happy. Do not concern yourself about the cost to others. The great lie of advertising exploits the hunger of the human heart, the need we share to fill that deep space within."

I said, "Everyone is looking for love. People say the passion fades but you grow in its place this deep, abiding feeling – which sounds very much like *agape.* The logical conclusion is that there's not much point in choosing a partner you feel passion for. On that basis, you might as well pick just about anybody, really, who seemed compatible, and start working on building up the *agape.*"

"That is how marriages have traditionally been arranged in the East. The kettle starts to boil after marriage and not before," said Ismene.

"Or doesn't boil at all. I'm good on the theory – but we all want that magic spark, don't we? The recognition that this person is the one we're meant to be with. But can it endure?"

"Love does endure. And it is wonderful when you feel you are with the companion for whom you have been searching all your life. The relationship becomes sacred when one reveals oneself to the beloved, by which I mean one's own Self, which is also the Self of God, as Julian says. When two people connect in that way there can be true love, because all love comes from God. I think when it does happen it may be because we have known that person before, in another life. But in a particular lifetime it may not be part of our life plan to have the continuous companionship of the beloved."

"I think that's terribly sad," I said, hoping I was not intruding on painful territory.

"Well, the purpose of life is not personal happiness. We ask the wrong question: how can I get everything I want to make me happy?"

"What's the right question?"

"What is my purpose? That's the right question. The purpose of life is to grow towards the wholeness God intends for us, as Julian promises. The aspiration towards God is common to all the great faiths. We are all going towards the same destination and it is sad that we do not see it."

"Do you have a faith?" I asked.

"Yes, I'm a Christian. I come from a family that took no interest in religion. My father was a self-made man who founded a business empire and made a fortune. He believed in the sweat of one's brow and material achievement through one's own endeavour – worthy enough aspirations if they are not one's sole existence. He relied upon himself and no one else his entire life. He used to say he felt no need for a god. I never felt moved to take any interest in religion myself – until something happened that made me think again.

"I was in my early twenties, travelling in central Brazil, and I stopped off in a small town to buy food. I noticed a little building at the end of the main street. For some reason, it drew my attention and I decided to investigate. It was a Baha'i meeting place… I knew nothing about the faith and know very little now, but as I entered I felt a deep sense of peace. The atmosphere of the tiny inner room was filled with what I can only describe as a spirit of holiness. I felt I could step out of the preoccupations of my life into another space, another condition, almost. It seemed nearly tangible. That was why I was so drawn to Anna's description of entering Julian's church. I know what she felt. Now, how was it possible that such a spirit could exist in a place if it was not a house of God? I tasted something that day and the taste remained with me and slowly became a hunger."

"I understand," I said.

"As I continued my travels, I met many people from diverse backgrounds and cultures. So many people who were living in desperate conditions had a faith that brought them through, that gave their lives meaning, despite everything they had to endure. Whether they were Christian, Muslim, Hindu, Jewish – they felt a connection with a God who sustained them. I began to want to share that certainty, that sense of being whole.

"What did I believe? I had doubts about the exclusivity of any faith. My experience in the Baha'i meeting place had given me that. My husband was a devout Muslim. I was attracted to his faith, to its spirit of unity. But I was still not ready. Nothing ever quite felt right in my heart till I met Julian. Meeting her was like coming home."

"Has your faith helped you to grow towards the wholeness you spoke of?"

"Oh, yes, very much so. And we grow by doing the work we came here to do. Each of us came with a particular purpose, a blueprint. But we are in uncharted territory and need to find our route maps! This is where Julian touches a deep chord for me. She speaks of our being fragmented, separated from our real selves. She says that God enfolds and encloses us, but we do not know it because we are not seeing the reality in which we are grounded.

"The earthly personality needs to reach up to the God within us, the higher part, as Julian calls it, to discover where our path lies. Julian tells us that nothing happens by chance, that God's hand is over everything. He allows things to happen to us only to the extent to which they can be turned to our benefit, so that we may learn and reach our true potential."

"Look at the candle." There was a large white candle on a brass plate in the centre of the table. "What do you see?"

I smiled and replied, "Well, wax."

Ismene struck a match and lit the candle, saying, "Look." As the burnished flame grew stronger and brighter, she said, "We begin with cold wax and we apply heat. The wax melts and becomes watery. The melted wax rises up the wick, makes contact with the air and bursts into flame. This is a metaphor for the way we are transformed through various stages until we are transmuted into light. We move from limited form to unlimited form, from mortality to immortality, because light never dies. It travels for ever. This is our journey. Candle after candle, we must light more and more, so that the light we create enlarges throughout our lives."

She asked, "Do you know the story of the phoenix?"

"You mean, rising from the ashes?"

"The story is found in Celtic Christian and Native American Indian traditions. The phoenix burns itself in the fire and is reborn. In other stories, it is represented by the pelican, which pierces its breast to feed its young with its own blood – an act of love, in which it pours out its heart's love to feed others. It is a symbol of what we have to do and keep on doing. Once you commit yourself to the path of initiation you cannot leave it and everything that comes into your life will test you, until you attain your goal. The lives we construct for ourselves fall apart so easily, at a fingertip's touch. Eventually, we come to realize that God's path is the only path."

After our meal, Ismene made green tea in an old silver teapot with fluted sides and a broken spout. We took our tea into the drawing room and sat together in companionable silence.

She rose and crossed to a small table, upon which was a package. She handed me the package, saying, "These are for you." Inside, I found a copy of Julian's book and the small, pale yellow *Enfolded in Love*, with its cover illustration of the homely figure leaning forward to gather up a kneeling child. She said, "That illustration reminds me of Gerard Manley Hopkins' description of God's tender, loving, all-encompassing care. Do you know his poem, 'The Grandeur of God'?"

"Yes. Yes, I do."

"'And though the last light off the black hills went, ah, morning at the brown brink eastward springs, because the Holy Ghost over the bent world broods, with warm breast and with, ah, bright wings.'"

I said, "It's a lovely poem. The teachers at my school were very fond of Gerard Manley Hopkins. I used to think they'd accidentally latched onto the wrong God – like a child, holding on to its mother's coat in a shop, who inadvertently switches to someone else's mum. That happened to me once. It took a few minutes for the two mothers to realize that they had each other's child. I burst into tears. Hopkins' God is loving but my teachers' God sounded a nasty piece of work, cruel and vengeful. An angry old man with a bad attitude. I wouldn't have wanted to go home with him."

"I think it's true to say that God has had a bad press!" said Ismene.

I laughed. "Maybe he needs a better press agent!"

"He does have some good ones, I think. Paul's work often reveals God's grandeur and his love... he finds God in small places, revealing the divinity in a human soul."

I felt my cheeks beginning to flush.

Ismene continued, "Paul said you were at university together."

"Yes."

"He and I are old friends. We have worked together on many stories. It was through a very old friend of mine that Paul met his wife, when he was out in Kashmir. Ranjit, Sushila's father, has for many years been deeply involved in human rights and the independence struggle. He's a truly extraordinary man. Indeed, the whole family have a special quality about them. Sushila was a lovely and remarkable child, both innocent and wise. And you know, as she grew up she retained all her beautiful qualities, her trusting and forgiving nature and belief in the intrinsic goodness of people. It was like watching the blossoming of a delicate and lovely flower.

"Now that was a love match. I remember Sushila saying to me, just before her wedding day, that, whatever happened, no matter what difficulties she and Paul might face or mistakes they might make, 'Paul and I will always be together. We cannot be parted.' Ah yes, yes indeed." Ismene looked sad suddenly; remembering, no doubt, how badly Paul had let his wife down.

I felt as though I were trespassing on private territory and quickly changed the subject. I said, "I envy you your certainty. I think I wish I knew your God."

"You will know him, Joanna, if that is your wish."

"Does your faith sustain you, does it help you to make sense of the past?"

"Oh yes. I was very angry. So much had been taken from me. I felt my life had been stolen. Munir's life certainly was. It was very hard. It would have been easy to become bitter. But I came to understand that anger would not help me. Anger is corrosive. It destroys one from inside. It is suicidal."

"But it achieves results."

"Not the best kind. Love is really the only thing that works."

12

Three days later word reached the foreign desk that Paul was on his way out of East Timor. The following day he telephoned the desk from Bangkok. I expected to see him in the office during the ensuing days, but there was no sign of him. I wondered how his wife coped with the long absences.

On the evening of Ismene Vale's East Timor reception, I parked my car and walked up the now familiar poplar-lined drive to her house. As the maid opened the door, I heard a hubbub of chatter and laughter from within. She directed me to the drawing room, where some thirty people were already gathered. I accepted a glass of wine from a waiter. Ismene spotted me, smiled and beckoned me to join her.

She greeted me warmly. "Joanna, I'm so glad you were able to come. I've been looking forward to our having a chat." She turned aside briefly from the group she was with and said, "Several people are coming this evening who are in a position to help East Timor and I know they'll enjoy talking to you. There are some other projects I'd very much like to discuss with you. If there's no opportunity this evening, may we meet for lunch or dinner?" I said I would love to meet up.

I spent the next two hours in the company of people who were deeply committed to helping others. It was a refreshing and invigorating experience. Among them was a field worker for a Christian aid agency, a member of the International Committee of the Red Cross and a peer, Lord Helpmann, who had dedicated his life to human rights. Ismene informed me that Lord Helpmann often played host to refugees from persecution. One of his regular guests was José Ramos Horta, East Timor's sole, roving ambassador, who operated on a budget of little more than largesse from sympathizers.

I met and immediately liked Gregorio, an East Timorese who had been imprisoned by the Indonesians and eventually left his country with the help of the International Red Cross. Gregorio was my height, five foot three, with long, curly black hair and deep brown eyes. He had an observant, gentle manner. I was later to discover that he was a deeply sensitive man, whose calm demeanour cloaked the pain of his experiences and the loss of his country.

Gregorio was a teenager in 1975, when the Indonesians invaded. Perhaps unwisely for the occasion, I asked him to tell me about that terrible day.

"We call it the day when death came from the sky," he said. The Indonesian army invaded by air. Hundreds of parachutes descended onto East Timor. The soldiers landed and the slaughter began. Gregorio saw soldiers murder his neighbour's two children, swinging them by their legs and smashing their heads against a wall. He saw another neighbour shoot dead an elderly woman, too afraid to refuse the order of a sadistic soldier. He saw a lake that ran red with victims' blood.

He had fled to the mountains to join the resistance. Later he became a bodyguard to their leader, Xanana Gusmão, the future President of a free East Timor. Now he was studying in London for a PhD. I learned a lot from him about East Timor and felt even more inspired to help. We agreed to meet and exchanged telephone numbers.

Gregorio's eyes suddenly lit up as someone entered the room. I turned and saw a lady in a nun's habit. "It's Sister Eleanor!" Gregorio said. The sister spotted him, smiled and raised her hand in greeting. "Excuse me," said Gregorio, before hurrying over to greet the Sister. They crossed the room together, in lively conversation. He introduced us, saying, "Sister Eleanor is a good friend to East Timor."

Sister Eleanor was tall – about five foot eight – and slender, with a fair skin and green eyes flecked with brown. She took my hand. Her grip was firm, her smile warm and welcoming. She had a gentle, homely quality that put me at my ease. She asked Gregorio if he had news of his sister.

He explained, "My sister is a nun. Sister Eleanor's convent gives great support to the Sisters. Yes, they are well, Sister. But it is a frightening situation all the while, as you know."

Sister Eleanor turned to me and said, "At our convent, St Etheldreda's, we have made a special link of prayer with the Sisters in East Timor." Sister Eleanor told me she was an artist whose paintings were sometimes sold in aid of charities. Several had been sold recently to help poor families in East Timor. The Sister had special dispensation to participate in activities that promoted the use of her work in this way, hence her acceptance of Gregorio's invitation to the reception.

Gregorio said, "Sister Eleanor and I met through the Sisters at Tyburn Convent, when they held a day of prayer for the people of East Timor. It is a strange coincidence that brought us together – and made us such good friends!"

Sister Eleanor smiled, saying, "If, of course, you believe in coincidence."

At ten o'clock, as I was about to leave, Paul Huntingford walked in. He went straight across to Ismene and they embraced like old friends. She introduced him to the people with whom she was chatting, who were evidently delighted to meet him. In moments, they were all deep in conversation.

I had not seen Paul since our university days, save for the occasional television appearance when he was receiving an award. He looked older and somehow stronger – more substantial, more muscular, a more solid presence. But his warm, humorous brown eyes were the same. And his voice sounded the same, deep and melodic. He had the same way of listening attentively, as though the person to whom he was speaking was saying something of great importance. All part of his technique, I thought.

Ismene caught my eye and called me over to join them. Paul turned, and I felt myself blush as he looked at me. I felt nineteen again, rather gauche and unsure of myself. It was very disconcerting, the way he had of looking at me, steadily, as though he were taking in the whole of me and nothing could be hidden.

As the members of the group continued their discussion, I became aware that Paul's eyes were upon me. My attention distracted momentarily by this, I suddenly realized that Ismene was replying to a question Lord Helpmann had asked about Kashmir. Paul joined in, saying to Lord Helpmann, "You must meet my father-in-law, Ranjit Kadir. He's a leading member of the human rights movement."

Lord Helpmann was nodding vigorously and saying that he knew Paul's father-in-law by reputation.

Paul said, "He'll be over here in a few weeks' time. Perhaps you'd like to join us at home for dinner? I feel sure Ranjit would like to meet you. It sounds as though you could be very helpful to one another."

Lord Helpmann said he would ring to make the arrangements and took Paul's business card. The focus of the conversation changed. Paul turned to me, with a warm smile.

"Hi, Jo. It's good to see you. Thank you for doing the story. I haven't had a chance to say this – it was a brilliant piece."

"I'm the one who should thank you," I replied. "You gave me a great story and I'm very grateful – "

"Because I knew you'd know what to do with it. And you certainly did."

Suddenly Paul was talking to me with the intimacy of an old friend. We talked together in a way I did not remember us ever doing before. It was really very strange, as though we were both remembering a relationship we had never had. I wondered if he had simply forgotten that he had stood me up.

Paul reminded me of people, places and events. We reminisced about our most eccentric tutor, Professor Setterington, an ardent socialist who used to give brilliant tutorials, often under the influence of his favourite tipple, Irish whiskey. He kept a cache in a cupboard under a portrait that he said was of a distant cousin. Since the subject of the portrait was Virgina Woolf, this seemed unlikely.

Paul said, "Do you remember how he used to tap his nose and wink, saying, 'The old girl's keeping an eye on me. One day the loot will be coming my way...'" I joined in to complete the sentence we both knew so well, "'... and then I can get shot of you miserable little buggers!'"

Paul said, "Dear old Red Setter. Were you there the time he got us all pie-eyed and fell off his chair?"

"No, but I was there the night he took us on a pub crawl; do you remember?"

"God, yes! Someone ended up in the canal – Scottish chap..."

"Jeremy McLannan."

"Yeah, of course. How could I forget? He couldn't swim, poor chap."

"How indeed? You were the one who fished him out. You came up the bank looking like a couple of bedraggled water rats and stinking of God knows what."

Paul laughed. "Yes, I did always like to cut a dash."

"I felt so sorry for you. People dumped all kinds of disgusting gunk there..."

"I had to throw those jeans away, I couldn't get the smell off them. And they were my most treasured flares!" I laughed.

Paul said, "We had a lot of fun. It was a good time. But one grows up." He looked reflective suddenly, and a little sad.

"Has being grown-up been less fun for you?" I asked.

"Oh, no, no, I've been lucky in many ways," he replied. "How about you? Are you married?"

"No. I nearly was, but we realized in time that we were not right for each other. It's not easy, is it? Living with another person."

I suddenly realized that I had strayed into dangerous territory and tried to change the subject. As I waffled on about nothing in particular, Paul suddenly said, "Joanna, it's great to see you again. Will you have dinner with me?"

Confused and thrown off course, I spluttered, "Why?"

Paul looked rather taken aback. "Because I think you're lovely and I'd like to see you again."

"Oh, would you now?" I replied, realizing that my cheeks were beginning to flush with anger. How dare he ask me out, when only minutes earlier he had been inviting someone to dine with his wife and father-in-law. What sort of a pushover did he think I was? Had he absolutely no conscience at all? His wife, I thought, must be the most downtrodden doormat on the planet.

"You haven't changed, have you, Paul?" I said angrily. "You just think you're such a big deal that you can get away with it every time, don't you? Well, you may fool a lot of people but you don't fool me. I've been round this particular mulberry bush once already and I didn't enjoy the trip. I have no intention of going round it again, thanks very much."

Paul looked very put-out. He said, "I'm sorry. I didn't mean to upset you."

"No, I don't suppose you did," I replied. "It's simply beyond your comprehension that someone, some time, might choose not to fall at your feet and do what you want them to do. Well listen and learn. I'm not impressed by what you're selling and I'm not buying." I turned angrily and walked from the room. Only as I was getting into my car did I realize that I had not said goodnight to Ismene.

13

I saw no sign of Paul in the office during the next few weeks. I wondered if he was keeping out of my way. I began to search for the mysterious Anna Leigh. I felt the need to meet her. I imagined us having lunch together, in a quiet country restaurant with a view into the distance of grass and trees. I imagined us liking each other, of my putting her at ease and persuading her to confide the rest of her story.

I was curious to know whether she had made a break from the past and changed her life. Had her encounter with Julian made a difference? Had Anna found what I lacked – a relevance and meaning to life? Was she still alive, even? If so, why had she not returned for her journal? I was afraid I might never get answers to the many questions she and Julian had raised in my mind.

I wrote to Frieda Bonhart's nephew, Charles Clemence, who had taken over the running of her publishing company, asking if he had any record of a writer named Anna Leigh. He wrote back saying that he had no knowledge of her.

I contacted the Julian Centre in Norwich, but the administrator had no recollection of Anna. Apparently, several hundred people visit every year, from all over the world. I telephoned Cambridge University and asked if there was any record of Anna. Again I drew a blank.

I tried the Office of National Statistics. They had records of twelve women in the right age group – the mid-thirties when she met Frieda Bonhart – who might be Anna Leigh or Lee; since my interview with Ismene Vale I realized it could be either spelling. A colleague in the reference library agreed to follow up the leads. Nick, our crime correspondent, suggested some other avenues of pursuit. But what if Leigh or Lee were her married name? What if she was not British-born? More important, what if Anna did not want to be found? Had I the right to try to track her down?

I wondered how someone could put so much work into a piece of writing and then just leave it, unfinished – indeed, give it away. It was almost as though Anna had found something more important than her work, something with more meaning. If so, I envied her.

I felt that Anna's story was autobiographical, but it could have been a complete fiction. If a fiction, then could I believe everything she had written about Julian of Norwich? No, I instinctively believed in Anna's integrity and that of the story she was telling. If I was to find out more, I must pick up where Anna had left off and read Julian's book.

But my good intentions went unrealized. The pressure of work was mounting and I did little more than dip into the books given to me by Ismene. Christmas came and went. Weeks and then months slipped by. I was asked to write a weekly column, in addition to my reporting duties. I felt tired and stressed most of the time. There seemed to be no room for anything extra. Matters were made worse by the continuing sense I had of no longer belonging at the *Correspondent*.

The ending of my affair with Patrick had left me sad and disillusioned. When I saw him on television I still felt attracted to him and I missed him, but now I also feared him – and there were so many other feelings of bitterness and resentment. Dr Newell had quietly faded out of the public eye. He had resigned and the government had succeeded in bluffing and spinning its way out of the story until the press had stopped pursuing it.

If Paul had come to the office since his East Timor trip, I had not seen him there. I had met Ismene a couple of times, to discuss other human rights projects. I had wanted to become involved but it was simply impossible to take on any more work. However, I promised to always try to write about any developments in East Timor, where the brutality and suffering continued, and I used my column to publicize this and other human rights causes whenever I could.

Then, in late April, something happened that changed everything. I was at my desk, working on a story, when Milo came over.

"Newell's croaked," he said.

"What?"

"Newell – bright eyes, bushy tail, y'know, the mole – he's croaked. Found in his garage, dangling from a beam – not the sort of DIY job the makeover shows have in mind, but no complaints from me. Get onto the wife and get some quotes."

I remained seated, in complete shock. I felt sick. My brain felt full of mush. I tried to stand up but my legs would not support me.

Milo, now back at his desk, shouted, "For Christ's sake, Meredith, get on with it! Jesus."

I could not reach Mrs Newell, for which I felt both sorry and glad; sorry that I could not express my sadness and sympathy, glad to spare her the ordeal of talking to me. I went through the rest of the day in a numbed haze. At home that evening, I cried and cried – for poor Dr Newell, his wife and his children.

Apparently, his brave attempts to deal with the aftermath of his disclosures had not succeeded. Things had not been nearly as good as he had optimistically led me – and perhaps himself – to believe. Accustomed from childhood to fighting through and depending on his own resources, he had tried to shoulder a burden that was simply too great. A sensitive man, he had lapsed into depression and sought solace once more in alcohol. In his confused state of mind, he had come to believe that he was nothing more than a blight on his family and that they would be better off without him.

I was swamped by guilt, regret, bewilderment and deep pain. I knew I should write to Mrs Newell, but could not.

I needed time to myself. I took a week's holiday in May and went to stay at a cottage in Hampshire, loaned by a friend who was working abroad. I arrived late in the evening, had some soup and went to bed. It was wonderful to rest in absolute silence. I soon drifted off to sleep.

I rose early the next morning, woken by the sun streaming through my window. I lay quietly for several minutes, listening to the soft rustling of the wind in the trees and the sweet, plaintive song of the birds.

The cottage was on a private estate that had been the home of the Earl of Longbourne. The main house had been divided into apartments and Rachel's cottage was a conversion in a corner of the old stable block. It was light and spacious, with high ceilings, exposed beams and windows that looked out onto a cobbled courtyard. I entered the bedroom through the original four-foot-wide wooden door. The windows on the other side of the house looked onto a small cottage garden and a path, framed by hanging blossoms, leading into the woods. Honeysuckle and clematis peeped in at the lounge window. The several acres of grounds were a mass of purple and pink rhododendrons.

Across the courtyard there was another, larger house, and in the opposite corner a barn, the door of which was kept open in summer for the swallows to nest. Away from the incessant buzz of London, I felt I could breathe freely and let go of the tensions that concentrated around my neck and shoulders.

The day was bright, warm and sunny. I took my breakfast and Anna's journal out into the courtyard, where there were chairs and a table. I had packed the journal as an afterthought, along with the books given to me by Ismene. My neighbour across the courtyard was away, his house shuttered, so I had complete privacy. It was a sublime day. Perhaps there never was such a perfect one. Perhaps there never will be again.

The floor of the courtyard was covered in rectangular grey cobbles, bedded in soft, brown, tufted earth, with dashes of mossy green. The cottages were constructed of cool, grey, rough-hewn stone slabs. Rachel's cottage encompassed the clock tower, the pointed roof of which had been hung with small curved and rectangular terracotta tiles, now browned with age, in a pattern of three alternate rows. Atop it was a grey, spidery weathervane, its letters shaky and askew.

The clock had long since given up any pretence of recording the hour. Its pale green attenuated hands remained fixed at twenty-three minutes past six – I wondered what momentous event had stopped time in that instant – and its wan, faded face seemed like a frail fragment, a reminder of what the place had been. The courtyard was surrounded by trees, some reaching forty feet into the sky. At the far end, in front of a potting shed, was a patch of wilderness, with beds of herbs and a bird table. Visitors to Rachel's cottage were required to put out food for the birds. Before settling to eat my breakfast, I replenished the bird table with seeds from the bag left by Rachel, and poured fresh water into the stone container. As I ate my breakfast, I watched two squirrels squabbling over territory, chasing one another up the pole that supported the bird table and snatching the food.

I was particularly attracted to that end of the courtyard. It was wild and untouched, a private, uncultivated place that had been allowed simply to be for many years, free of the attentions of the kind of gardener who likes to make nature neat. The rustling of the wind among the trees, now urgent, now caressing, seemed to be murmuring confidences about the times that had passed in this place. I remembered reading, a few weeks earlier, the obituary of Lady Helen, the Earl's aunt. She had stayed on at the house after it had been converted and sold, occupying an apartment overlooking the lawn and distant swathe of farmland. I remembered the obituary because it had described her as a woman of deep spirituality. It had struck me as a lovely and enviable tribute.

I savoured the fresh, delicious flesh of a peach, enjoying the soft, heavy roundness cradled in my palm, and wondered about the kind of life that inspires such a tribute. Though the daughter of an earl, she had led a quite ordinary life of childrearing and work in the community.

At the *Correspondent*'s last Christmas party I had met two men who were in competition for high governmental office. We journalists were amused to see how they avoided each other in the lively bustle of the affair. I went over to chat to one of the contenders, who was widely rumoured to be miserable about the manipulation of his career by the Prime Minister. As we shook hands, he said, "I thought you lot would be handing out Prozac," clearly smarting about articles in our paper that had said he was depressed. He was so different from his public image. On television he looked large and imposing, but in the flesh he was small and quite cuddly. The tough politician's persona was absent in real life. He seemed sad and lost and rather sweet really, I thought.

Later I chatted to his rival, who seemed rather the worse for the drink that was flowing freely. Whilst much allowance is made for eccentric behaviour in the cut and thrust of politics, I thought his flippancy ill-advised. As we talked, a famous entrepreneur joined us and warned him that his ill-considered outbursts were alarming the City.

Here were two men "who would be King". What, for goodness' sake, did they have to offer? What had they ever done to demonstrate leadership and sound judgement? They might want to lead, but why in the world would anyone want to follow them?

If people are, indeed, remembered for their effect upon others' lives, what mark would these men leave? Those saintly few who lead exemplary lives in the service of others are honoured appropriately when they die. Lady Helen was perhaps not among the saints, nor quite, I felt, among the sinners. The tribute to her was so simple and yet, as I sat in the courtyard and felt the spirit of the place, it seemed wonderful recognition of a life lived well.

This was a place I felt I must have dreamed of a million times. London had lost its appeal. There never seemed to be time and space to reflect upon my life, to think about what I wanted for the future. Time hurried by in a blur of deadlines. I pictured my life in London – my house, the office, the places I frequented. The memories held no moments like these.

I spent most of the morning reading Anna's journal again. She had written of pain, exposure, vulnerability and release. She had made herself vulnerable. She had made mistakes. Had it profited her? Or was she just another loser? In the evening, I prepared a chicken casserole and put it into the oven. I lit some candles, placed fruit in the bowl on the coffee table in the lounge and took from my suitcase my gift of books from Ismene Vale.

I took up my copy of *Enfolded in Love*. I remembered how Anna had described the way she handled the book, her longing to extract its meaning through its physical fabric. I thought of what Anna had written about books bringing messages from places that are difficult to reach to places that are hard to find. What could be more difficult, I reflected, than penetrating the layers of defensiveness and stale habit that surround the human heart?

As I read Julian's words, I realized that she was saying that we do not think we deserve to be loved, and so we do not accept the love that is freely offered. She was saying that self-acceptance is the first step towards wholeness, the elusive wholeness of which Ismene had spoken.

Julian tells the story of two people, a lord and a servant. The lord, who loves his servant dearly, sends him on an errand. The servant, who loves his master, rushes off at great speed to carry out the task. But he falls into a ditch and is badly injured. He struggles and cries out but can do nothing to help himself. And though his lord is close by and could save him, the servant cannot see him. So he stays in his ditch, feeling wretched and weak. I read that our own blindness prevents us from knowing the goodness of our own souls, so we despair. I read that the love is there for us, but our feelings of guilt and unworthiness prevent us from receiving it. Until the love of God penetrates us so that we know ourselves as lovable, we can find no peace.

When I had first read Anna's description of the illustration on the cover – the homely figure leaning forward to gather up a child in her embrace – I had been reminded of Rembrandt's *The Return of the Prodigal Son*. I had seen the painting several years earlier, at the Hermitage in St Petersburg. I had bought the poster of the painting and hung it in my study, and I had brought the poster with me to the cottage and hung it near a window that looked onto the courtyard. Why had I brought it? I cannot tell you.

In the painting, the father leans forward to embrace his son, who kneels at his feet. The father's face is a glow of internal light. He is old... he has been waiting a long time for this moment, I thought. He stoops to gather his son to him. The father's hands are firm and strong on the young man's shoulder and back. The son has fallen haphazardly against his father's lower body, after rushing headlong to him and dropping at his feet. If his father moved away, the son would collapse to the floor. Perhaps it was with his last ounce of strength that he stumbled towards his journey's end.

The young man's head is turned slightly, resting against his father's breast. His head is bowed and, though we have a three-quarter view, we can see that his eyes are closed. He has arrived, he has sanctuary, he is home.

In turning his head, he exposes the vulnerable spot at the nape of the neck. The soft beam of light that illumines his father's face spreads, as though directed from above, through the father's head and radiates from his hands across that vulnerable spot and the expanse of his son's back. Within the embrace, I felt, the pain and sorrow and sense of loss were being healed. I felt that this boy had cried many tears and been brought to utter humiliation before he could find his way home. I felt compassion for his pain and brokenness.

What punishment did he feel he deserved? What frailties did he bring with him that his father, but no other employer, would tolerate? What addiction, perhaps? He had spent years indulging in worldly pleasures. Julian seemed to be saying that it is these things that seduce us into forgetting our real selves. I knew how addiction took away control over one's life.

A friend had been addicted to gambling. Others I knew – among them my friend Alex – were addicted to drugs or alcohol. And what of those who are addicted to people? Anna's horrible experience with Mark had reminded me of my own reluctance to face the truth about Patrick. I had resisted relinquishing my dream. I had resisted being alone again.

The Return of the Prodigal Son is a picture of someone who has nothing left to lose, someone who has recognized his own nakedness under the sun. How much it means to us to be known and accepted as we really are. I longed for such a homecoming.

As the evening light faded gently, and the birds took over the trees with their evensong service, I looked again at the familiar scene of father and son – and suddenly I saw something else. I looked closely for the first time at another figure, who stands to the right of the embracing couple. This young man is tall and proud. He is well-dressed, with a rich, red cloak around his shoulders, and sturdy boots. He stands rather stiffly, looking awkward, puzzled, uncomfortable, and even disapproving of the emotional scene and what he may perceive as the senile, irrational doting of his father. For this is the other son, the prodigal's elder brother.

While his younger brother frittered away his time and money, this brother stayed at home and helped his father to build up the family business. He was the one who made sacrifices, who kept the rules, who did what the world expected of him. And what was his reward? To see his brother come back, having contributed nothing, and be given a hero's welcome.

How unfair. I could almost hear him saying the words. In his eyes I see the hurt, the bewilderment. What about me? he seems to be asking. His hands are clasped together anxiously. Suddenly all that he thought was sure and certain has been put in jeopardy. He thought he knew the rules of the game, the rules of his world, and now, suddenly, the world has been turned upside down. A scene of intimate love is taking place a couple of feet away from him and he feels excluded.

A feeling of profound sadness overcame me as I read this new significance into the scene. I had always identified with the prodigal, the rule-breaker, but suddenly I saw something of myself in the exclusion of the dutiful stay-at-home.

I had taken risks, forced myself to do things that were frightening and difficult, and my efforts had brought me success. But, like the elder brother, I had never risked everything, I had never allowed myself to be utterly vulnerable. I felt excluded. The prodigal must surely have dreaded meeting his brother, someone I imagined to have been less talented, less charming, someone whom he had perhaps teased as too conventional to take a chance in life. In the homecoming, the younger brother, who was once so confident and proud, so sure of his abilities to make it in the big wide world, is shown up in all his failure and vulnerability – and yet, in that moment, there is a nobility about him, because he confesses his weakness and opens himself to receive love.

Now the meaning of the painting became clearer than ever before. It is a story not only of love, compassion and forgiveness. It is also a story about allowing oneself to love and be loved. I remembered the words of a hymn we had sung at school: "Oh, love that seekest me through pain, I cannot close my heart to thee… I trace the rainbow through the rain…" Suddenly, they had a deeper meaning.

The last few lines in Anna's journal had been about the necessity to undergo a crucifixion, to go beyond vulnerability and exposure to redemption and release. Ismene had said that if we really understood how others felt about our actions, we would change. There seemed to be some common theme here, about understanding one's own feelings and those of others, about acknowledging one's loneliness and longing for love.

But I knew I was lonely, I had always longed for love, so where was I missing the point? Was Julian right? Did I perhaps not feel worthy of love? "You are beloved through all eternity…" the words from Anna's strange dream about Julian came back to me. Could I believe that I was so loved? Was I capable of believing it?

All of this seemed to connect, too, with an assertion I had heard somewhere that love was the solution to every problem. I wondered, if one dealt with every problem from the standpoint of love, and not fear, what would change? But a worrying thought nagged at me: had Anna been right? In order to grow, to find one's true self, must each of us, must I, undergo a crucifixion?

14

I awoke the following morning feeling troubled. I felt I was not going to be able to relax in my rural retreat. I felt out of place and out of sorts, as though I should be somewhere else, doing something else. It was disturbing to acknowledge how quickly my mood could change. As if in response to my sudden restlessness, the telephone rang. It was Ismene Vale. Even while escaping to the country, the journalist in me had been unable to resist leaving a contact number, in case of a sudden dramatic development in the East Timor story.

"Joanna, my dear, how are you feeling?"

"Oh, better. I've had some sleep."

"I'm very glad to hear it. Now I'm telephoning because you asked me to. The European representative of the East Timor resistance will be in London next week for a meeting with the shadow Foreign Secretary. The Portuguese Embassy is hosting a reception for him. Would you like to be invited?"

"Oh, please, yes. Thank you."

"Very well, I shall arrange it." I think Ismene was about to conclude the call, but somehow sensed that I did not want to be tactfully left to my own devices. I invited her to join me for lunch at the cottage. She readily agreed, and then said, "Well, now, would you feel up to feeding three of us? On Wednesday, Paul, Gregorio and I are attending an international human rights conference in Southampton. We could start our day early, join you for lunch and then travel on, if that would be convenient?"

I was taken aback but could hardly say no. In any case, it would be good to see Ismene and Gregorio. I had met Gregorio a few times for a drink or a meal and enjoyed his company. I felt he read people and situations with great perceptiveness. It never ceased to amaze me that this quiet, cultured man had once lived rough in the mountains, as a soldier and bodyguard, his life in danger at every moment. As always, the prospect of seeing Ismene gave a sense of purpose to the day. Perhaps it was the knowledge that I never met her without learning something, without my life making better sense afterwards. As for Paul, well, I would have to simply take things as they came.

On the Wednesday, at midday, I parked in the station car park at Longbourne, a village some five miles away, and walked to the platform to await my guests. Train doors opened and three figures emerged: Ismene and Gregorio, both tiny, and Paul, towering above them. Gregorio and Ismene both hugged me. Paul stood back a little, smiling. I felt uneasy. As I drove back to Littlechurch Mead, I realized that I still felt very tired and really quite unsociable. Much as I enjoyed Ismene's and Gregorio's company, I felt I had little to give. I had begun to take time for myself and it seemed that an unravelling process had begun, which would not stop.

I served lunch in the courtyard. As the time passed, I became aware of the deep bond of friendship between my guests. I realized that the bond was strengthened by their commitment to East Timor's struggle for freedom, the fact of a shared goal that mattered deeply to each. I understood why Gregorio and Ismene would have those feelings – but Paul?

As though reading my thoughts, Ismene asked, "Paul, what was it that motivated you to become a journalist?"

"Ah, well, curiosity, I suppose."

"Only curiosity?" Ismene persisted.

"Well, I reckon I was always a bit at odds with the world. My family are very middle class, solid, respectable people. Everything as I grew up was determined and clear. There was no uncertainty, no insecurity – a very happy childhood, I was lucky. But I was always dissatisfied, always feeling I wanted to achieve something not predicted and predictable, something of my own. I suppose we're pretty much the product of our upbringing, one way or another – even if we kick over the traces!

"A new idiom!" exclaimed Gregorio. We all laughed. Gregorio was very fond of practising his vocabulary of English idioms on us. Paul laughingly explained the literal meaning of kicking over the traces. I was impressed. I had no idea what traces were or how they got kicked over.

"You could have chosen a different kind of journalism – though I can't imagine it!" said Ismene.

"Well, I suppose the work chose me, in a way. I was very lucky – being in the right place at the right time. If I hadn't been, you and I would not have met, and I would not have had the benefit of your help and kindness when I was green and ignorant. My life has really been a series of coincidences, chance meetings that shaped what was to come."

"Now you are in Julian's territory, where nothing happens by chance," said Ismene.

Gregorio said "Julian of Norwich? I have met very few English people who have ever heard of her."

"Surely she isn't well known in East Timor?" I asked.

"Oh, no, not at all. But the Sister I invited to your party, Ismene, Sister Eleanor, she is a great expert on Julian."

"Oh, I do wish I had known when I met her!" said Ismene.

Gregorio had learned of the Sister's interest in Julian during their time together at Tyburn Convent, in London, on the day of prayer for East Timor. He said, "Sister Eleanor has given me a book of extracts from Julian's book. Her words are full of hope. I wonder what lies ahead for East Timor…"

"Freedom," said Ismene, placing her hand over his.

"Yes, it will come," said Gregorio. "One day it will come."

Paul said, "Until that day we will travel with you, Gregorio, my friend, to the end of the road."

"So I see God's goodness in the actions of my friends," said Gregorio, smiling, though there were tears in his eyes.

I was moved by the evident depth of feeling and commitment between the three friends. They had set their hands to a task and it was clear that they would not let go until it had been finished. I discovered that Paul and Ismene had made a valuable contribution to several human rights causes by bringing them to the attention of the world. I admired and envied them. They were doing work that was truly worthwhile. I was making a small contribution through my column – but suddenly it seemed almost insignificant.

I recognized again, just as when we were young, Paul's talent for connecting easily with others. He empathized with people in a way that went beyond the commonplace. It was a quality that drew people to him: a killer combination, empathy and ruthlessness, I thought, perhaps the perfect combination for a high-achieving journalist. I couldn't make Paul out. He was an enigma.

After lunch I took my guests on a tour of the grounds. It was a glorious day and the garden was at its loveliest. As we returned to the cottage, Ismene and Gregorio fell behind a little as Paul and I walked on.

Paul said, "Thank you for lunch. This is a beautiful place. How long will you be here?"

"Just this week."

"Then you'll be back in the swing of things?"

"Yes."

"I've been away for the past few months, on wall-to-wall assignments. I'm going to be around more now, at least for the time being. Perhaps we'll see each other." We walked on in silence. Paul asked, "Are you still angry with me?"

I felt irritated. I was not in the mood for a personal conversation and certainly not a confrontation. "Why should I be?"

"I don't know, but I seemed to have upset you last time we met."

Was he being deliberately provocative? Or was he just so full of himself that he could not imagine anyone objecting to his playing around? I began to feel so angry and exasperated that I felt sure I would say the wrong thing. It irritated me that I still felt attracted to him and that I was obliged to manage those feelings as best I could, as well as my annoyance at his behaviour. It was all making me feel rather ratty at a time when I felt I had no resources to deal with anything complicated. As I was wondering how to respond, the others caught up with us.

"We should leave soon," said Gregorio, glancing at his watch. I walked my guests back to the cottage, gave them tea and then drove them to the station. As I drove back to the cottage, I thought what a strange day it had been and how oddly Paul had behaved. I simply could not figure him out. I arrived back feeling distinctly at odds and uncomfortable in my skin. I needed to clear my head. I set off for the lake, walking around the gable end of the house and along the heather-lined path across the top of the lawn.

Everything was quiet now, and still. Everyone seemed to be away, all the doors and windows in the main house closed and shuttered, curtains drawn. I was glad to have the garden to myself. Birdsong and the soft rustle of leaves were all I heard as I walked across the lawn to the lake. I sat in my favourite spot, on the bench by the water's edge, and looked down into the depths, where dark green vegetation swirled softly, casting rippling patterns that stained the glassy, viscous surface. The wind gently lifted the light branches and sent a soft, hushing murmur through their leaves. I felt in harmony, a part of the spirit of the place, suddenly at ease after the tension of the day. The sunlight broke out from behind a cloud and everything around me shone, each leaf and ripple sparkled and the whole place seemed to be imbued with the radiance of an interior light.

After several minutes I rose and took the path to my left that circled the lake. I followed its contour between trees overhanging with the weight of their shadowing branches, past a rhododendron bush ablaze with vivid purple blossoms. Above me, high up in a tree, a blackbird sang. To my right, the water glowed mellow and still. The song of the bird was following me now, as though calling to me. Now at the far side of the lake, I stood in a clearing before a great redwood, whose outstretched arms reached high, as if in worship of the sky god. I continued on my walk and came to a small wooden bridge overhung by an oak. The bridge led to the little island in the middle of the lake, which I had come to think of as my private sanctuary. The bridge was stained green by the falling leaves and rain of countless years.

I opened the gate and walked across the bridge and onto the island. Dense bushes crowded either side of the narrow track that edged the land. The birds were busy, sweetly singing, twittering, calling in the boughs. I ducked under a canopy of leaves, enjoying the crunch and scrunch of leaves and twigs under my feet. Now the bank dropped steeply away. In the water I saw reflections of soft, cotton-wool clouds and delicately etched silhouettes of intricately leaved trees, patterned in charcoal green against the grey-blue sky. Protruding from the water, at the land's edge, was a goblin's boat with raised prow, a jagged piece of wood, deeply scored and fissured by long tongues of water, waiting for its goblin crew to come at nightfall and set sail across the lake.

A little way further and I came upon my place of rest, a seat fashioned from a piece of wood, supported by a tree stump and a log that had been hammered into the ground. From within the dense foliage in the middle of the island, where the ducks had built their nest, came a pittering, smittering sound. Across the bright water and the wide expanse of grass and trees, the Victorian Gothic house seemed magical, mysterious and full of secrets. The water was filled with its rippling reflections in a fracturing glass.

Above me, the flat, shiny leaves of a rhododendron bush moved with a gentle lulling motion, as though tenderly sheltering me from the chance of harm. The wind lifted and the leaves and branches tossed and danced gently. For everything within that garden was gentle and proportionate. I felt, as I had felt when I first saw Ismene's garden, that sense of everything being just as it ought to be, that all was well. In my heart I felt repose.

I rose and continued my walk along the sun-flecked path, beneath the overhanging, protective leaves of another sentinel oak. Ahead was the little bridge. I stepped onto it and reluctantly took my leave of the island's small sanctuary. As I walked back along the lake and towards the house I had a strange sense of being observed. Though no one had come during my walk, I felt as though this place was far from empty, never lonely, perpetually inhabited by life, a spirit of some kind. For how could a place be so alive without a conscious life force inhabiting it?

As I walked back along the heather-fringed path at the front of the house, I was surprised to see someone sitting in the little private garden at the gable end that had belonged to Lady Helen. She was a woman who looked to be in her eighties. She sat motionless and there was such an air of stillness about her that I could not help glancing her way as I passed by. At that moment she looked up and smiled.

"I'm sorry," I said. "I didn't mean to intrude."

"But you're not," she responded. "Why don't you join me?" I had never been into Lady Helen's garden. It was a patch of some forty square feet, tucked away among trees and enclosed by low wrought-iron railings. Roses and honeysuckle and wild flowers tumbled from nooks and crannies in a garden that was simple and unstructured, and yet possessed of a natural, uncontrived symmetry and grace. At the far end was an ancient summerhouse, and through its window I could see a faded pink parasol, folded and propped against the glass, as though its owner had left it there a few moments earlier. I pushed open the garden gate and entered.

The old lady offered me her hand. It was small and white, with knobbled veined tracery showing through the skin.

"I'm Molly Tillington. I'm an old friend of Helen's," she said. I introduced myself and offered my sympathy for her loss.

"Well, as I have been sitting here, remembering the many times we've sat here together, I don't feel as though I have lost her at all," she said. "Just before you came just now I had such a strong feeling of her presence. She loved her little garden and in a way I think she will always be here."

I said, "You seemed very peaceful. I hope I'm not interrupting."

"Not at all. It's nice to have company. You're new here, aren't you? I don't believe I've seen you before." I explained that I was there just for the week. "Do you like it here?" she asked.

"I love it. It's beautiful and the atmosphere is so peaceful; there's such a quality of serenity."

"Now that was cultivated. The family decided to create a place with a particular quality of harmony and sanctuary."

"Yes, I feel it. It's like nowhere I've been. It's a very calming, healing atmosphere. But at the same time there's a kind of clarity about it…"

"Something that makes you look inward? Many people have said so. There is a lot to be gained, on a spiritual level, from the very special quality of this garden. It's a good place to sit quietly and speak to one's heart. Helen and I used to sit here together and meditate on the heart. Do you meditate?"

"I'm afraid not. It's something I've often thought I'd like to try but never quite found the time for."

"I can thoroughly recommend it. It helps one to make sense of life and of the world. You see, by meditating on the heart, one can get in touch with one's intuition, and reach one's true self in the place where all knowledge is found. Would you like me to show you how?" Following Molly's direction, I closed my eyes and concentrated on my breath, then focused my attention on the middle of my chest, which she described as the spiritual heart centre.

"The heart centre is a point of awareness, where feelings enter. In its pure form it is empty, pervaded by weightlessness, absence of care, peace and a subtle light. This light may appear as white, gold, pale pink or blue. You need only feel whatever is there."

I was finding it difficult to keep my mind clear of distractions, but tried to follow Molly's lead. "Breathe gently and sense your breath going into your heart centre. Let the breath go in and out and as it does ask your heart to speak to you. Now – we will sit quietly and listen for five minutes or so. You'll find that your heart will begin to release emotions, memories, wishes, fears and dreams that have been stored there for a very long time."

I concentrated on the heart centre and slowly breathed in and out. As I sat very still, I became aware of, or perhaps imagined, a diffused light around the heart centre. I felt emotionally hurt.

I thought: *My heart hurts*. My heart hurt very badly. I thought: *My heart will break*. I experienced a very unpleasant feeling of profound sadness. I found myself thinking: *I had no idea you were so unhappy, that you felt so alone*. I thought of what Julian had said about not finding love until one could accept love, and that this was a matter of believing oneself to be lovable.

The haunting words from Anna's dream came to me: "You are beloved through all eternity and held safe in an embrace that will never let you go." Could I believe in a God of love? I heard myself saying inwardly, "I want to believe. I want to believe that I am loved. But how? Please, help me to believe." I felt a warm glow in my heart, a sense of fullness. Perhaps the fact that I had said "I want to believe" had made a beginning.

It came to me that what mattered was that I should do what I felt to be right in the moment, what I felt my heart wanted me to do. I sensed that if I followed this course the outcome could only be good. Suddenly, I no longer felt fearful about the future. Whatever came my way, I would find the strength to cope with it. If I could act from this new place, the heart centre, in generous feelings of love, perhaps some new beginning would follow, perhaps the wholeness and Selfhood would begin. I wondered: Must one find integration with the Self before finding happiness with another? I thought: *We are entering hallowed ground. We are talking about the sacred in relationships*.

I opened my eyes and saw Molly's eyes fixed upon me with an expression of tender concern. "How do you feel?"

"A little strange, but calm."

"Every time you meditate on the heart you make a connection with God's love. The more you do it, the easier it becomes to go to your heart for counsel and wisdom, or simply to feel that you are loved. By this means, we find silent assurance, self-acceptance, patience and an appreciation of simply being."

We spoke for a few minutes longer. As I rose to leave, Molly took up a book that was at her side on the bench. I gasped. It was *Enfolded in Love*.

"Do you know this little book?" she asked, seeing my surprise. I explained that I did and that I had become very interested in Julian. She smiled delightedly. "Helen was a great devotee of Julian's. She ran a local Julian of Norwich prayer group. How strange that you should have come to live in her home. But then, as Julian says, nothing happens by chance."

That evening, at the end of a disturbing and illuminating day, I considered how lucky I had been to find such a place in which to think and become stronger. I felt a most loving sense of harmony, a sense of homecoming. The memories of the events that created that atmosphere belonged to others, but the legacy of welcoming warmth and peace were mine.

15

My week at Rachel's cottage rekindled my long-held desire to move out of London. With Rachel's agreement, I started spending my weekends at the cottage. I loved the area and thought I could be happy there. It was a joy to step out of my front door and walk through the tranquillity of the garden and the woods. I would go for a walk three or four times a day, the last in darkness, my way lit by the stars. My walks brought a measured rhythm to my life, smoothing the jagged edges and calming my thoughts.

I had made a success of my weekly column. I wondered if it would be possible to continue it but relinquish my reporting duties, so that I could live in the country and work from home. It would entail giving up my employee status and I would have to accept a drop in income, but I would be free to have a life of my own. I put the proposal to Carol, the Deputy Managing Editor. After some negotiation, we reached an agreement and settled on a fee for the column. Because I would still be working for the paper, I was allowed to reduce my notice period to one month. I could not wait to make my escape.

In July, during my last week, I had a meeting with Carol, to sign my new contract. Carol led me into her office and closed the door. Then she dropped her bombshell. She could not offer me the fee we had agreed. The proprietor had made a sudden, unscheduled visit and demanded stringent budget cuts, though the paper was generating good profits.

"Why does Mr Sharkey want more money out of the paper?" I asked.

"To buy more toys," Carol said.

"Why does he want more toys?"

"To play with."

The fee she offered was derisory. I said that if I accepted it I would be too weak from hunger to do the work, and turned it down. Carol agreed to go back to the Managing Editor and try for an improvement. Later that day Carol called me in again. The offer was better but still considerably less than we had agreed. A few years earlier I would have made a fuss but there was nothing to be gained, so I accepted. The contract would allow me to move to the country and give me the space I needed to consider the next stage of my life.

I had changed, I had learned to act with prudence, but was the change for the better? I had always believed there was a line that people should not be allowed to cross. How close were the management to that line? How close was I to having my integrity compromised? How close to that loss of self that haunted me as a child, when I felt that the inner core of my very being was under threat and I must make myself very strong to withstand the assault?

This lingering childhood memory of the need to protect myself still informed the way I lived my life. And yet, surely some good had come of it: I had recognized the concept of Selfhood while very young and emerged from those difficult early years a strong person – at least, in some ways. I felt confident of my ability not to crack or crumble under the kind of pressure I had experienced so far. But, whilst Michael's early influence had strengthened me and still sustained me, I felt I was paying a price for learning to stand alone and not expecting to be supported or loved.

I had thought the Joker's card had worked with Dr Newell, but what had been the result? I had written to Mrs Newell and received in return a beautiful letter, in which she said that I alone had understood and tried to help. "If only others had been as understanding as you, I would not be in the situation I am in today," she had written. Her letter had made me feel better, but I still felt remorse for my part in his death.

I wondered about the proprietor's motivation. He was one of the world's richest men. Why did he feel the need to squeeze more and more out of the people who worked for him? Was it, as Ismene had said, an inner emptiness and lack of love that drove a person to always want more? Did all that money make him feel safe? Or was his greed a manifestation of fear? Love is generous and gives. Fear is jealous and wants to keep everything for itself. That would have been Julian's perspective, I felt sure.

I talked to Alex about the problem over my contract. He said, "Sharkey might even be surprised at how they're cheese-paring you. He puts people under such pressure, they're too frightened to question anything he says or even to tell him what's going on. I envy you your tunnel under the wire. I won't be in this business in two years' time. I'm thinking of retraining."

"As what?"

"Dunno. Something useful. I'm twenty-three. There has to be more than this."

"Shall we get out of here and have a drink? You can tell me about it," I said.

"I've given it up."

"Completely?"

"Is there another way?"

"Good for you," I said.

"I've been stupid. I don't want to end up like Milo. He's out of control. He was so pissed last week that people were dodging around him in the newsroom so he wouldn't fall on them. You were right. It's stupid to take stuff to get you through."

"I'm really glad to hear you say that, Alex."

"I know. Thanks, Jo."

"Maybe they'll sack Milo at last," I said.

"No way. He knows where the bodies are buried. I don't like working under him. I don't mind him being a bastard – I suppose I expected that – but he's a bloody sadist as well. When Imran went he gave him a real grilling, told him he was crap and wouldn't make it and not to expect a good reference."

"Why?"

"Because he could. Honestly, Jo, I'd watch him."

"Why would he want to get rid of me?"

"Because he can – well, not at the moment because you're well in with the Editor, but if you give him the opportunity he'll stick the dagger in. You stand up to him and he doesn't like it. You taught me how things work around here; I can't believe you can be so naïve."

Was Milo trying to get me out? If so, would my departure from the newsroom be enough for him – or was I making myself an easier target by moving away from the action? Should I change my plans and stay? But no, I did not want to give up my dream of a life in the country out of fear for the future. Julian would not have allowed fear to deflect her, once she had set her course. Staying with my plan felt good.

On the following Friday evening, Carol held a farewell party for me. I was presented with the traditional mock-up "special edition" front page of the paper. The main headline was "Meredith goes to country", subheaded "PM considers his position". Paul did not attend.

I arrived back at the cottage with a sense of relief. I felt much calmer there than I did in London. But I also felt restless. I realized that Longbourne House, though wonderful, was somewhere I was passing through. I wanted to find the place that was mine. Where would I go? What work would I do? What use would I make of the rest of my life? I did not know.

The business over the contract had brought to a head feelings that had lain dormant for years. I realized how bitterly I resented being treated in such a way and how compromised I had felt for a long time. Alex was right. There had to be more. But if I continued to be a journalist, could I find it? Could I find meaning?

16

I spent Saturday relaxing. It was a beautiful July day and the garden was in full bloom. I visited the little shop on the estate and stocked up on groceries, fresh bread, fruit and home-made apple cake. I also bought myself a bunch of imported red tulips. I put them in water and placed the vase on the pine dresser in the kitchen.

I rose late on the Sunday morning. As I sipped my first cup of tea of the day, I glanced towards the flowers on the dresser. The tulips had opened wide and extended themselves with an arched elegance, their sensuous, shiny red heads held proudly, as if proclaiming their beauty. Glossily darkened, like spreading blood, the confident scarlet blooms displayed themselves on stems stretched languorously outward and upward – no withholding restraint of shyness or modesty – desiring the attention of every eye. They expressed passion and excess, full-bodied, full-blown sensuality. If Anna loved her pale, fragile primroses, I loved these glorious, thrilling blooms that spoke to me of sexual and creative ecstasy.

On the radio, Billie Holiday was singing "Mean to Me, Baby". There was a completeness and certitude, a compactness, even, in her singing of the song. It was a perfect piece of art. I reflected that, like the tulips, she had created her own space, taken possession of it, inhabited it, owned it and extended into it. Now she invited me to join her there. I desired such moments in my life; moments of creativity and completeness, a place where everything in my life would be right and the balance would not be disturbed.

Could such a place be found? Was I capable of finding it? Thoughts of Julian returned to my mind. I knew I had long neglected her and my quest to find Anna. Now, at last, I had time and space, and my mind was free to give my attention to the books Ismene had given me. They were Julian's original text, in a version edited by Marion Glasscoe, a specialist in medieval theology, and the little compilation of extracts, *Enfolded in Love*. I had also brought some others that I had ordered from the Julian Centre.

As I read, I realized it was miraculous that Julian's book had been preserved. How had it survived the dissolution of the monasteries, when Henry VIII plundered the religious houses of their valuable artefacts and manuscripts? Why had someone bothered to save a small, plain book written in English, when there were gorgeous gold-leafed missals and psalters for the taking?

As I entertained these thoughts, a broad shaft of sunlight blazed across my closed eyes and my head felt as though it were full of light. I opened my eyes and found myself looking at the white cover, with its black inscription, of Julian's book. In the foreground is the figure of Jesus on the cross, with the risen Christ above him and a bird swooping earthwards.

Julian's first editor was Serenus Cressy, an English Benedictine monk. He writes "I was desirous to have told thee somewhat of the happy virgin, the compiler of these Revelations, but after all the search I could make I could not discover any thing touching her, more than what she occasionally sprinkles in the book itself." So he, too, had been curious, but had not had his curiosity satisfied. Was there something about this piece of work that made the individual want to shrink away into obscurity? For Anna, like Julian, had drawn back into the shadows.

Clearly, Julian had fascinated many people across the centuries. One expert describes "the sheer integrity of Julian's reasoning, the precision of her theology, the depth of her insight and the simplicity with which she expounds profound truths". In the language of my profession, her story carries conviction. So, when she speaks of God's abiding, unconditional love – is it true?

Cressy introduces Julian's book with a quotation from her last chapter. After her many years of patient contemplation, Julian received one final visitation. She was told, "Would you know your Lord's meaning in this thing? Learn it well: Love was his meaning. Who showed it to you? Love. What did he show you? Love. Why did he show it? For love."

Love was God's last word to Julian, the most persistent of questioners. The inimitable Julian had questioned Jesus' assurance that sin was inevitable but that "all shall be well". She had asked how that could possibly be, when sin causes so much pain. She had at last accepted Jesus' second assurance that what is impossible to man is possible to God, who will "make all things well". But the last message – love is his meaning – appears to be the most important of all.

Julian appears to have travelled beyond the limitations of her intellect to a place of greater understanding. Was this the place of the heart centre, the place that could be reached in silence, as Molly had shown me? I was curious. How far might I travel if only I had the courage? When it came to courage, Julian was a shining example. Julian the gentle revolutionary was my kind of heroine. She embodied the characteristics I admired most – courage, compassion and honesty. The more I saw of her, the better I liked her. How I would have loved to interview her.

I studied the books for three days. In the evening of the third day I looked towards the vase of tulips. I saw that the flowers had at last succumbed to the passing of the time they had occupied. Their deeply purpled fragile flesh had become almost transparent in places, smeared with goldened cream. In some parts, the glorious, brazen red had matured to a deep, dense plum colour; in others, the liberally spilt, thickly coated cream adorned the scarlet, silken velvet, falling like the folds of some rich magistrate's cloak, each tulip dropping its papered trumpets to the floor.

I lift one flower gently. It does not break. It curls, unyielding, against my palm. I place my finger within the bell, and touch that most exquisite, private softness, which lives still within the heart of the flower; but at the lightest pressure of my finger its integrity is broken, and, fragmented, the flower falls to the floor.

I felt the need to share my thoughts with Ismene. I dialled her number and felt comforted, as I always did when I heard her soft, melodic voice – a voice that conveyed great warmth and wisdom. She accepted my invitation to visit me the following weekend.

It was a glorious day, high summer, hot but with a gentle, cooling breeze.

"Have you seen anything of Paul?" Ismene asked, as we enjoyed an al fresco lunch in the little courtyard. I felt myself beginning to blush. Did she know about the difficult situation between us?

"He doesn't seem to have been around very much," I said. "They're keeping him busy."

"I have a lot of respect for Paul," said Ismene, "and, of course, great affection."

I was curious about her good opinion of Paul. She had known him a long time; yet she seemed not to know his real character. But then, I reminded myself, Paul always had been able to win admiration and approval, especially from women. Not that I imagined any such interest on Ismene's part. She was to Paul, as she was to me, a kind, wise guide and mentor.

I shared with Ismene the thoughts and questions that I had been pondering while reading Julian's book. I said, "Julian somehow was able to accept things that really didn't make sense to her. I could never do that. I always have to understand how things work!"

Ismene said, "She reported conscientiously what was revealed to her and accepted the validity of the message in faith. Not at first, of course, because she questioned things just as you do, just as I did. 'Sin is inevitable but all shall be well...' I wonder if we can make sense of that statement by learning from other cultures and faiths. Reincarnation and the outworking of karma, for example, might explain how someone can lead a wicked life – and yet 'all shall be well'. If we are given opportunities in future lives to learn by experiencing the behaviour we have inflicted upon others, then would that not be possible?"

"So it could be a long, long journey through many incarnations," I said.

"Through hundreds, perhaps thousands – leading in time to the perfecting of the human soul. It is the journey that we are all embarked upon, to be filled with the Christ, the pure force of love that was manifested through Jesus, and which can manifest through each of us, if only we will let it, so as to raise our consciousness and make it possible for us to enter the state of bliss called Heaven."

I said, "The most important part of the message was the last: 'Love is his meaning'".

Ismene said, "Precisely. Not retribution, because God is not angry with us. Just love, because only through love can we can follow his path, striving towards what the Book of Ephesians calls 'the perfection of the measure of the stature of the fullness of Christ'. Love is his meaning and Jesus' mission was to show us the example of a life lived in perfect love. When we emulate that, we find salvation."

I asked, "What about this really weird assertion of Julian's that the more we suffer for our wrongdoing, the greater our treasure in heaven?"

Ismene said, "That quotation continues '... for those that shall be saved'. Perhaps that means that when we become truly aware of the mistakes we've made, we have a choice. We can accept and assimilate what we have learned, and change, or we can choose to ignore it and carry on in the same old way. If we choose to change, we are the wiser and stronger and it has all been worthwhile."

I asked, "And yet she says God doesn't blame us and we're not meant to blame ourselves."

"Quite so. He looks upon us with pity, not with blame. Guilt is absolutely pointless. God wants us to simply repent and change. If we punish ourselves with guilt, Julian says, we dishonour God, because we are his darlings and he is sorry to see us giving ourselves a hard time. She also refers to each of us having a 'godly will' that never assented to sin, and she says that God and we are of one essence. Now, would you consider the possibility that the earthly self, which is separate from God, does things it would not do if it were fully conscious of its real self? Is it possible that the shame we feel when we do wrong raises our consciousness and opens our hearts and makes us more loving?"

Before returning home, Ismene joined me for a walk in the grounds. The heat of the day was cooling and the shadows were lengthening into evening. Everything was very still. Ismene took my arm as we walked. She said, "Joanna, I'm so very glad that we're friends. I know you've had a very difficult time recently, but you have behaved honourably and you will be the stronger for all that you endure, and endure well." She turned her head and smiled at me and said, "Love is his meaning. All will be well. Just keep those thoughts in your heart and they will sustain you through everything."

Later that evening I walked out again and looked up at the sky full of stars. Did I want to follow in Julian's tracks? If I did, it was clear that, if I must, like her, go forward in faith, and perhaps by grace, I must accept that there were places to which my intellect simply could not take me. Julian had found her path through suffering and sacrifice, of that I was sure. Nothing less could have brought her to such a depth of understanding. But Anna's gentle voice still haunted me. Do I dare to believe that I am beloved through all eternity? Is it true that Calvary is a place to which each of us must come?

The cedar of Lebanon outside my window inclines its lustrous branches. Each gently curving arc, shimmering with frosted paler green, is held in soft quiescence, tenderly reaching to keep me safe from wind and weather, with the quiet solicitude of a considerate friend.

There is a sense of knowing, of things understood, of something magical, perhaps... The trees are shadowing into night, surrendering their sunlit daily watch to the landscape of the stars.

The birds are resting, enfolded in their tiny wings. The trees come quietly in around me, and I know that it is safe to go to sleep. Gently, softly, I feel my heart begin to open. At its centre is a rose. I close my eyes, and drift into the place where dreams are made.

After I had been living at Rachel's cottage for a few weeks, writing and filing my column without difficulty, I decided to buy a place of my own and settle there. I put my house in London up for sale and had soon accepted an offer. I found a new home that was perfect. It was an eighteenth-century cottage in a quiet lane, a little way along from the church, on the outskirts of the village. It had a large, secluded garden and an organic vegetable patch. I made an offer and it was accepted. We arranged to complete the sale of my house and the purchase of my new home at the end of September. In the meantime, I remained at Rachel's cottage.

It was, a beautiful, hot August day. I worked at my computer in my room with its view of the wilderness across the courtyard and the high trees beyond, grateful to be away from the stultifying stuffiness of the city. The telephone rang, and I picked up the receiver to hear the affected, sexy tones of Felicity Garner, the Features Editor.

"Jo, sweetie. It's Fliss. How are you surviving down there among the Crimplene and cowdung set?"

"Oh, wearing it well!"

Felicity laughed. "I make a point of avoiding wide-open spaces. One breath of country air and I put on five pounds. Listen, darling, I'd like you to do a job for me. Interested?"

"I'm sure I shall be," I replied.

"Super. There's a two-day international conference of East Timor supporters next week – activists, non-governmental organizations, some notables, including a few celebs. What I want is a colour piece, people's stories, human interest, that sort of thing. Will you do it for me?"

I wanted to go. I was keen to work on the East Timor story again, and it was an opportunity to keep my name in the frame at the office. I said I would love to do the job.

"Heaven on a stick, darling! Knew you wouldn't let me down. I'll get back to you with a briefing. I'll want you and Paul to work closely together. We want a dramatic words-and-pics job. We'll talk later."

"Do you mean Paul Huntingford?"

"Yes. It's really to promote his exhibition of East Timor pictures at the ICA. That's why the Editor wants to cover the conference. It's all PR, darling, but isn't everything?"

I replaced the receiver with mixed feelings. I had not expected to work with Paul again. I had not known about his exhibition at the Institute of Contemporary Arts. I was getting out of touch with events in London. Having accepted the commission I could hardly withdraw because of Paul. It seemed that Felicity was being businesslike and setting her feelings aside. I could do worse than follow her example.

I spent the next couple of days bringing myself up to date with events in East Timor. The brutal oppression by the Indonesian army had intensified since the massacre at Santa Cruz Church in Dili, which Ismene and Paul had witnessed.

Many of those who had survived the army's bullets and beatings were languishing in prison, facing long sentences and even death, simply for participating in the peaceful protest. Indonesia continued to defy ten United Nations resolutions calling upon it to end its illegal occupation. Nonetheless, the government – which had managed to ride the storm over the arms scandal revealed by Dr Newell, and even his death – was continuing with its programme of aid and cheap loans. And it was still allowing the sale of Hawk jet fighter aircraft, which were being used to bomb East Timorese villages. The more I read, the angrier I became.

As I stepped out of Westminster underground station into bright sunshine, I was looking forward to my assignment, though a little apprehensive about seeing Paul again. I passed through groups of tourists, who were busy taking pictures of the Houses of Parliament, on my way to the Queen Elizabeth Conference centre, where the event was taking place. Paul had arrived before me. He strode across and greeted me in a warm and friendly manner.

We worked well together. Paul moved unobtrusively among the delegates. It seemed hardly possible that he was getting good material with so little fuss. He never got in my way. Indeed, he helped interviews along with the odd word and welcoming smile. I enjoyed working with him. Occasionally he would direct me towards someone whom he knew to have a story to tell. At lunchtime we snatched a hurried sandwich, as we talked over the material we had so far and considered our coverage for the rest of that day.

At six o'clock delegates began to drift away to their hotels. Paul asked, "Shall we have a quick drink to plan our tactics for tomorrow?" I agreed and we walked to a nearby pub. I sat on the terrace, which overlooked the slow, grey River Thames, and waited for Paul to bring our drinks.

He joined me and we sat quietly together for several minutes, looking out across the river. I wondered what he was thinking.

The initial awkwardness when we met that morning had evaporated during the busy day. It was pleasant to sit together, sharing a companionable silence.

I glanced at Paul and saw a faraway look in his eyes.

"Are you tired?" I asked.

"Tired? Me? Never," he replied, pulled suddenly from his reverie. "This is luxury, compared to what I'm used to."

I realized that to ask a war photographer if he was tired after a day photographing a conference must have sounded quite stupid.

"I know you have an interest in East Timor, but this must be boring for you," I said.

"Taking pictures is never boring. There's always something new and different, something one has never seen before. I don't even know sometimes why I take a particular photograph. I just know I have to. Later I find out why."

We chatted for several minutes; then he suddenly looked embarrassed. He said, "I mustn't keep you. You must have things to do."

"Yes. I mustn't keep my TV dinner waiting." It was my tiredness that caused me to make the remark. I regretted it immediately. Why had I made myself an object of pity to Paul, of all people?

"Well, you're welcome to share my boiled egg," he said. "Now I'm waiting for you to shout at me. And if you don't, I'm going to invite you to dinner."

"You know, Paul, I simply don't understand you. You're married – happily, from what I understand. You're not interested in me. You never have been. I don't know if it's some insecurity or whatever that makes you need to collect female scalps, or whatever it is you do, but it's childish and silly, and frankly you should grow up."

Paul looked dumbfounded. He said nothing. I thought I had said too much. There was a silence between us. We both stared across the river. Then Paul said, "This is very strange. It sounds as though you're talking about someone else."

"Come on, Paul; don't be cute. How do you suppose your wife would feel if she knew you were having this conversation with me?"

"She would feel sorry."

"Sorry?! I think she would put it rather stronger than that!"

"She would feel sorry that we're arguing. Jo, I was happily married, it's true. But my wife died three years ago."

For the first time in my life I knew exactly what people meant when they said they wished the ground would open up under them. I did not know what to say. Eventually I said, "I'm terribly sorry, Paul. Please forgive me."

Paul smiled his familiar smile and said, "Nothing to forgive." He paused. "Shall we have that boiled egg?"

I said yes, because I wanted to be with him. He suggested going to a restaurant but because I was tired and we had an early start the following day we agreed that he would rustle up something at his house in Islington, a ten-minute drive from my home.

Paul lived in a three-storey Edwardian house. The house was quite sparsely furnished. There was very little clutter and a feeling of space and light. On otherwise bare white walls hung beautiful photographs, many of indigenous people from Third World countries. He led me into the kitchen.

"It's a bit blokeish, I'm afraid," he said. "But there should be something edible around here." He peered into the fridge. "I seem to remember a scene in James Bond where he takes two eggs and a carrot from a lady's fridge and serves her up a mouth-watering soufflé. I'm afraid that isn't going to happen."

I laughed. "Just scramble the eggs."

"I would if there were any."

He peered further into the fridge. "There's some smoked salmon. There's also lots of salad. And there's some soup, delicious home-made vegetable soup from the kitchen of Ismene Vale."

"You're joking."

"She sent her maid over from Hampstead with it. She's convinced I don't eat."

The thought suddenly crossed my mind that no woman, not even the brilliant and sensible Ismene Vale, was invulnerable to Paul's charm. My mood was broken as I remembered how he had stood me up all those years ago, how he had betrayed his wife and let Felicity down.

"What would you like to drink?" Paul asked. I accepted a glass of wine and wondered what I was doing there. Paul put on some music and started to prepare the food. Suddenly the telephone rang. Paul took the call.

"Paul Huntingford. Oh, hi, Felicity. Yes, very well. You'll be pleased. Portrait stuff, and the interactive stuff you wanted of various delegates together." I flashed Paul a warning look, to communicate that I did not wish him to tell Felicity that I was there.

"Isn't she? No idea, I'm afraid. About three-quarters of an hour ago. I couldn't tell you. Any message to give her in the morning? Will do." There was a pause. "Absolutely fine, thanks. It's nice to have some time at home. It has been a long while. Yes. Yes. Mmm. Well, yes."

I affected not to be listening but was straining to hear. Paul's expression was serious.

"Really? Well, I'll be glad to do what I can. Yes, I was, very fond, and always will be. We'll arrange that, then. Great. When this job's out of the way. Great. Speak to you tomorrow, after you've had a chance to look at the pics. I'll give Jo your message." He replaced the receiver and smiled. "Your reputation is safe. Felicity wants a word in the morning. She's been trying to get you at home."

I felt angry and uncomfortable. What was Paul up to? It sounded as though he was planning to re-establish his liaison with Felicity. I said, "I probably shouldn't stay."

"Now that I've gone to all the trouble of taking the salmon out of the fridge and putting it on a plate? You can't go now. You're hungry. What a changeable woman you are. But I'm not saying I don't like it. Changeable is good."

Paul continued preparing the food. I listened to the music. It was Mozart's Clarinet Concerto… Why had he had to choose Mozart? Memories of that awful evening when I didn't get to see *The Marriage of Figaro* came back in sharp focus. I decided I would eat the meal, say a polite thank you and leave. After all, we did have to work together the following day. In my mind, I picked over Paul's conversation with Felicity. It had sounded as though they might be getting back together again. What was Paul up to? I realized that none of this should matter to me. What was I thinking of?

I ate the meal, drank a couple of glasses of wine and then said I must go. Paul offered to drive me home. I accepted, having thought about catching a bus but not feeling much like it.

As Paul's car drew up outside my house, I said, "Thank you, and thank you for feeding me." He smiled at me, and in his warm, humorous brown eyes I saw the same old Paul, the one I had liked so much and fallen in love with. I thought: *If only Paul were what he appeared to be, what a difference that would make.*

"Thank you for a lovely evening and a lovely day," he replied. "Being with you is always such fun." We said goodnight and arranged to meet at the conference centre early the following morning.

Fun? I thought, as I turned my key in the lock. Was he being sarcastic?

18

Our second day went even better than the first. I was happy with my interviews and Paul was happy with his pictures. Felicity wanted to see us, so we took a taxi to the office. While Paul was downstairs in the dark room, getting the last of his pictures developed, Felicity and I discussed the piece I was to write.

"How did you find Paul to work with?" she asked.

"Oh, great."

"Everyone does. I won't pretend I wasn't thrilled to get him to do this assignment for me. He may be a bastard – but what a photographer!" I was unsure how to respond, but was keen to get some information about Paul.

"So he's a bastard?"

"'Course. Aren't they all?"

I was perplexed. If she thought he was a bastard why was she arranging to meet him?

"Nice bastard, though." She smiled her big, wide smile and wagged a long pink fingernail at me. "Very cute, don't you think?"

"Oh, pff… in an obvious kind of way, I suppose," I said.

"So you fancy him, too!" Felicity laughed. "Join the queue. We were an item, you know."

"Really?"

"Bad timing, darling. But he's available now," said Felicity.

At that moment Paul walked in and Felicity gave him a dazzling smile. "Paul, darling – what have you got for me?" she asked. Paul handed her his contact sheet. She took it across to the window.

"Stunning, darling," she said. "You're a genius."

I wondered why Felicity was being so nice to him after he had treated her so badly. She discussed with Paul the pictures she would use, standing much closer to him than was necessary. Then she tilted her head to look up into his eyes and asked, "Time for a drink?"

"I can't tonight, I'm afraid," said Paul. "But I'll call you next week as we arranged, if that's OK."

As Paul and I walked out into the street, he said, "I wonder if you might like to come with me to a drinks do at the ICA? It's a reception for my exhibition. Do come. There'll be people I think you'll enjoy meeting."

I accepted the invitation and we took a taxi to the venue in the Mall, within sight of Buckingham Palace. The gallery where the party was being held was a hubbub of chatter. As we arrived, I spotted Ismene, and Paul took me across to join her. She greeted us both warmly.

Paul said, "Ismene, I think it's time I entertained you. You're always feeding me!"

I gathered that he was a frequent guest at her home. Paul invited us both to dinner the following week. We both accepted. In the circumstances it would have been rude to decline, I told myself.

On the evening of our dinner date, I picked Paul up; his car was at the garage. We dined at an expensive French restaurant. The food was delicious and it was a wonderful evening. It was inspiring to hear Paul and Ismene talk about the stories they had worked on together. I learned a lot about the independence struggles in Kashmir, Burma, Tibet and elsewhere. At the end of the evening I drove Ismene home, before dropping Paul off at his house.

"Will you come in for a nightcap?" he asked.

"Well, I – "

"Oh come on. I won't turn into a pumpkin. Though I might turn into a mangel-wurzel."

"What is a mangel-wurzel?"

"Come in and find out!"

I parked the car and followed Paul into his house. I declined a nightcap, because I was driving, and asked for tea. Paul put the kettle on and went into the lounge. Moments later, as he returned to the kitchen, I heard the strains of Mozart. Having decided not to spoil the moment, I did.

"You seem to like Mozart," I said.

"Mmm. Very much. He can usually lift my mood." Paul dum-de-dummed along to the Bassoon Concerto.

"Do you remember, years ago, inviting me to the opera?"

He turned, teapot in hand, and said, "Yes, I do."

"That was Mozart," I said, feeling my anger beginning to bubble up.

"Mmm," said Paul casually, pottering about with spoon and teacaddy. "*The Magic Flute*."

"*The Marriage of Figaro*, actually."

"No – *The Magic Flute*, I'm pretty certain. It was a very good performance for a small touring company, I recall."

"Well, I'm glad you enjoyed it."

"Er, yes – thank you."

"And it was *The Marriage of Figaro*."

"Is this important?" he asked gently. "This operatic performance that you didn't attend?"

"No, of course not. Why should it be?"

"I don't know," said Paul.

"But just for the record, it was *The Marriage of Figaro*, OK? Mozart's *The Marriage of Figaro*. Not *The Magic Flute*. Not *The Barber of Seville*. *The Marriage of* bloody *Figaro*."

"*The*, um, *Barber of Seville* is by Rossini," said Paul, scratching his head.

"I don't care if it's by Barry Manilow and his string quartet – "

"Now I think you're thinking of Mantovani – was that his name? Yes, Mantovani and his Music of the Mountains. My gran liked him."

"Don't tell me what I'm thinking! God, I can't even have a bloody argument with you without you interrupting!"

"Why are you angry with me?"

"Because you stood me up, you rat."

"No I didn't."

"Yes you did."

"I didn't. I wouldn't," said Paul.

"And now you've forgotten!"

"No I haven't."

"You have."

"I haven't."

"Can you stop sounding like the audience at a bloody pantomime?"

"Jo, I've never stood you up. You must be thinking of someone else. This other chap again, the one you keep thinking is me – or that I am," he said.

"You invited me to a performance of *The Marriage of Figaro*."

"I remember inviting you to *The Magic* – OK, OK, *The Marriage of Figaro* it was."

"As you well know, we arranged to meet in the foyer fifteen minutes before the performance."

"And you sent a note cancelling. Yes, of course I remember."

"I did not send a note. Why would I send a note?"

"I don't know. I got a note from you saying you couldn't come because you had to visit a friend in hospital. You said you'd catch up with me some time in the next few days."

"I didn't send any such note."

"Well, I got one and it was signed by you."

"How did you get it? Where did it come from?"

"I think, um, yes, it was shoved under my door."

"I would never shove a note under a man's door. How could you think I would do such a thing? Really. Well in that case, how come you went with Marcie?"

"Marcie? Oh, Marcie, yes. Did I go with Marcie? I don't remember. Yes, you're right, I believe I did. You know how she was always going on about how homesick and lonely she was? She turned up at my door, quite tearful, I seem to remember. Some chap had let her down on a date and she was at a loose end. She asked if I was free. I'd just got back and picked up your note, it was quite late and I had a spare ticket, so I asked if she'd like to tag along."

"Oh, God, no. Is this true?"

"Er, yes. I did always wonder why you were so distant with me after that. I assumed you'd decided you didn't want to take things further. Do you mean to say you turned up for our rendezvous?"

"Yes. In shoes that were killing me."

"How did we miss each other? We must have had a drink in the bar and gone straight to our seats. I think we did, she was still quite tearful."

"She must have known about our arrangement," I said. "Oh, God, Paul. I wish I'd known."

"So do I. But looking on the bright side, does this mean you're not angry with me any more?"

I smiled. "Well, I'm not angry with you at the moment."

"Then you'll have dinner with me tomorrow night."

"Will I?"

"Yes, of course you will. I'll cook something here, with ingredients this time."

Paul kissed me on the cheek as he saw me into my car. As I drove home, I began to imagine the following evening. My fantasy was brought up short by the thought that he seemed to have a date with Felicity the following week. I wondered what had happened between them, how close they had been and how he might feel about her now. I remembered, too, how badly he had let his wife down. That was something which he surely must regret, but it proved that he was capable of betrayal.

19

I arrived at Paul's house on time at seven o'clock. As he opened the door I heard a loud crashing sound coming from the direction of the kitchen.

"Not to worry!" he said cheerfully. "Everything's under control. Lovely to see you, Jo. You look gorgeous." He kissed me on the cheek and I followed him to the kitchen. A couple of pots were bubbling furiously on the cooker and pan lids were scattered on the floor. Paul picked them up, saying, "I'm an explosive but effective cook."

As I wondered what might come next, he offered me a drink and I accepted a glass of white wine. Paul turned his attention to his pots, saying, "This is chicken, one of my favourite recipes. You do eat chicken – God, I didn't think to ask you, you're not a vegetarian?" He looked so dismayed that I felt I must put him at ease without delay.

"Yes I do and no I'm not!"

Paul grinned. The pots behind him fizzed and popped away merrily. I observed that he had an interesting method in the kitchen of catching things just as they were about to boil over. Amazingly, when the food arrived it was cooked to perfection and mouth-wateringly delicious.

I said, "This is very good. You've got the job."

"Thank you, ma'am. Next time I'll cook you a curry – the best this side of Watford Gap."

"That I'd love. I developed a passion for curry when I used to visit my parents in India."

"When was that?"

"The late 1960s. My dad was there with the Welsh Guards."

"What did you make of India?"

"Oh, vibrant, passionate, exotic, disturbing – but in a good way…"

"Sounds as though you liked it."

"I loved it."

"Me too," said Paul.

"When were you there?"

"I was first there in 1979. That's where I met Ismene, on a train in Hyderabad. I was a green young stringer with an American news agency, a few months into my first assignment. I helped Ismene with her bags and we got chatting. She was very knowledgeable about the political situation and, typically, generous with her time. When we arrived at Rawalpindi, we went for a meal. I was headed into Kashmir and she gave me some very useful contacts, including a leader of the separatist movement."

"You lucky beggar. You got into interesting work straight away," I said.

"What were you doing?"

"Covering council meetings for the *Yorkshire Post*."

"I bet you winkled out some good stories of local corruption," Paul said.

"Well, I had my sources. I used to get offered Brie and Camembert as a bribe by a councillor who owned a cheese shop. Everyone knew what he was up to because we journalists would leave the council chamber ponging of smelly feet."

Paul laughed. I asked, "How did you get your start?"

"I was incredibly lucky. I got signed up with the agency straight out of Harvard and they liked to give people foreign experience as soon as possible. They assigned me to war photography early on. It seemed to be what I did best. They moved me around a lot, but always sent me back to Kashmir."

The evening passed pleasantly. We talked about old times, work matters and human rights issues. I felt very relaxed and comfortable in Paul's company.

"Did you always enjoy war photography?" I asked.

"I loved it. It gave me a buzz like nothing else. At the start I was scared. Untrue, I was always scared. But never bored. Boredom seemed to be the worst of all perils in those days."

"Didn't you mind the danger?"

"Didn't think about it. You just get carried by the momentum from assignment to assignment. When you're right in there, taking the pictures, the adrenalin seems to wipe out fear. The heightened feeling of aliveness you get when you don't know if you'll survive the day – it's addictive. It becomes the only reality, so that the bits in between – normal life – feel unreal, dreamlike. Nothing in normal life matters. No one is dying in front of you, so how can it?"

"But – all the terrible things you must have seen – how did you cope?"

"Hmm, not terribly well – though it took me a long time to realize it. I thought I was doing great. People liked my pictures. I was on a roll. But then – it just goes to show how wrong you can be... This is boring. Am I boring you?"

"No, not at all. What happened?"

"Well, things were changing. A lot of things happened very quickly. I fell in love, desperately, madly, totally – well, not desperately because luckily for me my feelings were returned. Sushila was the daughter of Ranjit Kadir, the contact Ismene had put me in touch with. Ranjit's a human rights lawyer, a very old friend of Ismene's. He was incredibly kind to me, bit of a father figure really. Life seemed perfect. I was young, I was doing work I loved, I was getting recognition for something I was good at, this wonderful woman loved me and I loved her and we got married. How could my life possibly be better? But things did go wrong, and I was to blame..." Paul looked terribly sad. He looked at me and said, "What went wrong was my fault."

"Oh Paul, I'm sorry. What happened?"

"I wasn't coping at all. I slept badly and would wake up screaming, in a pool of sweat. Awful. Sushila used to try to get me to talk about my work, but I thought it was a can of worms best left unopened.

"At home with Sushila, trying to have a normal life, I felt like an impostor. I'd be with friends and family, in a garden, drinking tea, making conversation, and all the while my mind was full of these unspeakable images; they invaded me night and day. I'd seen things you never forget. You can't just take pictures and stay outside. You're there, so you're involved. The obscenity and stench of violent death – that was my normal environment. I was getting crazy. I was on a roller coaster and I couldn't get off."

"But – how did you survive?"

"I became someone else. I was getting more and more foreign postings and it got to a stage where I was glad to get away from my life with Sushila, because then I didn't have to think about what I was doing and why. I didn't have to pretend to be normal. I didn't have to be. I just did my job and had a few beers in the bar at the end of the day. Then I started taking a bottle of whisky to my hotel room, to blot out the memories of the day. I used to think that if I drank enough I'd become unconscious and not dream – but you do dream. My life was starting to unravel, but I couldn't see it. I started having affairs – pointless, passionless affairs that were something to do to convince myself that I was still alive."

"Felicity mentioned – "

"Oh, yes, Felicity. That was a crazy business. I was in London, helping to edit a documentary I'd worked on. Sushila would have come with me but her mother was very ill. I was on the loose and I took up with Felicity. I'm deeply ashamed. It was a despicable, selfish, stupid, cruel act and I regret it bitterly."

"Felicity seems to still think well of you," I said.

"I didn't lie, at least. I've never lied. Not that that's anything to be proud of, considering all the rotten things I did. At least I have a chance to make some of it up to Felicity. She wants me to have a word with her son, Craig; he's seventeen now. He's a good lad. He and I got on well. Apparently he's gone a bit haywire, getting into the wrong company. Can't think why he'd listen to me! But I said I'd try.

"The affair started to fall apart very quickly. We weren't at all suited and I was starting to get crazy. I was spending more time with my parents – they're in Bristol – life was much saner there. Then I had a breakdown. Just like that, one day. I became this babbling, incoherent wreck. Other people had seen it coming on, but I was in a world of my own and wasn't listening to anyone. It must have been hellish for the people who loved me.

"My father told Sushila I was ill and she came over. While she was over here, her mother died. I couldn't forgive myself. But Sushila forgave me. She never spoke one word of reproach. We stayed with my parents while I got treatment – my father's a doctor – then Sushila took me back home to Kashmir. I didn't work for six months. Jo, I'm sorry. This is no fun for you, listening to a raddled old war correspondent bemoaning his lot."

"No, I'm interested. I've seen what war journalism can do to people. I've never really understood it because it hasn't happened to me. I suppose it's the price people pay to record the appalling things that happen in the world. I couldn't do that kind of work," I said.

"I'm not sure anyone can," said Paul. "It's like soldiering, in a way; people do it and nobody admits it's not an activity that human beings were designed for. Seeing terrible things, doing terrible things – it's dehumanizing. But you know, at the same time, taking pictures is awe-inspiring and a huge privilege, when you know that what you've done has made a difference.

"That recognition saved me. I came to understand that the work I was doing was absolutely necessary – but there had to be a way of doing it and remaining sane. It was then that my life began to change. One day something happened, and life was never the same again."

Paul was silent for a few moments. I realized that I must wait quietly because he was about to share something very special with me.

He said, "I had an incredible experience. I was walking across the brow of a hill. Way off into the distance there was a magnificent view, where the earth met the sky. Suddenly I felt a part of everything that I was looking at. I felt that the land and sky and trees, everything, and I were all one, one entity. It was extraordinary. And as I stood there, I had such a deep feeling of peace, a feeling of everything being right and as it was meant to be.

"I had always envied my wife and my in-laws their inner calm. There was an atmosphere of peace around them. Sushila had an air of being at one with past, present and future; she had a composure, a certainty, an acceptance of life and whatever it brought, good and bad. That moment of completeness on the hillside set me thinking, wondering about the source of that profound rootedness and contentment.

"Up until then, if anyone had asked me what my religion was I'd have said I was a Christian, because I grew up in a Christian family – but I realized that I didn't really hold any spiritual beliefs. Hinduism, my in-laws' religion, offered a sense of where I fitted into the universe. It offered a way of life. It made me see that there's a connection between all living things and that it matters how I behave twenty-four hours of the day because what I do affects the rest of creation.

"Things like Gandhi's stance on non-violence, trying not to exploit any living creature – those examples made far more sense to me than the way the Bible is written. In the *Mahabharata*, which is a Hindu epic, you're shown how deceit and dishonesty and vices like gambling can lead to your decay. I've become careful about what I do and whenever possible I try to look at cause and effect before things happen. What I've found just makes sense. It's brought me inner peace."

"I envy you."

"I think what excited me most was realizing that one person can change the world. It matters what we do, each one of us. If we buy Fair Trade coffee we can make a difference. We can make it fairer for coffee farmers and safer for the street children of South America, by petitioning our government and MPs and MEPs. Indifference is the worst thing, to simply not care."

Paul's passionate belief in his principles made him look strong and so alive. I admired the way he expressed his pure, unalloyed truth, the way he had turned his life around and used his faith to inform and inspire his work. But I was surprised at how easily he had adapted to a religion I had always thought of as strict and full of rules.

He said, "Hinduism isn't prescriptive. I still drink, as you can see – though I didn't for a couple of years, after I got well and realized that I'd been drinking to avoid dealing with my feelings. I intend to become a vegetarian. But Hinduism is relaxed about these things and about contacts with other faiths."

Paul told me that before his conversion he had visited a swami, or sect leader. "Ever the journalist, I took along a list of questions – all those questions about the meaning of life – that I needed to have answered. But I forgot the list and left it in the car. When we met, he just smiled and took my hand; it was like a charge of electricity. He gave me an incredible feeling of inner peace. He started to tell me things about how I should live my life. Then he said, 'You have been brought up as a Christian. Believe in Jesus.' When I saw the list of questions again, I realized that he had answered every one of them, and they were not obvious questions. Even now, it makes my hair stand on end.

"I never get angry now. Being a Hindu has taught me not to question what others tell me. Their beliefs are for me to either embrace or discard; there's no need for argument. I can now take in other ideas and evaluate them later, when I need to, rather than feeling I have to discount them – because I know now that one day I may have more knowledge, which will allow me to understand those ideas and maybe accept them."

"It's what Julian of Norwich had to do…" I said.

"Perhaps the hardest thing of all – because it's a matter of faith," said Paul. "I think the divisions between faiths are pointless. Everyone who comes with a message from God is going to challenge us. Hindus believe we follow a long path through millions of incarnations, as the soul evolves and grows closer to God. That's why we sometimes feel a strong connection with someone we're meeting for the first time. Have you never felt that sense of recognition? Have you never felt, intuitively, that you know someone's soul?"

At midnight I said I should leave for home. Paul said, "Thank you for coming this evening. Spending this time with you has meant a lot to me. I'm afraid I've been talking about myself all evening. I hope I wasn't too boring."

"I'm glad you told me about your life. I'm glad you felt you could trust me," I said.

"Jo, I always felt that, all those years ago – even when you kept rejecting me. I always felt at home with you. You always had a particular quality about you." He leaned across and took my hand, and suddenly his eyes were full of emotion.

"Dear Joanna," he said softly, and then he kissed me. It had been many years since I had first longed for him to kiss me. At that moment it seemed well worth the wait. I felt completely at one with him. He was exciting, passionate and gentle. I did not return home that night. For the first time in my life, I discovered how it felt to be with a man in complete, loving union.

In the morning he gave me breakfast. As I sat wrapped in his bathrobe, drinking his tea, I said, "What did you mean last night, when you said I kept rejecting you?"

"Well, you told poor old Alex not to give me your number."

"No, I meant when we were at university…" I said.

"Oh then, well, it was obvious you were seriously under-whelmed."

I was stunned. "D'you mean, you liked me?"

"Liked you! I was crazy about you. But you never gave me the time of day," said Paul.

"But – you never took the slightest interest in me – well, not until you asked me to *The Marriage of Figaro*."

"Are you kidding? I tried lots of times to talk to you. You were so serious. I got the impression you had higher things on your mind than wasting time on callow youths," Paul said.

"I just don't believe this. How could you have been so mistaken?"

"Do you mean you fancied me? Oh, no, that's hilarious." Paul burst out laughing.

"Well, I didn't think it was funny," I replied.

"Oh dear, oh dear, what a lot of fun we missed out on. Well, we're just going to have to make up for it now," he said. He gave me a hug and nuzzled my neck. "Lucky we've caught up with one another again before we lose our faculties. I wouldn't want to be pursuing you on a Zimmer frame – though, I dunno, it might be fun. It could be something to look forward to."

"If it comes to that," I said solemnly, "I promise to shuffle really slowly. Hey, was that why you gave me the East Timor story?"

"No. I gave you the story because you were the best person to do it."

"What if you hadn't thought that?"

"I wouldn't have given it to you. You can take that as gospel. I did allow myself to be easily persuaded into covering the conference, though, when Felicity said she was asking you to do the reporting."

"She may regret that," I said.

"Why?"

"Oh, Paul, really."

"Good gracious. I'd no idea. I'd better handle things very carefully. I've done enough damage there." I wished I had kept my mouth shut and said no more.

We did make up for lost time. During the following weeks we spent as much time together as we could. Paul helped me to move into my new house and we designated it our country cottage, with Paul's home in London as our town house. I had never been so happy.

20

As we got to know one another better Paul became my teacher. He taught me more about East Timor's long struggle for freedom and the suffering of her people, about the suppression of the Karen minority in Burma and the Kurds in Iraq. Paul had reported from Iraq after Saddam had bombed the people of Halabja with chemical weapons.

He made me aware of the world's lost, dispossessed and unloved. He inspired me to use my skills as a journalist to tell their stories – in his words, to give a voice to people who otherwise would not be heard. He also taught me to love him more and more, by being his very own self. I came to lose my fear of betrayal and loss. I came to trust.

Paul renegotiated his contract, to work part-time for the paper and spend the remainder of his time on independent projects. We worked from Magnolia Cottage, our home in Littlechurch Mead, and collaborated on several projects during those fulfilled and joyous months. As I watched Paul pour his heart and soul into his work I felt a strong desire to protect him. It was a fierce, almost primeval feeling – not possessive, because I loved the freedom of his soul, his refusal to compromise or conform. But I knew it was an instinct that would always put me between him and anything that might harm him.

My urge to protect spilled over into my own work. I now wrote human rights stories for the *Correspondent* and used my weekly column exclusively for that purpose. I often collaborated with Paul, who went away from time to time on assignments. Many of the stories I wrote had the same underlying theme: the Western world standing by and making money from other people's suffering. There were so many stories and sometimes words seemed futile. But now and again something would happen to show that things could change, and that made it all worthwhile. I had moved to another world, where my work and life had meaning.

Paul and I loved our cottage and our village. Returning from visits to London, coming off the motorway, there was always such a sense of homecoming as we traversed the roundabout and followed the B-road to the sign to Littlechurch Mead, where we turned left to drive through open fields to our home. It was with a sense of ease that we travelled along the familiar road, flanked by its sentinel trees, and into another world. We would pass the pretty white-washed farmhouse, thatched cottages and grey-stoned vicarage, before turning left into our little lane. One minute more would take us to our cottage, tucked securely among similar houses, all with gardens full of flowers, opposite the woods that fringed the other side of the lane.

Throughout the weeks we spent many happy hours walking and talking together, come rain or shine. My favourite walk took us along the lane towards the church. We would pass by the wooden lychgate, with its simple carvings that bore testimony to a centuries-old message of piety and sacrifice. We would pass beneath the branches of the oak that stood before the church, which had witnessed the celebration of love and prayer throughout the ages. We would pass the old school house, its gleaming windows looking out over the weathered stone wall, which was canopied with brightly dappled leaf upon leaf. We would then follow the lane as it bore to the left towards higher ground.

I remember how the sun glowed above and scattered its flags of light along the afternoon path ahead. I remember the sound of the wind in the high treetops and thickly leaved banks, a sound like rushing, tumultuous seas that were about to break and cover us.

From time to time Ismene would visit us for a weekend. Together, the three of us would walk and dine and share time, like the good friends we were.

Paul proved his prowess in the kitchen with delicious dishes from all over the world. I tended to leave him to it. His dexterous choreography around his bubbling pots was best left unimpeded. The music that often filled our home was similarly exotic: dazzling blurs of colour swirled across the pale background of our peaceful sanctuary in huge, generous swathes of vibrancy and exuberance.

I discovered a shop in the nearby market town that sold floating, drifty and sumptuous clothes made of silks and velvets in jewel-bright purples, blues and reds. I bought myself a red dress of the softest silk. When I wore it I felt as though a new personality emerged. I began to feel comfortable, more myself. When I wore my silks and satins from the shop I felt deeper and warmer, more serene, more sure of who I was.

Paul came to me one day in the garden, holding a photograph. "Look," he said. "This is my secret passion." It was a photograph of houses that had been virtually destroyed in what appeared to be a war zone. "Look," Paul repeated.

"What am I looking at?" I asked.

"What do you see?"

"Bombed-out houses, rubble – war?"

"What else?" asked Paul.

"Mmm. Fallen debris. Bits of wood," I said.

"Anything else?"

"Well – a bicycle."

"A bicycle. That's it." A bicycle was propped against a wall. Tied to its handlebars was a piece of red fabric – the one splash of colour in the photograph. "That's Petrovich's bicycle. I took this in Chechnya. It could be anybody's bike, but it isn't anybody's. The scarf shows that it belongs to Vass Petrovich."

Paul handed me a second photograph. It was an enlarged picture of the bicycle. Now I could see that the red scarf was patterned with tiny blue diamonds and its ends knotted with green cord.

"Vass Petrovich was a fixer, an interpreter, a gofer. He was a brave man. He helped me and others to reveal the atrocities being committed in Chechnya by Russia. Vass got us in to take these pictures – there's the proof. But he was accused of betrayal. The pictures I took, including this one, followed the massacre of Chechen freedom fighters who were meeting in the village. Vass was accused of betraying them to the Russians and then staying clear of the village to protect his own skin. But he was there. I didn't notice the bicycle when I took the picture. I had to get someone to smuggle my film out and it was days before I saw the pictures. Later, after I heard what had happened to Vass, I saw this. If I had seen it before I could have saved him. Now the proof of his innocence is there for all time and cannot be denied.

"Why did I take this particular picture? I don't know. Sometimes you know why you're bearing witness. Sometimes you feel compelled to take a photograph and don't know why. But something is always left, you know; there may be nothing you can hold in your hand, but there's always a marker, somewhere. Nothing is ever really lost."

"What is your passion?" I asked.

"Finding what's never really lost."

But there had been one great loss in Paul's life – his wife, Sushila. In his own time, he talked to me about it. "It was about eighteen months after my breakdown. Sushila was diagnosed with breast cancer. At first we thought everything was going to be all right and she would recover; then the doctors discovered that the cancer had spread to her lungs and stomach. I always expected her to pull through – though she tried to prepare me, in many ways.

"She became so very weak, so tiny and thin, like a little doll. It was pitiful to see her like that. She had always been my strength, my anchor. Over time, I came to realize that she was gradually moving away, her spirit was moving on. Her body was still there, but where was she? I came to understand that she needed me to let her go and I realized I had to honour her wish.

"One morning I went to her room and took her in my arms, and told her that I was setting her free. Her eyelashes fluttered. She was so weak, so fragile and frail. Her eyes opened for a moment. I knew we both understood. I felt such love coming from her. I held her, as her eyes closed. She died the following day."

Paul's eyes filled with tears. I put my arms around him, kissed his hair and rocked him gently. I remember that his hair smelt of celery; he had been cooking dinner. After a few minutes, he continued, "Later that day, I went into our little garden, where we'd had such happy times. I was numb with grief. Everything was a blur. Suddenly I heard birdsong. As I listened, I understood that it was a message, to tell me I had been right to give Sushila her freedom, to let her spirit go. I know now that, no matter how much you love someone, you have to be able to let go."

I released Paul gently, as he turned to look into my eyes. "Sushila never once reproached me for the way I hurt her. I deserved to be punished, but she never punished me. I learned so much from her. She's always with me. She's so much a part of what I've become. Sushila taught me that forgiveness is a kind of letting go. The hardest part is forgiving yourself. I never could, even though she had forgiven me. I didn't deserve to be forgiven, so how could I accept forgiveness?

"In her dying, Sushila taught me how to let go. I made the decision to let go my loathing of the people who committed all the evil acts I witnessed; all the bad feelings I had about my own involvement in terrible events that I longed to expunge from my memory; the guilt, the regret for the pain I had caused my wife. I let go the worst part of my life and the best part of my life. Sushila changed me for ever. She set me free. Don't cry, don't be sad. I've just told you a love story." Paul dried my tears and took my hand.

"Sushila has touched my life, too," I said.

"I know she's happy that we're together," said Paul. "I felt it from the start. All those years ago, when I first met you, I knew you. I have always known you. You and I are meant to be together and to be happy."

21

As autumn gave way to winter, I enjoyed the rites that marked the passing of the seasons, the harvest festival service, bonfires and brisk walks, wrapped up in jumpers and scarves. The year was coming to a close. We enjoyed a traditional Christmas, with holly and ivy, a log fire, carols in the church, cards and gifts, and friends calling to share food and drink at our home. There was even snow.

Winter became spring and spring melted into summer. In June, when we had been together almost a year, Paul asked me to marry him. We decided to marry a week before Christmas, in the little church down the lane. The vicar agreed to incorporate a Hindu blessing and prayers in the service.

Paul's parents were delighted, as were his brother and sister. Paul got on well with my father, who had moved back to our village in North Wales. To my astonishment, my father took a great interest in Paul's conversion to Hinduism. He had mellowed with the years. He told Paul he had known many good people of other faiths and had come to think that God, being just, would not debar them from heaven.

I gave my father a copy of *Enfolded in Love*. He became very interested in Julian and read her book. To my surprise, he revealed a hidden talent for writing and contributed articles to his parish magazine. He wrote beautifully evocative pieces about the way in which his faith had informed his life during his travels. He seemed to have decided to devote the latter part of his life to reflection and spiritual enquiry.

Paul and I married one week before Christmas. During the night it snowed hard. On my wedding day I looked out to see my little world softly cocooned in pure, glittering white. It seemed to signify that I was safe at last and that, indeed, all would be well.

I married in red silk. My beautiful dress was like a ball gown, long and swirling swathes of soft undulation which moved around me, lifted by the light breeze, as I walked to church on my father's arm. I carried red roses, for love, and wore a little coronet of red rosebuds in my hair. In deference to tradition, a veil of red embroidered gauze had been affixed to my headdress.

Paul said, "You look like a dark princess, my little princess." He looked irresistibly handsome in a white silk suit and pink and red waistcoat.

As my father and I reached the entrance to the church, tiny specks of snowflakes drifted down onto my dress, but we did not hurry. This moment meant such a great deal to us both; we wanted to savour every bit of it. We entered the church and it seemed as though the whole congregation turned round to greet us, in one big smile. The church was full of flowers. My friend Susan had taken charge of the decorations and she had made the place perfectly beautiful. Red and white roses and lilies were everywhere – in the window alcoves and in beautiful displays at the rear and front of the church. The pews were decorated with little bunches of red and white rosebuds, tied with white silk.

Susan's little granddaughter, Matilda, four years old and very conscious of the seriousness of her duties, was given the train of my dress to hold as we waited for our walk down the aisle. Matilda wore a white silk dress and a garland of pink and white freesias in her blonde curls.

As I walked up the aisle to the strains of Mozart – yes, it had to be Mozart – my heart seemed about to lift out of my chest. There was my Paul, waiting for me at the altar. I reached his side and he turned to me and took my hand. His eyes were glistening with the beginnings of tears as he looked into my eyes with so much love. My heart seemed to have floated up and kept me somewhere just below the ceiling as we went through the ritual that would make us one for ever. It was quickly over, and we were walking down the aisle through a sea of smiling faces. We stood on the church steps while our photograph was taken. A friend of Paul's was taking the pictures. He offered Paul his camera. Paul stepped forward and took it.

"Smile, darling," he said, as though there were any possibility of my doing anything else. He took a photograph that I knew I would treasure for the rest of my life.

It's an odd thing, how one can forget the day-to-day events when one is simply blissfully happy. The months flew by, Paul and I consolidated our news service and soon it was late summer once more.

In September, as we walked together in the garden, Paul said, "I'm thinking of going to East Timor soon." Because journalists were not allowed into the country, he would go in on a counterfeit Australian passport and meet up with the resistance in the capital, Dili. It all had to be done with great care, because any East Timorese seen talking to a foreigner could be in great danger.

The resistance would take him back up to the rough mountainous terrain north of the capital, where the guerrillas were encamped. The journey would entail a trip in the boot of a car to a meeting place, where he would hide in undergrowth – in case an army patrol passed by – until a resistance fighter collected him. Two weeks later, he left, with a promise to ring me from Bangkok when he returned there with his pictures. In the evening Ismene telephoned me.

"Joanna, my dear, you must be very proud of Paul. He'll come back with some extraordinary material, I've no doubt," she said.

Three days passed. I knew that by now Paul would be inside East Timor. It would have been far too risky to his companions for him to try to contact me from there. By the fifth day I knew that he would be in the resistance encampment, if all had gone according to plan. By the eighth day he would be returning to Dili, for his flight to Bangkok. It was important to get out of the country as soon as possible to minimise the risk of his pictures being seized. On the ninth day I could expect his call from Bangkok.

But the ninth day came and went and I heard nothing. The following day came and went and the day after that, but I had no news of Paul. Two weeks passed. I was becoming worried. Perhaps he had needed longer in the mountains. Perhaps there was some new development that he felt he should stay to cover.

One morning I awoke very early and, as usual, switched on my computer to check on the news agencies. I keyed in "East Timor" and a story flashed across my screen. "Australian national killed in clash between guerrillas and Indonesian troops." The story was datelined Jakarta. I read on. "An Australian man was shot dead six days ago, in a battle between East Timorese resistance fighters and an Indonesian army patrol in the mountains north of Dili. The man has been named as Alan Carter."

I froze. I stared at the screen, rigid with shock. The name on Paul's false passport – I seemed to remember that it was Alan something. But this could not possibly be Paul. It must be a mistake. How could someone in Jakarta possibly be sure about what was going on in East Timor? Journalists were not allowed in, so any information must be suspect.

Someone could have stolen his passport. It could be a bureaucratic mix-up; there were always itinerant Australian backpackers in East Timor. The thoughts raced around my brain, but I could not move away from the computer and the words that had not been there a moment ago but were now written across the screen.

I felt as though the wind had been knocked out of me and my brain numbed. It must have been several minutes before I rose from my desk in a daze. Nothing was wrong. There was nothing to panic about. I must carry on with my work, the research I was putting together for a story about Georgia. I moved around my office like an automaton, opening files and gathering together my notes. I became aware that the phone was ringing, but it seemed a very long way away. I suddenly realized that I should answer the phone. It might be Paul. I lifted the receiver. It was Ismene.

"Joanna, my dear. I'm sorry to ring you so early. I just wanted to have a word. Have you seen Reuters this morning?" As soon as I told her I had, she said, "Oh, my dear, I'm so sorry." Her voice sounded strained and shaky, as though she was trying to control tears. She said she had received a telephone call from Dili, from a contact in the underground, in the early hours of the morning. He had said there had been a battle and a foreigner had been killed. He had offered to go and check the details and telephone her again. He had just called again, confirming that the man who had been killed was Paul. But I knew that Paul had survived every war zone of the past ten years. He was indestructible. He knew his business and would never take stupid risks.

"No," I said. "You're wrong. It can't possibly be Paul. He simply would not have put himself in danger. He would never do anything silly. You know how experienced he is in war zones. Your contact has made a mistake."

Ismene said, "Let me carry on finding out what I can. I'll come down to you later."

"There's no need..." I started to say.

"I'll be there at around two o'clock," she replied softly.

A little while later the phone rang again. It was Paul's father. He sounded as if he had been crying. "Joanna, have you heard the news?" he asked. I was anxious to comfort him.

"I'm sure there's been a mistake," I said. "It can't possibly be Paul."

His voice broken with tears, he said, "I'm sorry. I wish I could believe that, but I have had a phone call from the Foreign Office. They think it was him."

"Please, you mustn't give up hope," I said. "It must be a mistake. The Foreign Office would phone me first. They've made a muddle. They couldn't possibly be sure of his identity so soon. It would take time for the British embassy in Jakarta to check something as complicated as this. I'm quite sure this is some mixed-up, garbled story. Paul is still working on his pictures and he'll be in touch soon."

Paul's father replied, "Jo, dear – I'll call you later."

I telephoned the Foreign Office but, at seven in the morning, could only get a recorded message. I rang Paul's father again, to get the name and number of the man who had rung him. The line was engaged.

Twenty minutes later Paul's father rang again. He said, "It's the worst news, Jo. The Foreign Office has confirmed that Paul is dead."

"No. They would have called me, as next-of-kin," I said.

"They didn't know Paul was married, a bureaucratic mix-up." I took the Foreign Office man's number and telephoned him. He sounded embarrassed.

"I was just about to ring you, Mrs Huntingford. I'm sorry about the mistake. I'm very sorry to say we've confirmed the identity of the victim. I deeply regret to tell you that he was your husband, Paul Huntingford."

I could not, would not believe it. I carried on with my work, while checking on agency reports every few minutes. Several minutes after the phone call, I looked at the screen to see Paul's name written there. But it could not be true. That would be too cruel.

At two o'clock Ismene arrived. She tried to comfort me. She stayed with me for two days, cooking me meals which I could not eat. I asked her to leave. I needed to be alone. She asked if I wanted her to ring Louisa or a friend, but I said no, that I would prefer to be on my own.

After she had left I walked out into the garden. It was evening, but still light and quite warm. I sat on the bench where Paul and I liked to sit together and watch the sunset. I don't know how long I was there, but I suddenly noticed that the stars were out.

I became aware of beautiful birdsong coming from the large oak at the end of the garden. Moments later, a tiny brown-flecked bird flew swiftly from the tree onto the ground a few feet in front of me. It looked at me for a few moments and then hopped up onto the arm of the bench. It began to sing, so quietly and sweetly, it seemed as though it was singing especially for me.

I closed my eyes and listened. Suddenly I had a strong sense of Paul's presence. I felt as I did when he held me in his arms – safe, comforted, loved... I knew that Paul was saying goodbye.

The feeling went, and in that moment I knew that Paul was gone for ever. I think I must have sat there for several hours, because I became aware that day was breaking. The feelings of loss and grief were so very deep, something inside me had broken. I could not cry.

As the days went by, the phone rang frequently. I did not answer it. Friends left messages, but I did not return their calls. One call that I did return was from Paul's father. He had promised Paul that, should he be killed on assignment, he would take care of the funeral arrangements. I agreed that he should carry out Paul's wish for a Hindu funeral.

We held the service at the little church down the lane. It was agonizing. All I can remember is the pain and the utter unreality of it. As we left Paul's graveside, I turned and tried to run back, to save Paul. Ismene held me and said, gently, "No, Joanna. He's gone. He's gone."

I arranged to take time off work and remained in the country. I saw and spoke to no one. I did not shower or bathe. I sent my cleaning lady away. She offered to shop for me, but I said no. She left me food anyway. I barely touched it. And it did not occur to me for weeks that I must owe her quite a lot of money that she could not spare.

I turned to the empty space within myself, turned away from life's movement, evading it, subtly and politely, excusing myself, with eyes averted, desirous only to be apart. Nothing could ever fill that space again. I had nothing to say.

I began to work again and then immersed myself in it. As the weeks went by, messages left by friends indicated that they were becoming increasingly worried about me. But I simply could not bear to be touched, to be in anyone's company. I felt that a skin had been removed. I felt vulnerable and could not face the world.

I received a letter from Alex, sending his love and saying he was thinking of me. He said he was leaving the paper to go to medical school. When he had qualified, he intended to go to Africa, with his girlfriend, to work for the needy. I knew I should respond and wish him well but could not bear to do so.

Ismene came once a week, bringing food and flowers. The first couple of times she knocked, but I did not reply. After that, she would place her gifts outside the front door and leave. Sometimes I would bring in some of the food and eat a little of it. I was losing a lot of weight and could see no future for myself. I tried to write but the words would not come. Then came the letter, brief and to the point. It was from the Editor. I was fired.

I came to my bed, hating myself and needing to escape myself in retreat and resignation. Fear pervaded me at the realization that I might lose everything, echoing my childhood fear of abandonment. For the first time in my life I was not in control. I turned my face to the wall. My bed was comfortable and warm and I saw no reason why I should ever leave it again.

The telephone was ringing. I let it ring and click into the answering machine. A moment later it rang again. And then again. I lifted the receiver.

"Joanna. Are you there?" It was Ismene. As she listened quietly, I told her how I felt, how pointless everything seemed, how great an effort to do the simplest tasks, how little I cared about myself and about the future. Ismene asked me to pray, and we prayed aloud together. She said, "Joanna, you are fighting for your life." That galvanized me and made me want to keep talking.

We talked through the night; sometimes I dozed off to sleep and then awoke suddenly to find Ismene still on the end of the phone line. It was early morning when she said, "Joanna, get out of bed. Go and run yourself a bath. Put in scented oils. Bring some candles and light them. Soak yourself in your bath, feel the warm water on your skin. When you have dried yourself, massage scented lotion into your skin, feel your body, be aware of it. Then dress yourself in something beautiful and go out to face the day."

And so I did. Raising myself from my bed was a monumental effort. I cannot remember any task ever being so hard. I did walk to the bathroom. I did run my bath. I did soak in the water and feel it on my skin. Almost without knowing what I did, I did all those things. Then I raised myself and dried myself and dressed myself in clothes that were beautiful, and I had taken the first steps on my road to survival.

Later that day I heard a car engine and peered from behind my curtains, to see Ismene's car draw up. She rang my door bell, but I still could not face speaking to anyone and did not respond.

As I watched from behind my curtains, Ismene returned to her car and took from it a bouquet of scarlet tulips, a vase and a bottle of water. In the clearing at the front of the house, she placed the vase on the ground, filled it with water from the bottle and arranged the flowers carefully in the vase.

Next she produced a hamper and placed it next to the vase of flowers. She opened the hamper and took out a blue-and-white-checked tablecloth, which she spread out on the ground. Then she took out a ham and a cooked chicken – I thought, how strange, when she is a vegetarian – a cake, salads and fruit, placing each in turn on the tablecloth. Next came napkins and cutlery.

Next came a basket, from which she took a bottle of wine and a single glass. I recognized it as one of a set of beautiful eighteenth-century crystal glasses that she owned. The wine and the glass were placed next to the hamper. Then she got back into her car and drove away.

I cannot tell you how profoundly that action affected me. I sat and listened to the hum of her car's engine as it grew fainter and fainter. I stared at the things she had left for me. I opened the front door for the first time in many days. The autumnsun streamed in and I stood in the doorway for several minutes, breathing in the clean, fresh air and feeling the warmth upon my skin.

I walked across to the vase of flowers, lifted it and brought it into the house. I placed it on a table near the window. I drew back the curtains and the sunlight revealed the deep, glistening red.

I brought in the food and the wine. I placed the single crystal glass carefully next to the vase of flowers. Then I cleared the papers and clutter from the table, took a cloth, dampened it from the tap and wiped the table top. I placed the crystal glass in the centre of the table, carefully, so that I should not accidentally break it. Next to it I placed the bottle of wine, which I noticed had been chilled.

I took the cooked chicken and salad from the hamper, along with the cutlery and a napkin. I brought a chair to the table. I uncorked the wine and poured myself a glass. I raised the glass to my lips and drank. Standing in a shaft of sunlight, I felt warmed and revived. I sat down at the table and I ate.

Later, I walked out into the garden. As I watched the sun setting I felt my legs losing strength, and sank to my knees. I began to sob, and suddenly I could not stop. The grief and loneliness and pain poured from me in a seemingly endless tide. It felt as though some poison were being washed away. That night, for the first time in weeks, I slept till morning.

It would be Christmas in two weeks' time and I dreaded facing it without Paul. Last Christmas we had married and been full of hope. Now there was no hope, because Paul had gone.

Louisa, my sister, had been begging me to allow her to come and look after me and finally I agreed. She came down the week before Christmas. She wanted to take me back to North Wales, to share the holiday with her family, but I could not bear the thought of it and felt I would only spoil their happiness. Though I did not want to be alone, it seemed the best option.

On Christmas Eve I attended a carol service in our little church, slipping quietly into a pew near the back. I had always enjoyed the atmosphere of Christmas, the sparkling frosty white on trees and Christmas cards, the way the snow silenced the land. It was a special time, when the world seemed to pause and take a breath. In the creation of that moment – or perhaps the acknowledgement of a moment that is always ours to take – I found great comfort. It gave hope that things did not always have to continue in the same way. People could change their lives. Even as a child, I had always hoped this was true.

Catherine, the vicar, welcomed us to the celebration of Jesus' birth with a warmth that encompassed us all. At the back of the church, I felt that I, too, was included. But I wondered how was it that the others in the congregation believed in a God of love when I had encountered only a God who did not seem to care? Anna had seemed to see truth and purpose in Julian's message of love, but had not she, too, been let down? I wished I could know the end of her story. She believed that Julian had touched her life – but had she found redemption and release?

As I puzzled over these thoughts, I realized that the choir was singing a favourite carol of mine, "Adam Lay Y'Bounden". This time I listened more carefully than usual to the words:

Adam lay y-bounden,
Bounden in a bond,
Four thousand winters
Thought he not too long.

And all was for an apple,
An apple that he took,
As clerkes finden
Written in their book.

Ne had the apple
The apple taken been,
Ne never had our Lady
A-been heavene queen.

Blessed be the time
That apple taken was,
Therefore maun we sing
Deo Gratias.

The words reminded me of what Julian had said about sin being inevitable and necessary and God's toleration of it honourable. Was it true that all the bad things that happen are allowed by God so that we may grow and learn? Was there really a purpose? Were there really grounds for hope, authentic hope?

Ismene sent me a hamper of food for Christmas. Being her usual sensitive self, she did not send one full of rich, traditional celebratory fare. Rather, her gift was a selection of organic produce, tasty, wholesome, nourishing food, fresh vegetables and fruit. On Christmas Day she telephoned me. We talked about Paul and the value of the work he had done in his life. She spoke of him as a man who had contributed a great deal to others, a man of conscience, a man who had left a lasting legacy to the world, a man who had loved me very much and whom I had made very happy. I was soon in tears.

She said, "This time will pass. We are never alone. In love there is no separation. We sometimes have to give up the ones we love, but it is only for a time. The people who love us are always close by, whether they are in this world or the next. And we are reunited with them, in God's time."

But if Paul really was still alive, in heaven, then surely he was with Sushila and might no longer want me?

"There are many things we cannot understand," Ismene said. "But in a place of love, everything comes right. Love for one does not exclude love for another. Love grows by love, and more love is the result."

Using Paul's contacts, I intensified my reporting of human rights stories, working as a freelance for several newspapers. It was my way of keeping some part of him alive. The work became my whole life. I tried particularly hard to push the East Timor story; but editors were reluctant to give it space. Despite the worldwide condemnation of Indonesia, following the massacre at Santa Cruz Church in Dili, East Timor was still not considered an important story.

The *Guardian* agreed to take regular opinion pieces from me, and as correspondents out in the field reported on the horrors of Bosnia, I wrote about the inadequacy of our government's response. The unspeakable atrocities being committed seemed too grotesque and appalling to believe. How could people who had once been neighbours do such things to each other? The UK – like other world powers – was talking but doing nothing. I wrote that we should arm the Muslims, so that they could defend themselves against the Serbs. But in my heart I felt there was no right answer. And words – in which I had once placed such great faith – seemed to be of no use or value. I confided in Ismene my feelings of helplessness and impotence.

She said, "It's water upon a stone. We cannot know what the outcome will be of anything we do. We can only do – and must do – what we believe to be right."

I missed Paul terribly. I lived and I worked, but inside there was a big, empty chasm, a desperate sadness and hunger and a pain from which I was never free. I hugged my sorrow to me, like a protective cloak. The place where I lived with my grief was private. Kind friends tried to persuade me to talk about Paul and how I felt, but I resisted. Nobody could possibly understand. Because I knew this, because I did not wish to be pressured into conversations that would cause me further pain, and perhaps because I wanted to disconnect the part of myself that felt and needed love, I distanced myself from people other than work contacts. My home became both sanctuary and prison.

My phone would ring at all hours of the day and night with news of a story that someone, somewhere, needed desperately to have publicized. I was glad of it. It gave me a purpose and an outlet for my energies. I came to care about people who were thousands of miles away, people to whom I could give practical help. I knew that meticulous reporting, rather than polemic, was my best weapon in their defence. One inaccuracy could undermine the authority of a piece, but the truth could not be refuted. Julian had taught me a lesson about reporting faithfully even those things I did not understand.

My thoughts often turned to Julian... Julian, who had been cheeky enough to question Jesus, as he gave her a message of love from the cross, as to how what he said about all being well could possibly be true when you only had to look around you to see how miserable people were, doing bad things and causing grief to themselves and to others; Julian, who piped up with a "Would you mind clarifying what you just said?" at a press conference with God. How could I fail to like her? She even had a great sense of humour. While miraculously recovering from her illness, after being given the last rites, an enquiry from her priest as to how she was feeling elicited the response, "I have been raving half the day!" which made him chuckle. It is all there, in her book.

Sometimes I would seek solace in my copy of *Enfolded in Love*. One quotation in particular touched me: "He did not say, 'You shall not be tempest-tossed, you shall not be work-weary, you shall not be discomforted'. But he said, 'You shall not be overcome.'" The words made me feel safe and at peace. They reminded me of a hymn we had sung at my mother's funeral, about travelling across life's tempestuous seas to a better place, and having no fear of the raging storm because *"Fy Nhad sydd wrth y llyw"* – my Father will be at the helm.

In the spring Ismene invited me to the annual Julian Lecture. It was to take place at St Julian's Church on 8 May, the anniversary of the visions. Sister Eleanor, Gregorio's friend, was to give the talk. Ismene told me that her convent, St Etheldreda's, had helped Gregorio's sister to set up a Julian prayer group in East Timor. I accepted Ismene's invitation, wanting to believe there was some pattern, sense and meaning to life and hoping it might be revealed to me on that day.

I met Ismene and Gregorio in London. Over lunch, Gregorio shared with us his worries about his country, where the brutality of the illegal regime continued unabated. His family had been influential under the Portuguese, before the Indonesian occupation, but today, like everyone else, they lived with the constant fear of imminent death. Almost every day a neighbour or friend disappeared. He felt helpless, believing he should be able to do more.

We travelled by train to Norwich and arrived at St Julian's Church half an hour before the lecture was due to start. The church was already packed. Everyone seemed to know everyone else and there was a lively buzz of conversation. Sister Eleanor was intro-

duced by Sheila Upjohn, a local writer. She announced the title of
the lecture as "Julian and the God of the Wayside". Sheila spoke
briefly of her own experience of Julian, saying, "Once she gets her
hooks into you she won't let go until you've done the work she
wants you to do!"

I loved this description. Practical love was such an important
part of my maternal family heritage. Stories about my grandmother
and great-grandmother were all about how they helped others.
Giving a helping hand to someone in distress was so natural to my
mother that there was always a little gift here, a word of kindness
there, some small act of generosity, done without fuss.

She used to tell me how my grandmother would give money to
the miners employed by my grandfather when they ran out of cash
before pay-day. She told me how my great-grandmother had carried
clean bedlinen on her back across the mountain at Senghenydd, in
South Wales, to a woman who was bedridden and neglected, with a
houseful of children. "And the doctor said, 'For heaven's sake, Mrs
Jones, cut her bloody toenails!'"

People used to joke about Blodwen, my aunt, that if you wanted
to find her you should look in the house of the person in the village
who was in most need. Like Blodwen, Julian was a practical woman.
Surely such a woman would not let me down with promises that
would not be kept? Julian, the person, had become important to me.
Was she someone in whom I could put my trust?

Sister Eleanor stepped up to the lectern. She gave us a welcoming
smile that seemed to embrace each one of us. I was astonished to
hear her hit upon the very subject that had been on my mind. She
said, "When life is painful and we suffer, it may seem impossible that
there is any pattern or plan and that there is a God who cares for
us. But it is our blindness that makes us think this way. Because we
are poor in love, we cannot comprehend God's love, which is great.

"When we know his love and have seen it at work in our lives,
then we begin to see clearly. We begin to understand that our Father
is very much in charge, and indeed so intimately involved in our
lives that he lives within us.

"We have Julian's testimony for this. Julian tells us how her spiritual eyes were opened and she saw her own soul, in the middle of her heart. She says, 'The soul was as large as if it were an eternal world, and a blessed kingdom as well. Its condition showed it to be a most glorious city, in which God was seated, in rightful peace and rest. His Godhead rules and upholds both heaven and earth, and all that is, and is supreme in might, wisdom and goodness. Nor will he quit the place he holds in our soul for ever... for in us is he completely at home and has his eternal dwelling.'

"When I first encountered Julian, there was a great deal that I did not understand. And yet all the while, I felt I could trust her. I felt I had come home. The better I have come to know her, the more I have come to understand her, and to love her, as so many of you dear friends here today love her.

"I love her because she loved me first. There can be no doubt of that. It's so clear in the way she speaks of her 'even-Christens', the ordinary people whom she loved. And it's clear in the diligent way she carried out her sacred task of interpreting her message. From the pages of her book shines a mother's love.

"But for some of us, it is very hard to simply accept her assurance of God's love, her insistence that God regards us as his darlings and never stops loving us, no matter what we feel and no matter what we do. Because many of us have never experienced anything approximating to that kind of love.

"We are living in a new Dark Age, in which the world is enduring a loss of love, a loss of tenderness, a loss of imagination, a loss of trust, a loss of soul. For so many, the pain is so great that there can be no trust in relationships and no safety in the universe. The yearning to love and to be loved is stifled and replaced by a constant watchfulness and a defensiveness. Lonely people, belonging nowhere and to nobody, cope as best they can.

"The search for intimacy has never been so desperate. Yet many people go in fear of ridicule, condemnation and rejection. Others carry the burden of self-hate. They pass the ultimate judgement upon themselves, as if, somehow, to deaden the pain of intolerable anxiety. They are filled with inner desolation and feelings of failure and worthlessness. Yet they are beautiful, and they are truly loved and they have reason to hope."

The Sister's message touched something deep within me. I quietly searched for tissues in my handbag.

Sister Eleanor continued, "How are we to take into our hearts the unconditional love that God offers us? How does a hungry vagrant approach the table of a generous host who has thrown open his doors and said, 'Come in, you are welcome! You are the honoured guest we have all been waiting for. You are the prodigal returned and we are longing to kill the fatted calf!' How can he believe that he is really wanted? He knows what he is – or at least, he thinks he does. Why should anyone want him?

"It is hard to accept the limitless love God offers us, because we do not understand the nature of that love, because we are so poor in love. So God comes to us in small ways that we can understand. For the great God who rules heaven and earth is also the God of the Wayside.

"If we want to find the truth, to encounter God, we must look in hidden places – the kindness of someone who offers us a seat on the bus when we are tired, who notices the need of another and goes out to meet it. When we keep our eyes open for small acts of kindness and generosity and consider where the impulse to perform those acts originated, then we meet the God of the Wayside. For such acts always spring from a loving heart. As Julian says, all goodness comes from God, and it reaches the 'lower self', or human personality, from the higher self – which is the soul of God who lives in us.

"And so, to grow in love, we must learn to recognize God in others and to find God in ourselves. We are asked to accept the kindness of others. We are asked to do those things that the heart tells us to do, so that in time those actions become second nature and we grow in compassion.

"In this way, we learn to give love to all people, not just the special few. We come to see people in a different light, each as an individual, each deserving of love. And we come to see ourselves in the same way. This is how the world is saved, and how we are saved.

"But when we refuse to acknowledge truth that has been revealed to us, when we resist the impulse to be kind, perhaps through fear of being misunderstood; when we reject the kindness of others, perhaps because we suspect the giver's motives or think we do not deserve it; then we quench the Holy Spirit, as we are cautioned against in the Book of Thessalonians, and we stop the action of love. By giving and receiving love, we come into God's way of life, we open our hearts to him and allow him to enter and change us, we grow to become what we were made to be – part of God – a destiny that will bring us joy and peace and the true fulfilment of being our real selves."

Sister Eleanor explained that when Julian said nothing happened by chance, she was saying that we should accept and embrace all that came our way, however painful it might be. We should not try to protect ourselves from life, but take it all as an opportunity for learning.

"Julian assures us that God will not allow anything to happen to us that cannot be turned to our good. Life is our teacher and we learn and grow through our relationships with others.

"So we must not hug our pain to us, but strive to learn the lesson it brings us. We have Julian's assurance that one day we will be glad that everything happened in just the way that it did. If we seek the companionship of the God of the Wayside, he will walk with us along our path through life, showing us that, despite the difficulties we face and the suffering we endure, it all makes sense, and that, as Julian promised us, all shall be well."

As the lecture ended, I hurriedly wiped my eyes, hoping no one had noticed my tears. It was extraordinary. It was as though Sister Eleanor had fashioned her lecture precisely to meet my need and had been speaking to me personally.

The lecture ended to warm applause. The audience members were quickly on their feet and gathered around the Sister, congratulating her. Tea was served and we mingled with the crowd. I noticed a tall, distinguished-looking elderly man talking to Sister Eleanor.

"There's Robert Llewelyn," Gregorio said. I knew his name, of course, as the editor of *Enfolded in Love* and the former chaplain of Julian's cell.

"Would you like to meet Robert?" asked Gregorio. It transpired that Gregorio had been several times to visit Robert Llewelyn at his home nearby. I said I would love to. Mr Llewelyn, who was helping himself to a cup of tea, greeted us warmly. He had the kindest eyes I had ever seen. I told him I had derived great comfort from *Enfolded in Love*. He thanked me and then questioned Gregorio solicitously about his sister.

"She is well, thank you, Robert. The Sisters are very brave," said Gregorio.

Mr Llewelyn asked me about myself, and before I knew it I found myself telling him, hesitantly, without meaning to, about Paul's death. As I did so, Gregorio quietly left us together. If kind looks can heal a heart, mine was a little healed in that moment. Mr Llewelyn seemed really to care about my unhappiness. He asked if he could do anything to help. Perhaps I would like to visit him. He gave me his telephone number.

"Would you like to meet Sister Eleanor? I think you would enjoy talking to her," he said.

"I have briefly met the Sister and I would love to meet her again," I said.

Mr Llewelyn excused himself and a few moments later returned with the Sister.

"I hope we will meet again. Do come and visit me," he said, then shook my hand warmly and left me with Sister Eleanor.

The Sister's smile was gentle and tender. Her presence seemed to envelop me, like a circle of love and healing light. I felt better, simply being with her. I said that I had enjoyed her talk. She thanked me and said, "I'm glad you came here today, to Julian's little church. It's such a little wayside place, isn't it? You'd never notice it unless you were looking for it."

"I was looking for it – very much so," I replied, beginning to feel terribly sad.

Sister Eleanor touched my arm gently. "I'm glad you found it, found us, today." She paused, and then said, "Robert told me about your great loss. I'm very sorry." She looked as though she really meant it, really cared. Tears started to prick at the back of my eyes. Sister Eleanor continued to speak softly to me, words of comfort and reassurance, all the while looking into my eyes with kindness and understanding.

She placed her right hand on my arm. It felt almost as though she was about to embrace me. In that moment I thought what a relief it would be to be swept up in that loving embrace depicted on the cover of *Enfolded in Love*.

"I would like to offer you my help. Will you let me?" asked Sister Eleanor, looking at me with great kindness. "When we're bereaved, there's a particular kind of help we need, and I would feel honoured if you would allow me to offer it to you. At our convent we have a guest house. Will you come and see us when you feel ready? At the very least, it will be a quiet, peaceful place where you can rest."

Just being in the presence of someone so gentle, kind and loving made me feel a little better. I said I was grateful for her offer and would come if I could. She pressed her hand gently against my arm and said, "I hope you will."

23

A few weeks later, in mid-June, I telephoned Sister Eleanor's convent, which was at Brancaster, on the north coast of Norfolk. I arranged to spend a few days there at the end of the month.

I travelled by train to London and then on to Norfolk. I took pleasure in leaving London behind me, anticipating the peace and quiet that awaited me at St Etheldreda's. The journey passed peacefully. I read the paper, drank tea and began to look forward to time away from the telephone and the demands of work.

At King's Lynn station I hired a taxi to drive me to Brancaster.

"How long will it take us to get there?" I asked.

"Half an hour'll do it," the taxi driver replied.

After some twenty-five minutes we arrived at the coast, and turned left, onto a narrow road that edged the line of the land. I looked out across the cold, grey sea. A few minutes later we arrived at a village.

"This is it," said the driver. "Brancaster." He continued through the village and for a further half-mile. A little way ahead I saw an old farmhouse, protected by a low hedge.

"Here it is," he said, stopping in front of a farm gate, on which was written "Convent of St Etheldreda". He unwound his window and leaned out to press a buzzer next to the gate, which swung open. We turned into the drive and he pulled up in front of the door.

I stepped out onto the driveway. Beyond the house, I could see farm buildings. I had expected high walls and Gothic turrets. This was a surprise.

I rang the doorbell and waited. The door was opened by a woman of about fifty. She wore a traditional floor-length black habit, with a black veil and a white wimple. On her feet were sandals and woollen socks. "Sister Eleanor is expecting me," I said.

"Do come in," she replied with a warm smile. "Come along into the parlour and I'll tell Sister you're here."

I followed her to a little room just inside the door, and she left me there. A few minutes later, the door opened and Sister Eleanor entered.

"Hello, Joanna. Welcome. I'm so glad you could come," she said, giving me a hug. "Did you have a good journey? You must be hungry. I'll show you to your room. Then we'll have some food."

Sister Eleanor took me through a series of corridors with pale, whitewashed walls and wide windows, saying, "It's quite a labyrinth here!" We came to a courtyard, crossed flagstones and entered a low building that might have been a converted barn. "This is our guest house," she said. "I hope you'll be comfortable." She led me into a small, cosy room with simple furnishings and a crucifix on the wall. She left me there for several minutes, to settle in, and then returned, saying, "Come, let's go and get some food."

The Sister took me to the refectory, which was furnished with trestle tables and benches. After a few minutes, a nun entered, bearing on a tray two bowls of soup and a plate of bread. She smiled and put the food on the table before us.

The hot vegetable soup was filling and delicious. The bread was home-baked and still warm. I complimented Sister Eleanor on the meal. She replied, "I'm glad you're enjoying it. We grow all our own vegetables here. I don't think anything tastes as good as something one has just taken out of the ground."

When we had finished our meal the Sister asked, "Would you like to see my work?" I said I would. She led me out of the front door and around the corner of the house. Just ahead was an exterior staircase. "Come up," she said. I followed her up the stairs and into a long room with a high ceiling and large windows, including an enormous one in the roof. As we walked into the room, I saw that the rear windows had a view into the far distance, over the marshes.

"This is where I work. I share it with two other Sisters. Each of us has her own space. This used to be the hayloft. Our chapel is below, in what was the stable."

Below the window in the roof was an easel. On it was a half-finished painting. More paintings were hung on the walls, several were resting against a wall and a little pile of smaller canvases was on a low shelf. They were paintings of angels, quite exquisite, done in pale pastel watercolours. Those that hung on the wall appeared, almost, to be in mid-flight, swooping down from the heavens into the room.

On a table were little pots of paints, brushes and paint-smeared rags. There were two wooden stools, one low and one high, another table and two old wicker armchairs by the window. In a corner was a sink. The room was cluttered, but tidy.

"I painted these," said Sister Eleanor. "The Sisters I share the space with are also painters. We banged a hole in the roof to make a skylight for the northern light. Those are their canvases." She indicated the far end of the room, where paintings of birds and seascapes hung on the wall and were propped up against it.

I looked at Sister Eleanor's paintings. They were like nothing I had seen before: delicate, imaginative and quite tender. The faces were extraordinary, suffused with radiant love.

Sister Eleanor said, "Many of the women who are drawn here have some kind of artistic talent, which we are encouraged to develop. One of the sisters I share with is a trained artist. The other found she had a strong urge to paint that she had never felt before.

"Gifts tend to emerge that people didn't know about. Some sisters draw. We have two wood-carvers. One of the Sisters is a potter. She made me this. Lovely, isn't it?" She handed me a beautiful pot, decorated with delicate swirls in varying shades of blue and green. "We sell our work, just as we sell eggs and produce from the garden, to earn our living as a community. And, of course, we like to do what we can for those in greater need."

She asked, "Shall we have some tea?" Someone had left a tray, with a pot of freshly brewed tea and cups and saucers on the table by the window. Sister Eleanor indicated that I should take a seat in one of the wicker armchairs. She took the other chair and poured the tea.

I looked out of the window, across the garden and at the marshes beyond. Sister Eleanor said, "I often sit here, looking out. It gives me a deep sense of peace and freedom. Here there is always time enough. Out in the world people have so little time to make sense of it all, to think about what they want from life… I think your world of journalism is a particularly hard world, isn't it?" I agreed. "But the work you do is very important. You can change lives."

We talked about the work Paul and I had done together and my efforts to continue it, in his memory. Sister Eleanor listened quietly and attentively. Something about the directness of her gaze, the gentleness of her countenance and the softness of her voice touched me, breaking through my protective shell. I felt the pricking of tears and a lump forming in my throat. I tried to speak, but no words came. Sister Eleanor put her hand gently upon my arm.

Suddenly, I found that I was pouring it all out, all the pain and anger I felt about Paul's death. The Sister said very little, and yet she asked just the right questions to make me feel safe to continue. I felt she understood. I confessed that I did not feel up to the job of following in Paul's footsteps. I could not hope to report human rights stories in the way he would have done.

Sister Eleanor said gently, "But why do you feel you have to be other than what you are? Paul loved you for yourself. His work was his and your work is yours. So long as you do the work that is yours to do, using the talents God gave you, you do not fall short. On the contrary, you fulfil his plan for you. God gives us all we need. I know that yours is a harsh world. If people criticize you, let them. Try not to focus on the anger you feel towards those who do bad things. If you keep patiently on your path, you will find peace."

I joined the Sisters for supper and walked in the garden for a while before returning to my room. I was soon asleep.

Love bade me welcome: yet my soul drew back,
Guilty of dust and sin.
But quick-eyed Love, observing me grow slack
From my first entrance in,
Drew nearer to me, sweetly questioning
If I lacked anything.

"A guest," I answered, "worthy to be here."
Love said, "You shall be he."
"I, the unkind, the ungrateful? Ah, my dear
I cannot look on Thee."
Love took my hand, and smiling did reply,
"Who made the eyes but I?"

"Truth, Lord, but I have marred them: let my shame
Go where it doth deserve."
"And know you not," says Love, "who bore the blame?"
"My dear, then I will serve."
"You must sit down," says Love, "and taste my meat,"
So I did sit and eat.

(George Herbert)

I returned home from St Etheldreda's feeling more relaxed
and at peace. As the summer months passed by, from time to time

Sister Eleanor would send me a beautiful little hand-painted card, inscribed with a text from Julian's book. I pinned them up above my desk. They comforted me.

As September approached, I dreaded the anniversary of Paul's death. When it came, the day was so painful, I felt I needed some succour and sustenance that would heal my heart. My thoughts turned again towards Sister Eleanor and St Etheldreda's. I knew that I needed to be away the week before Christmas, the anniversary of our wedding. I arranged to spend a few days at the convent.

This time I drove to Brancaster. It was a long, tiring drive and I was glad when I recognized the flat landscape that would soon give way to the north Norfolk coast. In the distance the sky was thick with what looked like a rapidly moving black cloud. Flocks of birds were sweeping along the horizon, coming in to seek sanctuary for the winter.

I arrived at St Etheldreda's feeling tired and hungry. I gratefully received a warm welcome from Sister Eleanor, who quickly settled me by an open fire with a bowl of hot soup. Soon after, she took me to the refectory and saw to it that I was fed with a nourishing meal of fish, vegetables and rice, followed by hot apple pie and custard. In my little room, my head had barely touched the pillow before I was asleep.

I spent the following day resting, and the next day I drove to Norwich. My first stop was the cathedral. I entered its precinct, leaving behind the noisy rumble of traffic. Ahead, the cathedral appeared like some fairy palace of mellow golden stone, intricately carved, its portico flanked by crumbling figures of saints or martyrs, their features obliterated by the weathering of centuries.

A bell pealed and struck the chimes of the hour. As I entered, I read a notice by the door, which told me that the cathedral had been founded in 1096, by Bishop Herbert de Losinga, as the mother church of the diocese.

Just inside the door, a woman was watering a large display of yellow and white chrysanthemums, below which had been placed a profusion of forest greenery. There came to my mind the stained-glass image of the crucifixion in Chartres Cathedral, in which the cross is painted green. It is green to symbolize the fact that this is a story about life, not death.

The cathedral was being prepared for Christmas. In every nook and cranny there seemed to be someone buffing or polishing, or attempting to vaccuum quietly. The woman with the watering can continued her duties among the many displays of flowers.

I was struck by the ordinariness of things, the need for practical tasks to be carried out, seemingly endlessly, in order for us to snatch the time we need for the things that matter to us. How is it possible, when this is the reality of our lives, to find the time and space for each of us to consider his or her particular journey?

Among all that I had read since encountering Julian, I frequently had come across the concept of taking time out to go within. Somewhere there had been a promise that, through those stolen snatches of time, if only one were persistent enough, something real that gave succour could be established and increased. Was it a place or a state of mind, or a state of being? It seemed as though there was a way to return time and again, to revisit and reinforce that beingness, to build up that body of soul-truth-light – a citadel in a city that I could one day make my home.

It was a place that now was hard to reach, but might one day be easy to find. Seeing through a glass darkly, but then face to face, to know even as I am known... How readily the Christian teaching of my childhood came back to me. It seemed that, despite my rejection of it, something had taken root.

To my left was a curved staircase leading to a vault, built, said the notice, in the early fourteenth century. Would I find there the atmosphere of Julian's world? I climbed the narrow staircase and found myself in a kind of little chapel, full of glass cases containing medieval ecclesiastical artefacts. In one case, I saw a silver plate, decorated with a hand raised in a gesture of benediction. Beyond it, reflected in the glass, I saw myself. I looked into my own eyes and caught sight of the depth of my own yearning for a glimpse of the truth, for meaning.

I was taken most of all with the wall and ceiling decorations, the processions of angels and saints. I had thought that church decorations from that period were inspired by dread of hellfire and damnation, but these were not. They were full of celebration and beauty. In one corner was a sweet-faced angel, with calm, reflective eyes and the gentlest demeanour and a blue halo edged with golden light. I thought: *Perhaps when someone was painting those graceful, green-leaved garlands on the ceiling, Julian was growing up.*

I had been told there were two windows in the cathedral with depictions of Julian. One was in the chapel dedicated to the Norfolk Regiment. I found her there, with a ginger moggy at her feet. This Julian was beautiful, but serious and rather saintly, I thought, not really my idea of Julian. She wore a rich red cloak, edged with gold and silver. I did like the cat, though. He seemed to be peering inquisitively at the observer, as though thinking: *Well, I see you having a jolly good look at me, but who are you?*

I moved on to the little Bouchon chapel. This was a much simpler portrayal. Julian kneels, her hands raised in prayer, looking towards heaven. I preferred it, for its simplicity, though she is in the rather grand company of Henry I, St Bede and St Augustine. As I stood before the window, I suddenly felt a sense of great joy – a brief perception, it seemed, of the glory of heaven. I felt I was standing in a pool of radiant light. I knew it was the product of my imagination, but it was a beautiful sensation. My eyes filled with tears. I asked Julian to help me make what I should of the day.

As I left the cathedral, I picked up a leaflet, perhaps identical to the one Anna had taken on her visit there, which had begun first her journey and then mine. A map on the leaflet showed me the route to St Julian's Church.

I walked from the cathedral and headed towards King Street. I passed the shabby buildings that Anna had described, and found the little narrow alleyway, St Julian's Alley, that would lead me through to the church and the little complex that contained the Julian Centre and All Hallows Convent. I passed St Julian's Church, which I was saving till later. I walked on, and turned left at the top of the alleyway and into the Julian Centre.

The administrator greeted me cheerily. I told her what I was hoping to find. Within a few minutes I had been supplied with a cup of tea and biscuits, followed shortly afterwards by books and documents. I was there for some three hours – and several cups of tea.

I made copious notes and felt I was filling in the gaps in my knowledge – but I was still dissatisfied. Where were the answers to my questions? It seemed as though I were being driven by some part of me that was empty and desired to be filled. I was no longer sure what I was searching for. I only knew that I needed to find it. I bought copies of several of the Julian lectures. I also bought two more books, including a new translation of both the short and long texts. I had done my work and now I could visit the church and Julian's chapel.

The church was small and unexceptional. It felt to me in no way special. I walked across to the little chapel and entered. The atmosphere was peaceful and calm. There was the table covered by a white cloth, with two candlesticks containing heavy white candles. There was the little window looking out onto the garden. A plaque was set into the wall, commemorating Julian's sojourn. Before it were some dozen votive candles in red glass containers, their tiny flames flickering. I had been by no means the only pilgrim in search of Julian that day. I lit a candle and placed it with the others.

There, too, was the crucifix. To me, the sense of vulnerability lay more in its simplicity than in Jesus' expression or the way his head was inclined.

I thought: *It is such a simple thing*. A young man was put to death by crucifixion two thousand years ago. We still remember it. The symbol of the man on the cross is imbued with such meaning. Did he open wide the gates of heaven? I felt a sense of welcoming quiet, but no ready-made answers to my questions. The chapel was snug and warm, but outside the day was rough and blustery. I imagined, way beyond the church walls, the seascape described by Anna, of wildness, wind and weather.

I was glad to return to the comforting warmth of St Etheldreda's. Sister Eleanor greeted me and invited me to join her for tea in her studio. I told her about my day and my curiosity about Julian, her fascination for me. My head was buzzing with ideas and impressions. My curiosity had for a while displaced my sadness, and suddenly I wanted answers. Most of all, I wanted an answer about Julian's loving God who did not condemn me and was never angry.

Sister Eleanor handed me my teacup and said, "Before I met Julian, I used to believe in the wrath of God and the mercy of God. I believed that we repented and then God forgave us. But Julian's version is that God's forgiveness is there the whole time and we've only got to accept it."

"Then – why does the Church preach repentance and forgiveness? Why doesn't it preach Julian's version?"

"Julian's message is revolutionary, and most of us don't much like change, do we? The truth is indeed shocking – God can't forgive our sins. He can't forgive us because he has already done so. There's no doubt about Julian's meaning. She says no fewer than ten times that God doesn't blame us for our sins. She says, 'Between God and our soul there is neither wrath nor forgiveness in his sight.' It's we who create an angry God, by projecting onto him the anger that's in us, which we haven't allowed God's compassionate love to quench. But you're right, this isn't an acceptable theology to some people and I doubt if it's often preached in our pulpits."

"Why is it that the Old Testament focuses so much on God's anger?"

"Well, I think we have to see it as expressing a relative truth, something that serves us well until we're ready to move on to something more absolute. Do you remember the hymn about heaven being above the bright blue sky? When I was a child that was enough to be going on with but it wouldn't satisfy me now. I believe we must hold ourselves open to be taken on in God's time to the more absolute truth which Julian offers. And by the way, Jesus never said God was angry. When I came to Julian's truth it was a great liberation for me. It gave me a new vision of God."

"But theologians have known about Julian. Why has the Church ignored her message?"

"Why indeed? One small voice is easy to ignore. But things are beginning to change. The Church is coming to see that Julian, perhaps more than anyone, has the undistorted image of God. She's on target. She recognizes that the way we treat one another depends upon our vision of God. If we think of God as angry and judgemental, that's how we'll behave towards others.

"Many dictators have been religious men. Their tyranny has been a reflection of what they saw in God. Saul of Tarsus, when he was persecuting the Church, was a deeply religious man acting consistently with his distorted image of God. If we see God as a tyrant, we'll become tyrants – not, for most of us, on the world scene, but in the family, the church, the school, the hospital, wherever we are."

I said, "That's the problem, isn't it? That's what's happening. This awful self-righteous arrogance, this certainty of being right and everyone else being wrong causes so much trouble in the world. It's what's put me off religion."

"And many others. I think it may be much better to be an atheist than to be a religious person with a seriously distorted image of the one we worship. Though, of course, atheists can be tyrants. It's from seeing ourselves as lovable that all growth begins. And love is a response. If parents love their children, it evokes love from the child. If we can enter into the reality that God loves us, our own love is evoked. Then our relationship with God is not a duty but natural and a joy."

"This is the part I find very difficult."

"We all do, Joanna. It's a hard road that you've chosen. The mental concept that God loves us is one thing. The absorption into the heart of the belief that God loves us and is not angry is something else. That's why we need meditation and prayer – to go within, to reach the state of love, to contact God. In this way, our prayer life develops at the level of the unconscious and we become more loving.

"I've found that Julian's undistorted image of God – all-compassionate and free of anger, whose forgiveness is always coming to meet us – develops characteristics of gentleness, forbearance, patience and understanding. Many people in discovering Julian feel, with me, that they have come home."

"That's what I want, so much – to feel I've come home. That's my Holy Grail."

"And it's your birthright. Your home is there. Your place awaits you, a place where you will be received as an honoured guest, a place where you are so much loved."

Tears came into my eyes. "I can't believe it. I can't believe I deserve it…"

"Then Julian would say you dishonour God." Sister Eleanor placed her hand on my arm in a comforting gesture. "Julian says we're blind as to the nature of love and in consequence make a mistaken response to God. Our horizons are limited by our poverty in love. We have to break through the barrier by faith, so that we may reach God's perspective. Then we'll see guilt and self-blame for what they are, indulgences that enable us to live within our sterile limitations, at the expense of honouring God."

"But what about God's justice?"

"In the logic of Julian's thought, God's justice has to go. God is unjust – if we measure justice by our ordinary, accepted standards. In Julian we find that justice is swallowed up in mercy.

"The prodigal son's elder brother, how would you picture him? I see him as a diligent, dutiful, hard-working young man, a fair overseer on the farm, a moral and upright person. And yet he was judged by his failure to respond to his father's mercy. He couldn't accept the compassionate, forgiving love of God shown to his brother, so he was excluded from the celebration. With the elder brother, God may not come into it, but with the younger brother God is there when he comes back to the father.

"The labourers in the vineyard – they, too, were judged by their incapacity to respond to the compassion of the owner of the vineyard. Of the two dying thieves at Calvary, one was judged purely on his response to God's mercy. His companion couldn't receive the promise of paradise because he was unable to respond to the mercy which was equally available to them both.

"This is how we change the world. Not by opposition, but by mercy and grace. We touch people with our forgiveness, as Jesus did on the cross, so that they open and become able to receive it. It's only because one is forgiven, because one is loved, that one can begin to change; not the other way round. But we so often fail to take possession of the release God is offering us. We mistake our self-blame for humility and in doing so we deny the generosity of God's love."

"So – forgiveness is the key to everything?"

"Forgiveness is an unlocking of the door and a setting free. The primary meaning the Greek word *aphesis* is letting go. Let me give you an example of Julian's work in mediating God's love to people who are burdened by their sins. Several years ago, a blind man visited Julian's cell. His blindness had been caused by the cruel treatment he had suffered as a wartime prisoner of the Japanese.

"As he knelt in the cell, Julian appeared. She brought with her the Japanese soldier who had caused the man's suffering. The dead soldier had come to seek the forgiveness of his victim, who was still full of bitterness. The blind man's companion heard him speak to his visitor in Japanese. During the conversation, the two enemies were at last reconciled. The blind man let go of his resentment and lapsed into an ecstasy of joy.

"He and his friend then went to All Hallows Convent guest house, next door, where they were given tea by one of the Sisters. In her presence, the vision was repeated – though no one else saw Julian or the soldier – and the blind man poured out his heart once more in Japanese. Imagine how he must have felt, to release the burden he had been carrying for so many years. That release and freedom is available to each of us."

We talked for a while longer. As I was about to leave, Sister Eleanor said, "Wait. I wonder if you would like to borrow this little book? It's by Robert Llewelyn. I think you would enjoy it."

Later that evening, seated by the window in my little room, I took up the book. Its title was *Love Bade Me Welcome*. I opened it and found an inscription written by the author. It said "For Eleanor. It has been a joy meeting you and sharing Julian and a time of silence with you. I hope this book may bring a blessing. Pray for me. With love, Robert."

I turned to the preface, and read that the book's subject was the life of prayer. The methods outlined, it said, included a brief examination of a Zen practice. I read "It is a great advance that we live in a time in which openness to what is good in other traditions has been encouraged at the highest level by both the Roman Catholic and the Anglican Church."

The book's title was taken from a poem by George Herbert, a poem of deep tenderness and beauty. The reader's attention is drawn to the surprise twist in the poem's last few lines. "We are here reminded how our first impulse on accepting Love's welcome is to look about for some form of service. Yet there follows at once a gentle rebuke. May it not be that Love wants to serve us, and, if so, are we too proud to submit!" Robert writes. "'You must sit down,' says Love, 'and taste my meat.'

"It is only as our love takes on the nature of God's own love that we can offer to one another the nourishment which alone can satisfy. And while our love must be mainly expressed in daily living, its roots are discoverable in the depths of the prayer life. The feeding at God's table precedes the command to go out in peace to love and serve the world."

I saw little of Sister Eleanor during the following few days. Some of her work was being sold for a local charity and she had two canvases to finish, though she made it clear that she would most gladly give me time if I wanted to talk. However, it was a relief to have an excuse not to delve into my feelings.

I returned home from Norfolk feeling more at peace. But the feeling did not last. I was quickly thrown back onto the treadmill of work, with the familiar tension and stress – though the pressure that caused the stress was self-imposed. I did not need to work so hard. I was driven by my anger about all the injustice in the world. In my heart, I felt restless. Sister Eleanor continued to send me her beautiful hand-painted cards. I meant to visit St Etheldreda's again, but I had found a way of managing my sadness and preferred not to reopen old wounds.

The seasons changed one into another and after three years of supplying a steady stream of stories, I persuaded the Editor of my old paper to appoint me as human rights correspondent. There had never been such a post on the paper and it felt like a worthwhile achievement. Paul would have been proud of me.

I wondered occasionally what had become of Anna. My enquiries and those of my colleague in the reference library had drawn a blank and been abandoned long ago. But at the back of my mind there remained the knowledge that I had begun a piece of work – my quest for Anna and Julian – and left it unfinished.

25

It was the summer of 1999, almost eight years since I had picked up Anna's journal in the antiquarian bookshop. Ismene and I had been in touch a great deal in recent weeks. The people of East Timor, after their many years of struggle and suffering, were at last about to have the opportunity to vote for independence.

However, supporters of the East Timorese were very worried. In the weeks leading up to the referendum, Indonesia's brutality was intensifying. We were hearing terrible stories about the increasing violence and savagery of the government-backed militia. The Indonesian military resented bitterly the prospect of giving up the territory, which it saw as its fiefdom, and was determined to sabotage the referendum. Ismene was among those who had warned the United Nations of the risk it ran by failing to put in place adequate security measures.

It was Saturday morning. I awoke at seven. I had checked the agency reports the previous evening, and the situation was clearly deteriorating. As I poured my first cup of tea, I heard the phone ringing. I lifted the receiver. It was Ismene.

"All hell has broken loose in East Timor," she said. Her contacts in the underground had been emailing her for the past few hours, with details of horrific attacks on civilians by the military. "I'm afraid we're facing a bloodbath."

As the hours passed, Ismene emailed me with information as soon as she received it. I passed it to a friend, a politician who was known for her support of human rights. I wrote articles for my paper and provided backup research for leader comment. By this time, though, our foreign correspondents out in the field were hard at work, risking their lives to provide on-the-spot cover. Again, I felt inadequate. Why was I not out there, following the story, as Paul would have been?

As one o'clock approached I switched on the television for the news. Horrific, shocking images flooded across the screen. Engraved for ever on my mind was the sight of two toddlers, sobbing and terrified, trying to clamber across rubble to safety, and not an adult in sight to scoop them up, comfort them and save them. It had been shot from a distance, so there was no certainty that the person filming the event had been able to help.

I saw children hanging from razor-sharp barbed wire around the United Nations compound. Their desperate parents, who knew that they were bound to die, had tried to save their children by flinging them over the wire. One little girl hung, screaming, from the wire – too far for away anyone in the compound to reach across and save her. I imagined how her parents must have felt.

Hundreds, perhaps thousands, were being slaughtered and no one was trying to save them. The pity of it. The shame of it. If I could have run across to where the child hung from the wire, I believed I would have risked the bullets to do so. Was this just easy, brave thinking from a distance? Perhaps. Perhaps not. But why did God not save her? It would have been so easy for him. Why did he allow an innocent little child to suffer and die?

I telephoned Gregorio, who was now a lecturer at a university in the north of England. He asked, "Did you see the images on television?" He sounded broken-hearted. We talked for a while. I tried to comfort him. His sister was missing. There seemed so little that I could say. I said, "I'm so sorry," and repeated it, feeling the inadequacy of my words. Shortly after, I spoke to Claire, his girlfriend.

She said, "He's distraught. He's been so brave all these years; I've never seen him so upset. He's up in the early hours, watching the news. I come downstairs each morning and find him in floods of tears."

The following day the news was worse... children slaughtered, along with the nuns who were trying to protect them. A young priest had gone out to meet the soldiers, police and militia – those terrible forces of violence and destruction that terrorized a people who had been brave enough to vote for freedom. He had pleaded with them to spare the people sheltering in his church. Mercilessly, they had hacked him to death, and then slaughtered every man, woman and child to whom he had given sanctuary.

I imagined the young priest going forward with such courage and no doubt such fear in his heart. Another image from the television footage came into my mind, of another young priest, the sacred purple of his office around his shoulders, walking swiftly and quietly among a group of terrified East Timorese, carrying a cross. He displayed such dignity, despite his evident fear. What had brought this tender young man to such a fate? Had he been able to make sense of the horror visited upon him and his people? Had he survived? If so, had he kept his faith?

I could not watch the news without breaking down in tears. I could not bear to see the East Timorese suffering so terribly. They were, in some strange way, my people. I had made myself a promise to protect them. Why were these things allowed to happen? I felt helpless. But God was not.

Julian had accepted the paradox that sin was evil but necessary, and that, despite everything, "all shall be well". Intellectually, I could just about accept that sin was necessary, because it allowed us to learn and grow from our mistakes. What I could not understand was how God could help intervening. If you feel for another and see that person in desperate need, it is a natural, instinctive thing to help, to save them. If such behaviour comes instinctively to us, so that we will on occasion risk our own lives to save others, how is it that such behaviour is not instinctive to God? If the goodness that inspires such behaviour comes from God, how is it possible that he is not ruled by it?

I suspected that these questions would never be answered. I could not, would not believe in a God who expected me to accept such horrors. All shall be well? Tell it to the East Timorese, I thought. I felt that I, like them, had been betrayed.

26

Ismene held a party to celebrate the freedom of East Timor. It was a time for joy, but we all knew there was a long road ahead in rebuilding the country and healing the wounds of the trauma of the past twenty-four years. Ismene took me aside for a quiet moment. We had not spoken about personal matters for several months and she wanted to know how my life was.

I confided in her my continuing sadness and raw anger about Paul's death, about the cruelty in East Timor, about all the injustice in the world.

"If I'd had a faith, I would have lost it during these past weeks," I said. "How could a loving God let that happen?"

"I understand," said Ismene thoughtfully. "I have a different interpretation. I think what we have seen underlines the truth of Julian's message. The East Timorese have every reason to hate not only the Indonesians but us, too, for colluding in the invasion and supporting the illegal occupation. The international community has again failed to protect the East Timorese, during the referendum. But even now, the East Timorese speak not of retribution but reconciliation. They know that this is the only possible way forward."

"You're saying we have to forgive because there's no viable alternative? That may be true, but it still doesn't explain God's part in all of this."

"What would Julian say? She would say, look again to the cross. If you think God betrays us, then what greater betrayal could there be than sending his own son to be crucified? And yet, great good came of it. I suggest you look closely at the cross. And remember the parable of the servant in the ditch. The mystery Julian reveals is that we are blindly ignorant of our own true will. God is keeping his side of an agreement that we made with him, which we have forgotten. He waits patiently for as long as it takes to achieve his intended aim of welcoming us home.

"Julian gives us an eye-witness description of the crucifixion and it's as harrowing as anything you will see in any war zone. I suggest you go to Julian. Then I'd like to discuss this more fully, in a quieter place. Why don't we meet for lunch in a few days?"

That evening I took up Julian's book and read her account of the crucifixion. Julian describes Jesus' face as having the pallor of death, then becoming blue as the flesh mortified, the nose shrivelled and dried, and the whole body became dark.

There was a bitter, dry wind and it was terribly cold. All the blood had drained away, but there remained some moisture in Jesus' flesh. The body was as discoloured, dry and withered as if he had been dead a week.

The body was abandoned and drying for a long time, becoming distorted because of the nails and its own weight. The nails had made the wounds bigger and the body sagged under its own weight from hanging. The crown of thorns was baked with dried blood, the hair and dry flesh clinging to the thorns, which enlarged the wounds.

The skin, with the hair and blood, was raised and loosened from the bone by the thorns, where it slashed through, like a sagging cloth, as if it would fall off. This caused me great sorrow and fear, and I would not for my life have seen it fall off.

The garland of thorns was dyed with the blood of wounds, and the head was the colour of dry, clotted blood.

The pain was hard and grievous, but much more so when the moisture was exhausted and everything began to dry and shrink. I saw four ways in which the body had been dried up: the loss of blood; the torment which followed; being hung in the air, as is a cloth to dry; and his need of liquid.

I saw pain so terrible that no words could describe it.

With a first-hand report such as this, it is difficult to remain an observer and not become a participant. I understood what Paul must have felt about witnessing scenes that he could not expunge from his memory. "You see something and you know you must tell others what you have seen," he had said.

Ismene and I met for lunch and discussed Julian's description of Jesus' crucifixion. "Your question is, why does God allow bad things to happen? I would say the things that happen to us here are often things to which we have agreed at soul level. Not at the level of the personality, of course, which understandably fights against the torments it undergoes. At soul level we can profit from pain we endure because it's always an opportunity to learn and move forward.

"But Jesus didn't need to learn, surely?"

"That's true. He did it for us, to enable us to feel compassion and to understand the nature and necessity of love and forgiveness. Look at what has come from Jesus' sacrifice. Everything is always in God's plan. Absolutely everything is in his hand. He will allow nothing to happen to us that cannot be turned to our good. The Bible says, 'All things work together for the good of those who wait upon the Lord.' Julian says, 'All shall be well.' Suffering is somehow consecrated and transmuted into a balm that can heal. I believe that the East Timorese nation, at soul level, chose to do a great thing for the world. It is their gift to the rest of us. Haven't you always felt that they were, in some way, a special people?"

"Yes, always. Their determination to be free, their courage and endurance – no matter what cruelty they suffered, it never dampened their spirit. I saw it in so many men and women."

"The children, too. Does that begin to make sense of things?"

"I'll have to think about what you've said. Perhaps."

Good has come of Jesus' sacrifice. That cannot be denied. Am I a beneficiary of that sacrifice? Someone endured cruel execution, for me. The mystery of why may be hard to understand, but the nobility and generosity of the sacrifice cannot be ignored. If I am so loved, why cannot I love myself? Perhaps I simply need to stop and be aware of that love, not to try to deserve it, but simply accept that it is mine.

27

Christmas passed and we were at the start of a new millennium. As midnight approached I looked out of my window across the garden to the tall trees beyond. I felt a sense of completion, which surprised me, because man-made boundaries of time always seemed to me confected and meaningless. As I stood in darkness, looking out and up towards the stars, it suddenly occurred to me that Julian and I were women of an age. She, who had lived so many hundreds of years before, and I belonged to the same time-frame, the same millennium. It made her seem closer.

As I returned to my lounge and watched television pictures of the celebrations around the globe, the world seemed very small. It reminded me that we were all part of one community. And yet, the sight of millions of pounds going up in smoke in spectacular firework displays seemed to reflect an inherent lack of meaning. Where was the sense of ourselves, of our place in the world's history, in time and in space?

How much had we really learned since Jesus' time? I wondered how many of those celebrating shared my feelings of emptiness. I felt restless, but did not know how to make myself feel more at ease. I continued to derive comfort from my copy of *Enfolded in Love*, but it was several years since my visits to St Etheldreda's. Every now and then I would think of the mysterious Anna Leigh and wonder what had become of her.

Then something happened. By the oddest of quirks, I was reminded of a dream I had had some fifteen years earlier. I was watching an old Hollywood film about the American Wild West, and on the screen was a low stone building, surrounded by trees. I had seen a similar scene somewhere, and for some reason it made me feel anxious. What was the source of the memory? Suddenly I remembered the dream. It all came flooding back.

I had been thoroughly frightened at the time – so much so that I had been afraid to go to sleep for several nights, in case the dream recurred. It had not been the content of the dream that scared me, but the fact that it had seemed absolutely real. I had been there, in some place I did not recognize; but I had known that this was no dream, that this was actually happening.

I recalled the small, low, roughly built structure, set in dense countryside, far away from anywhere. I had gone into the building and met a group of men. They seemed to be soldiers – or fighters, at any rate – dressed in combat fatigues, the sort of camouflage clothes that might be worn in the jungle.

They welcomed me. They asked me to take a message for them. I said I would. They said I must remember it, because it was very important. I asked one of the men to write down the message. He wrote it on a piece of paper, which he gave to me. I began to come out of the dream, but as I did so realized that I could not bring the piece of paper with me, so I went back into the dream. I asked them to tell me in words that I would not forget, and they gave me the words "Pacific Rim".

Afterwards, whenever I read about investment in the emerging economies of Australasia and came across the words "Pacific Rim" I would shudder. But the memory eventually passed from my consciousness and the words ceased to have the same connotations.

On that Sunday afternoon, when I saw the low stone building, I remembered the dream and connected disparate fragments of my life. East Timor was in the Pacific Rim. The people who had been fighting for freedom had lived in the mountains, in dense jungle. Was it possible that in my dream I had promised those men to bring out the message about their struggle? It seemed fanciful, vain even, to consider it, and yet it was a compelling explanation. Was the dream, vivid as it had been, nothing more than a coincidence? Could Julian have been right when she said that nothing happened by chance?

My equilibrium had been disturbed. I put Blue, my beautiful blue-black Labrador-collie cross, on his lead, and we went for a walk. The air was cold and crisp. The ground was hard and unyielding and a light dusting of frost sparkled on the leaves. As I walked, I realized that it was time to take stock of my life.

I began to feel that somewhere along the way I had missed something important. Sometimes, in investigating a story, one might overlook a vital clue; then the whole picture would fail to come together. Only when one backtracked and double-checked every step would one find the missing piece of the jigsaw, make that important phone call or read that one particular report and be able to piece together the whole story. I felt that way about my life. Somewhere I had failed to connect and, without noticing, wandered onto the wrong path.

I let Blue off the lead and watched him career away into the distance, relishing his freedom. I walked on through the wood, and Blue soon returned and padded softly alongside me, making sporadic dashes to investigate anything that took his fancy and then running back to my side. As we walked, Julian's words came into my mind: "He did not say, 'You shall not be tempest-tossed, you shall not be work-weary, you shall not be discomforted.' But he said, 'You shall not be overcome.'"

Suddenly, my neglect of Anna's journal seemed lazy and selfish. Doing something constructive with it had been too much trouble, too difficult. But, I reflected, what is a journalist, after all, but someone who brings messages from places that are difficult to reach to places that are hard to find?

Could I really trust Julian and believe her message? I certainly had no confidence to engage with theology. It would have been a nonsense. Besides, many far better-qualified people had already produced wonderful books that analysed and communicated Julian's message. But the story had come my way and I had promised Ismene and myself to try to do something with it. I wished there were something I could do. Most of all, I wished I could believe Julian's assertion – whether spoken by her or imagined by Anna – "You are beloved through all eternity and held safe in an embrace that will never let you go."

As I lifted the latch on my front gate, the overcast sky was turning to rain. Blue and I hurried up the path to the warmth and sanctuary of our home. As I turned the key in the lock, I heard the telephone ringing. I picked up the receiver in the hallway and heard the low, soft tones of Ismene Vale. The line was crackling. I knew she had gone to Peru.

"Hello, Joanna. I'm calling from Lima. This line's bad. Can you hear me?"

"I can! How are you? It's wonderful to hear from you."

"I'm very well. How are you?"

"Very well," I replied. It was not true. I had been feeling unwell for several months. In recent weeks everything had begun to feel too much of an effort. I felt as though I were carrying a weight of tiredness accumulated over years.

"I have some intriguing news," said Ismene. "I've had a call from Charles Clemence – Frieda Bonhart's nephew, you remember? Frieda, sadly, died two weeks ago – though perhaps I should not say sadly, because she is now free of her burden, free to be all she really is… The news that will interest you is that Charles has found a note from Frieda about Anna's journal in a trunk in her attic.

"The note is addressed to Charles. It asks him to return the original journal to Anna, should she ever ask for it, or, in the event of Frieda's death, to give it to me. But unfortunately Charles can't find the original journal. Then he remembered that a friend of mine had contacted him several years ago, asking about Anna, and that you'd mentioned that you and I both had copies of the journal.

"Anyway, it seems as though Frieda wrote the note when she was becoming ill. Charles also found a number of old, unopened letters. Now this is where it becomes fascinating. One was from someone who signed herself 'Annabel Leigh', asking for the return of the manuscript."

"No! How amazing," I said.

"It had been posted some eighteen months after Frieda was given the journal, which does seem strange. I think that even then Frieda's Alzheimer's must have been causing short-term memory loss because the letter went unopened.

"Charles has written back, and is now awaiting a reply. I'm going to be away for several more weeks, so I explained your interest to Charles. I hope you don't mind. He asked me to give you his number and said he would be very happy to meet you."

"This is absolutely extraordinary. I'd love to meet him," I said. "I expect he'll want both our copies. Shall I collect yours from your house and give it to him?"

"Would you? That would be most kind," said Ismene.

The following morning I rang Charles Clemence. We talked about my attempts to trace Anna – or should it have been Annabel? He expressed great interest and promised to ring me the moment he had any news.

That evening I took up my copy of *Enfolded in Love* and read part of Jesus' message to Julian: "I am the ground of your praying. First, it is my will that you should have this; then I make it your will, too; then I make you ask for it, and you do so. How then should you not have what you pray for?"

It was two weeks before I spoke to Charles Clemence again. He called from Gatwick Airport, where he was about to board a plane to Frankfurt. He spoke for only a few moments, to tell me his secretary had just left a message on his mobile phone, saying that a reply to his letter to Annabel Leigh had arrived. He invited me to lunch in two days' time, when he would be visiting Basingstoke, about an hour's drive from my home. Then we would read the letter together. I readily accepted.

On a bright February day I sat and waited in the little country restaurant where we had arranged to meet. The door opened and in walked a tallish man, in his mid-forties, dressed in a well-worn green corduroy jacket, a clashing blue and brown jumper and brown slacks. His appearance was enlivened by a wispy bit of his collar-length, fairish, greying hair that was sticking up from his crown, like a little antenna.

The restaurant was almost empty, and he quickly spotted me and came across. He introduced himself in a warm and friendly manner. His twinkling grey-green eyes seemed to suggest a light-hearted curiosity, and yet he had a quiet containment about him – as though, I thought, he knew a secret. I hoped that he did.

He sat down and took an envelope from his inside breast pocket, saying, "I haven't read it yet. I thought it only fair to save it up so that we could read it together. Here, you do the honours." He handed me the envelope, adding, "My secretary opened it when it arrived. I told her not to tell me anything so that we could discover the contents together."

I took the envelope with great excitement. Inside was a letter, another, sealed envelope and a business card. I unfolded the letter. It was from an address in Bath and signed by a Mrs Irene Bridger. I read the letter aloud: "Dear Mr Clemence, I am returning your letter to Miss Lee, which was forwarded to me by William Grasmere & Co, the local agent that manages Myrtle Cottage, of which I am the owner.

"'I am very sorry to be the bearer of bad news, but I am afraid Miss Lee died some years ago. If your business is of a personal nature, I do hope this does not come as too great a shock. She is buried in the local churchyard, at Cley.

"'Mr John Grasmere has offered to give you every assistance, should you wish to visit Miss Lee's grave, and asked me to send you his business card. I am sorry I am unable to be of more help and wish you well, Yours, Irene Bridger (Mrs)."

I stared at the letter. I felt immensely disappointed and cheated.

Charles Clemence said, "I'm sorry. This must be a big disappointment."

"Well, I think I never seriously expected to track Anna – or Annabel – down. I feel so sad for her. So things never did work out."

Charles looked at me with curiosity and compassion. He said, "Well, perhaps they did. We can't really know, can we? Let me cheer you up while I give you lunch."

Charles' considerate, attentive manner did cheer me a little. He was clearly generously determined to try to make up for the disappointment. He asked about my life and my work, and told me how much he was enjoying running his aunt's business.

"When I took over I'd never actually run anything before, so I'm very reliant upon my colleagues who've been there years. There's a bit of an antiquated way of doing things, but by and large it seems to work."

"What were you doing before?"

"Writing. I've written some books on the environment. I'm an anthropologist by training, and I've gradually moved from people to places. Ismene's early influence on my life."

"Oh, what a fool I am! C.W. Clemence – is that you?"

Charles lowered his eyes, smiled bashfully and nodded. C.W. Clemence was a very distinguished author. He might even have won major prizes. I felt embarrassed by my failure to make the connection.

"I'm so sorry," I said.

"No need to be. I much prefer it when I'm taken for what I am."

As I reflected momentarily on the logicality or otherwise of that statement, Charles was telling me that he had extended the range of Bonhart's to include spiritual and esoteric writing, in which he had a great interest.

His boyish, rather bumbling manner fell away when he talked about something that captured his imagination. Looking at him more closely, I took in a square, longish face with a strong chin. His nose was straight, with a surprising slightly upturned tip. His wide-set eyes, glinting with enthusiasm for his subject, crinkled at the edges, as though well accustomed to laughter. He had kind eyes, and his smile hovered about the corners of his lips, as though reluctant to leave.

Charles' directness and high intelligence were wrapped in a persona that was almost other-worldly in its abstractedness. His clothes gave the impression that he really did not care what people thought. His air of detachment, as though slightly surprised to have been deposited unexpectedly where he found himself, was at odds with his lively talkativeness when enthusing about a subject. In those moments, as he gestured expansively, the oversized pepper mill looked to be in peril.

He said, "I'm fascinated by other people's enthusiasms. People achieve such extraordinary things when they put their heart and soul into something they love."

He still had not located Annabel's original journal. However, he had found a translation of Julian's book and a copy of *Enfolded in Love*, which he had been reading.

He said, "It's inspiring, isn't it?"

I took from my bag the two copies of Annabel's journal and handed them to him, saying, "You must have these."

"I'd like you to tell me about the journal. Would you? Ismene has whetted my appetite." When I had described the contents of the journal, he said, "I can see why you and Ismene got caught up in Annabel's story. You know, I think there could well be a market for a book about Julian's relevance for us today; something that would touch people who have no interest in theology or even religion. Joanna, would you keep your copy and think about it again in that light?" I said that I wasn't really sure what kind of form such a book would take but that I would be glad to give it some thought.

We passed a pleasant couple of hours together. Charles was easy to be with and his sense of humour infectious.

"I do enjoy the ridiculous," he said, telling me a very silly story, chuckling with amusement and then laughing long and heartily. I suspected that his habit of making a joke of things covered an innate shyness. It had been a very long time since I had laughed so much. Charles was good fun in an eccentric sort of way and really, I thought, rather endearing.

Charles told me about his aunt. "It was very sad when she became ill. Frieda was such an independent woman – a free thinker.

You know, she started Bonhart's from nothing. My grandfather thought it was a mad idea and wouldn't give her a bean, but Frieda took no notice. Nothing daunted her. Such an attractive characteristic, don't you think?

"You know, she was the kindest person in the world, would do anything for anybody – but let someone try to be super-clever and pull a fast one, and they'd have the rug pulled out from under them so fast they wouldn't know what had hit them. And she wouldn't care who it was – it could be the Prime Minister. When she was in crusading vein she'd say, 'Right is right, and wrong is no man's right!' This will sound silly, but whenever I see the statue on the top of the Old Bailey, with the scales of justice in one hand and the sword of truth in the other – I think of dear Frieda."

Charles looked sad for a moment. I was about to speak, when he said, with an air of cheerfulness, "Her old cat's still around. It must be at least eighteen. It's used to being in the office and I'll swear it's still under her influence. It's a funny thing, you know, but whenever I'm about to do something incautious and possibly unwise, it clambers onto my desk and gives me what Frieda used to call an old-fashioned look."

"I'm sorry. It's a terrible thing to lose someone you love."

Charles, his voice a little throaty, replied, "But you know, love never goes. I still feel Frieda about me; I sense her presence. You know, death really does have no dominion."

"Ah, if a Welsh boy said it, it must be true!"

"Are you Welsh?"

"Oh, yes, very much so. Can't you hear the accent?"

"There's a faint trace there, but you sound pretty standard English to me."

"I'm travelling on false papers. But I don't sound so English when I get worked up about something!"

"Well," said Charles, "I shall have to wait and see. I shall mind my Ps and Qs so as not to annoy you."

I said I planned to visit London soon and suggested that I call into his office then, to discuss my thoughts about ways in which the journal might be developed.

Charles said enthusiastically, "Splendid. I shall look forward to it."

Despite my promise to Charles, I allowed the days to slip by without calling in at his office. The disappointment over Anna had brought everything to a head. I was worn out, exhausted by years of pushing myself, of dedicating every waking hour to my work and seeing time spent in contemplation or relaxation as time lost. I longed for peace. As I was thinking these thoughts, the letterbox flipped open with the arrival of the post. There on the mat was an envelope addressed to me in Sister Eleanor's handwriting. I took from the envelope a folded card. On the front was a beautiful watercolour picture of an angel, who sat, with wings outspread and a golden circle around her head, playing a lute.

Inside the card the Sister had written, in beautiful script, a quotation from Julian's book: "A mother may sometimes let her child fall and suffer in various ways, so that it may learn by its mistakes. But she will never allow any real harm to come to the child because of her love. And though earthly mothers may not be able to prevent their children from dying, our Heavenly Mother Jesus will never let us, his children, see death. For he is all might, all wisdom, and all love…

"When we fall he holds us lovingly, and graciously and swiftly raises us. In all this work he takes the part of a kind nurse who has no other care but the welfare of her child. It is his responsibility to save us, it is his glory to do it, and it is his will we should know it. Utterly at home, he lives in us for ever."

It had been such a long time since I had visited St Etheldreda's. Suddenly I thought how much I would like to see Sister Eleanor. I would take a few days off and visit the convent, where I could be sure of peace and rest.

As I packed my bag, as an afterthought I slipped in the journal. The following Friday my taxi pulled up outside the convent's gate. Soon I was in the little parlour, being served tea in a pretty china cup on a tray covered by a white, starched cloth. As I sipped my tea, the door opened and Sister Eleanor came towards me, arms outstretched. She looked hardly any older than when we had last met. "Joanna. It's lovely to see you again. We've missed you," she said.

After I had put my bag in my room, I accompanied the Sister to the garden. Together we walked along a path that led to a barn, and beyond it to a secluded area with a wall to one side.

"In the summer we grow such lovely flowers, as you know," said Sister Eleanor. "But there's not much to see at this time of year. Just some poor little snowdrops and winter jasmine." Patches of delicate yellow jasmine were splashed along the wall. "But I like to walk in the garden in this season. It always fills me with wonder to reflect on how life begins in the dark soil, when everything looks so unpromising; how from nothing comes everything."

Eleanor led me along another path and into the vegetable garden. "We have cabbages, Brussels sprouts, parsnips, leeks at the moment – lots of good, warming vegetables to keep out the cold." We walked along the edge of the garden, where it met the marshes. In the distance, along the horizon, the dark clouds of birds were wheeling in to find sanctuary. We watched them together, in silence.

I asked, "Do you believe that each of us must come to a personal Calvary?"

"There comes a point when the worldly self must be sacrificed upon the cross," said Sister Eleanor. "We spend a long time in the Garden of Gesthemane before resolving to take the road to Calvary. But yes, Calvary awaits, and beyond it lie peace and freedom."

"I've been troubled by doubts and questions for a very long time. There's something I'd like to show you. A journal. Not written by me, but by a woman who has died."

"Is it something you would like me to read and discuss with you?"

"Would you?"

"Of course, if it will help. I shall be going to prayers in a little while. Why don't you leave the journal in my studio, so that I can collect it later?" After a few more minutes, Sister Eleanor said, "It's becoming a little cold." As we returned indoors, she said, "Shall we see one another tomorrow, after you have rested?" She invited me to join her for afternoon tea. That night I was able to let go of my habitual tension and slept soundly.

29

The following morning I awoke feeling greatly refreshed. I had been thinking about visiting Annabel's grave and had brought with me John Grasmere's business card. His office was at Sheringham, some forty-five minutes' drive to the east along the coast.

Was this another of Julian's not-really coincidences? Chance had brought me to Brancaster; should I follow through? Did I feel up to the visit? Would it make me feel better? I was so unsure of my emotional condition that I did not want to risk doing anything that would make me more sad. But, as I savoured my filling, nourishing breakfast of porridge and fruit, I began to feel stronger and almost bold. Curiosity began to overtake me. I would go. I would finish my pursuit of Annabel, pay my respects and put the affair to rest.

I telephoned John Grasmere and arranged an appointment for eleven o'clock. I took a taxi eastwards along the coastal road, passing through one pretty village after another, my eyes drawn continually to the vast expanse of calm, rippled sea that spread to the horizon.

I was at Sheringham in good time and John Grasmere was waiting for me. He greeted me solicitously, clearly unsure of my relationship with Annabel. I felt disinclined to explain. As we talked, he shook his head sorrowfully, as though in disbelief at life's cruelties. He offered to take me to Annabel's grave in the churchyard at Cley, a coastal village several minutes' drive to the east. I thanked him and said I would prefer to go alone.

The church at Cley was tucked away on the outskirts of the village. Here, at last, I would say my goodbye to the woman whose life story had puzzled me for so long. There should have been relief, but there was only sadness. The crunch of my footsteps on the gravel path leading to the graveyard sounded intrusively loud and I was glad to step onto the grass.

I made my way round the central holly tree, past the great oak, taking the track that wound round to the left, as I had been directed by John Grasmere. Birds sang plaintively in the tall trees, as though respectful of the dead who occupied that sad and lonely place. I continued towards the low, moss-covered wall that flanked the row of headstones to my left. And there, past the wall and beneath a great Scottish fir, stood the small, plain headstone of Annabel's grave.

I approached quietly, feeling an empty ache in the pit of my stomach. I stepped closer to read the inscription – "In loving memory of Annabel Lee, died 1986, aged thirty-eight years. Out of the darkness and into the light." Poor Annabel had been dead fourteen years! She had been dead five years when I first started looking for her. I felt sad, compassionate, angry and cheated, all in one muddled emotion. I felt as though I had been looking all along for a ghost. How was it that she had seemed so real, so flesh-and-blood, so alive? I felt a deep sense of loss, mingled with pity, for this woman, who felt like a friend, whom I had never met.

She had died young, no more than a few years after her meeting with Frieda Bonhart and those sad, last entries in her journal. No name of anyone who would miss her was on her headstone. No flowers were on her grave. She had been forgotten by the world. Here she had come to the end of her journey and here my quest for Anna – Annabel – ended. At the edge of her grave was a patch of snow-drops, their delicate white bells trembling gently in the keen, light wind. I shivered. It had become cold. It was time to leave.

At the appointed time of three o'clock I returned to Sister Eleanor's studio. Once again, we settled ourselves comfortably in the old wicker chairs by the window. As she poured the tea, the Sister asked, "Did you sleep well?"

"Better than I have in months, thank you, Sister."

"I'm so glad that you decided to visit us again. I hope this is a place where you find sanctuary."

"It is. But it's also a place where I find I ask myself lots of questions…"

"About a personal Calvary?" Sister Eleanor handed me my teacup and offered biscuits. With the kindest expression of loving concern, she said, "We need to come to Calvary so that we may reach a depth of understanding. We become whole through our existence in the body, experiencing the joy and pain of life and learning through our relationships."

"It sounds as though we're meant to suffer…"

"No. But we all do. Don't you agree that most of us only learn the hard way? Julian says we were made to be happy, that we were made for love. We are given a means of living in peace and love, whatever the world may throw at us, through the practice of contemplative prayer."

"Meditation?"

"Yes, it's the same process. Through contemplative prayer Christ carries out his redemptive work, which is to reconcile our outward, everyday consciousness – our thoughts, impressions, desires and emotions – with the inward depths, the part that is already at one with God in peace and love.

"Through the power of Christ, we're saved from the futility of trying to fabricate meaning and a sense of self out of the world of everyday experiential consciousness. And this is salvation: a state where our outward selves live in harmony with the inward depths, in divine union, peace and freedom. The primary meaning of the Greek word for salvation is wholeness."

"But the world is still a painful place to live…"

"It is. Julian understood that very well. But, once we have found that place of unity, when the time of great suffering comes, our personal Calvary, as it eventually does for all of us, we can accept it and live with it. We are enabled to do so because we know that our acceptance brings healing into our world, our time, our space. Julian explains that God makes us the great gift of allowing us to share in the re-creation of the world through love."

"Do you mean that when someone raises his own consciousness, he raises the consciousness of the world?" I repeated Ismene's assertion.

"Exactly so."

"I'm still not sure I understand why God allows bad things to happen."

"This question is at the heart of Julian's book. She was told by Jesus that she must trust God's word that, despite everything, all shall be well."

"From what you're saying, it seems we have to simply trust that one day it will all make sense…"

"Contemplative prayer gives us the means by which we are able to trust. We find a place, another consciousness, where we are nourished. We are given grace, and by grace comes faith. It cannot be done by intellectual endeavour. This is the work of the heart," said Sister Eleanor.

"Then the writer of the journal – you've read it?" Sister Eleanor nodded. "She could have found the redemption and release she wanted so desperately?"

"If she had called upon God to bring her safely through, yes."

"She didn't, though. I don't believe it's likely." I told Sister Eleanor the whole story: how I had come across the book, become intrigued by Annabel and fascinated by Julian, tried to trace Annabel and finally, by means of the letter, visited her grave.

"I wanted so much to believe that it happened for her, that she found meaning," I said. "Now I'll never know the truth."

"How can we discern the truth of any situation?"

"By knowing the facts – and we don't."

Sister Eleanor shook her head gently. "Facts alone are not enough. They have to be interpreted. And only through God's grace can we interpret them truly, for only God has the whole picture, only God sees into our hearts. That's why we're told not to judge one another. The imagination can bring us closer to God, to see through his eyes, to see what is real. The imagination is the instrument of the soul. So, shall we use our imagination to try to touch upon the truth? Shall we try to make sense of Annabel's situation? How exactly does she finish?"

She handed me the journal. I turned to the end of the narrative and said, "Well, she says she has reached the conclusion that she's on the trail of the Holy Grail, and that the Grail is the cup that gives everlasting life, and the search for the cup of Christ is the search for the divine in each of us."

I read "'But the wine in the cup has a bitter taste. In Gesthemane, Jesus asked if it might pass from him. He knew, as I am beginning to understand, that those who drink from the cup must undergo a crucifixion. And beyond that, I trust, the other side of vulnerability and exposure, lie redemption and release.' And there she stops. It's so frustrating. My feeling is that if she'd got her life back together she would have finished her story. She would have written her play. The abrupt ending seems to suggest that things went badly wrong for her and she went under."

Sister Eleanor said, "It looks very much that way, doesn't it? But let me offer you an alternative possibility. Let us suppose that when Annabel left the journal with Miss Bonhart all those years ago she was at a very low ebb, as the evidence seems to suggest. Perhaps she went to the Winchester literary festival in an attempt to hold on to what felt like the remnants of normal life, to assure herself that there was still a world to which she belonged.

"She might, in search of succour and solace, have visited the cathedral, as she did in Norwich. Perhaps she might have heard the choir rehearsing for evensong. They might have been singing a familiar hymn, with words that touched Annabel – such as, perhaps, 'Oh love that will not let me go'. Do you know the hymn?"

"Yes, I do…"

"Let us imagine that as Annabel sat listening to those wonderful voices, singing with such purity of expression, she may have felt she could not bear to go back to the life she had lived. Her search for something she needed desperately but could not find may have become too much for her. Perhaps she felt she must assuage her desperate inner hunger and loneliness, either fill that empty space inside or obliterate everything. Perhaps she had come closer to the edge than she realized. That is easy to do."

"Yes."

"Let us imagine Anna walking out of the cathedral and finding her way to some peaceful place, perhaps the city's water meadows. She may have walked along the bank of the stream for several minutes, not really quite sure why she was there. Then, can you imagine that she may have gone right to the water's edge?

"She may have looked at her reflection in the water, and wondered if there was any point in going on. It was late afternoon, and becoming dark. The water looked cool and inviting. She thought: *It would be so easy to simply stop, to put an end to it all, to quietly slip away.*

"Suddenly she hears again the beautiful singing of the cathedral choir… 'Oh joy that seekest me through pain, I cannot close my heart to thee, I trace the rainbow through the rain, and feel the promise is not vain that morn shall tearless be…' She realizes suddenly that in the crucifixion love and grief co-existed, and hope was born out of suffering and apparent failure. It was possible."

I said, "Sister, how can you be so sure… you're not imagining this, are you? You know the story… You met Annabel. It's true, isn't it?"

"Yes, I knew her. I knew her well." The Sister leaned forward, put her hand over mine and pressed it gently, saying, "I am Annabel."

I was stunned. How was it possible? Sister Eleanor was Annabel?

"But you can't be. You can't possibly be. I've seen her grave!"

"I'm sorry to give you such a shock."

"But – what happened to you, after Winchester? This isn't possible. How can you be Annabel?"

"The only answer to that is, by God's grace! I can't tell you how much it meant to me to see my journal again. Let me tell you the rest of my story. But first, I think you need another cup of tea!"

While I tried to take in Sister Eleanor's astonishing revelation and make sense of it, she poured me more tea and handed me the cup.

"I am sorry. This is a dreadful shock for you," she said.

"But – I saw your grave!"

"The grave is that of a dear friend who borrowed my false identity. Let me start at the beginning. I shall tell you everything. Are you all right? Would you like some air?"

"No. No, please. I want to hear your story."

"Very well. While I was in Winchester, I saw, in the festival programme, that Freida Bonhart was to give a talk on how to get a book published. I decided to go. I'd been thinking I might do more research on Julian and write a novel, rather than a play. When I arrived back from the water meadows it was almost time for the talk, so I went straight there. I had the journal in my bag.

"After the talk, on an impulse, I asked Miss Bonhart if she would read my manuscript and give her opinion. I hadn't put my name on it because really, at that point, I hadn't intended showing it to anyone. As you'll have observed, it's more a personal journal than anything else. I'd thought of it as the basis for a piece of work, nothing more. If I'd been thinking straight I would not have had the temerity to foist something so raw and incomplete on poor Freida Bonhart.

"When I walked up to her, I realized that I ought to introduce myself and the name Annabel Lee came into my mind. In the hubbub, she must have heard it as Anna. I seemed to remember that the poem was about obsessive love and a girl who drowned. I was feeling confused and uncertain. I don't know why I didn't simply give my real name. I think I felt I had no identity, and so my name had no relevance. It's Eleanor Thornton, by the way; that's my old, worldly name, at any rate. There was some thought in my head about finding a new identity. I really wasn't thinking clearly.

"That night I had a very strange dream. I was in a vast library somewhere, and someone was showing me rows and rows of books. This person was guiding me, it seemed. He or she took me along row after row, and all I can remember the person saying was, 'Can you find the one you are looking for?' Then my guide said, 'Don't forget, this library is open all the time; you can come here whenever you wish, night or day.' I didn't understand the meaning of the dream, but it left me feeling calm and peaceful." I was startled, remembering my almost identical dream.

"The following morning I went to the cathedral again. I sat there for quite a long time. When I looked at my watch I saw that it was midday. I hurried to Frieda Bonhart's hotel, with the intention of retrieving the manuscript, or, if she felt inclined to read something so raw, to at least give her my name and address. But they said she had already checked out and returned to London.

"As I drove back to London, I realized that I would not be able to tackle a new play or anything else. I became aware that I was losing my grip on all the things that were familiar to me. I didn't feel able to concentrate on anything.

"What was I to do with the rest of my life? Could I continue to try to make a career as a playwright? Should I return to teaching? I had done very little work for several months and was running out of money. I felt I had achieved nothing with my life. There had been times when I had felt I was making a worthwhile contribution: when I was teaching, and when I saw one of my plays performed and watched the audience – it happened once or twice – motionless and silent, engrossed in the action on stage. But all that had gone.

"My change of heart in the water meadows at Winchester had saved my life. I had been given hope. But though I never forgot that there was hope, I had not yet completed my journey to Calvary. In my dream about Julian she had spoken – or I had imagined she had spoken – of hope… 'Hope always lies through and beyond despair…'"

I said, remembering the words, "'To discover hope, we must move into the darkness and risk the loss of the few remaining reference points that seem to make some sense of the bewildering landscape.' I've read the passage many times."

"I really came to understand the meaning of those words," said Sister Eleanor. "I had lost my reference points – career, success, reputation… what Julian calls 'these things that are so little, in which there is no rest'. I had let people down and was no longer considered reliable. I had always taken pride in my work and felt deeply ashamed of my failure.

"But failure is an opportunity for God to come in, to heal and to love. Only when we become vulnerable do we allow him to reach us. When people asked Jesus why he ate with publicans and sinners, he replied, 'Because I'm here to tell sinners that God loves them.' Only when we see no way forward and know we're helpless do we at last allow God to take charge.

"Some part of me knew I was about to disappear from the world and would not want to be found. And that's still true. I don't want to return to the old me. I have a new identity, in the real meaning of the words.

"You know, the odd thing was – another coincidence, if you still believe in them – the odd thing was that though I chose the name Annabel Lee on the spur of the moment, because I was feeling depressed, much later, after I had come here, I saw the connection."

"Annabel Lee, in her kingdom by the sea..."

"'... her highborn kinsmen came and bore her away from me, to shut her up in a sepulchre in this kingdom by the sea,'" Sister Eleanor continued, quoting the poem by Edgar Allan Poe. "And here I am, in a kingdom by the sea. And this is, after all, a kind of death to the world, like Julian's enclosure."

"Yes, I get it now," I said, wondering what kind of investigative journalist needed to have every last detail pointed out to her.

"Don't blame yourself," said Sister Eleanor. "You were seeing things in a different light. We all do that at times. We see the literal truth and miss the creative possibility. I could never have painted angels in my old life. I would not have been open to the possibility of what angels might look like. If I couldn't imagine them, how could I paint them?"

She looked towards her canvases. One, which hung near a window that looked out onto the garden, was of an angel with outspread wings. Eleanor had infused it with what seemed almost an internal light. The angel's expression was full of serenity, joy and love. It was a very beautiful painting and I wanted to keep looking at it.

Sister Eleanor said, "God's messengers are everywhere. Sometimes they come from heaven and sometimes from earth. What I missed was the point of the poem, that Annabel is loved. She is the beloved, as we all are. I missed that connection. But perhaps some part of me did not."

"I was never quite sure how much of your story was autobiographical – "

"Oh, all of it was."

"Frieda Bonhart couldn't find any trace of your plays."

"They were performed in some very obscure theatres! A couple were done in Ireland, one in Prague, another in Miami. There are an awful lot of playwrights out there – and an awful lot of plays! And of course, you didn't have my real name. Poor you. I'm sorry to have inadvertently put you to so much trouble," said Sister Eleanor.

"Oh, and the Welsh song! I was so amazed to find it. Why was it with the book?"

"Oh, I wrote the song for a character in a play. A woman called Jane, who was Fool to Mary Tudor. I don't speak Welsh myself. A friend translated it for me."

"It felt so strange. Because I am Welsh and Welsh was my first language."

"Well, now perhaps we know why I decided that Jane should be Welsh!"

"At the very end of your journal it seemed as though you were getting your life back to normal."

"I hoped so, but it was an illusion. I had a long way to go… The day after I attended the literary festival I became ill with a viral infection, which turned into pneumonia. Because of the weakness of my immune system – the lupus that caused my childhood problems – the infection didn't respond to antibiotics. My depression over Mark and the rest of my life had weakened me further and increased my vulnerability. I think attitude has a lot of influence over disease, particularly anything affecting the immune system. I was ill for three months and was not expected to live. Then, unexpectedly, the doctors located a new antibiotic drug. I was a beneficiary of the research into Aids. That worked and I steadily got better.

"Although my health was improving, I was left with a residue of depression and unhappiness. Having been close to death, I became acutely aware that I could easily pick up an infection that could kill me. I felt vulnerable. I went to recuperate at a cottage on the coast."

"At Cley…"

"Yes. I wrote the letter to Miss Bonhart some eighteen months after I'd met her, after I had begun to recover my strength. I wrote again but never received a reply. Several years later I learned that she had developed Alzheimer's and I decided she had probably thrown the journal away – after all, there was no name or address on it. I thought it best to let it go, with the past."

"But who is buried in the churchyard at Cley?"

"My friend Frances is buried there. Frances lived with me for several months, when she was going through the final stages of cancer. Sadly, she had fallen out with her family. There was something about Frances' life that her parents could not accept and it caused great bitterness and enmity. She wanted to spend her last months in peace.

"I had mentioned that if a letter addressed to Annabel Lee came while I was out she should keep it for me. It amused her to borrow my stolen identity. She said it was an appropriate choice. She even changed her name by deed poll, so that she could not be traced. Frances made me promise not to reveal her secret to her family if they should ever come looking for her. I thought that a mistake, but I am bound by my promise. So, now, are you, Joanna.

"But before then, living by the sea, I gained strength. I went for long walks and came to love the area. I had a little money left and my plays were earning me meagre royalties. I started painting again, for the first time in years. Painting was always my first love as a small child. I had lost it on the way.

"During my second year at the cottage, I began to work part-time as a volunteer at a home for young women in King's Lynn. Someone whose portrait I had painted arranged it. I was really only there to do a little administration, as a way of regaining my confidence. But as it turned out I received far greater blessings there.

"I was so humbled by what I saw. Young girls who had been prostituted were trying, with great courage, to piece together their broken lives. Their childhood had been stolen. They needed loving support from adults who would not exploit their vulnerability. Gradually, the girls came to trust and confide in me. Most were addicted to drugs, but determined to end their addiction. Where did they find the strength to fight for control of their lives? The home was truly a place where, just as at Calvary, hope and sorrow met.

"Once a week, a sister from St Etheldreda's would deliver vegetables to the home. She would stop for a cup of tea before her return journey and we'd talk for five or ten minutes. I found myself looking forward to those conversations. I started to go to church again.

"Over the course of that year, my conversations with the Sister who brought the vegetables made me more and more certain that I had at last come upon the way of life that was right for me. Eventually, I plucked up courage to ask for an appointment with Mother Abbess. I think it's fair to say that she combined a kind welcome with an unwavering insistence that I consider all the sacrifices and difficulties the life would entail. She was very generous. Each time we spoke, the stronger my conviction became that I wanted to dedicate the rest of my life to prayer and that this was the right place for me.

"Three years after I had moved to the cottage I came here as a postulant, a candidate. Then I became a novice, a trial member of the order. After that I had three years under simple vows before making my final vows.

"So… Annabel did find meaning," I said.

"She did, most assuredly."

"This is not the end I expected to my search for the lost lady…"

"When is anything what we expect it to be? Has it brought resolution, and acceptance?"

"In a way. Yes it has, of course. Julian has kept her promise. I still have a million questions, though – more now, perhaps."

We sat in silence for a few moments, looking out across the marshes. I said, "Julian has certainly made me see things in a different light. She gives me a sense of acceptance and welcome. She makes me feel that I'm not some supplicant with her nose pressed against the glass – which is how I've always felt about religion – but someone who's expected and wanted."

"That's exactly what you are – the beloved child coming home, if you so choose," said Sister Eleanor.

"I'm still a journalist. I still need to rationalize what I've heard, even though I know that isn't how it works. According to Julian, Jesus didn't die to pay for our sins – which is what I was taught as a child."

"That's the orthodox view, but the idea of Jesus paying a debt doesn't make sense to me. You've only got to look at what Julian says to realize that Jesus didn't die in order to appease God's anger. Julian tells us fourteen times that God has no anger within him. She tells us four times that this vitally important message was given in each of her sixteen revelations. It isn't a matter of Jesus' death enabling God to change his mind. God never needed to change his mind. His mind has always been one of inexhaustible love. It's a question of our minds being changed and us coming to him."

"But what about all the stuff about hellfire and damnation – and remission of sins…?"

"Julian says she didn't see hell in any of her visions. The atonement is a great mystery. Jesus said he gave his life as ransom for many, that his blood was given in remission of sins. But you have to accept that in the context of the time. All the references to the wrath of God in the Book of Common Prayer and the Old Testament – I can't accept any of it. It's just not possible in the light of Julian."

I said, "It's strange, isn't it, to think of her spending her life locked away from the world, and yet having such a profound and revolutionary message that she can become an abiding influence on people's lives hundreds of years later."

"Julian is the witness whose voice is never still. She is a woman for today, perhaps more than any other time. She sees how miserable and desperate so many of us are, and, for love, must communicate what she has learned. She would like to shout from the rooftops the truth that we are loved. But the devil continues to do his best to undermine those few who catch a glimpse of the truth about themselves. When he gives you a God you're frightened of, he makes his job easy."

I reflected for a few moments; then said, "We're all searching…"

"We're all searching for the Holy Grail of Selfhood and integration, but most of the time we're not aware of what we're searching for. Finding Selfhood, integration with our real selves and with God – finding the divine within ourselves – that's our purpose here. That was the gift Jesus offered us; he opened the doors of our perception and showed how we could achieve what God had planned for us. And it's something that can be achieved only through living a human life. That's why the Grail contains wine that has a bitter taste. Julian really understood how hard life can be. She said, 'This place is prison, this life is penance' – and she wasn't referring to her cell and her particular way of life. But she went on to say, 'The remedy is that our Lord is with us, protecting us and leading us into the fullness of joy.'"

I said, "I suppose it's just a question of trusting – and that's so hard, when you've been let down and always counted on yourself to get through…"

"Yes, it takes a leap of faith, and faith takes courage. You know, I always think the most convincing argument for God's love is the evidence of his work in lives changed. I have seen people transformed. They've become so different from their former selves – physically, even – you would hardly believe it was the same person." I smiled. Sister Eleanor said, "Yes! That does include me. I was changed through my experiences."

I said, "And – you've reconciled everything and found contentment? I'm sorry. I don't mean to offend you." I was wondering how the Sister had moved from a passionate love affair to apparently not needing a close relationship with a man.

As though reading my thoughts, she said, "The experience with Mark brought me to Calvary, so I thank him for being my teacher. I know that when you read my story it seemed as though the experience only detracted from me – but in reality it was the process of polishing one facet of a jewel. It brought me to a realization, for the first time, that there could be such depth of feeling. It was a necessary part of my journey. I realized quite a long time later than I no longer wanted an exclusive partnership with one person. But had I wanted such a partnership, I would have taken better care of myself, because I have learned to love myself – by learning to perceive myself as lovable.

"My experience with Mark showed me that that kind of attachment is an addiction. To get clear of an addiction takes time and distance. Something happens then – not just a fading of memories but, I believe, a physical change. I think perhaps the body stops producing the chemicals that feed the addiction.

"During my time at Cley I met someone and could easily have become involved. But I knew it was wrong for me, that he was wrong for me. I realized that – even if unconsciously – he was draining my energy. These things can be so subtle. And so I decided against it. I decided not to give him my attention. From the point where I nearly became involved to the moment when I decided not to, I could almost feel the shift of energy, the reclaiming of my own space and integrity. There were probably psychological reasons for my decision, but there were spiritual reasons, too."

"Do you never feel, if you don't mind my asking, the need of that kind of love?" I asked. I was thinking how much I still longed for Paul.

"No. Not any longer. I have no regrets. This life is not in any way an escape from failed relationships. It's about more love, not less. It's a freedom, not a constraint. It's a prize, not a consolation. It's a way of finding happiness that comes from within – which is the only place it ever comes from, in reality. It's a blissful experience, a way of getting closer to oneself, by coming into a closer knowledge of God."

I said, "You said that time and distance will heal an addiction. But if it's genuine love between two people, I've heard that love always remains…"

"Exactly so. Sometimes, when lovers part, there is a deep spiritual fracture; some connection deep inside them is broken and that's why it hurts so much." She looked at me with great tenderness and compassion. "But in love there is no separation. When someone loves you, their spirit is always close by. How could it be otherwise?"

After a few minutes' silence, I said, "I think I must learn how to pray."

"I will show you," said Sister Eleanor. "We shall pray together. Prayer is powerful. I believe it's an energy that scientists will one day learn to understand and measure. And you know, this is also something Julian says. The more one looks into Julian the more one discovers. Julian perceived her own prayer to be part of something greater and more powerful than herself, part of a great flow of energy which comes from God and can carry us back to him."

"It sounds very New Ageist…," I said.

"Many people would agree with you. Through prayer and meditation, one can become a channel for God's light and love, sending it out to the world or to individuals who need help or healing. When we channel the light, we lift all humanity. Nothing is ever wasted. One person can change the world."

"You know, I'm surprised that these ideas are accepted here," I said.

"I've been very fortunate. Mother Abbess allows me to use my prayer in the way I believe I'm meant to use it. There are other orders where it would not be permitted. With Mother Abbess's agreement, my whole life, everything I do, including my painting, is offered up as a prayer," said Sister Eleanor.

After a few more moments of reflective silence, the Sister said, "I am so very grateful to you, Joanna. When I saw my journal yesterday I could hardly believe my eyes. I've prayed a great deal about it. I always felt that my experience of searching for Julian could be of use to others. I believed that some day the right person would come across the journal and take up where I had left off; someone who would complete my story about the search for Julian and the truth of her message of God's abiding love for each one of us."

"But it's your journal, Sister, and your story. Why don't you complete it yourself?"

"Please call me Eleanor. I feel as though we're friends. It seems that you became the absent friend to whom my journal was written. No, I've completed that part of my journey. My way is now a way of prayer – that is my contribution now. My life will be lived in this quiet place. But Julian's message of love needs to be told out in the marketplace, by someone who lives in the everyday world."

I did not know how to tell Eleanor that I was sure I was not the right person for the job. I said, "I wish I could bring you your original journal, but it can't be found."

"It's not important. Who knows what may have become of it? Perhaps it still has work to do and when its time comes it will emerge. Someone will take it from a shelf full of books and begin her – or his – journey. One day, perhaps, the book that began it all, so many journeys, yours and mine, and who knows how many until now and in the years to come – Julian's great book – will come to light in just the same way.

"Thanks to you, Joanna, God has answered my prayers wonderfully. Loose ends hamper the contemplative life. I wanted to see my journal again, so that I could finally close that chapter of my life, but there seemed no possibility of it ever happening. And yet, you have come here and put it into my hands. That is a small miracle – an everyday miracle, performed by the God of the Wayside." Eleanor took my hand and said quietly, "Thank you".

I looked out of the window, across the garden and at the marshes beyond. Eleanor said, "I love the view from here. There's something about the East Anglian light; it has a particular quality. When I sit here, looking out across the land and sky, I feel I'm in the right place at the right time. From here, you do see the world in a different light."

We sat together quietly for a few minutes; then Eleanor said, "The world is looking for love today perhaps more than ever before. I feel as though the planet is moving away from the old dominating energy, personified for some by an angry God, towards an awakening to his Motherhood and to the Christ light and life that manifested through Jesus – the traditional character of the Second Person of the Trinity, of wisdom and the Divine Feminine. That, perhaps, is the lady who has been lost for so many years and who is about to be found. This is Julian's time, because now the world is ready for her message."

After a few more moments of quiet reflection, Eleanor turned to me and asked, softly, "And what about you, Joanna? Have you found answers to your questions?"

"I'm not sure. Sometimes I think I'm meant to have only questions."

We were both silent for a few more minutes; then Eleanor said, "What is it that you're looking for?"

"Meaning, I suppose. You've given me a lot to think about."

"And to feel about?" she asked softly.

Eleanor rose and came towards me. Bending down, she put her hand gently upon my arm. "Dear Joanna," she said. "You have travelled so far and carried such a heavy burden. Let it go now."

Suddenly the tears came flooding from me. I found myself sobbing like a child. Eleanor knelt down and gently took me in her arms and rocked me like a baby. We remained like that for several minutes, while the pain and anguish continued to pour out of me, in tears and in words, as Eleanor soothed me.

"I feel so alone. There seems to be no one and nothing I can turn to. I don't know what the future holds. I feel as if I've just been abandoned, just been left here to struggle through as best I can. But whatever I do, however hard I try, nothing comes right and one year goes by after another and I never achieve anything worthwhile, I never have any certainty in my life, I'm always on the edge of a precipice, I'm always running hard, trying to catch up with what I should do and who I should be and where I should be. I've never not tried. I want to belong somewhere, I want to know that what I can do is of use to someone, that there was some point in my coming to this planet. What I see and feel is pain and uncertainty and despair. I feel as though I'm trembling inside, all the time, and trying to get a grip on things and force some sense and meaning into my life. I want to know that my work is of value, that I am of value. I want to be happy. I want to be loved. And I am so, so tired…" I sat back in my chair and Eleanor gently released me from her embrace.

"What can I do? How can I change?" I asked.

"Love is his meaning. Love yourself. Dear Joanna, you are overwhelmed and exhausted. You have struggled alone for so many years, relying on yourself, trying always to do the right thing. God has let you come to a point where you simply cannot cope any longer, so that, at last, you will turn to him." She smiled. "Only when God finally prises our hands off the driving wheel can he get into the driving seat and steer us in the right direction!

"You know, Joanna, Julian's challenge is still waiting to be answered, by each of us: Do you believe that you are beloved through all eternity? When you believe that you are so loved, and put your trust in God, that is when your path will open up before you. All other roads lead nowhere. But first, you must let go. You must stop fretting and worrying, because while you do so you remain in charge and cannot find your direction. Let go. Then there will come a pause and in that pause something will move. You may find that different work awaits you. But if you continue with the wonderful work you do, how much better it will be if you do it not from anger and fear, but from love."

I said, "I need to make some kind of sense of Paul's death. If I can do that, then perhaps I can move forward."

"Dear Joanna, go to that quiet place within yourself and you will find the answers there."

The next few days passed peacefully. I spent my time walking in the garden, thinking and setting time aside for the quiet contemplation that Eleanor had recommended. By the time I was due to leave for home I felt a great deal more at peace. I felt I was drawing into my life something substantial that would comfort and sustain me.

I telephoned for a taxi to collect me at two o'clock. My last half-hour was spent with Eleanor in the garden. We sat together, looking out across the marshes.

"You have brought me such a great gift, Joanna," she said. "Because of you, my prayer life will now be fuller. My calling will be enriched, my contribution greater than it might have been had I not met you. And your work, out in the world, will also be blessed. Take Julian with you. Tell people about her. I believe that's why she brought us together. She would like her message to be heard in the hustle and bustle of people's troubled lives. She is saying to each of us, 'You are beloved for all eternity. Believe it, for it is true. Accept this gift and place it in your heart and be at peace.'"

A few moments before my taxi was due to arrive we walked round to the front of the house. As we turned the corner, I heard the car's engine and saw it draw up at the gate. Eleanor walked with me towards it. I suddenly remembered something I had meant to ask her. "When you said you heard the hymn, while you were in the water meadows at Winchester, did you mean that you actually heard it, or imagined it?"

"Something between the two, I suppose. I heard it, if you can understand, with my inner ear. Yes, I heard it," said Eleanor.

"I think I understand."

"I'm probably not explaining it very well. Perhaps you'll experience something like it one day."

I thought of the bird that sang in my garden after Paul had died. I said, "I think perhaps I already have."

Eleanor looked at me and smiled gently, as one might smile at a much-loved child. "God bless you," she said. She took me in her arms and kissed me on the cheek and then, from her deep pocket, took out my copy of her journal and placed it in my hands.

I said, "I'm thinking of writing something about Julian. I've had a few ideas. I promise to do the best I can for her."

"I know you will." As I was about to get into the taxi, she said, "Wherever life takes you, Joanna, never forget that you have a friend here, in this quiet place…" She smiled. "A friend who was lost, but now is found."

As the taxi pulled out through the gate and into the road, I turned to see Eleanor raise her hand in a gesture of farewell.

30

At home once more, I needed time to reflect upon my meeting with Eleanor. It felt like a completion, but also a beginning.

It suddenly seemed extraordinary that I had never been to look at the three copies of Julian's book in the British Library. I determined to go as soon as possible and put a date in my diary for the following Wednesday. I rang the library, to arrange to view the manuscripts held there – the short text and two of the three long texts.

I travelled by train from Hampshire to Waterloo station, and then by underground across London, to King's Cross station. I walked the short distance along the Euston Road towards the British Library. There, among millions of books, the three copies of Julian's book awaited me. I felt excited at the prospect of handling the books that had brought Julian's message safely through the centuries.

In the manuscript reading room, I selected a desk at which to work, gave its number to the librarian and waited. After a few minutes the three books were brought to me. For several minutes I could do no more than look at them. I hardly dared to touch them. I thought: *I am looking at some of the most precious things in the world.*

Is there another book in some library, hidden, forgotten, tucked away on a dusty shelf, kept safe for another time? Is it perhaps a book written in Julian's own hand? Is it another, later version, with even more profound insights, the fruits of further years of contemplation by Julian? If so, it surely must resonate with a power that will draw someone to it, some seeker after wisdom, as Serenus Cressy was drawn to the manuscript in the library in Paris more than three hundred years ago.

If the book exists, I hope there is someone, perhaps someone a little restless, whose life has left unsatisfied some quiet desire, who pauses on a cold winter night to look across the land into the unfathomable distance, searching for a particular star. I hope that he or she is already engaged in the quest for something hidden that will bring meaning.

I reflected again on the way in which precious things can be protected by being surrounded by ordinariness. To many people, Jesus was just another young man who would pass unnoticed in a crowd. Others, like the woman who touched the edge of his robe in order to be healed, knew him for what he was. Eleanor's childhood image of the hidden primroses came into my mind.

The short text was in an anthology of late medieval religious writings – MSS Add. 37790, from the Amherst collection. It was copied in the mid-fifteenth century from an original dated 1413, which says that at that time Julian was still alive. It contained many partially illuminated capitals.

I handled the two long texts – the Sloane MS2499 and MS3705 – both dating from the seventeenth century, both copied in ink on parchment, simply, with no embellishments of gold leaf or colour.

It was the MS3705 that particularly touched me. It is copied in two hands, one neat, artistic and feminine; the other large, masculine, plainer, less careful, more daring. In the sweet, feminine hand there was the most wonderful sense of reverence, of such love. The scribe honoured and treasured the work that she or he copied. If you can read a personality in a hand, then I encountered a beautiful soul in this. There was something so diligent and quiet and true in the careful copying of, perhaps, Julian's original work.

As the word "diligent" came into my mind, I was reminded of the homely figure in the line drawing on the cover of *Enfolded in Love*, and the way in which Julian writes of the mother's hands being diligent about her child. The words describe so well the way in which one's hands are always busy about a small child – wiping a nose, handing a toy, caressing – with a ceaseless, watchful readiness that anticipates the child's needs. How reassuring that constant, loving touching must be to the child who receives it.

I wondered, were these pages that I was turning, so carefully, for fear of damaging them, turned by someone whose fingers touched Julian's original work? There was a quality about the book that inspired reflection and deep respect. But then, how could one write such words, such wonderful words, without resonating to their meaning?

"I desired often times to know what was our Lord's meaning," writes the copyist scribe. "More than fifteen years later I was answered in spiritual understanding, saying this: Do you want to understand your Lord's meaning in this thing? Understand it well. Love was his meaning. Who showed it to you? Love. What did he show you? Love. Why did he show it? For Love. Keep yourself in that love and you shall understand and know more of the same. But of this you will never know or understand anything else. In this way I was taught that Love was our Lord's meaning.

"And I saw with certainty in this and in all the showings that before God created us, he loved us, and this love was never diminished and never shall be. And in this love he has done all his work; and in this love he has made everything beneficial to us; and in this love our life is everlasting.

"In our creation we had a beginning but all the love in which he created us was in him from without beginning, and in this love we had our beginning. And all this we shall see in God without end, which may Jesus grant us. Amen."

I sat for some time with the books, just enjoying being in their presence and having them briefly in my care. Then I suddenly wondered if, in this library that contained so many millions of books, there might be a copy of the little book that Eleanor had mentioned from her childhood – if, indeed, the book had existed at all – *The Isle of Wirrawoo*.

I asked the readers' adviser, who looked it up in the catalogue and said, "Yes, we have it. Do you want to order it?" I did. Twenty minutes later the book was handed to me. On the flyleaf I read "*The Isle of Wirrawoo*, an Australian fairy tale, by A. L. Purse, published by Oxford University Press in 1923".

It was, indeed, the story of a little girl who was lost on an island. Her island was, like East Timor, off the northern coast of Australia. The book was full of quirky poems and I found Eleanor's reference to "the beetle in the big gum tree". I read:

> *There's an island that I know of*
> *Where there are no aches or pains;*
> *Where it's always hot in summer*
> *And it's winter when it rains.*
>
> *There are fishes in the rivers,*
> *There are dingoes on the plains,*
> *And a beetle in the big gum tree.*
>
> *If you hear a wiffle whoffing*
> *Or a sound like someone coughing*
> *That's the beetle in the big gum tree.*

But the story was not quite as Eleanor had remembered it. When the little girl meets the strange sea creature, the dugong, he tells her, "You see that path running up the beach? It leads to the top of the mountain. Follow it. If you reach the top by sunset, all will be well. But if you do not, and the sun sinks behind the mountain before you are at the top, you will never see your home again. On the top of the mountain you will find the beetle, and he will show you the way home."

However, in contradiction of Eleanor's memory, the little girl's companion, the elf named Mys, did not help her to reach the summit of the mountain. In the book, Mys-elf keeps leading her astray and makes her miss the path. When the little girl at last arrives home, she says she realizes that she could have arrived a lot sooner, if only she had not allowed Mys-elf to get in the way.

I chuckled at Eleanor's mis-memory of the book. Presumably, she, like me, had been a child who preferred to rely upon her own resources and had taken a different message from the story. But the lesson struck a chord with me; for had I not always allowed myself to get in my way, rather than follow my true Self, the part of me that is part of God?

How extraordinary that a childhood image from Eleanor's life should have such resonance in my own. In particular, the connection with East Timor felt powerful and strange. It seemed, though a small thing, to confirm that something bound the two of us together, a marker put down long ago to tell us that we had work to share – for nothing happens by chance.

31

It was dark when I arrived home. Blue, who had spent the day with my neighbour, gave me his customary rapturous greeting. My cat Canticle, who was curled up on the couch, stretched a languorous paw as I entered. Seren, my black cat with twinkling, coal-black eyes, padded towards me and rubbed her head against my leg. Seren had turned up at my door one morning several years earlier, little more than skin and bone, seeking sanctuary. She was a star, and so I had named her.

Blue pushed his soft, wet nose against my hand and demanded to be fussed over. As I went to the kitchen, Blue, Canticle and Seren followed me. I gave the animals food and then heated some home-made vegetable soup. I cut some hunks of bread and cheese and poured a glass of wine.

I suddenly felt I would like to hear the sea, and put on a cassette that intermingled the sounds of waves with gentle, tinkling, faraway music and what could have been a chorus of angels.

I lit several candles and brought my meal and wine and placed them on the small table by the sofa. I plumped up the cushions and made myself comfortable. Canticle curled up beside me and Seren settled down to snooze on the rug. Blue climbed onto the sofa and pushed his nose against my arm, asking to be stroked. I made a fuss of him for a few minutes, and then eased him gently aside and began to eat my meal.

The candles glimmer. I sink into the cushions and let the music flow over me. Peace takes hold of my heart, as a hand clasps an old, familiar book.

Today I have yellow tulips in my room. Splashes of luminous sunshine yellow rise on stems of spring green. The petals open wide, to reveal the intimate detail at the flower's heart. I take up my copy of *Enfolded in Love*.

There, on the cover, is the familiar, homely figure leaning forward to embrace the child, who shelters in the loving warmth, wrapped in the folds of the adult's cloak. I see the bare, vulnerable spot at the nape of the child's neck and the bare soles of his feet.

Then, in the background and a little way off, I notice for the first time another figure – the figure of Jesus, with welcoming arms outstretched. I read again Jesus' words, repeated by Julian: "All shall be well; and thou shalt see for thyself that all manner of thing shall be well."

Can I now let go of my legacy of hurt and bitterness? Can I at last turn aside from the image of an angry, vengeful puppet master who has found me wanting and cast me out into the abyss? Can I trust in the promise made by Jesus to Julian of a secret, great deed that God will perform on the last day, through which we will be made to understand all the things that are now beyond our comprehension? Can I believe in Julian's promise of God's unconditional love, that I am held safe in an embrace that will never let me go?

For Julian's book is a passionate love story, "And in the joining and the union he is our very true spouse and we his beloved wife and his fair maiden, with which wife he was never displeased, for he says I love you and you love me, and our love will never divide in two."

Dear Julian, you have brought me to this place of peace and love… On the table before me, the flame of the heavy wax candle flickers, and I feel my heart opening.

I came to Calvary and endured the crucifixion that awaited me. But only now do hope and sorrow meet. Only now am I able to reach through my failure and despair, to claim the promised redemption and release. A feeling of deep peace pervades me. I lay the little book upon my heart.

I close my eyes, and I imagine a gentle presence within the quiet space that I am entering. Could there be someone waiting, at the edge of a circle lit by a candle's golden rays, with arms outstretched in loving welcome? The space is suddenly filled with dazzling light, white and golden powerful beams of love that flood my being and lift me to a state of happiness that is new to me. I feel comforted, secure, calm, content.

I am in a garden where it is always summer. I am made to understand that in this place I am known and loved. In my mind, I walk along a path that takes me into a meadow, and feel the soft, fresh air upon my skin. Alongside the path there are blossoms of gorgeous colour and scent, like none I have ever seen.

I stoop to lift aside some heavy, fringed leaves and find, in a cool, still place, a perfect violet. Each tiny purple flower glows with an iridescent sheen. I touch the petals' velvet softness and know I have found something that was never lost. It was merely waiting, in the shadows, for the right time. How intimate and faithful a lover will patiently await such moments. The lady was never lost. She has always been there. I believed her to be lost because I was looking in the wrong place.

I still have many miles to travel, but a star shines over the road that lies ahead. I fix my eyes upon that star, which lights the path that takes me home. Love is his meaning. In the candle's crystal light I see that through faith, by grace, we come to know that it is not how rich or clever or famous we are that counts, but how much we care. I have no fear of what tomorrow may bring because I know that, whatever comes, all shall be well.

APPENDIX

The first known copy of Julian's book was discovered in Paris, at the Bibliothéque nationale, in the 1660s. Experts surmise that it was taken there by one of the nuns and monks who fled to Europe during Henry's sacking of the monasteries. Julian's first editor was Serenus Cressy, an English Benedictine monk who was chaplain to a convent of nuns in exile at Cambrai, north of Paris.

In 1753, two more copies of Julian's text came to light in a collection sold to the British Museum by Sir Hans Sloane, a physician and scientist. So now there were three, one in Paris and two in London. One of the Sloane manuscripts appears to date from the early seventeenth century; the other from the end of the same century or early the next. Then, in 1909, a fourth version was discovered, when Lord Amherst's collection was dispersed and sold. This text is shorter than that reproduced in the three other manuscripts. It was Julian's first draft. She explains that the longer version was written after some twenty years of pondering the meaning of the revelations.

In 1843, Serenus Cressy's edition was reprinted. Then, in 1877, the Reverend Henry Collins brought out the first printed version of one of the Sloane manuscripts.

Like Cressy's original, it is unlikely that either of these two versions attracted many readers. But all the while, Julian's book was preserved, as though intended to blossom into life centuries later. And who can say what its influence may have been on the lives of

those who read it, even if they were few? One of Julian's readers was
Florence Nightingale, who took the book with her to the Crimea.

In 1901, a new edition of Julian's book was published by Grace
Warrack. Thanks to her, Julian's book became readily available for
the first time in six hundred years. It was reprinted over and over
during the next seventy years.

In the 1980s, as though her time had finally come, new transla-
tions and books about Julian's work began to proliferate. Julian had
suddenly become interesting.

ACKNOWLEDGEMENTS

I would like to thank Denise Treissman, who manages the estate of the late Reverend Robert Llewelyn, and Lay Canon Professor Brian Thorne for allowing me to include extracts from their Julian lectures. I would also like to thank my editor, Mary Tomlinson, for her invaluable help.